THE MASADA FRANCHISE

THE MASADA FRANCHISE

Chris Drewitt

The Book Guild Ltd
Sussex, England

The Book Guild Ltd
25 High Street,
Lewes, Sussex

First published 1997

© Chris Drewitt, 1997

Set in Baskerville by
Rowland Phototypesetting Ltd
Bury St Edmunds, Suffolk

Printed in Great Britain by
Antony Rowe Ltd.
Chippenham, Wiltshire

A catalogue record for this book is
available from the British Library

ISBN 1 85776 144 8

1

Ghosts

LONDON

Stuart looked down at the granite face of the film star staring grimly from the hotel television screen. He'd seen the old film many times before, but was always fascinated by the poetic licence and glorification of death the scriptwriters and directors had conjured up, in order to turn one of his greatest failures into a Robin Hood adventure.

He punched the remote control and turned down the volume. The actors launched into their fantasy once more as Stuart stalked into the bathroom and turned on the shower.

Standing naked in front of the misting mirror, he stared at the deeply tanned body. Not as hard and fit as it used to be, but the old wound scars still gave the slightly overweight frame a hint of interest and mystery to the opposite sex, on the rare occasions that he felt the deep yearning for female company.

As the steamy mist closed off the image, Stuart's mind drifted back to the real operation and his best friend, Yanders de Beer. Stuart had been forced to cut him down with a short burst of automatic fire, to save him from a long and terrifying death at the hands of rampaging Zimbah warriors.

It seemed as if it was light years ago. How many wars and undercover operations had there been since then, for Major Thomas 'Trapper' Stuart? They all seemed to float into the

1

mists of time, to become one homogenous excuse for a life. All except for Yanders . . . and the woman. He saw their faces every day and every night as though it was just yesterday. The pleading in Yanders' eyes and the haunting repeated scream of *Kill me, Trapper. For God's sake, kill me!* was branded into what was left of his soul.

Chris Marker was early. It was a habit. He had time to find a convenient seat with his back to the wall and observe the comings and goings of those around him. A very large single malt whisky sat in front of him, untouched, as the attractive Polynesian waitresses at the Park Lane Hilton's Trader Vic's restaurant fluttered around the adjacent tables in their long silk cheongsams. Marker loved women, and they, more often than not, loved him.

He saw Stuart as soon as he came into view, descending the curved stairs from the Hilton's foyer. The green eyes, under a full head of straight pepper and salt hair, radiated an unfeeling coldness that was not warmed by a complexion forged by many years in the tropical sun.

Those eyes had taken in the whole room before the last stair was negotiated and Marker's table for two, with an empty seat and a whisky for one, had been noted.

Stuart took the longest route to the table and sat down in front of him. 'Vasco,' he said in a level voice which would have only been recognised as a greeting by his closest associates.

'Trap,' Marker replied, with a smile. 'Welcome back to England.'

TEL AVIV, ISRAEL, the previous year

Yani Bar-David had sand in his eyes. For operational reasons the trip from Washington hadn't been direct and there had been the usual delays passing through Milan and Athens. He looked across the desk at his old mentor. Avraham Sharon slowly re-read the report his younger operative had sent earlier in a diplomatic bag.

2

'So, Yani.' Sharon sighed in his deep growl. 'It looks like the American Bear has lost something in Sierra Laputu and is not asking his friends for help to find it; whatever this *it* may be.'

Yani didn't answer, he knew the old man too well. The pause was for reflection, not an invitation to interrupt his thoughts.

'As far as we can ascertain, the Americans have made absolutely no contact with any Western or other agencies around the world. The only traffic has been between CIA headquarters at Langley and their diplomatic staff in London, Pretoria and Freeman. The communications have been scant, but with a GETIM prefix, indicating that the Director should be called immediately. Our people in Freeman have heard nothing and everything appears calm, except for the on and off border skirmishes with their neighbours to the south-east. President Mokomo continues to grow fat as his people starve. I suppose that can be considered to be calm and normal in that part of the world – or here, for that matter.'

Sharon leaned back in his high wing-backed leather chair. He slowly slipped the half-moon tortoiseshell glasses off his nose and massaged his weary eyes with the finger and thumb of his other hand.

'What d'you think?' he asked the younger man, as he looked up.

'Our deep-cover agent in Langley only has level two access, but is a West African specialist, so I am hopeful that an invitation to the top floor will be forthcoming soon,' Yani offered, spreading his hands in the universal gesture of *maybe*.

Sharon rose and walked over to the window. The summer heat left a haze over the city, which from his farm in the clear air of the hills could be seen as a faint orange dome. His second wife, Hannah, always compared it to her home town of San Francisco, but it would be years before *this* dome became as thick as the one over there.

'You have a feeling about this one, don't you, Yani?' Sharon asked.

'Yes, sir. The communications are all short and clipped. I haven't seen them so' – Yani searched for the right word – *'frightened.'*

3

'I have,' the old man said, as he turned to Bar-David, 'but that was a long time ago. Keep onto it, Yani. Keep onto it, but report only to me, verbally.'

The old man held out his hand in a gesture of affectionate dismissal. Yani took it, once more feeling the strength of the pioneer, one of the men who had relentlessly continued to carve out a nation against the will of many and the treachery of so-called friends. As he turned to leave, the old man called to him.

'Yani!' Sharon growled, as he searched the younger man's face over the top of the replaced half-moons. 'To me only!'

'To you only,' the young Mossad agent replied softly.

The old man smiled and turned away. While Israel had young men like Yani Bar-David, she would remain in good hands and all the Devil's hoards couldn't destroy her . . . Sharon was tired. He had been at war for over 50 years.

LANGLEY, USA

The President of the United States of America sat at the end of the oblong table in the level one operations suite. He'd sat here many times before as the CIA's Director, but only three times as President. People came to see him these days, not the other way around.

Officially, he was on his way back from a presentation and campaigning trip to the Naval College at Annapolis, but his mind had been raking through the details of a covert operation under his direct control many years past, before the heady days of his striving for, and finally winning, the most powerful position in the world. Everything he'd achieved was now under threat. Everything he reached for in the future was drifting away from him like the light at the distant end of a distant tunnel.

'Is there any doubt?' he asked the assembled meeting.

Admiral Carlton Hess, the Deputy Director, shook his head. 'All indications confirm that material from the Masada operation is in the hands of the Sierra Laputu government and the said government consider this fact to be a convenient way to create, in the words of their President, *significant amounts of foreign exchange for his starving people*. No doubt into a numbered Swiss bank account under his direct control.'

'What options have you considered?' the President asked, looking directly at Hess.

'In a situation like this,' the admiral answered, 'there is only one option available to protect the security of the United States and remove the threat to this country and the potential threat to others, which would have the same damaging effect on us and, if I may say so, to your good self, Mr President.

'You mean direct action,' the President stated rather than asked.

'No, sir,' Hess replied quickly. 'What I mean is *deniable* direct action.'

'Holy shit, Carlton! It's election year next year – d'you want another god-damned scandal ?'

Hess lowered his eyes and his voice before answering. 'I am not suggesting we use anyone from the NSE or anyone else from the inside, but wouldn't underestimate their access. Although they got caught badly once, the people who *really* did the job for them didn't.'

'I've heard enough for today,' the President said. His voice had a resigned ring to it, as though the events surrounding him were directing themselves rather than being controlled. 'Admiral Hess!'

'Yes, Mr President.'

'The role of the Central Intelligence Agency is defined quite clearly within the laws of these United States of America?'

'Yes, Mr President.'

'You're fully aware and conversant with its defined role and position within the laws of this country and the Constitution?'

'Yes, Mr President.'

'The oath I took is also quite clear, Admiral. I suggest that I return to my other duties and you, Admiral, continue with yours.'

'As a naval officer I –'

The President of the United States lifted his hand and smiled as he rose to leave. 'Carlton, you're a good man. That's why you're sitting here. But don't give me all that naval crap. It's like that famous drinking man Winston Churchill said, *Don't talk to me about naval tradition. It's nothing but rum, sodomy and the lash!*'

'He also said something else, sir,' Hess returned with a cold stare. *'It's a good thing for an uneducated man to read books of quotations!'*

The President frowned, turned and walked slowly towards the door. As one of his Secret Service men opened it for him he turned towards the Deputy Director and in his adopted Texan drawl said, 'Carlton, you're a spook – go spook somebody.' Then he was gone.

Hess sat down heavily and turned to his Operations Director, Mark Cappricci. 'Where's Stuart?'

'Stuart? In South Africa, the last time we heard anything about him.'

'Well, find him and organise a meet . . . Oh yes! And get our best intelligence guy on West Africa up to my office in one hour. Who is he? Conners?'

'It's a she, actually, sir. Michelle Christie.'

'Where's Conners?' the Admiral sighed.

'Having his gall bladder out. Quite painful, I hear.'

'Shit, I need a close-knit team on this, Mark, not a bunch of learners!'

Cappricci walked around the far end of the cheap table and punched three numbers into the telephone keyboard.

'Charlie, it's Cappricci. Please send Michelle Christie's pink file up to the Deputy's office immediately and have her report there at' – he looked at Hess – 'nineteen thirty hours?' Hess nodded. 'Yes, nineteen thirty hours, understood? . . . Fine . . . Ciao.'

'Sir?' Cappricci hesitated. 'D'you think Stuart is the right freelance operative for this job? I've always felt that his reputation was more fiction than reality. Many of the things he's reported to have done have very little corroboration on file.'

'You've never met him?' Hess asked with a whimsical look on his face.

6

'No, but I've read up on him, along with others of his ilk. I've rejected him in the past for stability reasons if for nothing else. They call him The Wild Goose, don't they?'

'Only the gutter press, and even then not to his face,' Hess replied. 'His friends call him Trapper.'

'Another measure of his ego, no doubt?'

'Ahhh, not quite, my boy, not quite. More a warning to those who underestimate or double-cross him. Just remember, he is alive. Those who broke his rules are dead. He's like an elephant. He never forgets and always, even if it takes years, balances the distorted scales he carries around in his head. He's a son of a bitch, but if he takes your money he's *your* son of a bitch, until the job's done. He's yours, Mark. Use nobody else to find him. No records. No signals. I give you seven days.'

Michelle Christie had been on the top level only twice before. Both times with her section leader, Bill Conners. She spoke four African dialects, French, Italian, poor Arabic and good Hebrew. Having been brought up in the Diplomatic Service, her time had been spent in Washington, England, Israel, South Africa, West Guinea and Nigeria. She was five feet ten inches in her bare feet, with medium blonde hair that had highlights. In the office it was usually worn up in a French or Swedish pleat. She had just returned from a holiday in the South of France, with a healthy, smooth tan which would take at least two months to fade and had no lines.

Hess liked her immediately. She radiated the confidence that comes from known ability. When he threw her new level-one pass onto the table, she never flinched.

'Thank you, sir,' she offered. 'How can I help?' She noticed her pink file had been placed in a strategic and obvious place on the admiral's desk, along with a red operational file.

'Read that file, in this room. I'll be back in two hours,' Hess replied.

'Would that be the pink file or the red file, sir?' she asked with her lips, whilst answering the question with her eyes.

'Cute, lady,' the admiral smiled, 'cute.' Have your fun now, because by the time you've got through that lot, in the *red* file, you may wonder if you're ever going to have any fun in, oh, the next one or three years.'

Hess got up and left the room. He left the pink file on the edge of his desk. It would still be there untouched, he thought, when he returned.

Michelle Christie spun the red file round and picked it up. It was three inches thick. She started to read. Her life would never be the same again.

2

Spirits and Players

FREEMAN, SIERRA LAPUTU

Two of the women on the bed were native Sierra Laputu beauties: medium dark skin, tall and slim with fine regal features. The third was slightly smaller and lighter, reflecting her Lebanese genes. All of them were naked, except for a smattering of expensive gold and diamond jewellery and a fine coating of body oil.

President Mokomo, for 24 years the ruler and raper of the country's wealth, lay entwined amongst them. He was sweating and out of breath.

The Lebanese girl made little cooing noises as she tried in vain with her lips to raise his manhood once more to the game. She needed the white powder. Only by his pleasure could she win the prize. Her efforts became more urgent as she detected a stirring in his loins, and her *sisters* entered the play.

Mokomo pulled the Lebanese up to him by her long, thick hair. As she thrust her tongue deep into his mouth, another of the girls, the one with the Mandingo blood, mounted him and tried to bring him to another climax, but the man was finished and couldn't maintain his physical presence any longer.

'Enough,' he snapped. The women peeled off him, clucking pathetic endearments as they faded into the adjoining room. He shouted for his servant. 'Alpha, where are you?'

'Here I am, your excellency,' the young man replied, as if he'd appeared from nowhere.

'How are my guests?' Mokomo asked.

'Mr Jamayal is in the pool with his ladies, and the American would appear to have never had it so good. He's even promised to take Camellia and Celestine back to America as soon as he can.'

'Good, good. Our two *Cs* work well together. The equipment is functioning?'

'Oh yes, your excellency. Would you like to check the screen?'

'That would give me great pleasure, Alpha, but first I will bathe. There is always time to savour the capture of a senior official of the World Bank in a compromising position – for the good of the people, of course.'

Mokomo walked off across the cool tiles to his private bathroom. It was half the size of an Olympic swimming pool and had seen many outlandish sexual events over the years.

Alpha Benjamin watched his master disappear, and then returned to a small room at the end of the striking marble hall which linked the President's quarters to the rest of the palatial residence. He had a degree in English law and was a colonel in the country's military intelligence service. His prime job in life was to act as the President's adviser in matters of a delicate nature, which would potentially enhance both the President's significant wealth and therefore his own modest fortune by the use of bribery, corruption, theft and, always most regrettably, murder. Alpha enjoyed his job, especially when the fools being trapped were fat, sweating, pale skinned Americans who called him *boy*. Yes, he would enjoy seeing this one squirm. Jamayal had pulled in a good fish this time. Alpha wondered how much the President would pay him when the sting was complete and how much would go to the Lebanese's uncle Jamayal in London, the joint owner of Sierra Laputu and 60 per cent shareholder of every asset-bearing industry in the country.

Alpha sat down behind a range of electronic screens and recording and communications equipment. The automatic door locked shut behind him. In a country where the capital

10

city's hospital operations were conducted by candle-light, he found the irony amusing.

On the only colour screen, the American was busy telling the girls how rich he was and bragging about the introductions to the top names in show business he could arrange for them.

'Yes,' whispered Alpha to himself, 'I can see the headlines now in the *Herald Tribune*, "Famous Banker Introduces Two African Prostitutes to Manhattan Society". Pathetic!'

As he switched the screen off, he smiled to himself. Camellia and Celestine were both HIV positive. Neither of them knew, of course. He required all his female employees to have regular medicals, but never revealed interesting results. That kind of information was far too valuable. Alpha had decided a long time ago that his own survival in this regime was based on what he alone knew. He protected this knowledge with extreme prejudice when he deemed it necessary. The German doctor who had conducted his ladies' examinations and tests had got too greedy recently. He had gone missing on a field trip up-country to one of the Jamayal diamond mines. Alpha would find a new one soon; he always did.

THE SIERRA LAPUTU BORDER

Major Valentine Nelson drove into the overnight camp, just as his troops were stirring from their short sleep. Most of them were just boys. Each of them lived with an AK47 or AK58 assault rifle of Russian design and Far East manufacture, instead of going to school.

Their communist neighbours had attacked Sierra Laputu to rid the country of the Mokomo regime some 20 years ago, so these boys of his were actually fighting to keep in power the very man they would most like to see deposed, but dared not even think it. The war itself had become more of a border skirmish, punctuated with accidental firefights with other African peacekeeping forces from countries like Nigeria and Ghana.

Rations from Freeman were scant and no pay had been

11

received for months. The rainy season was almost due, and everyone just wanted to go home.

As Nelson's aging Toyota Landcruiser pulled to a halt, a sergeant came over to meet him. Many eyes looked expectantly for any sign of a good news smile. The smile didn't come. In fact, the earnest and urgent manner in which the sergeant received orders from their major prepared them for the kind of operational orders they didn't want to hear. But this time they were wrong.

There were 52 officers, NCOs and men in the jungle camp. The regimental sergeant major arrived two hours after Nelson, driving three other officers from camps within 20 miles of the gathering. Now, Nelson was standing on the hood of his Toyota. Even the background noises of jungle life seemed to be holding their breath for whatever news was to be announced in this unusual fashion.

'Men,' Nelson called in a clear and articulate baritone, 'our families have no money because we have not been paid. We have been virtually living off the land for months, because rations and stores do not arrive. We fight a war with too few bullets and no equipment spares. All our messages to staff headquarters seem to drift into the sky with the spirits of our dead.' He paused and looked all around him. Not one man moved or spoke.

'Your officers have decided to appeal directly to the President himself, by sending a delegation to State House in Freeman today. We ask for volunteers to come with us on this journey, in case our superiors think we are in mutiny and try to stop us before we achieve our goal. We are *not* in mutiny. We ask only for men to protect us on our journey to State House, to deliver our plea.'

Whisperings began to flow through the ranks. Nelson held his breath and stared long and hard at the three other officers standing by his vehicle. Their futures were now in the hands of their men. Would loyalty overcome the desire to gain from informing and the chance of short-term profit? They were all so young.

A tall, rangy soldier lifted his rifle past his shoulder. Nelson

12

knew he could be dead in a split second. The rifle continued to move up above the youth's head and he started to chant, 'Nelson! Nelson! Nelson! Nelson!'

The cry was taken up and a flood of emotion welled up inside him. Everyone had turned towards him, and his name echoed off the jungle's walls, time and time again. They were all smiling and jumping up and down. His fellow officers joined him on the Toyota's hood and they linked hands and held them aloft.

By 1600 hours the camp was deserted and a small convoy of trucks and three Landcruisers were heading along the dirt track, west and north towards the capital, Freeman, and President Mokomo at State House.

As the journey began and the elation subsided, Nelson's doubts flooded over him. What if the President was not there when they arrived? What if his superiors found out their plan before they arrived, and sent troops to stop them? What if . . . ? What if . . . ? What if . . . ? It was all too late now; the venture was launched and would roll like a ball downhill. He had to keep control. He just had to!

CANNES, FRENCH RIVIERA

It was a pleasant surprise for Michelle Christie to be back in the South of France so quickly. When Hess had asked her to suggest a meeting place she was very familiar with, it was with studious calm and crossed fingers she'd suggested her beloved Cannes. It was the Fourth of July weekend and the USS *Saratoga* was at anchor in the bay for the holiday. You couldn't move for dashing F18 pilots on the promenade. They looked 18 years old, but rode one of the world's most advanced fighter aircraft at speeds which made instinct an examinable qualification.

The male guests sunbathing on the Carlton Hotel pier were also pleased that Hess had approved the meeting location. There were many bronzed, topless and thonged beauties on the Carlton beach, but Michelle was one of those ladies who would look good in sacking and was spectacular naked. It was all down to God – she hated exercise, thought joggers were mad and considered sweating under a 90-degree piercing sun drenched in old-fashioned sun oil maximum effort, excluding sex, in which she indulged rarely, but totally when aroused.

The expense account Hess had given her indicated the importance of the meeting. It was the first time she'd been given a CIA credit card and she intended to make an almost unrespectable dent in Uncle Sam's account while she was here. A dark blue designer cocktail dress had already been purchased for the famous Fourth of July reception in the Carlton, the venue for her meeting with Stuart.

Currently, a 200-dollar coral-coloured thong was all that complemented her golden brown body. As she rolled over on the sunlounger, Stuart noticed that her breasts hardly moved with the change of gravity's force on them. He'd been watching her from his rented apartment next to the Carlton for over an hour and was almost satisfied she was alone.

It took him ten minutes to reach the lounger next to her, even though the distance from the apartment entrance was only 150 metres. He turned left out of the building and ambled past the open-air restaurants on the Croisette, glancing at their excellent but overpriced menus, crossed the promenade's dual carriageway about 150 metres east of the Carlton pier and descended the beach steps to the sand. He'd rented the lounger position next to the girl, by phone, after previously tipping the beach attendant, within five minutes of her arrival on one of the most exclusive sunbathing piers in the world.

When he quietly eased himself onto the thick padding of the lounger to her left, she didn't move from the face-down pose which left her tight, unlined buttocks proudly standing to attention on either side of the minute thong that disappeared almost instantly. Stuart wore a swimming costume under his shorts and was thankful for the control their tightness gave over his unexpected erection. After another five minutes, during which time partial physical control returned to him, he spoke to the figure lying next to him. 'You're a very beautiful woman, Ms Christie. But of course you know that, don't you?'

She instantly spun her head around, but the sun was directly behind him and she was partially blinded for a moment. Turning, she rose up onto her left elbow. 'I beg your pardon?' she said, shading her eyes with her free hand.

'I said, you're a very beautiful woman. It was meant to be a compliment.'

Recognition betrayed her, from within the depth of her eyes, for a split second. Stuart saw it instantly and knew that he would remain in control of the mind games to follow. Unless he'd witnessed a momentary and uncharacteristic lapse in concentration, this lady was not an experienced field operative – and Langley's declaration that her role was as a briefing contact only could very well be genuine.

She moved her position to see him more clearly. 'You weren't arriving until this evening, I checked your booking at the Carlton.'

'Not staying at the Carlton,' Stuart replied, looking for another eye reaction. It didn't come, and Stuart became angry with himself for being disappointed. He might have to be more careful with this little lady than his first impressions indicated ... at least for now.

'Why not?' Michelle asked. 'We had an arrangement.'

'We have no arrangements. Your people advised me of their, and therefore *your* arrangements. My only agreement was to meet. Now we've met! What d'you want? It's been a long and sleepless journey from Jo'burg and I return tomorrow.'

'I can't tell you here. Anyone could be listening.'

'Pack your tits and your arse into something and follow me. If you come closer than fifty metres, you'll never see me again and your bosses will be really pissed off.'

Stuart was moving before she could attempt an answer. In her haste to dress, she sat on her extremely new and expensive sunglasses and broke them.

'Shit,' she said, too loud. Uncle Sam hadn't bought them for her, she had. 'Shit, shit, shit!'

Stuart paced himself ahead of the girl's faltering progress, until he was sure she'd seen him enter the apartment block entrance. He rose to the fourth floor in the lift and held the doors open until its sister started to ascend.

When Michelle stepped out of the second lift, she surveyed

15

the empty access floor on both sides. An apartment door at the south corner of the building stood ajar by about six inches. She slowly walked towards it, her medium heeled beach pumps quietly slapping against the bottom of her bare feet. The sound seemed deafening. It matched the thumping of the pulse in the echo chamber of her temples. She'd never felt so exposed, so alone. All her years of training hadn't prepared her for this feeling of . . . controlled panic?

Stuart silently placed his hand on her left shoulder as she reached forward to knock on the apartment door. The thong beneath her beach sarong amplified the sound of her discharging bladder. It was the most embarrassing moment of Michelle Christie's life. As the warm fluid rushed between the tight thong and her expensively smooth inner thigh, she swore to a God that she hadn't spoken to for a long time that one day she would take revenge on this man who had humiliated her and without doubt taken pleasure in the action.

'Tch Tch,' Stuart almost whispered, as he slid past her into the small but well-appointed living room. 'Do come in, when you've – ahh – finished.' He paused and looked back at the pathetic figure holding onto the door frame. 'Can I get you a drink,' he smiled, 'or a towel, perhaps?'

She steadied and straightened herself into a poor copy of the lithe creature that had adorned the Carlton pier just a short time before.

'You, mister, can go fuck yourself. I'll see you at the appointed fucking place and at the appointed fucking time, and if you and your incredible ego can remember where and when that's supposed to be, you might just be able to make enough blood money to pay for your return ticket back underneath whichever fucking stone you happen to be hiding under at this fucking time! Do I make myself perfectly clear, or are you as stupid as you appear to be fucking ignorant?' The tirade stopped and she took a deep breath.

'Pardon?' Stuart said with mock concern.

The man and the woman stared at each other for what seemed an age. Michelle reached under her sarong and peeled off the wet thong, slowly folding the garment into a small

16

package. Stuart thought she was going to throw it at him, but she walked into the bathroom and carefully, with theatrical emphasis, wrapped the material around his toothbrush.

'Swill your cavities in that, asshole,' she fired back, striding past him with a renewed spring in her step. She thought about slamming the door for a second, but decided silence would have more effect, and it did.

Four hours later, when Michelle walked into the Carlton's cocktail reception, every man in the large marbled room paused to take a second glance. Stuart was standing diagonally opposite her in the far corner, across from the host's reception group near the entrance. It was the last part of the room anyone entering could observe. She looked straight at him and through him, as though they had never met.

The hotel's host raised her hand to his lips. Stuart should have turned away but he couldn't. He knew it was a mistake, even as his will failed; the hidden venom in her eyes trapped his own at the instant he came into view, privately enhancing her beauty.

An F18 pilot, who looked about 12 years old to Stuart, was rabbiting into his ear about aces, Spitfires and Hurricanes during the Battle of Britain. Stuart was smiling and nodding, while the condensation on the outside of his untouched glass of champagne soaked his hand.

'Tell me, lieutenant,' Stuart asked, 'what d'you hold most dear, a ground zero flight at Mach 1 in the mountains, or an incredible night of lovemaking with a beautiful woman who knows how to make love all night?'

'Well, sir,' the young man replied earnestly, 'I have to say that flying at Mach plus, with the land's horizon above you, is almost the ultimate erotic experience. No woman I've made love to has ever come close to that.'

'What about *that* woman?' Stuart offered, as he lowered his head ever so slightly towards Michelle. 'Have you ever made love to a woman like that?'

The young man smiled and looked up at Stuart. 'Sir, my father has a theory about women who look like that. He thinks

17

that they're either frigid or lesbians and we just waste our time, efforts and mostly cash on trying to trap them. What do you think, sir?'

'Ask me in the morning,' Stuart answered, without looking at the pilot. 'Here, take this glass, it's on the house.'

The young knight took the glass before realising what he'd done and then watched the older man stalk his way across the large room. The stunning lady in the blue dress was talking to two of his fellow pilots and the chief of maintenance, who kept the *Saratoga*'s birds flying. She was smiling and laughing at polite intervals and the young heroes were completely besotted.

Stuart arrived at the group with a hidden menace that belied the calm and friendly introduction.

'Michelle?' he asked in a feigned form of apology. 'It can't be you, surely? I thought you were in the Far East until the end of the year at least!'

'So does everyone else – ahh, – Mervin. How are you, darling?'

'All the better for seeing you, my sweet. How is your husband the Admiral keeping? Still got the prostrate problem, or did he go in to get it sorted out?'

The naval uniforms instantly began to melt away from around the good looking couple. Many a promising career had gone aground due to a bored senior navy wife's sexual needs. F18 pilots could get it anywhere and any time. No one was going to go anywhere near an unannounced admiral's wife on the loose on the French Riviera.

As the last of the brittle white uniforms made their polite exits, she turned to Stuart and raped him with her eyes.

'I should never have approached that open door, should I?' she asked, in a voice slightly deeper than normal, a minute but recognisable rasp straining inside its dampening tones.

'No,' he replied. 'You were completely exposed from the front, rear and both sides.'

'I broke every rule in the book. '

'Yes.'

'I could have been killed. '

18

'Yes.'

Her replies were statements of fact not questions. 'You must think that I'm a complete waste of time – a beginner.'

'No, I know you are.'

'Not at everything,' she retorted, whilst confidently making a mock attempt to straightening the red carnation in his left-hand jacket lapel. 'Not at everything, Major Stuart.'

Stuart smiled at the beautiful form in front of him. Her lips had darkened under the shiny pink lipstick, betraying the animal instinct which was drowning training, ego, duty and any other label a desk bound administrator could find to file the compromise she was willingly, but almost unknowingly, slipping into.

'We have business, Ms Christie,' Stuart whispered in defence of them both. 'Business?' The woman leaned against him, slowly increasing the pressure of her body as she raised her face to his. 'What business, soldier boy?' she cooed, in an out-rageously fake Southern Belle accent. 'What business could a gentleman like yourself, and a little lady like myself, possibly have together? We haven't even been properly introduced! Lordy, Lordy!'

Stuart had let his hands rest on the woman's upper arms, just above her elbows. She was turned slightly to her right and it was to the opposite arm that he slowly increased his grip. At first she thought it was a sign of response, but the pressure became pain, a pain that would bruise if it continued for more than a few seconds. Her rising passion was drowned with the emptiness which often precedes foreboding. Then the moment was lost.

'Come with me, my dear,' Stuart almost ground through his teeth, whilst etching a comfortable smile onto his face for the benefit of any observers. 'Come with me, and look happy – we're happy, we love each other. It's the Fourth of July, and the only reason we've got all dressed up like this is so that we can take all sorts of time undressing each other. That's what lovers do, isn't it? Make the audience believers . . . We're just a couple amongst many other couples who tonight will move off anonymously to their rooms to do whatever turns them on.

19

Kiss me and then leave the hall. I'll be outside your room in twenty minutes. Leave the door unlocked.'

Michelle looked into the man's green eyes and at that moment wanted him more than any man she'd ever met, but her feelings were murdered by the pain in her left arm. Stuart was speaking, but she didn't take it on board. His pressure increased as she pulled herself towards him. The whole scene had only taken seconds, but she was aware that she'd lost total control once more. It was this man. She must concentrate, her whole future depended on it.

Almost before she knew what was happening, his lips crushed hers for just a second and she was obeying instructions she hadn't quantified. She hated herself for it, but was passing the second floor in the Carlton's lift before her full capacity to rationalise returned.

'Jesus H Christ! This man is one dangerous son of a bitch, Michelle,' she said to her reflection, which struggled out of the lightly smoked glass that protected the pictures and menus mounted on the lift's walls, each of them holding a distorted reflection of the beautiful woman within. 'Watch yourself, girl. You haven't won a round yet!'

Stuart moved slowly back through the crowd to the complimentary bar which served the pink champagne. His glass filled, he engaged himself in conversation with a small man in a white dinner jacket. He was of Indian or Pakistani descent, a breath of fresh air in a hotel which seemed to be almost exclusively filled by jewellery dealers from all over the world. They spoke for only a few minutes, of the weather and suchlike; of New York in the fall.

Having parted with a smile and the most formal of pleasantries, Stuart finished his only drink of the evening and left the reception, nodding to all encountered on his route who warranted superficial, calm and polite attention. He headed out of the hotel, around the famous Carlton Terrace and into his apartment block.

After quickly showering and packing his leather case, he stood in front of the dressing table mirror to adjust the soft Italian shoulder holster which held his 14-shot P7M13 automatic, made by the Heckler & Koch Company of Oberndorf in the Black Forest. The weapon was small and smooth, but built to target competion standards, with the safety mechanism housed inside the butt for quick draw-and-fire action. Stuart could place a round between a man's eyes at 70 metres from the draw, while in a 180-degree spinning turn to the left or the right. It sat easily in wait underneath his left shoulder. Three spare magazines sat equally at home underneath his right shoulder, balancing perfectly the designer-quality shoulder rig that sat comfortably beneath his casual jacket. It was made by Ritex of Switzerland and bought from a discreet but exclusive tailor's shop in Aberdeen.

A quarter of an hour after leaving Michelle Christie in the Carlton's reception hall, he was opening the door of her room on the second floor. The suite lounge was covered only by the light from an old standard lamp that had seen better days and a table lamp which was tastefully set to one side of an imitation Regency cupboard that housed the TV. The bedroom door was open. Stuart moved forward quietly and entered the bedroom. As he had expected, she had changed into something more comfortable and was removing her make-up in front of a round mirror which sat on a china stand on a dressing table at the foot of the, high-built, king-size bed.

'Hi,' Stuart said.

'Hi,' she replied, without pausing from her task. 'Going somewhere?'

'Ahmm, elsewhere, as soon as you've finished passing your message.'

'What's your hurry?' Michelle asked, as she lowered her head ever so slightly to look into his eyes through the mirror.

'You are. Get on with it,' Stuart replied, in an aggressive manner which was not deserved, needed or warranted.

She lifted her head to remove him from her line of sight, and followed her instructions from Hess to the letter. It took 20 minutes. Stuart took no notes. When she'd finished she sat in silence, awaiting the mercenary's reaction. He was silent for a two-minute period which seemed like ten, during which time he walked over to the veranda and looked down onto the dusk of the Croisette's promenade. Cars were passing in both directions, and people were continuing their parade from one end of the strip to the other. Groups of the beautiful set who had decided to remain for the evening, still lolled around the terrace, sipping more of the house champagne that they'd started on hours before. Now, it was nine dollars a glass.

'Who's the controller for the operation?' Stuart asked.

'Mark Cappricci.'

'Do you know him?'

'He's my direct superior.'

'I didn't ask that. I asked if you knew him.'

Michelle turned and looked at the distant man standing to the right of the veranda. He continued to stare out into the night as he waited for an answer.

'He's just my boss. We don't mix socially.'

'Have you ever read his file?'

'Of course not, for Christ's sake. As soon as I pulled it he would know, and anyway, why the hell would I want to?'

'Never mind,' Stuart cut in. 'Is that it, lock stock and barrel?'

'That's it, Major.'

Stuart turned and smiled at Michelle. 'You've done well, little lady, for a first time. What's the contact route?'

'No route until you have accepted the contract.'

'I send my answer through the route,' Stuart replied with a small sigh.

'No answer, no route. Those are my orders.'

'Can't be done until I check availabilities. That's a fact of life and no amount of administrative, covert bullshit can change it.'

'I have my orders.'

'So you do, my dear, so you do. Be careful, though. Obeying orders can get you killed in this business. Tell Hess I'll contact him through the *widow* within forty-eight hours.'

'But Cappricci is the controller,' Michelle began. 'He –'

Stuart cut her off with a raised hand. 'Enjoy Cannes, Ms Christie. Turn right after the Festival Restaurant, off the strip, if you want to find the *real* Cannes and her food.' Then he was gone.

CASTLE STUART, THE GREAT GLEN, SCOTLAND

Stuart rolled the hired Range Rover to a stop in front of the ancient castle that had once been his home. The white cross of St Andrew flew proudly at the ramparts' head, as a tribute to all those lost at Culloden Moor at the hands of the English and their mercenaries, the hated Campbells. The treachery of Glencoe – the massacre of the MacDonalds in their sleep – and the inevitable result on the moor at Culloden echoed down the centuries and lay fresh in the hearts of all who were proud to call themselves Highlanders.

The irony of the situation never ceased to amuse Stuart. Dishonourably discharged from the Special Air Service, deposed by his own family as the true laird of Castle Stuart and the 25,000 acres of land that went with it, entry could not be denied him under Scottish law and the family charter it supported. He, the black sheep, one of the most famous mercenary leaders in the world! His family referred to him as a 'security consultant'. That was when they felt they unfortunately had to refer to him at all.

The days of many servants at Castle Stuart had long gone, as they had at most Scottish castles since the end of the Second World War. One still remained: Silas Urquart had been a delivery boy, a bush pilot, a gun runner, a bar owner in Hong Kong, and a hundred other things in between. Now, he was an elder of the Scottish Presbyterian Church, an expert in the golden liquid, the scourge of the Inverness Over Sixties Ladies' Club and general live-in caretaker and general factotum to the laird and family of Castle Stuart. His situation was further enhanced by the fact that Stuart's younger brother, Geordie Gordon-Stuart, his wife and the three pretentious children preferred to spend 90 per cent of their time in the comfort of the family's South Kensington apartment in London. This left Silas as good as the lord of the manor for most of the year and Castle Stuart a haven for Geordie's elder brother, *persona non grata* in the land of his birth.

The single, rather small front door of the castle opened before Stuart stepped down out of the Rover. Silas watched this man; the man he and all the local community called the true laird, step forward. His rare smile lit up a tanned face that hid a thousand screams. He caught himself wondering once more what life would have been like at the estate if the Major hadn't refused to give any testimony in his own defence all those years ago, and had thus fallen under the might of the Establishment in both the UK and the United States. His thoughts were clipped short...

'Silas, you old bugger! It's good to see you again. How's the love life?'

'The love life is adequate, if not a wee bit patchy, sir. You're looking disgustingly healthy as usual, if I might say so. Please come in. It's a wee bit parky outside today, don't you find?'

Stuart took Urquart's hand and felt the strength that still remained in the aging frame. 'Yes, *parky* is the word all right, Silas. It's cold enough to be October not July.'

'Aye, sir, nothing changes up here. It'll likely be a heat wave tomorrow. Come in, come in. A not so *wee* dram will clear the cobwebs and put lead in your pencil.'

'So it will, old friend, but let's get the gear out of the car first. Then, we can settle down for the evening and have a good chinwag.'

In fact, it was a couple of hours later that Stuart sat down beside the fire in the small great hall of the castle to a very large Smith's Glenlivet on the rocks and a supper tray which almost overflowed with Silas's mince, neaps and tatties, hot bread rolls and real butter. The two old friends sat in almost complete silence on either side of the fire, until a significant proportion of the fare had been consumed. Stuart placed his tray to one side, stretched and relaxed into the deep leather wing-backed chair, a heavy Caithness Crystal glass balanced on his left knee.

'The old mistress could never get you out of that habit, sir.' Urquart smiled as he nodded towards the precarious glass.

'Never dropped one yet, Silas,' Stuart replied, as he opened his eyes and smiled at the old man. 'Tell me, what's happening these days with my beloved family?'

'The family, sir? They're alive and well, living in that country to the south. The only time I see them is during the shooting season for a few weekends. On occasion, the young mistress comes during the summer to fish, but as you know, Castle Stuart suffers like many others from the absentee landlord syndrome. An estate has to be lived in and loved like a women in order to flourish, not be treated only as an asset to be borrowed against for ventures elsewhere. Still, sir, I do very well and visits like this by yourself are very much looked forward to, infrequent though they are.' The last was said in mild rebuke and Stuart chuckled as he took a light sip from the whisky glass. 'And you, sir, are you, ah, coming or going, so to speak?'

'Going, old friend, going.'

'Am I to expect any house guests in the next few days, or will I only have the pleasure of your company?'

'Just me, Silas. I'm on a tight schedule.'

The old man sighed and rose to return the trays to the kitchen. 'That's a pity, sir. I rather look forward to your friends' short stays. Is there anything else you require, sir? Another dram, perhaps?'

'I'll take one to bed, Silas. I have a few telephone calls to make first.'

'Use the gunroom, sir. I have the fire lit in there also, tonight.'

Stuart got up and went into a full stretch. This was the only place in the world he felt safe. A typical Highland castle, the building was tall and narrow with six levels, including the main keep and the corner turrets, all joined by spiral stone staircases which would preclude anyone who was afraid of heights even going to the toilet. The gunroom was where Urquart had chosen to have his living room. It wasn't small but had a good fireplace and was easy to heat. Even though the building had had modern central heating fitted in the early seventies, Stuart's brother didn't allow him to use it when he occupied the castle alone.

Stuart picked up the liberal dram that still sat inside its sparkling glass and strolled through the seventeenth-century archway which led him back through the entrance passage and into the west stair-tower. Climbing one flight, he entered the warmth of the gunroom. Two of the walls were encased by cabinets with upwards of a quarter of a million pounds worth of best English shotguns, side-by-side stalking rifles and big game rifles locked within their leaded glass doors. Their vintage echoed back to when the map of the world was covered in pink and the British Empire was set to last for a thousand years. The other walls were covered in the dusty trophies from beautiful animals butchered by the lairds of Castle Stuart, in the name of sport, across two centuries. In one of the corners there was the castle's pride and joy. A cage hung from a chain attached to one of the high beams, in which was purported to be the preserved and polished skull of an ancient Campbell laird whose history was as dubious as the origin of the skull itself.

'Cheers,' Stuart said to the smiling skull, as he raised his glass. 'Here's to you and all who are not welcome in this stony pile.' He took a large pull at the glass and sat down by the telephone.

His calls went long into the night. When finally he went to bed, a full glass of whisky sat in a clean glass on the bedside table. Silas Urquart was long asleep in the east tower, the castle protected by one of the most sophisticated alarm systems in the country and a loaded Webley and Scott 25-inch-barrel shotgun under his four-poster bed.

Stuart slept the sleep of the blessed and awoke late to the bellow of a red deer stag high on the moor, the true lord of the glen.

3

The Game

'Ding dong', the aircraft tannoy called, and most of the 193 passengers on the British Airways flight to New York automatically raised their heads for a second or two.

'We're now making our final approach to John F. Kennedy airport, New York and would ask . . .'

The usual announcements followed and Stuart left his club class seat to freshen up in the forward cabin toilets.

He'd been dropped off at Glasgow airport by Silas Urquart, from where he'd booked a full-fare seat to the Big Apple for late that day. As soon as Silas had departed he caught the next Glasgow-to-London shuttle. Two hours later he was on the next BA 747 to New York, landing three hours and forty minutes before the Glasgow flight took off. The passenger manifest held the name Johnston, as did the passport in his briefcase.

When the aircraft rolled to a stop on the apron and the forward door swung open, the sticky, smelly heat of New York in summer cascaded into the cabin. Stuart let the initial rush to disembark subside and then fell in behind a couple and their two overweight, overnoisy and overindulged children. He carried only a small brown leather briefcase and a matching suit carrier, so he had no need to descend to the baggage reclaim area. Indeed, he never reached any of the formal entry areas, but turned into the tunnel marked Gate 27 and walked down to the end of the ramp. No airport personnel were present in the concourse. At the closed end of the articulated arm a door was latched back. The sun shone through, printing a lopsided rectangle on the sliding plastic screen which covered the articulated snake's mouth.

Stuart's eyes were shielded from the glare of the sun as he emerged from the tunnel into the light. The sunglasses hid not only his eyes but the intent beneath them. Walking immediately down the outside service stairway, he didn't pause or stop until he was seated in the TWA van which had been waiting for him on the tarmac. The driver and his companion were known to him, and whilst no one spoke, the former smiled a wide grin before pulling away. The smile held no warmth. In fact, there was little room for anything in the smile due to the large amount of gum that was continually being mashed, in high-fidelity stereo sound.

Disgusting habit, that, thought Stuart, but kept his thoughts to himself. The Gambino Family soldier wouldn't have the sense of humour to take a curved ball comment, and he was too tired to enter a macho verbals contest with a punk who normally wore a silk suit and white socks as a uniform, instead of the over white overalls currently cramping his style. This kind of street slime probably thought the only handgun worth having was a Smith & Wesson 0.44 Magnum, because Dirty Harry had once carried one in the movies. He wouldn't have considered that anyone entering a fast-fire exchange with a 0.44 would probably end up being knifed from behind, because he would be so deaf after loosing off six rounds that a herd of wild buffalo could creep up on him.

He settled down in the plastic seat and resigned himself to an hour of bad music with a chewing gum accompaniment.

The road north out of the city was engulfed in unusually heavy traffic for the time of day and it took longer than expected to reach the turnpike to the Gambino-owned estate, which was tastefully sited on an East River tributary. They changed cars en route, but Smiler stayed with them all the way. Stuart had been right, he wore white socks.

On arrival, the car drove past the New England-style mansion to a redeveloped laundry house which had been converted into a guest lodge some 20 years before. It was about a quarter of a mile behind the main house, but only a hundred metres from the running water.

The style of dress on the two fit-looking young men who lurked around the front door of the lodge said government not mob. On closer inspection they even had those silly little badges on their left lapels which helped the bad guys recognise the good guys more easily before they whacked them.

'This way, Major,' the blond Secret Service man said to Stuart as he got out of the car.

'Is there another?' Stuart threw back at him, as he passed and entered the wooden vestibule and strode on into the drawing room beyond. Hess was seated behind the desk and Cappricci slouched at the well stocked bar.

'Admiral, Cap, how are you both.' Stuart held out his hand to Hess.

'Still got my back, Thomas. You still got your overdraft?' Hess laughed.

'Yeah, but you're going to put that right, aren't you?' Stuart replied, with the same degree of mock warmth.

Mark Cappricci held up a glass in greeting as the exchange dwindled out, and Stuart returned his pretend salute by raising an eyebrow.

'I could certainly use one of those, Cap, if you're in the chair,' Stuart smiled.

'Your wish is my command. Admiral, can I get you something?'

'Bourbon and branch, Cap. Heavy on the branch, if you please,' Hess replied, as he sat down heavily behind the desk once more.

The drinks were poured and the men settled in their seats. Hess opened a red file in front of him. 'Operation Masada, 1965,' he began, 'to develop, and deploy in North Vietnam, a virus which would live for only twenty-four hours. During this short period of time it would infect the female of the species and render same incapable of bearing children for ever. Dropped by air onto the enemy, no toxin was to survive after the design period, thus protecting friendlies and rendering the

29

weapon a localised deployment facility with total deniability.'

Stuart let the typical official gobbledegook pass without comment. 'Why Masada?' he asked.

The admiral sighed and swung his chair around to look out of the drawing room window behind him. 'They all died in the end,' he replied quietly.

'Genocide,' Stuart stated, rather than asked.

'Strategic zoning,' Hess corrected.

'Strategic bullshit! In the Queen's English it's genocide,' Stuart repeated, 'You're beginning to sound just like your namesake.'

'Don't you give me that, I'm a Democrat and a good Catholic boy. The USA has not, nor will it ever, condone genocide of any colour, shape, kind or creed.'

'Well, good for the good old US of A,' Stuart smiled, 'but no people equals no people, and no people equals genocide in anybody's language. What's this got to do with the mission anyway? You obviously didn't perfect or deploy the weapon, or it would have been all over the media sometime over the last thirty or forty years, and some high-flying arses would have been sacrificed in the most public manner. I can see it all now, Hessgate.'

'Hey, Trap, that's below the belt,' Cappricci cut in. 'Let's all chill out and get down to basics. Ethnic cleansing has been an imperialist tool from the year dot.'

'*Chill out?*' Stuart mimicked. 'You've been listening to your kids too much. So, OK, what's the bottom line? Forget this Masada business. Only the *actual* target's detailed position in SL was missed out of the briefing in France.'

'Well, that's where we have a slight problem – the target.' Hess shuffled.

'What's the problem?' Stuart asked. 'You know I don't like curved balls from the home team.'

'No curved balls,' Cappricci defended, 'no curved balls.' He was walking up and down the room slowly, swilling the remains of his drink around the bottom of his glass. 'It's just that we have reason to believe that there's a chance, an outside chance, that the target is, ahh . . .'

'It's hot,' Hess finished for Cappricci.

'What kind of hot?' Stuart came back.

'Real hot,' Cappricci confirmed, without actually confirming anything.

'So, let me guess. What you're telling me, if your lady's briefing was correct, is that a very small sixties vintage nuclear warhead has fallen into the hands of the government thugs in SL, due to their discovery of the wreck of a long-lost flight that nobody has tried to find or retrieve for donkey's years. Now, you're telling me that on top of that, the unit itself might be compromised, throwing a hot zone out for some unspecified distance around the crash site. Tell me, why has no one gone in before, and what has this Masada weapon got to do with all this? It was never mentioned in France. Surely you had the flight covered by satellite and had it pegged before it even crashed, and wasn't it standard practice to have a fighter escort in those days? What the hell happened Carlton? Somebody must have really fucked up!'

Admiral Carlton Hess closed the file and stood up. *'Fucked up?'* he said quietly. 'Yeah, somebody fucked up. A guard on a security gate fucked up. A fuelling truck NCO fucked up and an overtired air traffic controller fucked up.'

'What are you trying to tell me?' Stuart asked.

'Trapper, they stole the fucking aeroplane, right from under our noses in England. We couldn't do a thing because of the cargo that was on board. They flew over Europe, city hopping as they went, to offer maximum threat to any attempt to down them. The French challenged them and a hero in an RAF Lightning actually flipped wings with them to try to scare them into landing. It appeared in the end that they were heading for Libya or Chad, but she just kept on going right to the edge of her fuel range envelope. Then, down she went in the north of SL. Hey, another thirty minutes and the whole episode would have been buried for ever in the Atlantic, where our research vessels could have picked up the evidence at leisure.'

'You still haven't answered the question as to why nothing has been done until now,' Stuart insisted.

'The area has been regularly monitored from space. Only

31

recently has the possibility of a hot spot turned up. The region, as you well know, is a close-knit area of variety. Jungle, swamp and savannahs all exist within a few miles of each another. We had every hope that nature would suck in or dissolve the problem away.'

'Still seems a bit thin to me,' Stuart sighed.

'Well, four million pounds in cash isn't a bit thin, especially when the terms are fifty per cent upfront,' Hess turned on Stuart.

Stuart was just going to cut in but Hess beat him to it. 'You've accepted the contract, Major Stuart, your down payment is in the next room. Cap! You fill him in on the operational details from our side and any intelligence he's not got. I've got to get back to Langley tonight. Good luck, Major. Pick reliable men this time, for God's sake, and do it quietly!'

'They're picked already, and if you're referring to the problems on the last operation, it was the men you asked me to take along with me that blew it, not my own people.'

'Gentlemen, gentlemen,' Cappricci cut in once more, 'the meeting started so well, with an air of mutual co-operation. Let's finish it the same way.'

'Just so, Cap, just so.' The Admiral shrugged. He held out his hand as he finished buttoning his coat. Stuart took it and the two front-line men gripped each other's hand, confirming the respect that all professionals retain above their personal feelings.

'Enjoy the money, Trap. On my calculations you're charging us double for everything. For God's sake keep it, this time. Retire – we're both getting too old for this bullshit.'

The old man and Stuart grinned at each other, then Hess released his grip and was gone with a shout to his driver, the young blond doorman.

'Come with me,' Cappricci said to Stuart's back, 'into the library.'

Stuart turned and followed the younger man into the multi-shelved room. It had been converted into a field operations room. The day was going to be a long one and the night even longer. As he closed the door, which melted into the shelved background, Cappricci threw in the curved ball that Stuart had known was buried somewhere.

'Oh yes, we forgot to mention, the Masada weapon was also on board the aircraft. Inconvenient really!'

Mist swirled low over the river's early morning sounds as Stuart and Cappricci opened the terrace doors to take in the rejuvenating morning air, untainted by the chemical reactions that the sun's heat would initiate in just a couple of hours.

'I think we can do it, Cap. That's all I can say right now, but I'm going to need more men to carry the hot gear for protection against whatever cocktail is brewing at the landing site, and we'll need much closer air penetration than you've planned.'

'Remember, the Sierra Laputu forces are thick on the ground without suit protection,' Cappricci encouraged. 'Officers trained in China, but the troops are very young and unmotivated. We assess that Western-trained units of Special Forces calibre will have a fifteen to one advantage on the ground. They have a few converted old British Hawk fighter trainers, but any air support is likely to be via French built Puma choppers, if they're working. A parachute descent from the height you're considering should have you at the LZ before the air intrusion has been picked up – if it ever is. You still think Gambia is your best springboard?'

'It's the only springboard just now. That in itself is a danger, but if you want to go *now*, then that's where the dice have fallen. My aircrew fly part-time for Air Gambia anyway, so there are extra gains on the table there as well.'

'They'll be flying commercial jets then?' Cappricci asked, almost as small talk.

'Between them, they're cleared on just about everything except modern, single-seater fast-jets. Bill Shanks flew Phantoms in the RAF, but not for long. Having said that, he can put a maximum payload Hercules down in your back garden and a DC3 down your chimney . . . *and* get them out again.'

'He drinks, doesn't he?' Cappricci asked.

'Been rummaging, haven't we, *friend*.' Stuart smiled back. It was a sneer really and the third-generation Italian knew it.

'Noticed it in a file once, that's all,' Cappricci loosely defended.

'Well, you're wrong. Old Shanksy boy doesn't drink, he goes on the raging piss! But not when he's working. He'll be dry from the moment he signs on.'

'And falling down drunk the moment he signs off?'

'Yeah, something like that.'

'It's just that I am supposed to approve all personnel profiles, due to the sensitive nature of the project,' Cappricci threw in.

Stuart put his head back and laughed. 'Cap, don't give me that Langley bullshit. Right now, you're Uncle Sam's number one potential scapegoat. From the moment you were given this assignment you became just as expendable as the rest of us and very likely to land in shit at any time. You're not behind your grubby desk, in that grubby building in Virginia, rising through the ranks on the back of the Harvard degree that the Family bought you. You're in the killing zone now. The only friends you have in the world are my team and the Family. If we win, you win. If we lose . . . well, you could always go back to the old country.'

Mark Cappricci looked deeply into Stuart's eyes. 'I guess you're right. Take the goddamned money and get outta here, Trap.'

The sun was well above the skyline of trees when Stuart pulled on to the freeway in the hire car they had had delivered to the lodge. All the briefings were over. All options had been considered and the plan approved by the President of the United States, by deniable proxy. All that was left to be done, was to do it. However, he would make one more visit before he returned to the UK.

Don Falcone was an old acquaintance. As well as being Mark Cappricci's great-uncle, twice removed, he was allegedly the head of the most powerful Mafia family on the East Coast, with tentacles that stretched round the globe, threading themselves through every niche of every government where ambitious men sold their souls for power, influence and the trappings that went with it.

34

As Stuart sat down to drink wine with the old Mafia godfather, Major Valentine Nelson was calling his small convoy to a halt.

The Suya River was swollen and the bridge to the east of Ngelun was almost awash, but still standing. Like all bridges in the country, it was too weak for modern traffic, which, although not frequent, was often far too heavy for the old foundations and wooden slats that made up the basis of the load bearing surface.

'Let the men out to have a break,' he said to the NCO driving his Landcruiser, as he slid out of the right-hand front door into the light brown mud of one of the country's main roads – a ribbon of narrow dust or mud peppered by a million potholes. Speeds above 30 mph were achievable, if permanent spinal damage was a serious aim.

Men and boys peeled out of the vehicles, and soon were lounging around or relieving themselves in the general vicinity of the trucks. Nelson watched a small group of them laughing and joking with each other. It didn't seem to make any difference what hardships these young men had to put up with. The reason was simple: living at home was worse. You starved, or died of a simple ailment which in the West could be cured by just popping into a chemist's. Watching their families die had become a normal part of life, and most of them had never known any government other than the current one. Most were devout Christians, with the odd Muslim thrown in. Nelson himself was a lay preacher when duties allowed. He knew that all this was just a trial by the true God, who eventually would deliver them all from evil.

Suddenly, the group of five soldiers he was watching dissolved into a mêlée of fire, mud, flesh and bone, their laughter and joking drowned for ever by a Chinese-made hand grenade. AK47 fire raked the rest of the convoy as the troops cocked their weapons and took cover behind the trucks and the neighbouring line of trees.

Knatcha, the senior NCO, slid in beside Nelson. 'They're at our rear and to the left, Major.'

'Take your platoon and work down the river bank for two

hundred metres, dropping off men on the way,' Nelson ordered. 'We will drive them down to you like wild boar. Take no prisoners unless you can pick up an officer.'

'Yes, sir,' the sergeant answered quickly, and was gone.

What had been a lounging rabble broke into two units. One returned fire and made a lot of noise, and the other slid away like a snake to the river bank to set out the killing ground to come.

Nelson left two platoons with the vehicles and moved northeast, upriver. Nothing larger than a grenade had been set against them, so he assumed they'd come upon an enemy search-and-destroy unit which was deeper into SL territory than recently experienced. Two hundred metres upriver they swung east towards the road, rolling out into a fan which quickly covered the enemy retreat to the north. As the last soldier in the fan reached the road, he stopped and clicked his radio switch twice. He received two clicks in return, and Nelson, at the head of the fan, signalled his men forward. Simultaneously, the holding troops at the vehicles ceased fire and pulled back to the river.

The attackers were now the quarry, but didn't know it. Their commander was a Nigerian mercenary who had deserted from a peacekeeping unit in the north. He took the silence by the vehicles to mean success and pressed home his attack.

As soon as the attackers moved forward, Nelson's men laid down an intense blanket of fire and launched themselves towards the river. Caught unawares, some of the attackers turned to defend themselves but were cut down in the intensity of the fire. The remainder ran forward, towards and past the trucks, into a hail of bullets from below them on the river bank. There was nowhere for them to run. They were caught in a classic crossfire configuration, allowing their killers to fire at will without risk of friendly-fire casualties.

The final headcount was 23, with 5 wounded on the enemy side and 6 dead lost to Nelson. The enemy wounded were collected behind one of the Landcruisers, but no officer's insignia could be found. They were quiet, with even their pain seeming to be of no concern. They were dead men and they knew it. This was Africa, not a white man's war with rules of engagement.

Nelson strode up and down in front of them. 'Where's your officer?' he asked, in a quiet, almost unconcerned way. Only blank and sullen looks greeted him. He studied their faces intently. His training in China had been thorough, and had never failed him in any interrogation to date.

'Well?' he repeated, but the blank stares never flinched. Taking out his pistol, he shot the soldier to the right of the group in the middle of his face. Blood and shattered bone blew back onto Nelson's uniform. He looked down and made a theatrical show of brushing it off with the barrel of the revolver. Neither the death nor the show made any dent on the blank faces.

'Knatcha, this man here is their officer,' Nelson snapped, pointing at a tall, thin, atheletic looking man with a dark black skin. 'Question him and then we will take him back to Freeman. Shoot the others.'

Hope flickered in the eyes of the man next to the executed soldier as he was dragged off. The remaining two were despatched with a single shot each from an AK. The Nigerian had tribal scars on his cheeks that were not of SL origin. This hadn't signed his death warrant, only the manner and route to it. After about 30 minutes the man's screams subsided and Knatcha returned from the bush with his platoon.

Nelson was resting in the driver's side of the Toyota. His eyes were closed, but his ears could see all around him in the fading light and he counted 43 steps as Knatcha approached him.

'Sir,' the NCO called.

'Yes, Knatcha, what do we have?'

'Nigerian scum. He and these rebels crossed the river last night and were just getting ready to break camp when we arrived.'

'Any Nigerians other than the officer?' Nelson asked. 'Any paperwork.'

'No to both questions, Major. Just these field maps,' the NCO replied as he held up a leather map case. Nelson's own was made of fraying green webbing. He took the case and threw it into the back seat of the vehicle.

'Get the men together, Knatcha. Let us see if this bridge is held up by steel or just God's will.

Major Nelson and the remainder of his men were safely over the bridge and well on their tortuous journey to the capital when Michelle Christie heard the tapping on the door of her hotel room. She'd fallen asleep on the bed, curled up in one of the hotel's extra-large towelling dressing gowns, after soaking and bathing away Washington's city grime.

'Yes . . . I'm coming,' she called, running her hands through her hair as she slid off the bed. 'Just a moment.'

She tightened the gown's belt and opened the door. There was a loud clunk as the automatic lock deactivated. Mark Cappricci was leaning on the door jamb. His suit was crumpled, he needed a shave and his Moschino tie knot lay loose below the open neck of a silk shirt that should have been changed at least 24 hours before.

'Buy your boss a beer?' he smiled.

'What's in it for me?' she joked.

'Dinner at McDonald's.'

'No sale.' she answered, and pretended to close the door.

'OK, OK. I give in. We'll drive out to Louie's, but if I don't get a beer now I'll never make it.'

'Sold,' she grinned, and bounced into the bathroom. 'The minibar's on the other side of the desk. Help yourself. Hey, you look a mess! Been meeting with the tax man or something like that?'

Cappricci broke the seal on the minibar door and pulled out a bottle of beer. It was a German brand.

'What's the matter with this country these days, when you can't get American beer in an American hotel bedroom.'

'Same all over the world, Cap. Same all over the world. Where are you staying?'

'One floor up,' he answered, as he clicked on the TV and took a deep pull at the neck of the frosted beer bottle. CNN materialised onto the screen. An attractive Barbie Doll clone, with a hard edge to her voice, was once more reiterating the problems surrounding Saddam Hussein's hidden nuclear capabilities and the threat to Israel and world peace in general. A picture of Saddam was hanging in a box in the air above her sculptured and well-sprayed blonde head, projecting from within yet another Japanese-made colour TV screen.

'We'll get you yet, you black-hearted bastard,' he said to the TV screen.

'What did you say,' Michelle called from the bathroom, 'I can't hear over the television.'

'Nothing,' called Cappricci. 'Just dreaming. I'm going to go and get cleaned up. I'll come down for you at eight – we can talk then.'

Michelle popped her head round the door. She'd almost finished her make up. 'Cocktail bar at seven thirty. Go on, you'll have to be quick.'

'Hey, who's the boss around here anyway?' Cappricci sighed, as he finished the last of the beer.

'Oh, you are, *sir*, but if you want to get a table at Louie's you're going to have to call right now and we're going to have to be there on time. '*Capisce?*'

'*Ho capito*, lady, *ho capito*,' he replied in bad Italian. 'Seven-thirty it is. See you later.' He pressed the room's door-lock button before he left and took the stairs to the next floor. A hotel messenger had left a note under his door. It was from Stuart. Cappricci called the number but it was engaged. He tried every minute for 15 minutes without luck and then went for a shower.

Stuart had spent the evening assembling his crew from all over the world. The hotel phone was red-hot, but he only had to confirm the meeting place with Bill Shanks and the initial logistics for personnel and equipment were complete. Shanks was in the air, due to land at London Heathrow in about an hour.

The telephone rang. It was Cappricci.

'How's it going?'

'Just about tied up, Cap. How's your end? Extra equipment on the road?'

39

'The aircraft is en route. Red Cross markings and a bellyload of UN aid marked for Upper Volta. Should be at Banjul by daylight, the day after tomorrow.'

'Why not tell the whole world, Cap? Perhaps you should come along with us? It might intensify your security interest.'

'Well, Mr. Johnston, ah do declare, the redcoats are restless tonight!'

The phone went dead.

Cappricci called Carlton Hess at his home. 'The Franchise has been sold. Contracts are in the post.'

'Good. That's good, my boy. Thank you for calling. Everything quite on the wires?'

'Oh yes, sir. Deathly quiet.'

'Well, let's hope it stays like that. When are you due back in the office?'

'If all goes well, in three days. We meet with the Sierra Laputu Commissioner to the UN tomorrow at three p.m.'

'In New York?'

'No sir, here in Washington.'

'How's the girl doing?' Hess asked, his voice rising in pitch ever so slightly.

'Good prospect, Admiral, but nothing has gone wrong yet.'

'And it better hadn't. I doubt your career could stand it. Keep me informed. Oh, and good luck.'

The line went dead. It was the second time it had happened to him in the last ten minutes. He stood in his shirt tails and ankle socks, staring at the phone, looking a little ridiculous. 'What the hell,' he said to the mirror over the desk. 'Bunch of prima donnas. Everything's under control.'

He dropped the phone into its cradle and grabbed a different expensive silk tie. It was seven fifteen. He didn't want to be late for cocktails.

Michelle was sitting at the bar when Mark arrived. She'd gone down early for two reasons. She liked to play the singles game and being early would make her boss late, even if he was on time. Her dress was a strapless black velvet, Helen Storey number, which was body-hugging enough to require tights or self-supporting stockings. Suspenders were out of the question, they'd ruin the line of the hips and thighs above the short tailored hemline. Janet Reger underwear completed the feel, and a single pearl, hanging from a flat gold neck chain, rounded off the look. Her hair was down, but pulled to one side by a diamond clip over the left ear. Chanel had designed their No.5 for a woman like Michelle and she wore it as a body perfume as well as in the normal areas women aimed its delicate fragrance. As a result, all her clothes held a residue of the perfume and it was always there as a background to her life. She was simply and naturally stunning.

'You look wonderful, my dear,' Cappricci said, loud enough for all to assume she was spoken for.

'Being inside a suit that doesn't look like it's been slept in does a lot of good for you too, Cap.'

'Well, the cab awaits. We'd better make a move.'

She slipped off the stool and straightened her dress for a second or two longer than necessary, but long enough for every man's attention in the room to be drawn from their own partners. Mark Cappricci's ego swelled as he escorted her out through the crowd.

The journey out to the Italian restaurant took 20 minutes. During the trip, most of the conversation came from Michelle. Mark was very much aware of her body next to his. This, combined with the lack of food, and three beers in 45 minutes, made his stomach rumble and ache.

'Someone sounds hungry,' Michelle smiled.

His pupils were dilated. 'Yes!'

She reached out and held his hand. He lifted it and kissed it. Her pulse lifted a few beats and her hormones reminded her that she hadn't had a man for a long time. Looking at her attractive boss, she knew it would be easy tonight, but Mark Cappricci wasn't the right man, in the right place, at the right time.

She squeezed his hand and then removed it from his grip. 'It'll be nice to have an escort tonight without having to fend him off, boss. Thanks for the invitation.'

Cappricci's eyes registered real disappointment for only a

second. It was replaced by mock horror. 'My heart is broken! I shall kill myself!'

'Don't do it, buddy,' the cab driver called over his shoulder. 'I don't got insurance for bloodstains.'

Everyone laughed. The moment was gone and no harm had been done.

The evening went well and they returned to the hotel at around 11.30 p.m., both as fully up to date on the operation as Cappricci wanted. They said goodnight at the lift and Michelle went to her room alone. As she closed and locked the door a voice said, '*Shalom*, Miriam.'

Yani Bar-David was sitting in the armchair by the bed. He'd been there within ten minutes of Michelle leaving for the cocktail bar before dinner. After sweeping the room for listening devices, he'd sat in the dark, awaiting her return.

'Yani,' she began.

'I have very little time,' the young Israeli said quietly. 'Fill me in and then I must go. I have an early flight out in the morning and much to do before I leave.'

They spoke for an hour. Bar-David wrote nothing down.

'So now we have it. The Americans have an illegal weapon and a small nuclear device lost in Africa. Not only have they lost them, but they lost them a long time ago. My God, if this irresponsibility hits the world press, it will bring down the President and the Administration. They use the name Masada well. It will be those on Capital Hill who will not survive this time, if the mission is a failure.'

Yani rose and held the girl at arm's length, by both shoulders.

'Be careful, Michelle, and be ready to run at a moment's notice. I don't know how our people will react to this news, but they have been desperate to have a lever on this President for some time. I can't see that they won't use it in some way.'

'I will, Yani,' she said, and kissed both his cheeks. 'Be there for me if I need you.'

'Always.' Then he was gone.

Hours later, Yani Bar-David watched Stuart check into the Concorde desk, before following the same ritual with the smart British Airways hostess.

'Good morning, Mr Davidson,' she smiled, as he passed over his ticket. 'Could I also see your passport? Thank you.'

She punched away at her console and then passed Yani's ticket and Canadian passport back to him. 'Seat 2A has been pre-booked for you. Is that OK, sir?'

'Yes, that's fine, thank you very much.'

The console threw out a boarding pass from its printer.

'Have a pleasant journey, Mr Davidson. Do you know the way to the lounge?'

'Sure do,' Yani answered. He didn't, but it seemed the right thing to say.

Yani took time out to make a long-distance call before settling down to champagne and strawberries. He sat within earshot of Stuart, who sat alone, reading the *Herald Tribune*. After a few minutes, Stuart rose to get a tomato juice from the complimentary counter. Yani noticed the stance and the walk. Yes, he thought, all hunters have the presence of the leopard and the aura of the lone stalker. They are never clumsy and, except to a trained eye, merge into the background with ease.

The flight was called.

Six hours later, Yani was inside the Israeli Embassy in London, Stuart was on a flight to Brussels and Major Valentine Nelson was one hour from Freeman.

4

The Death Kiss

The last person to arrive at Stuart's room was Bill Shanks. He'd been drinking, but not too much.

'Well, if the devil could cast his net . . .' Shanks laughed, as he entered the room.

There were a few 'Hi' and 'Helloes' from the gathering. Stuart called them to silence.

'Right! Shut up, you lot. Everyone here knows everyone else, but I'm going to run through specific duties before I run through the operation. Shanks, you're flying a C130 Hercules. You're in command of it and its security. You drop us in, return and come back for us at the pick-up point. Pick up is considered hot. Any problems so far?'

'Normal,' Shanks replied, looking around the room for a sign of drink.

'Petey, you're explosives, mines and the heavy-calibre machine-gun.'

'Biggest load, as usual,' Pete Van der Merwe, replied.

'That's because you're the biggest son of a bitch north of the Caprivi Strip,' Shag Skinner called from across the room.

'Cool it, Shag,' Stuart cut in. 'We haven't got time for the pleasantries. Anyway, you're his and Chet's back-up. You're not getting away with only carrying your blades and an AK.'

John 'Shag' Skinner was a natural assassin. He preferred the knife and was only one ounce away from being crazy. In the complicated confusion of a hand-to-hand firefight, Skinner was often thought lost. He would emerge after the battle was over, covered in blood and mud from one of his famous crawls through the enemy positions. Often, he despatched more of the enemy than the liberal sprayers of automatic fire. Using the knife, he could see their eyes when they died ... Many couldn't control him. Stuart could.

'AKs, eh? I hate that Russian stuff. Must be Africa, right?'

'Yes, it's Africa again, but a new patch,' Stuart answered. 'Just hold on. Let me do this my way.'

'Hey, you're the boss man; no problem,' Skinner deferred.

'Right. You're Petey's back-up with the equipment. Dave, Mitch, Steve and Mike, you won't be surprised to learn you're anything and everything. Chet, you, of course, are riding point or hanging back as sniper.'

'That's good, Trap. Anything that keeps me as far away from you mad mother-fuckers is all right by me,' Chester 'Chet' Maclazowitz replied with a smile. The only non-European in the group, he was an extraordinarily skilled long-distance sniper from Wyoming, via the Green Berets. He'd killed at 1700 metres with a modified Galil 7.62 mm semi-automatic sniper rifle. Only he remembered when he last missed.

Recent new investigations into JFK's assassination claimed that it was impossible to fire the three shots that officially came from Oswald's rifle and hit the target within the timeframe available. Chet could do it in his sleep. He knew of two others who could also do it. When he was killing at long distance, after he'd lain in wait for a long, long time, he sometimes got an erection just before he pulled the trigger. Once he nearly had an orgasm. He sometimes wondered if the kill would actually make it happen one day.

'OK, I'll run through the operation, then you'll all know why the pay is so good,' Stuart said, as he uncovered a large map of Sierra Laputu.

'Who's done the planning and logistics programme?' Van der Merwe asked.

'Combination of me and the client,' Stuart replied.

'I miss Yanders,' the Dutchman said to nobody in particular. 'Best at that kind of stuff. I trusted Yanders to get me home.'

'So did we all, Petey,' Stuart said to the same ghost. 'So did we all.'

'We never paid our dues on Yanders,' Skinner cut in.

'Forget Yanders. He's dead!' Stuart shouted.

'Yanders isn't dead until we get the little shit that pulled the rug from underneath us. Dying for money or a cause is one thing. Betrayal is personal,' Pete Van der Merwe insisted quietly.

'So it is,' Stuart agreed, 'but not on this caper. Now, can we get back to the job, or do you guys want to bullshit all night?'

'Hear, hear,' Shanks added. 'We're wasting good drinking time and I have to go on the wagon tomorrow.'

'Yes,' Mitch Carter said, 'get on with it. The past is the past.'

'Right, gentlemen. This is a recovery or destroy mission, and the target can turn round and bite you for the next twenty-five thousand years.' The room fell silent. Every man had taken money upfront; they were in, whether they liked it not – all the way there and, God willing, all the way back.

The operational briefing lasted five hours. It identified the mission: to recover, or if all else failed destroy, a small nuclear source; the means available; risks; route in and route out. The Masada weapon was not included in the briefing. Several extra items of equipment were identified as desirable, if not necessary, by the team. Stuart immediately ordered these items through Cappricci, who advised they would be made available at the C130's fuel stop in Malaga, by the Sixth Fleet, which was on NATO exercises in the Mediterranean.

'Well, fellas, that's it. Any more questions?' Stuart asked, finally.

'I think we've just about cooked the goose,' Bill Shanks replied for everyone.

'That raps it up then. There's a bar in the next room, but remember, the next time we meet together will be in Gambia. Tickets on departure at the designated desks tomorrow. From now on you're on your own. Don't let me down.'

The meaning in the last statement was not lost on the gathering. From the moment they left Stuart's room they were under battlefield orders. A court martial consisted of a bullet in the

46

head. They had witnessed Stuart dispense judgement in the past, in the field or later – much later, when the offender thought he was safe and home free.

The party didn't last long, much to Bill Shanks' disappointment. The men peeled off in ones and twos to get rest. Bill Shanks waved goodbye to Stuart and partially fell into his ordered taxi. Stuart watched him disappear round the corner and then returned to the operations room. He went over the plans time and time again through the night. His flight was the last one out the following evening. He would have plenty of time to sleep during the day . . . plenty of time.

Shanks left the taxi quickly, passing too much money over the seat to the driver, who shrugged, smiled and drove off.

Catching the lift to the third floor, he fumbled for his key and was still fighting with the lining of his jacket pocket when he reached the door of his room. Having successfully negotiated the door and the bedroom, he staggered into the bathroom for an emergency discharge.

The ritual having been fulfilled, he followed the remainder of his regular post-drinks procedure: shit, shower and a shave. The three S's. It saved him the bother in the morning, when the hangover was singing and the hands were unsteady.

The shower felt good, and afterwards he rubbed himself very hard all over with the lush white bath towel. All he needed now was the shave and a liberal splash of aftershave to send him to a clean, smooth and comfortable sleep, which would allow him to awake refreshed and ready to fly to the moon, or any other godforsaken place on the flight plan he was given.

He plugged in his old Braun shaver and looked into the mirror. 'Well, old son, let's make our handsome, debonair and only moderately crinkly white hide ready to screw as many of those lovely dark beauties as we can find, shall we?' He switched on the razor and ran the smooth blade cover over the day and a half's worth of beard growth, the vibrating blades feeling good on his cheek. There was a separate sideburn trimmer on the shaver and he noticed a rogue hair sticking out across his left ear.

47

A split second after he clicked the trimmer on, plastic explosive inside the shaver blew two-thirds of his head clean off. Brains, bone chips and one eye slowly ran down the outside of the singed shower curtain and the peppered tiles beyond.

The charge had been expertly weighed and placed to kill, but not to create panic. Several guests were awakened by the noise, but when a noise is over, it has to be repeated to a newly wakened person for them to associate the noise to the wakening itself. In this case it wasn't, so they turned over and went back to sleep. Henry Windman, a salesman in the very next room, was watching a late-night porno movie and he thought the explosion was a car backfiring in the street.

Mark Cappricci rang Stuart's room number five seconds after the latter's bedroom alarm had burst into life.

'Yeah,' Stuart growled, from a very dry mouth.

'Shanks bought the farm.'

'Say again?'

'Bill Shanks died,' Cappricci repeated.

'Tell me,' Stuart replied, almost awake.

'Bomb in the hotel room.'

'How big?'

'Enough to take his face off and require a certain amount of interior decorating in the bathroom.'

'That's it then, we have to delay until someone like John Sandys is available.'

'There is another option,' Cappricci offered.

'None that instantly hits me between the eyes,' Stuart replied, now fully awake. He was staring into space as he listened and noticed a damp spot on the ceiling. The thought crossed his mind that it was a bad deal for the rate charged.

'Well, we could give you a pilot from the SEALS in the Med . . .'

There was a long pause, then Stuart said, 'Same price?'

'Same price? I do not fucking believe it! A guy you've known for years has just been whacked, the day before you go live on an operation and the only thing you have on your mind is the fucking price?'

'Haven't got time for a dead man now. I can – *will* – audit those books in the fullness of time. Who've you got?'

'The C130 delivery man.' Cappricci offered.

'Cleared?'

'Cleared? This guy is from F18 training and passed through Air America, Laos.'

'Oh, a regular nutcase who didn't have the brains to make a million on the side and is still flying?'

'He's all you've got and a damned sight better than some of the old crocks you hang around with.'

'What's his name?'

'Hartman – David Hartman.'

'Same price?'

'Yes, OK, same price, you – Christ, I nearly said *mercenary* bastard.'

'Quite, and don't you forget it. Tell him to stay by the plane and not to do anything until I approach him.'

'How will he know?'

'Need to know, Cap. He'll know, believe me.'

'I'm the controller of this operation, for Christ's sake, *I* fucking need to know!' He was wasting his breath, the line was dead. 'Stuart, I'll have your ass in a sling if it's the last thing I do,' Cappricci said to nobody, and then threw the phone into its cradle. A small piece of plastic broke off it and flew across the room.

At 2 a.m., Cappricci had to go to the toilet. On the way back to his bed he stepped on the sharp sliver of white, jagged moulding. The wound it made was deep and it bled for a long time. Cappricci cursed Stuart to Hell and gone. The sooner this operation was over, the better.

On the approaches to Freeman, Major Valentine Nelson felt the same as Cappricci did. The problems were different, but the basic reasons the same: fear, trust, betrayal.

Nelson's men had their orders. They were to stay in the vehicles unless called for, but to be ready to defend themselves if it all went wrong.

As they sped past the Freeman barracks, a strolling corporal noticed the very dirty and muddy vehicles because they were too dirty and too muddy for Freeman deployment. It was obvious that these speeding vehicles were straight from the front. He mentioned it casually to an MP in the guardhouse just inside the gates. He, in turn, called the duty officer to ask if any units were due at the base that day. The officer knew of none, but he would check. It was something to do.

Nelson's column drove past State House and out to the point past the Tumani Palms Hotel. Everything looked as it should be. There were two ceremonial guards at the entrance to the seat of power and an army Land Rover parked to one side. A couple of well-to-do looking business types were entering the building. Everywhere else, within a stone's throw of the grounds, had the smell of the crushing poverty that spread throughout the countryside like a poisoned snake.

The column drove up to State House too fast, reflecting the nervousness of everyone in the vehicles. As the second truck pulled to a halt, the left rear wheels kicked over a pothole in the roadway. The shock unlatched the truck's tailgate, and it slammed down onto the chassis. Under normal circumstances the *crack* would only have turned a few heads, but the tension in the forward truck snapped and the soldiers poured out, cocking their assault rifles as they fanned out in the crouch position. Nelson couldn't believe his eyes, nor could the Presidential Guards. The two soldiers threw down their shiny rifles and held their hands on their heads. Nelson screamed at his troops to halt and withdraw, but some were already inside the building.

Inside, Alpha burst into the President's office. 'It's the army. There's a mutiny!'

'Where?' President Mokomo asked sharply.

'Here, my President, here! They're downstairs now. We must leave.'

The President was a large, overweight man, but he moved like a ballroom dancer across the office to his safe. Within minutes he had a briefcase full of his most personnel documents and a handful of high-denomination dollar bills. Soon, in the background, he could hear the rotors of his personal

Puma helicopter starting up. Alpha would be at the controls.

Downstairs, Nelson had a mêlée of different noises searing in his brain. The blood was pumping in his ears. Every door and passageway was full of officials and army personnel, but no resistance, just smiles and calls of support. The only problem was, support for what? All they'd wanted was their pay.

Outside, in the grounds, Mokomo and two of his wives loaded their children into the helicopter. Boxes and suitcases were thrown inside in a haphazard manner. At the controls, Alpha was urging speed to the fleeing family.

'Go, Alpha, go,' Mokomo cried out, as he tried to slide the door shut.

The chopper lifted almost immediately. Nose down, it swept out to sea, climbing all the time; north over the estuary, over Bpungi airport and onwards towards the neighbouring country of West Guinea. By the time they landed in Albertville, an official friendly welcoming party was at the airport to meet them. They were free, safe and very, very rich. Mokomo had only one thing on his mind though: the manner of death that he would impose on the upstarts on his return. They had nothing. They wouldn't last two minutes.

Nelson looked out to sea as the chopper disappeared. Turning to a young captain beside him, his fears welled up. 'Well, Cassa,' he said quietly, 'what will become of us now? We came for pay and food, and instead we appear to have inherited a country!'

'We will lead it, Major,' the young officer asserted. 'The people will be with us. Listen, it's happening already.'

In the immediate vicinity of the government building, people were chanting and weapons were being fired into the air. Nelson looked at his watch. It had taken less than 90 minutes. He suddenly felt weak and drained. What next?

Out of his depth and feeling as though he were being carried along on an uncontrollable wave, he turned and returned across the lawns to the house.

'God give me wisdom,' he whispered, under his breath.

Captain Cassa strode out alongside him. He was only 27 years old, with the fire of youth still in his heart. Destiny held him in the cup of its hand, but he didn't know it. There was just the excitement of a new beginning, pumping untold adrenaline through his veins.

David Hartman watched from the cockpit of the Hercules as the last of the equipment pallets were forklifted up the rear ramp of the aircraft. He hadn't delivered the C130 Hercules, as Cappricci had advised Stuart he would, but had landed at Malaga in the right-hand seat of an Intruder two-seater light bomber despatched from the fleet some 12 hours before. Four of these hours had been spent in high-security clearance briefings and the rest checking equipment lists and the mechanical integrity of the weapons.

The Herc was in dark bush camouflage colours, sporting markings of the air force of Ghana. It was an early model, but in good condition. The orders to change its markings to that of the Red Cross had been cancelled. On board, one of its extras was a satellite navigation package which included a direct satcom telephone link to Cappricci's operations centre. Only Hartman was to be aware of the call facility. No one on the operation, including Hartman, was aware of the satellite tracking beacon within the system which allowed Cappricci to know the aircraft's position at all times to within a hundred metres, anywhere in the world.

When the last of the ground staff had gone and the fuel tanker had completed its discharge into the aircraft, Hartman locked all the cargo doors and entrances from the inside. Slinging a sleeping cot across some of the cargo webbing, he settled down to charge up his batteries with some badly needed sleep. He could allow himself nine hours and still be well in time for the rendezvous schedule in the Gambia.

When he awoke, the early morning light gave witness to mist which had drifted in from the sea.

He dropped into the pilot's seat and called the airport tower. The news wasn't good. The airport was closed and was likely to remain so for some hours. All flights and taxiing were suspended.

Looking out of the forward windscreen, Hartman was

reminded of the misty morning flights from the secretly public airbase in Laos, carrying anything, anywhere, anytime, in support of the American war effort in Vietnam. It seemed just like yesterday. A far cry from being a SEAL instructor, with his pension not far away. Martial arts had kept him fit and his genes didn't open the door to baldness, but the last thing he'd expected was to be called back into clandestine direct action.

One of the problems of not fighting a major war every 20 years was that real experience was hard to find. Very few people had Hartman's varied skills and experience.

He strapped himself in and commenced the start-up procedures, just as if he were going to take tourists up on a flight over Disney World. The visibility was about 50 metres, but enough to keep the white lines of the runway in sight. The controllers in the tower didn't hear the engines over the whine of their radars, but an engineer in one of the hangars heard the initial start-up and called his supervisor in the office block.

By the time the tower was alerted, Hartman was already pulling out of the stacking apron and onto the runway approach. The air traffic controller in the tower was going crazy on the radio, trying to stop an unknown aircraft heading in an unsure direction.

'Malaga Tower, this is Ghost Rider on your screens approaching runway south. Confirm gateway clear to 20,000 feet.'

'Aircraft calling Malaga Tower. Please confirm your call sign and shut down immediately.'

'Malaga Tower, this is Ghost Rider exiting gateway to the south to 20,000 feet. Confirm clear flight path.' Hartman smiled, as he eased the throttles forward and the scream of the engines hurled the C130 down the runway.

'Aircraft on runway south, this is Malaga Tower. The gateway is closed. Do not, repeat do not, attempt a take-off.'

The Hercules rose in a steep climb and came out of the fog at about 5,000 feet, headed east for 30 minutes and then curled to the west, climbing to 15,000 feet to join the submitted flight plan. He called Cappricci on the direct link. *He* could make the arrangements to calm Malaga. But Hartman wasn't sure who was going to calm Cappricci.

5

Cocktails and Bitter Ice

'Well, Michelle, what are the wires telling us today?' Admiral Hess growled.

'Our little team have all arrived safely in the Gambia, sir.'

'Good, good . . . Anything on the pilot Shanks?'

'Nothing yet, sir. The Brits are passing it off as an IRA thing of some kind. *"Reports sketchy. No claims for responsibility"* and all that kind of stuff. The usual.'

'Those Irishmen have given the Brits an excuse to do just about what they wanted to do, or cover up, for the last 20 years. No wonder they don't find themselves a settlement. When are they going in?'

'Cap should be along with an update directly, Admiral. We have a commslink scheduled in, well now, actually,' she replied, looking at the brass cased ship's clock on Hess's wall, or bulk-head as the Admiral insisted in calling it. 'There's been no contact from Stuart at all. If Hartman wasn't there we wouldn't have a clue what the status is.'

'You won't hear from Stuart until it's over. Why should we? We don't *know* him, do we?'

'Well, not officially, but what if he needs help?' Michelle asked.

'If he needs help he'll be dead. He wouldn't call us, anyway. He trusts us no more than anyone else, even though we are paying him.'

'Well, we're certainly doing that. The contract price is outrageous.'

'He'll have put a cool mill away on the side,' Hess chuckled.

'He's a shithead,' Michelle said, surprising herself as much as Hess.

'Yes, but avoid telling *him* that, if he gets back.' Mark Cappricci walked into the room with a scratch pad in his hands. His face was grey.

'Well, Mark, what's the SITREP today? Did you get the comms-link?' Hess wanted to know.

'Yes, the schedule was made. They're going in early.'

'What do you mean, "they're going in early"?' Michelle asked, startled.

'How early?' Hess followed up.

'They're in the air now.'

'The hell they are,' the Admiral spluttered. 'What the fuck's going on around here? I thought you were supposed to be controlling this operation, Cap. What's wrong with your man Hartman? Why didn't he call in? Is he sleeping out there? We went to a hell of a lot of trouble to get a man on the inside of this operation. We need to know.'

'Well, sir, Hartman isn't sleeping, he's dead.'

The room fell into complete silence. It was Michelle Christie who spoke first.

'It was Stuart,' she said, in a level voice.

'Yes,' Cappricci answered.

'Some way he found out, but how?'

'As far as we can tell, Hartman arrived on time in the Gambia, after a somewhat unorthodox exit from Malaga. They all boarded the plane, it taxied out to the runway and suddenly Hartman was dumped out of a side door during take-off.'

'Dumped out? Who the fuck's flying the goddamned plane, for Christ's sake?' shouted Hess, his frustration exploding.

'We, ah, don't know, sir. No one else in the party is supposed to be capable,' Cappricci offered. He looked like a schoolboy who'd been brought up before the headmaster in a Dickens novel.

'So, let's get this right. We have a bunch of cut-throats, with a C130 full of some of America's and Russia's best killing equipment, flying on the most sensitive mission we've launched since ... since ... Hiroshima, and we've no intelligence on what's happening. Marvellous! At least we can track where they are.'

'The beacon's been disabled as well, sir.'

'Of course it has, Cap. Wait a minute, you said the scheduled commslink was made. If Hartman is dead, who made it?'

'Stuart did,' Michelle Christie answered for Cappricci.

'I'm afraid so,' he confirmed.

'Then, children, I'm afraid that everyone in this room is now on a very select list.'

'Sir?' Michelle asked.

'The hit list of one Major Thomas Trapper Stuart.'

'But why? We can say that we put Hartman there as back-up, not as a spy,' Michelle said.

'It's not Hartman,' Hess replied, 'he was just the victim. Shanks is the problem. Stuart will believe that we killed Shanks to substitute him with Hartman.'

Michelle was startled. 'I thought we did.'

'No,' Cappricci cut in, 'we just took advantage of an opportunity.'

'Nobody told me,' Michelle almost spat out. 'Who did, then? Who killed Shanks?'

'We don't know, Michelle. We need to know, but we don't,' Hess answered.

'And you let the operation continue?' she asked.

'No choice ... timing. Now you two get off each other's backs and come up with a new operational strategy, pronto. *Capisce*, Italian?' Hess threw at Cappricci.

'Yes, sir,' they both answered in unison.

As Hess went out of the room, leaving his two agents in partial shock behind him, Stuart was savouring the African night through the Herc's cockpit window. John Sandys smiled at him from the left-hand seat. The team was complete again.

6

Broadswords and Magic

The Hercules took the inland route, to avoid traffic control at West Guinea's Albertville airport, and cut the northern Sierra Laputu border. There was a red hue in the sky over the horizon as they latched onto the River Seti's tributary to the north of Bakia, keeping the Koma Mansa range to the south.

The operations plan called for them to land at a disused mine's airstrip, abandoned long before the Jamayal Group got their hands on the majority share of the country's diamond assets. This, they would *not* do. Stuart and Sandys strained their eyes through the dawn to find a strip of low bush that would allow the Hercules a successful landing. It didn't take long. Stuart signalled with a down-turned thumb to Sandys, who nodded and pulled the Hercules over to starboard to clear his view. One pass told him that he could slot her in fairly easily and he called into the intercom for the rest of the men to strap in and brace themselves in the crash position. A red light appeared in the cargo area.

Ibex ran ahead of the aircraft as it skimmed the light brush with its undercarriage down. As soon as he hit the dirt, Sandys triggered the rear ramp and it started it's slow descent. If the hydraulics were damaged, they wanted the ramp down, not up. They were doing about 90 knots when they touched down, and the cloud of dust thrown up behind them in the red dawn made a back drop worthy of a great master's palette.

Two hundred metres into the landing, one of the nose-wheel

tyres burst and threw her sharply to the left. Sandys was up to it and he controlled a potentially damaging slide to bring her to an incredibly noisy, but safe, standstill.

When the engines were cut, a deathly hush returned to the savannah. It lasted only seconds as the mercenaries in the cargo area quickly unstrapped to jump out of the three-quarters-open cargo door and throw up a picket around their area. Skinner ran forward and Carter ran aft 150 metres from the aircraft then hit the dirt. They, and all the rest of the men except Sandys, were wearing SAS-specification personal communications equipment, allowing whispered calls across long distances. After about two minutes, Skinner called in first.

'Skinner. All clear forward.'

They only had to wait a few seconds before Carter echoed the call from the rear position. It had taken him a little longer, because Skinner had been able to range his scan into the light of the east. Carter's security arc looked straight into the retreating night sky. The whole area was supposed to be deserted and apparently this intelligence was correct.

'OK, everybody out,' Stuart called into his microphone, as soon as Carter clicked in his clearance.

Their vehicles were 4-litre Jeep Cherokee open-topped four-by-fours, with a mounted 50-calibre machine-gun on the lead vehicle and a towed equipment trailer on the second.

Van der Merwe gunned the lead Jeep out of the ramp exit, which was still six feet above the ground. The vehicle flew out of the aircraft and landed with consummate ease in the dust.

'Take it easy, Petey,' Stuart snapped, 'or you'll be lugging that fifty earlier than you planned.'

'No problem, Trap. This baby can fly.'

'Well, this one can't, ' Steve Rider chipped in from the second vehicle, with the trailer.

'It won't have to,' Mike Landau laughed, as he put his huge frame behind the manual descent lever. 'Two minutes and you're out.'

'Fifty quid it's three,' said Dave Tomlins under his breath.

'I heard that,' Landau called. 'You're on!'

Stuart let them get it out of their systems before he called them to order. The LZ was safe and adrenaline was flowing in rivers.

As Rider's combination rolled out of the fuselage, Stuart and Sandys dropped out of the cockpit into the hold. Chet Maclazowitz was still sitting in his webbing seat, chewing gum, with his long legs stretched out and crossed in front of him. The deadly sniper's rifle lay across his knees.

'Don't overdo it, will you, Chet,' Stuart said, as he and Sandys strolled past him.

'You got it, Trap,' Maclazowitz grinned. In the days to come, he would walk many miles alone, sleep lightly and act as their guardian angel; point man when the squeeze was on and sweeper when they were pulling out. Now, he rested.

'I wouldn't hang around too long, Chet. It's going to get hot in here quite soon,' Stuart called over his shoulder.

'So what's new?' Maclazowitz threw back, as he rose to follow them out.

Inside the aircraft were two more Jeeps. They were loaded with fuel cans and plastic explosive. They weren't going anywhere.

'Outfielders come home,' Stuart called into his radio, as he walked down the ramp. 'Let's roll.'

Within a minute, all the team were mounted in the Jeeps and ready to move off. Sandys took the wheel of the lead Jeep and Rider the second. They pulled away for about 70 metres and then stopped. Stuart swung out from beside Sandys, lifted the Herc's flare gun and launched a red flare into the hold of the aircraft. He was back in the Jeep, and the wheels of both vehicles were turning, before the flare landed. They were at least 200 metres away before the explosion racked the aircraft and the surrounding countryside. Anyone who found the remains of the Hercules, with the vehicles inside it, would assume it had suffered a fatal crash, along with all aboard. The group turned south towards the target. If all went well, they should be within stalking range by sundown.

Stuart loved Africa, but not what he'd helped do to it. The whites had raped it and left it armed to the teeth, to become the playground for the cold war factions. Tribal feuds which had lasted for hundreds of years had been turned into mechanised civil wars, to become the testing ground for the white man's skill in creating sophisticated weaponry. At first, he'd fought for those he perceived were the good guys. They needed training and planning skills to add to their instinct as guerrilla fighters, which initially hadn't easily been transferred to the skilled use of weapons that killed at long range or could be scattered ad lib over the countryside, to maim man and animal alike with indiscriminate disinterest.

As the years went by, he'd become a product of Africa herself. There were no good guys. The African value of life was from a culture so different from that of the white European that it had taken the Afrikaners several hundred years to understand and survive in it. They were just another tribe on a continent of tribes. Who knows what this spectacular continent would have been like now if Washington, Moscow and Peking had chosen not to play their war games there. Now, it was the home of children who killed each other to eat, rather than bother to grow or ask for food. This would be his last job. It would pay for his recent losses and leave him with enough money to live comfortably for the rest of his life. A new identity . . . a new passport . . .

Stuart's thoughts were interrupted as Sandys stiffened beside him. 'Company!' he called to Stuart, lifting his head to see more clearly ahead of the vehicle.

The low sun, in the early morning sky, threw easily seen shadows across the tracks they had just crossed. Stuart flagged the small column to stop and waved Maclazowitz out of the second Jeep to join him.

'How many? How long, Chet?' he asked.

The tall man got down on all fours and inspected the vehicle tracks carefully. He delicately pushed the high rim of one side of a track over with his little finger, rose and slowly wandered off down the track route, pausing now and then to confirm some detail or other on the lined earth. Stuart stayed where he was and the rest remained silent in the shut-down vehicles.

'Chet?' Stuart asked, without impatience.

'I'd guess two light vehicles, same as us, plus three trucks . . . all heavy.'

'How long?'

'We're right up their asses, buddy. I mean right up.'

Both men scanned the horizon ahead.

'No dust,' commented Stuart.

'Yep. They've been travelling all night. Why stop now?'

'Could be water?'

'Could be anything.'

'OK, big man. Hit the road. We'll pull into that scrub over there and wait for you to send a postcard.'

'Call sign. Hawkeye?'

'Roger on that . . . Go!' Stuart pointed down the track lines.

The big man moved off at 45 degrees to the tracks themselves. He would stalk the prey with the sun at his back.

'Into that scrub, Steve,' Stuart called softly to Rider in the second Jeep. 'We'll follow.'

The two vehicles pulled under cover and Van der Merwe checked the action on the 50 calibre machine gun, mounted on Stuart's Jeep.

'Skinner, take the watch.' Stuart ordered.

'Yo!' replied Skinner, already moving.

'Silent running, guys. No smoking. Petey, you stay with the fifty. Everyone else out of the Jeeps and lie low.'

Stuart positioned himself so that he had a clear view of the target zone. Hawkeye was already nowhere to be seen.

Maclazowitz had travelled just over a mile and a half, downwind of the tracks, when he smelled the food cooking. The stalk would be easy. He moved silently south and east. A group of trees and lusher vegetation were to the north of him and he expected to find water and the target under their shade.

A small herd of white-tailed deer appeared across his path. He wanted to access a small bluff behind them, which should give him enough height to complete his surveillance from a good distance. They were grazing at right angles to his intended path, but as they were already upwind he decided to wait.

Five minutes after the last deer had passed, he broke cover

61

and walked calmly and slowly towards the medium-high brush which latticed the base of the bluff. The deer ignored him completely. Instinct told them that the demeanour of this other animal was not threatening. No special smell haunted their memory.

He reached the crest of the bluff almost an hour after the target's tracks had first been seen. The rifle's scope fitted snugly against his right eye and he focused it without powering up the laser, in order to save battery power. The crosshairs focused on the front of a Mercedes 40-ton truck. It looked almost new but he couldn't see its military markings because of the angle. The second was rear on to him, its canvas flaps tied back and the tailgate down. The third truck was older and looked Japanese in style. It was sideways on and some markings were in view. Chet clicked the magnification up two notches and reassigned the cross-hairs.

'Broadsword,' Chet said quietly, into his small mouthpiece.

'Go,' Stuart replied immediately.

'About forty. Heavily tooled up. Part of the pan-African peacekeeping force. Some of Gerry's boys.'

'Ghana?' Stuart half stated, half questioned.

'Bang on.'

'Shit! What's your status?'

'Well clear . . . high, with a wide eye.'

'Stay put. No action. Broadsword clear,' Stuart closed out. If the Hawkeye heard nothing from them for one hour, he would call in. Communications were to be kept to a minimum at all times.

'Outrider?' Stuart transmitted.

'Yo,' returned Skinner.

'Front's covered. Watch the back door at five hundred.'

'I'm gone.'

'OK, guys,' Stuart said to the waiting men. 'They came, they'll eat, they'll go. We wait. Rest but keep tight. We want in and out with minimum contact.'

They settled down in the cover of the brushy copse. Stuart could have done without this delay. So far he'd been ahead of the game. Any delay was bad. He looked up at Petey on the back of the Jeep. He was slowly scanning the skies. Peace-keeping forces usually had air support around. The last thing they wanted was to have a chopper drop in to see them.

'This is bad shit, Trap,' Van der Merwe said, over his shoulder.

'Can it, Petey,' Stuart growled. 'Just you keep your eyes open for unwelcome visitors.'

The Dutchman scanned the skies to the south-west. Bad shit was bad shit. Even the man couldn't change that.

Pete Van der Merwe settled down on the back of his Jeep.

Chet Maclazowitz lay motionless in the rising heat of the day.

Stuart counted every second as it passed.

Caesar Falcone – Don Falcone – sipped ice-cold champagne from a thin glass, at home, with a guest.

'Is the champagne to your liking, Samir?' he asked.

Jamayal lifted the fluted glass and ran the index finger of his left hand down its dewed contour. 'Perfect temperature, as always, Don Falcone.'

'Refill Mr Jamayal's glass, Mario.' The old man indicated to his long serving retainer.

The aged servant carefully extracted the bottle from its ice bucket. He wrapped the linen towel around it accurately, with practised ease. Not one drop of water fell to the floor or dripped onto the polished, eighteenth-century dining table that separated the two men by 20 feet.

Jamayal nodded his thanks as the glass was filled, but left it in its place on the table.

'I have ordered lamb, in the style of the Yemen, my friend,' Falcone offered.

'You're too kind. It's my favourite dish. But when you're next a guest in *my* home you must allow me to offer you the best of your own Italian food and wine.'

'I accept your kind offer, Samir. The delights of good food and wine are one of my few pleasures in these changing times.'

'Just so, Don Falcone, just so. Is it not a great disappointment that a man must go to such lengths to care for and feed his family, nowadays.'

63

'Ah, yes, a family is indeed a great worry. The young have new and dangerous ideas. They have to be controlled if business is to continue in an organised and focused way. Discipline, now more than ever, is of paramount concern to our interests, in every corner of the world that we operate. This business in London, for instance, has caused me great concern. I personally guaranteed the safe passage through Europe of the, shall we say, *tourists*, to your adopted country.'

'The unfortunate accident to the pilot was an act of utmost disrespect,' Jamayal apologised.

'It must be redressed.'

'And it will, Don Falcone. It will. I'm confident that my people in London will have a name soon. It's just a matter of time.'

'Time? What is time? How much of it do we have left in this snapshot we call life?'

'It is as Allah wills, my friend,' Jamayal said, raising both his hands in the universal sign of resignation.

'But, old friend, things must be as *I* will. However, let us not talk of will, or God. How are your wife and the beautiful girls? How many now.' Five?'

'Six,' said the Lebanese multimillionaire, his pallor a shade lighter than when he'd arrived at the sprawling estate. His eyes were unblinking as the food was served. These Italians, he thought. One day they would show him, Samir Jamayal, respect. First, he must stay alive. These businessmen made the savagery of butchers like Saddam Hussein look like a Jersey kindergarten. He believed Falcone would kill his own daughter in the name of Sicilian honour, if convention required it. Also, he knew that behind his back, Falcone called him 'the pale nigger.' One day there would be a reckoning . . .

'Oh, the lamb! The chef has surpassed himself. It is exquisite.'

'You're too kind, Samir, too kind. I do so look forward to our little chats and too infrequent meetings. This month's diamond shipments were of extraordinary quality. It's so comforting to know that De Beers remain under stress and continue to fear our potential volume.'

'Just so, Don Falcone, and if the situation in the Soviet Union continues to relax, the volume end of the medium to low quality diamond market will be flooded. High-quality, large-carat merchandise from Sierra Laputu remains the very best in the world.'

'What of these Zambian pirates?' Falcone asked.

'They continue to import their stones into SL to have them re-exported as original Laputu stones, but we continue to track them down.'

'The leaders?'

'The leaders never leave Zambia and have protection at the same level as the Colombian drug barons. We would have to go to war to stop them at home.'

The meal they ate was of a standard equal to, if not better than, the most famous tables in the world. The two men talked of many things, from investments to politics.

Murder was never mentioned, but hung over the proceedings at every level, a tool to be used after great consideration of need, effect and the consequences of the action. In these modern days, it was an ultimate sanction not a habit. Of all the requirements of their trade, its unwise use could result in unexpected market ripples which were, bad for business.

Mario served Louis XIV brandy and the two settled down into the depths of leather wing chairs, which guarded a small bay window at the far end of the room, away from the double-door entrance.

'And so, Samir. What of our unexpected stroke of fortune in your jungle?'

'Hardly jungle. It's a combination of thick brush and lush vegetation in the high water table areas. I always feel that the word *jungle* represents something deep, dangerous and unending for many miles.'

'Like the Bronx, you mean?'

'Ah, Don Falcone! You expect me to say *no*, but I say *yes*. A jungle can have many locations, but its essence remains the same. It has depth and height, which makes an interloper expect some hideous creature to be lurking in the near distance, or watching from a camouflaged canopy. The

65

undergrowth and towering cover can be vegetable or mineral, but the constant danger is always animal. My real home is an example. Lebanon was the jewel of the Middle East. Beirut its Paris. The animals that lurked in the cover were vicious, from different lands. They chose to treat a garden as a jungle and the weeds grew; their tentacles strangled the garden until only a perverted jungle was left, inhabited by the predators within it.'

'So you left and went to Africa.'

'We Lebanese are traders, educated traders. Who can make trade in the middle of a war whose cause has been lost in the mists of time and changed by the warriors themselves to meet their own changing ends, as the conflict grows and is sustained like a living animal within the living jungle itself?'

'But life is a war, Samir. In fact it is a constant kaleidoscope of different but interconnected wars, each one a tributary of the river which flows to the ultimate destination, the seat of power.'

'Don Falcone, *you* have great power and influence. This height of control means different things to different men. Tell me, what does it mean to you?'

'To me?' the old Sicilian answered. 'It is very simple, my friend. It means a great responsibility. Many people and families rely on my guidance. The Family is me and I am the Family.'

'A family built from the blood of its enemies?'

'Blood? Yes! Blood, sweat and tears, Samir. But the old days are over. The dinosaurs are nearly all dead. I consult these days with lawyers and accountants, governors and senators. Only rarely do the men from the old country sit at this table, and when they do I see reflections of the empty shell that I have become inside. My children despise me, but take my money. My wife lives in luxury, but still remains a peasant from a mountain village at heart. We all remain foreigners in a foreign land, because we live within this Family which together sustains us and brands us at the same time.'

'So it does not bring any comfort or happiness?'

'These luxuries are dangerous in our business. We may have

66

them, but never appear to have them. We must deceive ourselves as well as others.'

'And if we deceive ourselves, what do we have left to hang
on to in this life?'

'Just the power, Samir.'

'And the insanity to use it?'

The old don rose from his chair and walked towards the bay
window. 'Insanity? Yes, I believe you're right. The insanity of
ultimate power, wielded from the shadows to mould, corrupt
and influence the powerful; to create and nurture more power
for its own sake.' He turned and looked at the fine-featured
Arab sitting opposite him. 'There must be no slip-ups in Africa,
Samir! You do understand that, don't you?'

Jamayal started to rise, but Don Falcone held up his hand
and signalled him to stay where he was.

'There is much at stake of which you do not know. The
very fabric of the White House can fall into our hands, if we
succeed.'

'If a small band of white mercenaries succeed,' Jamayal
shrugged.

'They are some of the world's best, in the kind of terrain
and the type of country we are dealing with. If they fail, the
CIA will be blamed. They always are.'

'If they fail?'

'I have already said they must not!' He turned to stare out
of the window. 'Thank you for your company, Samir. Go back
to Africa. I hope we meet again.'

Jamayal rose and walked towards the dining room's magnificent double doors and the hallway beyond. Mario appeared
from nowhere with his coat and scarf. 'Your coat, sir,' he smiled.
'Have a safe journey, sir.'

'Oh, I will, Mario. You can count on it,' Jamayal replied with
an exaggerated smile. 'It is written.'

'Allah, sir?'

'No, old man, Samir Jamayal! Samir Jamayal!' He turned on
his heel and in a second he was gone.

'Goodnight, sir,' the retired assassin called after him politely,
as he closed the outside door slowly. The large brass catch

confirmed the oak door shut with a deep *clunk* and he turned to attend to his master's needs.

'Can I get you anything more, Don Falcone?'

'Yes, old friend. Get our ambitious young associate in West Guinea on the line. It's time for him to go to work.'

'Another brandy while you wait?'

'Why not, Mario, why not? The night has just begun. My slippers also, if you don't mind.'

Mario returned to the brandy decanter and poured a triple measure into the don's large balloon glass. He laid it on the small chestnut table which sat beside the leather chair and then walked over to a 1920s-design telephone on his employer's old and spiralled yew desk. He rang an international-length number from memory and waited. The lines to West Guinea were engaged and he tried again immediately, but it was almost an hour after the first attempt that Mario heard a phone ringing at the other end and a sleepy voice answer. 'Hallo.'

'Alpha?'

'Yes.'

'Hold the line.'

Falcone lifted himself in his chair and cleared his throat. He took only the handset from Mario and spoke quietly into it.

'All the players would appear to be in the ring, my young friend,' Falcone said, across the echoing link. 'It is time for you to earn your pay.'

'We are ready,' Alpha answered.

'You have everything you need?'

'Everything except the timing.'

'The timing is now. You can make history and a great deal of money. Not many men have an opportunity like this in their lifetime, my young black friend. Use it wisely; the prize is awaiting you.'

'You can rely on me, Do—' Alpha stopped. He was strictly forbidden to use Falcone's name during any calls or on any communications.

'I know I can. You have so much to lose,' Falcone replied, returning the handset to its cradle.

'That will be all for tonight, Mario,' Falcone smiled. He spoke in Sicilian Italian and Mario thanked him in the same dialect.

Mario left the room and Falcone followed him out, turning to climb up the sweeping staircase. At the mezzanine floor he stopped and reflected on the display of pictures and works of art. They were his pride and joy. Many witnessed the battles and leaders of centuries gone by. His eyes came to rest on a picture of the Scots King Robert the Bruce watching the arrival of his world-renowned spider and the web it spun in his cavern hideout. The picture was almost ten feet long and had once graced the walls of a castle in the Highlands of Scotland. It had been a gift from an old friend. He wondered if the web he, Falcone, was weaving, would trap the intended fly or suffocate all within its complex and sticky depths. The web was spun. The die was cast. The consequences would arrive with the inevitability of the rising tide. Who drowned and who floated was, for the time being, in the hands of others.

The old man smiled at the picture. 'Goodnight, my kingly warrior. Beware of your companion. *He* may be a *she* and bite off your head !'

'Company!' Pete Van der Merwe called, and swung the 50 calibre machine gun into the sun.

'Shit!' Stuart spat under his breath. 'What and how many?'

'Two choppers, fast and low.'

'Hawkeye, this is Broadsword. Make like a chameleon, we got birds of prey incoming.'

'Hawkeye, copy. Our friends hear them also,' Maclazowitz replied from his sniper's nest.

The two Bell helicopters were many years old, but their distinctive blade throb stirred memories of other flights and other wars as they slid over the bush like carrion crows on the lookout for someone else's kill. The pilots were white but the markings were Nigerian.

'More peacekeeping wetbacks,' Stuart passed on through his comms system to the rest of the team. 'Keep loose and blend.'

The Hueys flew straight over Van der Merwe's position. Both pilots were veterans and picked up the barrel of the 50-calibre easily as they swept over the thicket.

'We've been made,' Petey called, as his eyes met those of the second pilot.

'OK, everybody move out. Hit the metal,' Stuart ordered. 'Hawkeye?'

'Yo, Broadsword.'

'Waste anything that moves. We're coming for you.'

'How's my backside?'

'In the wind, buddy, in the wind. Don't miss!'

'OK, I'm live,' Maclazowitz confirmed. 'You-all don't sneak up on me. It looks like it's going to get exciting outside the nest. Hold on, the choppers are here . . . OK, they're splitting up. Number two is doing a one-eighty back to you. Door gunners are harnessing up and he's hauling rocket pods.'

'We saw the pods,' Stuart confirmed. 'Do your thing now, Hawk. Do it now!'

For Chet Maclazowitz, time went into slow motion. It always did when the need to kill arrived. No matter what was going on around him, whether hand-to-hand fighting or the silence of a high tree nest, the cross-hairs of his rifle scope were the centre of his being. They were his eyes, connected to his retina by invisible threads.

As he settled the cushioned eyepiece to his right cheek, the familiar swelling in his loins greeted him and comforted him in the same way that an infant clings to, and searches for, the safety of its mothers nipples. The rifle was silenced with a removable muffler. In Chet's hands it was spectacularly lethal. The peacekeeping contingent from Ghana wouldn't know what had hit them.

The first group of soldiers to come into Chet's field of vision were loading equipment into the back of the second truck. There were six of them. The first two fell almost together; shot in the middle of their backs. One was killed outright, the other suffering a shattered spine which would leave him paralysed from the waist down for the rest of his short life. Their companions dropped their loads and looked around with helpless looks on their faces. One bent down immediately to attend to his fallen friends. Chet passed him by and placed a round in the left side of the man's head behind him. It exploded in a crimson shower that sprayed the remaining soldiers in the group into terrified shock. As they paused, they died.

The first helicopter had remained over the camp but didn't land due to the confusion below. The pilot strained through the dust. He tried to fix the direction of the incoming fire to the camp and the combined unit below, but his hover was too low and created too much dust and noise; all the elements of panic and confusion that Chet thrived on. His kill rate was in excess of one soldier for every four seconds. One soldier, one father, one son ... He had 27 kills before Stuart's group engaged and 5 more before he was spotted by the helicopter pilot.

Stuart knew his first priority was Maclazowitz, and the assault group sped at full speed towards his position. The pilot in the second chopper had expected them to take up a defensive position against his attack. He was taken completely by surprise when the vehicles shot out of the thicket towards, not away from, the unit from Ghana. The four-litre Jeeps were hitting close to 80 mph before the Huey even started to turn out of its overshoot. No shots were fired by either side. As the pilot banked, Van der Merwe homed the 50-calibre onto the sliding bird.

'Nail him, Petey. Don't let him loose those pods off, or we're fucking mince-meat. Hawkeye, what's your status?' Stuart called down the comms link.

'I'm made by the bird, but he hasn't got any teeth.'

'Personnel carrier?'

'Roger, it's a *Slick*.'

'We'll be there in five.'

'Make it four, he's putting up a dust cloud all over me and I can't attain target status. The blacks should be all over me in seconds, unless they've got shit for brains.

'No way, you big freak,' Van der Merwe cut in. 'We can't let the Kaffirs get you, you might give them indigestion. Just let me shoot a high "pheasant" and we'll be right with you.'

'Clear the air, you lot,' Stuart shouted. 'Petey, we're waiting!'

A 50-calibre machine-gun is an awesome mobile infantry weapon, easily capable of taking out the side of a building. As a close-up anti-aircraft weapon, it has a speed-to-kill ratio better than most anti-aircraft missiles.

Pete Van der Merwe loosed off a blistering blanket of fire, just as the Huey was approximately 20 degrees off completing its attack turn on the convoy. The type of ground the Jeeps were covering was level and medium hard, so his aim was hardly compromised.

As the pilot died, his fingers cramped over the rocket launch trigger. The pods on both the port and starboard sides of the aircraft systematically disgorged their lethal cargo into the air as it started a fatal spiral into the hot savannah. Rockets lanced harmlessly around the compass rose as the dancing chopper fell to its death.

'Hold on, Hawk,' Stuart cried. 'Bird 1 is down and we're right up your backside breathing fire.'

'Roger, Broadsword. I'm putting a grenade blanket down to buy time and make me feel better.'

'Feel better, buddy, we're here,' Stuart shouted.

Skinner was the first out of a Jeep. He had three Master Tanto killing knives in a shoulder sling which had once held a pistol in its original incarnation as a shoulder holster. In his hand he held a customised Trailmaster which sported a 9-inch blade made of Carbon 5 steel. He disappeared in the dust of the chopper's down draft before the second Jeep came to a halt.

'Hawkeye,' Stuart called. 'Skinner's out. We're coming to you from the front. No frills. Can you see us?'

'See you? I can smell you! Tell Petey not to take the bird out until I'm clear, or he'll drop it right in my lap.'

'Got you,' Van der Merwe cut in. 'Get the fuck out of there, you big girl's blouse, I'm on a roll!'

'Up yours, Dutchman,' Maclazowitz laughed.

'For God's sake keep it down,' Stuart called again. He was right on the edge. His men had walked into a firefight before they'd got past the starting blocks. Their adrenaline was flowing in almost lethal doses. Clear thought was under extreme stress.

'Landau's hit, Tomlins bought the farm,' shouted Rider,

suddenly. 'I need cover at the water's edge right now! Where the hell's Chet?'

'Right by your side, baby,' the big American replied into his microphone, as he touched Rider's shoulder.

'Trapper?' Maclazowitz called.

'Go, Hawk,' Stuart replied.

'Take the chopper, I'm clear.'

'It's history,' Van der Merwe chipped in, and raked the unarmed aircraft with decimating firepower. One of the main rotor blades disengaged from the main drive shaft and careered through the waterhole's treeline. The Slick Huey rolled over onto its back but the 50-calibre kept on firing as the tail section started to part from the fuselage pod and its rotor screamed in self-destruction. It exploded on the rise where Maclazowitz had been nesting, but the explosion itself suffocated most of the fire that could have caught hold. A sudden silence fell on the veldt and the dust started to settle.

'Headcount and status,' Stuart ordered over the air.

Everyone except Skinner, Landau and Tomlins called in. Landau was going to be a problem, he was gut shot. The men came in from their final assault positions, and the standard weapons and personnel checks commenced. It was Carter who came upon Skinner. He was washing his right arm and the Trailmaster in the waterhole. His face was splattered in blood. The Tantos were still housed in their leather scabbards.

'You OK?' Carter asked.

'Who, me?' Skinner giggled through glazed eyes. 'OK? Sure, I'm OK. Are you OK? Is everybody OK? Of course I'm OK! What's the matter with you, Carter? Shit yourself?'

'Fuck you, Skinner,' Carter replied. 'You need some serious fucking help.'

'We'll all need some serious help if we don't sanitise this site quickly and haul ass,' Stuart cut in. 'We must assume they got a radio call out and that even in Africa someone is going to send someone to check what happened . . . Now let's get with it!'

Every body was counted and confirmed dead. Those that were not dead were despatched by a shot to the head, saving

73

at least one of the wounded from a lifetime in a wheelchair. Stuart shot Landau, while giving him a drink of water and assuring him the wound he had was minor.

The bodycount was 47, including Landau and Tomlins. The corpses were left where they fell, but the two dead mercenaries were covered in gasoline and burned. No one spoke over their bodies. Their shares would be spread equally between the survivors. Neither had any family.

As they regrouped and prepared the small convoy for its continued journey, John Sandys found himself next to Stuart at some distance away from the others. 'If Yanders were here, he would be advising you to cut your losses and pull out. They know we're here now. They may not know why we're here, but this operation is not a quick seek-and-destroy mission any more.'

'Who told you it ever was?' Stuart asked with a cold stare.

'Well, no one actually, but the way you described the mission it felt kind of quick, clear and surgical.'

'Well, the patient can claim malpractice, because we are up to our arses in political alligators and you would be surprised how little I care! We're going all the way.'

'To where?' Sandys asked sarcastically.

'Wherever I say. All right?'

'Yeah, yeah. Wherever you say,' Sandys conceded.

Pete Van der Merwe's Jeep approached them. 'Mounted up and ready to roll, Trap,' he said softly.

'About time,' Stuart quipped, forcibly changing his mood. 'Let's get the hell out of here.'

The assault group pulled out of the waterhole and headed back on course. They were way behind schedule and moral was generally low, except for Skinner. He sat in the back of the second Jeep with a vacant smile on his face.

'Shit!' said Stuart under his breath, when he saw him. Nobody heard.

7

Falcons, Foxes and Freshmen

Avraham Sharon's motor yacht was modest but comfortable. It rarely went to sea with Sharon on it, but appeared in various Mediterranean ports for extended periods during the year. He used it mostly as a weekend getaway. The sophisticated, microfrequency communications equipment fitted on board kept him in touch with all his contacts throughout the world. Today, the vessel was tied up in a familiar marina, just below the Carlton Hotel on the Tel Aviv seafront.

Sharon sat on the aft deck under the shade of the bridge deck canopy, reading a book. A plastic bottle of Highland Spring water sat in an expensive silver-plated ice bucket to his right and a small wickerwork table to his left. Two deckhands were going about their business around the vessel and another was sitting in the pilot's seat inside the navigation bridge, watching the world go by.

They were expecting Yani, but only nodded acknowledgement as he walked down the pier and mounted the short gangway.

'Find a seat,' Sharon growled, without lifting his head. 'Just let me finish this section and I'll be right with you. Only a page and a half left. Have a drink.'

Bar-David looked round and picked a film-director-style folding chair from a pile of half a dozen stacked at the entrance to the saloon lounge.

Sharon finished reading and studiously folded over the corner of the page he'd just completed.

'We used to get a smack round the ear for doing that at school,' Yani said, with a smile.

'Me to,' chuckled Sharon. 'I think that's why I do it.'

'Bad example, sir,' Yani joked.

'I don't have to set examples any more, Yani, just make them,' Sharon replied, bringing the conversation back to street level.

'Speaking of which?' Yani asked.

'Speaking of which,' Sharon confirmed.

'Well, the game has become very complicated.'

'Are we still in it?' Sharon cut in, looking at the young specialist over his half-moon glasses.

'Yes, but only just. Stuart's team are in and should be at their target about now. The target remains as intelligence suspected.'

'The nuclear source?'

'Yes, but there's a twist.' Yani waited, expecting a comment from the old man. None came, so he continued. 'There's a lot of peripheral interest. In fact, so much that I wouldn't be surprised to see the operation advertised in the International press.'

'That bad?'

'Well, perhaps not that bad, but you'll see what I mean as I go on . . . Stuart has stolen a jump on Cappricci and probably blames him for the death of the pilot Shanks.'

'As planned?'

'As planned.'

'So the assault group will be working alone, trusting nobody?'

'Also as planned.'

'And the twist?' Sharon asked, without impatience.

'The Mafia.'

'The Mafia! Whose Mafia?' Sharon asked.

'*The* Mafia.'

'Which family?'

'All of them,' Yani said, almost under his breath.

'What do you mean, all of them?'

'Falcone himself, the capo di capos, boss of bosses –'

'*The* godfather,' Sharon finished the sentence for his young gladiator.

76

'Yes, *the* godfather.'

'So, my young friend,' Sharon said, stretching his arms and legs and settling back in a half-sitting, half-lying position in the wooden and canvas chair. It creaked heavily as he moved. 'Let me get this right, Stuart is *in*; we have succeeded in destablising his relationship with his employers, the CIA; the government in SL has unexpectedly changed and we don't know what their knowledge of the situation is . . . or do we?'

'Not yet, sir.'

'Not yet. OK, so *they* are wild card number one; the Mafia are wild card number two?'

'Not quite,' Yani said uncomfortably.

Sharon, the old SABA fighter, had an uncanny and simple way of bringing complicated issues down to success or failures in his officer's competence. Yani was beginning to feel exposed. 'We have discovered there is an uncommon link between some of the major players, but we haven't closed the loop on it yet.'

'What is this . . . uncommon link?'

'Stuart met Falcone before the operation began and it has been known for many years that Cappricci is distantly related to Falcone.'

'It has also been known for many years that Stuart and his kind have the highest connections in the underworld all over the globe. This is not news, Yani.'

'Not in itself, but after tailing Stuart to the Falcone estate, we left surveillance there just in case.'

'And?'

'Samir Jamayal was a lone dinner guest just a few days ago.'

'Jamayal?'

'Yes, sir. Samir Jamayal, The Fox of Beirut.'

'God! Stuart, Falcone, Jamayal and Cappricci's lot all involved in this operation in some way? Yani, we're missing something; something which is probably staring us smack in the face but we don't see it.'

'Something more important than a nuclear warhead?' Yani questioned.

'More or less important, who knows? What I do know is that we've a nest of the most unsavoury vipers I could think of, all

77

mixed up together in some kind of unholy marriage, or possibly separate marriages for a prize, or prizes, that we've not yet identified.'

'Then the warhead is a smokescreen?'

'No, no, my boy. The warhead is very real, but someone is using it as a cover for something else. I'm sure of it.'

'What do you suggest we do?' Yani asked, raising his hands in frustration.

'The door we have to open will be in the files at Langley. Stuart may or may not have the key. Our operative there will have to be put at risk. She must be proactive, not reactive. She must dig, take risks. We must discover what the vipers in the nest think their prize is.'

'And if we do find out, what then?'

'Then, Yani, we decide if we wish to claim the prize for ourselves.'

'So, we can add one more viper to the list, sir?' Yani asked.

'No, no, we are not vipers, Yani,' Sharon chuckled. 'I prefer to hunt from the high ground. The snake has only one enemy on the edge of our Israeli deserts and it comes from the sky. We must fly high and see far, and when the time is right, strike fast and silently with talons which are sharp and strong. No, not a viper, an eagle, Yani . . . more like a desert eagle.'

Sharon smiled at Bar-David, taking pleasure from being in the game. The young man rose and folded up the deckchair, placed it where he'd found it and turned back to his boss.

'We haven't much time, sir.'

'Call her now. Tell her we need information within twenty-four hours or we may be too late. Use the white phone in the saloon. It's got a standard scrambler, but I suppose she's got a clean phone in case they do an internal security scan on her apartment?'

'Right in one. They check people with her level of clearance on frequent occasions. They even went through her laundry last month to check for evidence of sexual activity.'

'Did they find any?' Sharon asked.

'No, and neither did we.'

Michelle Christie was in bed in her new Washington apartment, when the phone call from Yani Bar-David came. Her security file at Langley showed that she had a brother who lived and worked in Durban. Yani played the brother, affecting a slight South African accent in case the phone calls were recorded.

'Michelle, it's Eugene . . . You awake?'

'No, little brother, I'm asleep. I talk in my sleep, didn't you know?'

'No shit?'

'No shit! Before you ask, I can't send you any more money this quarter. I just bought the flat and my pay cheque just made me solvent.'

'It's just a couple of hundred bucks, by wire.'

'Why? No, on second thoughts, don't tell me. When do you need it? I'm too tired to argue.'

'Within twenty-four hours. You can wire it to me through American Express.'

'Sounds like you're in a mess again. What on earth makes you do these things?'

'You know me, sis. Always getting let down by so-called friends and finding myself out on a limb, with no time to sort things out.'

'OK, but this is the last time . . . and I am going to tell Father.'

'Too late, he knows. I asked him first and he got real excited. Wants you to call him, but please send me the money first.'

Michelle looked at the clock on her bedside table. 'It's three a.m. I'll wire you the money from the Amex office as soon as it opens and call Dad tomorrow. OK?'

'Sis, I love you. Come see me soon. Bye.'

'I love you too,' she said to a dead phone.

The coded play-acting over, Michelle lay back on the bed, stretched her legs and arms and ran her hands through her hair. It needed washing. Too much hairspray for the reception last night. Too much hairspray, but who for? She'd had lots of male attention as usual, but almost before she knew it herself she'd put up the hands off signals, resulting in her being alone once more in the immaculate bedroom.

Her right hand strayed to the moist lips between her expensively smooth thighs.

She was in the habit of bringing herself to orgasm at least three or four times a week. A man had never managed to do it to her during full lovemaking. She'd been close, but never fallen over the edge. The couplings always ended with him satisfying himself and her making the right noises. Suddenly, she felt pathetic and removed her fingers from their comfort zone.

'Shit,' she said under her breath, as she threw the silken covers off the edge of the bed and stomped into the bathroom.

The room contained a separate fully tiled power shower. It was big as showers go; as was the shower rose. The water was hot, but not too hot, and she stood with her back to the energised spray. It massaged her neck and relieved the muscle knots she'd gone to bed and awakened with. The orgasm would have helped, but the tension was deep-seated and her new instructions had turned the knots from rope to steel. She tried to fall back on her training and close out the seriousness of the risks into which she was about to launch herself. It was for this reason that she was here, to step into the dark alone; out from behind the false lifestyle and identity to betray all she'd been. This, for a country that had taken her under its wing when her parents were killed in a bus by a terrorist bomb. Taken? No, not taken – nurtured and educated in another country. Built, constructed and moulded by the Mossad web, to be loyal, questioning but obedient, silent, patient but deadly, for the good of Israel.

Her training had been second to none. She knew that because the CIA had trained her as well. Parallel training for the same reasons and the same job, for two different countries who were supposed to be friends. The country she was to betray was always going to be the country that she'd lived the majority of her life in. It was the country she knew, liked to live in, understood . . . *home!*

If she had to run, would she like to be an Israeli in Israel? Her mind flew through the options and uncertainties, the biggest worry being her certain knowledge that under extreme stress, in Cannes, she'd had rings run round her by a disgraced soldier whose IQ and intellectual persona probably wouldn't get past the fifth grade. Could she survive, in the probing, amoral tinderbox that awaited her now that she was really to become fully active, in the depths of the most famous and tarnished security service in the world? Suddenly, it all seemed unfair on *her*, not the people on both sides who had trusted her and extended the best opportunities of twentieth-century living to her.

She switched off the welcoming waterfall and stepped out of the gold-framed glass door. She would make a special effort to look attractive today. If people were looking at her, they might only see the picture and not the treachery that stood at her shoulder. Let them see what they wanted to see. The Trojan Horse? Well, not quite. Perhaps the Trojan Filly. She would be careful not to overdo it. As she looked through her wardrobe and planned her outfit, confidence started to return. If she got caught, she'd be the best-looking arrestee that the grimy corridors of Langley had ever seen.

'OK, kid,' she said, 'stop stalling and get to it.'

She dressed with practised ease. The designer suit was a Chanel original and the matching heels had cost her 700 dollars in Beverly Hills. She was always smart when she went to Langley. Today, she would let her eyes hang for that extra second on the eyes of those who looked at her longer than necessary. She would smile. Not a big smile, just enough to say she'd noticed them as well, men and women alike.

The word *Langley* is bandied about in novels and movies all over the world. It conjures up visions of romance, intrigue, James Bond. In truth, it's a grubby place which resembles a well-used Midwest high school rather than the hub of a nation's intelligence and covert operations front line. Like a hospital, Langley has its own smell, from countless years of sweaty bodies working long hours; acres of Brazilian rainforest transformed into a billion files that will never manage to get converted onto floppy disks because there's never enough time; coffee-stains in the carpet that never quite come out, but blend with the cleaning agents to add unspecific depth to the background aroma; dirty windows with their cosseted collection of dead flies; the hint of water stains on a few of the walls; clean, but tasteless washrooms; smoke . . . Michelle's perfume was light and fresh, but it cut into Langley's invisible smog like a plastic surgeon's knife. The smell was there and you couldn't miss it, but when it passed by it only held your attention for a second or two. The surgeon's scar is fine and almost invisible.

She signed in with casual purpose and made her way to the corner office on the third floor which had been her home since the operation commenced. Mark Cappricci was struggling to access a cup of coffee from a vending machine, known as 'Capprici's folly', lodged in a little alcove next to his office and opposite hers. There was also an aging photocopier which broke down every two days and a shredding machine which could perform murder one if not treated with respect. The coffee the machine produced was very strong, but tasted more of the plastic cup it was served in than the beans that had been sacrificed to make it.

'Kick its ass, Cap,' she called, as she passed by.

Cappricci gave her the bird, smiled and promptly burnt his tongue with his first sip of the day.

'Ten minutes, if you aren't posing for *Playboy*,' Cappricci called after her.

'I'll be there, Mr. Hefner. Don't forget to bring a clean silk dressing gown.'

'Dressing gown?' Cappricci sneered back. 'More like dressing down by the time Hess has finished with you, chickadee.'

She spun round at him and smiled. It caught him completely by surprise. He took a sip of coffee in an unconscious reaction and burnt his mouth again. She saw it happen, but closed her door in time for him not to realise it. The adrenaline in her body was running at Mach 2. She took a few seconds to control it, without dampening it. If she could get through the meeting with Hess, without any uncontrollable diversions, she was ready. The Amex office was only a short drive away. She could have details of the assignment from her contact there before lunch time. That gave her 12 hours to perform . . . what?

Stuart also had 12 hours on his mind. He'd started 24 hours ahead of his schedule and now he was 12 hours behind.

Major Nelson had a report on his desk that was 12 hours old.

Something was going on upcountry that didn't make sense. There were two Pan-African peacekeeping force helicopters reported overdue and a confused report about a burnt-out Hercules.

'Cassa!' he called down the corridor. 'Do we have anything more on these lost aircraft reports?'

'No, sir,' he replied, entering the room. 'We haven't had time to follow them up. Reports are coming in all the time about the war and our forces' reaction to our revolution.'

'Hardly a revolution, Captain. We were handed the keys to the door on a plate. Now where did these reports come from?'

'I, ah, don't really know, Major. D'you want me to drop what I'm doing and proceed with an investigation?'

'What *are* you doing, Captain?'

'I'm organising the distribution of food to our villages.'

'Our villages? What about all the other villages? What are we doing about them?'

'But Major, what can we do in such a short time?'

'Call an officers' conference as soon as possible. We must organise *all* our resources to protect our position and start to organise the people to help themselves. Continue with what you're doing. Call the meeting and let me know when it's confirmed. Peacekeeping force problems can wait. We have so much to do, and Mokomo will not be sleeping.'

The young officer spun on his heel and left the room. Nelson sighed and returned to the desk that his ex-President had imported from England. He didn't want the responsibility of running a country. He was a soldier, and happy being so. Something must be done soon. Offers of help from all over the world were flooding in, but he knew they only wanted access to the country's massive natural resources. His people could continue to die like dogs, as far as the 'civilised' West and East were concerned, and the commercial factions within the country were starting to call in their worldwide influence already.

83

The Jamayal Group, he said under his breath. They owned most of the country's assets. As friends of the ousted President, they held the key to the success of the takeover. He – *they* – must do a deal with Jamayal, even if the deal was short-term or even broken. It would give some form of tenuous breathing space while a new government was formed and control of some kind created and maintained.

'I'll be back in an hour,' he said to Cassa, as he passed the captain's desk in the corridor.

'I will organise the meeting while you're away, Major.'

'Good, good, that will be fine,' Nelson answered over his shoulder. 'An hour, maybe a little longer . . . I'll drive myself.'

Outside, there was a breeze and the skies were only 50 per cent covered by cloud. It was humid, but the movement of air made Nelson feel fresh and renewed. He climbed into his green Shogun and pulled away from the front of State House. Young soldiers were everywhere, lounging around the grubby streets, drinking beer and chatting to girls . . . prostitutes. The city must be cleaned up; it would give the Freeman-based troops something to do and keep their minds from straying to unachievable dreams. They were all so young, he thought.

The Jamayal offices were close to State House, but Nelson headed for their Victorian mansion, which overlooked the sea far enough away from the city to avoid the inconvenience of the putrid smells and beggars that adorned its streets like Christmas decorations in a European town. Nelson had seen them on CNN more than once. As he rolled up the drive, the contrasts of wealth and desperate poverty overwhelmed him. The grounds were not deserted, by any means. Gardeners, servants and workmen ambled about their loosely defined duties. When he stopped in front of the columned portals, a uniformed servant ran down the majestic steps to greet him.

'Good day, sah. Can I help you, sah,' he fawned over Nelson.

'I have come to see Mr Jamayal,' Nelson answered calmly.

'Which Mr Jamayal, sah?'

Nelson suddenly realised he didn't know. He hadn't considered the large family and the potential availability of numerous Mr Jamayals. He paused for a second.

84

'Don't be insolent, boy!' Nelson snapped. 'Tell Mr Jamayal that Major Valentine Nelson, Provisional President of Sierra Laputu, is here to see him and doesn't intend to be kept waiting.'

'Immediately, sah. Mr Samir is sleeping. I will have him woken immediately, sah. Please follow me, sah.'

The similarities between the decor in the Jamayal house and the luxurious sections of State House were not lost on Nelson as he waited in the wood-lined, air-conditioned library. Unlike the large Victorian houses in England itself, the floor was made of swirling marble, maintaining the air of coolness and rich quality that went with the colonial architecture of the age. It had originally been the property of an English timber merchant who owned his own fleet of ships and a country estate in Cheshire within an easy carriage ride from the port of Liverpool. Those were the days when that English port's miles of wharves handled hundreds of vessels each year, trading everything that grew, could be mined or made. The trade in human flesh was also a thriving business and every merchant on the West African coast dabbled in it, even if it was not his primary business. Nelson wondered how many souls had passed through the financial coffers of this old house's owners, past and present.

His thoughts were interrupted by the slapping of soft shoes on the marble floor. A servant, dressed in a white jacket with brass buttons, carried a tray with a sterling silver tea service on it and two bone china cups and saucers into the library and laid it down on the small round mahogany table beside Nelson. The man didn't speak, but ensured that the table's lace tablecloth was in an exactly symmetrical position, before lowering the tray onto its protective hand-made layer. He nodded to Nelson and left the room. Seconds later, another servant, with a purple jacket and more extensive brass finery, entered the room.

'Mr Jamayal sends his apologies and hopes the tea is to your liking. He will be with you directly and asks if there is anything else you need or wish while you wait.'

'The tea is very nice, thank you,' Nelson answered without touching it. 'Please tell Mr. Jamayal not to rush. I am aware that I did not call ahead and that he was not expecting me.'

'But very pleased to receive you in my home, Major Nelson,' Samir Jamayal smiled, over the top of his servant's left shoulder as he entered the room. Nelson remained seated. His host noticed the slight.

'How is the tea,' Jamayal asked, pouring himself a cup. 'It's a special blend I import from India myself and sell at inflated prices in the finest stores all over the world, to the very rich, the pseudo-rich and the nouveaux riches, all of whom mostly wouldn't know one fine tea from another. Don't you find that sad, although a little amusing?'

'I find the plight of the pickers of tea more sad,' replied Nelson, holding out a cup.

'Yes, some of them do have less than ideal conditions, but unfortunately I have no control over these things. I am but a humble trader,' Jamayal replied with a shrug and a sickly smile.

'Ah yes, *control*,' Nelson replied in a level voice. 'It is of control that I come to speak with you, Mr Jamayal.'

'Please call me Samir, Major. There is no need for friends to be so formal and I do hope that we are going to be friends.'

Nelson came right to the point of his visit.

'Mr Jamayal, your companies effectively control the finances of this country. My army now controls you. We have martial law, administered by a military government. No one has any rights at this time, unless I extend them that courtesy.'

'It would appear so,' Jamayal fenced.

Nelson didn't reply, but just stared at the Lebanese with hooded, cold eyes.

'And?' Jamayal continued.

'And I want you to do a few minor services for your adopted country.'

'Oh, is that all?' Jamayal laughed. 'But of course, it will be an honour. Tell me, what d'you, ah, what can I do for the country?'

'You can use your influence to support the new government, *not* the certain aspirations of your past protector to return.'

'And for the gift of this influence, I get what . . . Major?'

'For now, your life. Later, who knows?' Nelson replied. 'But be quite clear that you will never leave Sierra Laputu again if you do not comply with my wishes.'

86

'You come to *my* house, alone, and threaten *me*, Samir Jamayal!'

'I am not alone, Jamayal. Today, every man at arms born in Sierra Laputu is at my shoulder. It is very early days, but all bank accounts are frozen for international transfers from noon. We are considering the pros and cons of nationalising certain strategic assets, in the national interest. Shall I continue?'

'I get the picture, Major. Let's cut the bullshit and get down to specifics.'

'If you're found to be supporting the old regime, you will be shot. If you attempt to remove any assets from the country, you will be shot. If any of your servants, employees or relations do either, you will be shot. That covers my side of the bargain,' Nelson finished, with a face of stone.

'Very, ah, *concise*. What other little duties would you like me to perform?'

'A C130 Hercules transport has been found near one of your major diamond concessions on the edge of the Valley region. We didn't have one and it looks as though it had military equipment on board.'

'Had?'

'It appears to have crashed and burned, but it's close enough to the mine's airstrip to indicate that this was its destination,' Nelson continued.

Jamayal's heart started pumping at double time and the back of his neck became hot. 'Were there any bodies, or recognition markings?'

'No,' replied Nelson, 'but the heat was intense and I don't suppose a detailed search was completed.'

'What did you say the cargo was?' Jamayal asked, almost coyly.

'Oh, trucks, Jeeps; basically, light ground forces' equipment,' Nelson replied, in an offhand manner that hid the intensity with which he was straining to catch a glimmer of recognition or betrayal in the Arab's eyes.

'This seems most strange, Major. As you know, we do have extensive security arrangements at all our concessions, but we don't throw money away chartering large cargo aircraft to deliver light equipment. This – what did you call it. Hercules?

– must be from another origin. Perhaps from the airforce of one of the peacekeeping factions?'

'Yes, we had thought of that, of course. In fact, there are vague reports that one or maybe two of their helicopters are overdue, but nobody seems to have lost a Hercules.'

'In these times, communications are difficult and often confused,' Jamayal offered, a light dew appearing on his forehead.

'Yes, communications are difficult,' Nelson agreed, 'but coincidentally, the reports all indicate the same general area.'

'There you are, Major. I'll wager you find that the large aircraft has indeed come from the peacekeeping force and that the messages have been misreported in their handing down.'

'Perhaps. As I said, these are early days and the reports are new and unconfirmed, but not for long. Prepare yourself for a helicopter journey up-country, Mr Jamayal. You will be picked up here at 0900 tomorrow morning. Let us find out together what has been going on in your backyard, so to speak.'

Jamayal looked Nelson square in the eyes and knew that to object would be to no avail. He smiled and raised his right hand off the arm of his chair. 'What a good idea, Major. It's so important, in these difficult times, that anomalies are cleared up as soon as possible, in order that they don't turn into something more – what shall I say, *Sinister*?'

'Just so,' Nelson replied, rising. 'Tomorrow, then. I will see myself out.'

Jamayal rose and bowed his head in almost mock deference. 'Until tomorrow then, Major Nelson – Mr President.'

As Nelson returned to the humidity outside and the blinking of fleeting sun, he smiled to himself. The Beirut Fox? A fox could be trapped, no matter how sly he was. Yes, a *fox* could be trapped . . . but a *wolf?* You had to kill a wolf, and somewhere out there Nelson knew there was a wolf, lurking in the shadows, only allowing his scent to drift into play; using this to herd his prey into a dark cave from which there would be no escape. Until this wolf was found and his prey identified, the new Sierra Laputu would have his scent drifting into every aspect of the country's life. He must be hunted down . . . now.

8

Hunters, Witches and Sleepers

The South Seti tributary was running quite high. It had been raining hard up country for several days, with little let-up. Stuart called a halt.

They were close now. The charts showed that there were two or three villages ahead and the mine complex to the north. They had been running hard, trying to make up time. A little rest, a stretch and a meal, although cold, would revitalise the men for the job ahead. The next rest, the next meal, could be very close or very distant. On top of this, there were too many curved balls. Stuart was sure they were being set up for something, but he didn't know what, or where it was going to happen.

During the last half-hour of tearing across the African savannah he'd resolved on a course of action, but to put it into play he had to make a telephone call.

'A *what?*' said Pete Van der Merwe, pulling aside the Arab headdress he used against the biting dust.

'A phone call,' repeated Stuart as they pulled to a stop.

'Hey, John, the governor's finally gone AWOL in the head,' Van der Merwe called to Sandys. 'He's going to make a phone call from the middle of nowhere!'

'That's right, big fella,' Sandys replied, 'and I'm the magician who is going to make it possible. Want to call your mum?'

'Come on, John, get cracking,' Stuart snapped.

'Got you, boss,' Sandys called back. 'Come on, Petey, help me with the gear.'

In the other Jeep, Skinner was searching for his shaving kit. He liked to be fresh and clean when killing.

'What they up to, Chet?' he asked.

'Rigging that Satcom stuff they found in the Herc,' he answered. 'Going to run it off the Jeep batteries if they've got the location spec on the satellite sorted out. It'll take a while setting up. Put your feet up, buddy. Y'all have some grits!'

'Sounds good to me, Colonel Sanders. Get frying,' said Skinner, mocking Maclazowitz's loaded Southern boy accent.

It took the pilot, Sandys, and the ex SAS officer, Stuart, over two hours to rig the communications gear and get a tone on the satellite. Stuart phoned Scotland.

'Good morning, Castle Stuart,' Silas Urquart's familiar tones echoed down the satellite link.

Stuart waited the obligatory one second for the Satcom delay and then answered.

'Silas, it's me. No time, just listen. Tell Vasco that I've got a double-cross brewing. I need him in Freeman and a boat off Palm Island at twenty-two hundred hours the day after tomorrow. Finance whatever he needs from the Hispaniola account. Usual radio channel.'

'Very good, sir. Can I be of any further help?'

'Yes, you've not heard from me if any of the white or black hats call.'

'Miss Michelle has called, sir.'

'There are no friendlies, at this time.'

'Understood, sir. Extreme prejudice?'

'And the rest, old man. Over and out.'

'Good day, sir,' Urquart replied, and replaced the receiver. 'Looks like we're going to have a wee bit of excitement,' he said to the black Labrador lying on the antique Persian rug which adorned the teak parquet floor in front of the fireplace.

Nigger was named after the dog owned by Guy Gibson, the leader of the RAF's famous Dambuster Raid during the Second World War. He rolled over when Urquart's tone and direction of voice changed, wagged his tail and farted.

'Oh,' chuckled the old man, 'do you really think so?'

Nigger smiled with his eyes, wagged his tail for two half

90

hearted beats and drifted back to sleep. Humans were so easy to please!

Chris Marker was doing just over 90 mph in the two-month-old convertible when the car phone rang. Years before, as a ship's captain, he'd navigated the Barrier Reef in an emergency, with no equipment, just the stars and raw instinct. That was another story, but the cook on the ship had called him Vasco da Gama after the famous Portuguese navigator. It had stuck.

'Hallo!' he shouted over his favourite BB King tape, as he turned the German sound system down a couple of notches.

'Hi,' his PA, Danny, called. 'It's me.'

'Hi, yourself. What's happening?'

Danielle Taylor had worked for Marker for many years. When he changed jobs, she changed jobs. There were always whispers about affairs and suchlike, but it was always the speculation of the rumour mongers. She'd a great guy as a husband, whom she loved very much, and neither she nor Marker had even got close to straying together. Their mutual trust, however, was unimpeachable and special.

Marker worked in the shipping and oil business, chartering ships all over the world for a myriad of reasons and uses. As a trader and shipbroker, his word, commercially, was his bond. The majority of ship contracting, or fixtures, were done by word of mouth worldwide, with most of the paperwork following up days or weeks behind. You can only do this kind of business, worth millions of dollars a year in turnover, if your word and the word of your staff is accepted as sacrosanct in the market place.

'We got the Shell fixture and the ICI spot contract. I'm still waiting for news on the Epirokatiki Line sale of the *Jason*. Gibson's got the BP enquiry again,' she reported.

'Don't hold your breath on the *Jason*, time's running out. Anything else, kid?'

'Only one, Chris. Urquart called from Scotland.'

'Was it urgent?'

'He asked me to contact you in the most expeditious manner.'

91

'It's urgent!' replied Marker.

'He's by the phone,' Danny replied.

'OK, I'm gone,' Marker called into the hands-free mike. 'Looks like it might be show time again,' he said to himself. His heartbeat started to rise.

Marker pulled off the road at a large country house hotel which had a long winding drive covered by a high canopy of European hardwood trees. He parked the Jaguar close to the entrance and pressed the automatic roof button. Country houses have lots of birds around and they all seem to be attracted to the driver's seat of a convertible car when deballasting their waste products. He didn't lock the roof down, or the car itself. It wasn't required in a place like this.

Crossing the entrance hall, he noticed that there was a public phone booth, in the old-fashioned wooden style which had been popular in the nineteen twenties. He side stepped in and sat down. As he closed the door, a light came on automatically over a phone; the only modern item in the alcove.

He called a telephone pager number. After receiving instructions from the phone company's recorded message, he dialled in some numbers and waited. Three minutes later, the phone rang and Silas Urquart's unmistakable tones came down the line from Scotland.

'Castle Stuart, can I help you?'

'It's Vasco, you old bugger. How are you?'

'Better for hearing a friendly voice, sir. How are *you?*'

'Fine, fine, Silas. How's the hunting these days?'

'Well, it's funny you should ask, sir. The laird has recently asked me to forward an invitation to you for some shooting this week. It's a spur-of-the-moment thing, so please don't feel that the short notice is due to you being asked to fill in for a guest who has dropped out.'

'Perish the thought, old chap, perish the thought.'

'Does sir have a facsimile machine at hand?' Silas asked.

'Stand by one!' Marker replied, laying the phone down on its side.

Through the glass of the booth he could see a rather dowdy lady engrossed in the onerous administration details of the hotel reception. Behind her, looking a little out of place in the environment, was a Canon facsimile machine. He left the booth and crossed the hall to the reception desk.

'Excuse me,' he said in a friendly tone, crowning it with his renowned disarming smile, 'I don't suppose it would be possible for me to receive an urgent fax here, would it? I would, of course, pay for the courtesy.'

'Are you a resident, sir?' the lady replied in a rather condescending tone.

'Ah, I'm considering it,' replied Marker, gushing charm.

'Perhaps sir will be taking lunch here?'

'What a good idea,' replied Marker.

'In that case, sir would be a temporary resident and able to avail himself of the hotel's facilities. May I write the number down for you?'

'How kind,' he beamed.

Fully armed with the fax number, Marker stepped quickly back into the booth.

'Silas?'

'Still here, sir.'

'Sorry to keep you waiting, I had to fight myself past a remnant of the female battalions of the British Raj to get access to the fax,' Marker explained.

'One should not underestimate the hidden charms of such ladies, sir. Many generations of hockey and early years of sexual depravation can provide one with a very fit and somewhat morally abandoned bedfellow. That is, of course, once one gets beneath the tweeds, pleats, brogues and expensively engineered undergarments.'

'You dirty old bugger,' Marker laughed.

'Quite so, sir. The number?'

Marker passed the fax number to Urquart and rang off with the usual pleasantries. The hotel fax rang almost immediately, and both Marker and the receptionist stood over the machine as it scraped out a single sheet of A4 paper.

As it finished, Marker went to pick it out of the machine's tray, but the guardian of the hotel beat him to it.

'This fax may be for you, Mr . . . ?'

Marker,' he conceded.

'And so it is, Mr Marker,' she announced, as she inspected the address section of the fax and handed it over.

Marker took a second to check that the fax had been received ungarbled and then turned back to his collaborator. 'Lunch?'

'Through the double doors in the Knight's Room, sir. You may order in the bar if you wish,' she answered, with the first attempt at a smile and a nod towards a single door next to the dining room entrance.

'Perfect,' Marker answered, manufacturing yet another beaming smile. 'Could you order me a large Scotch, while I make one more quick phone call?'

'Of course, sir. A large Scotch and a menu?'

'So kind,' Marker replied, as he recrossed the hall to the phone booth. He rang the pager again, but this time left the number 666. When Silas received it, he would know that the message had been received clearly. All Marker had to do now was to understand it and confirm that he could deliver within the time-frame required.

Time was also on Michelle Christie's mind. It was slipping away.

The morning had been full of meetings and communications regarding the operation. Hess and Cappricci had been her companions from the moment she arrived in the office. No opportunity had presented itself to allow her to access the secure file room alone.

Currently they were in a status meeting. These were held twice a day, or more frequently if required. Hess was concerned about Jamayal and Falcone.

'So, we still haven't got a handle on the focus of their alliance?'

'Their alliance is manifest in its dealings. It's their involvement in our operation that remains unclear,' Cappricci corrected.

'Then we must assume they know *everything*, until we can define their actual knowledge,' Hess instructed. 'Have we had their profiles updated from the files, or are we working from our general field knowledge?'

'Field knowledge is extensive,' Michelle replied.

'But not subject to automatic OIDC.'

It didn't matter which targets were included in any operative's report, the Operative Intelligence Data Compilation service co-ordinated the new material into their personnel files within 15 days of receipt, or 24 hours if the security codes designated.

'What's the last entry date for Falcone?' Hess asked.

'There are almost daily entries for the don,' Cappricci answered.

'Then what about Jamayal? Surely the last congruent incident wasn't their meeting in New York?'

'I'm afraid it was,' Michelle cut in quickly. 'Shall I go down and get a computer priority on the last available correlations?'

'Yes, but do it yourself. You can operate the system, can't you?' Hess asked.

'Oh yes, sir. No problem.'

'Then go now, we'll be here until you get back. Cap, you fill me in on the satellite shots of the target area and these reports that our party may have exploded on landing. I don't believe it for a minute, but fill me in anyway.'

Michelle left the room as Hess and Cappricci huddled over the latest shots of the target site and 50 kilometres around it. 'I'll be as quick as I can,' she said over her shoulder. No one answered.

She passed through the corridors with an air of urgency that reduced banter to zero. Carlton Hess had his office on the south-east corner of the building and Michelle took that route to the stairs. As she passed his office she swung in and solicited the help of his long-time secretary, assistant and lover, Nancy Carmichael.

'Nancy, help! I need a compilation check for the boss immediately and he has a file missing from his Ops briefing folder. It must be on his desk. Have you got a listing?'

'I gave him everything he asked for, as usual. Here's the index. What's not there?' Nancy answered, with a bit of a fluster. 'I always give him his briefing in one folder. By the time he's read it and messed about with it, God only knows what order the files end up in! I'll bet it's in the file, but not in the indexed order.'

'Wouldn't surprise me at all, Nancy, but would you call Archives and tell them to call up the latest on these two characters; all points. The last call-off was 18 hours ago. I'll check the boss's desk,' Michelle called over her shoulder as she swept into the Admiral's office.

'Check the window sill behind his desk,' Nancy called after her. 'He uses it for cataloguing – his way.'

'Roger on that,' Michelle replied, as she made sure that the door partially closed in her rush.

Nancy got busy on the phone. The admiral's office was almost clinically empty. 'What does he *do*, for Christ's sake,' Michelle whispered under her breath. There was nothing. She looked down the index sheet that Nancy had given her. Item number seven hit her straight between the eyes, *Operation Masada, access code 987/r/356-q*. It was in the computer section's q files. The 'q' designation meant that only one hard copy was allowed to be printed and in existence at one time. The copy was under continual track and the paper it was printed on was light-sensitive, allowing no legible photocopies to be taken and rendering the print unreadable after about eight hours. To access the file, you also needed a personal security code as well as the access code. 'Shit,' she said out loud.

'Any luck?' Nancy called, as she entered the room.

'It's a maximum restriction computer file. If he hasn't got it, we can't help,' Michelle sighed.

'Which one is missing?'

'This one.' Michelle pointed out with the end of her gold Cross pen.

'Typical!' Nancy chuckled. 'It's in Cap's file not his. I made them both up and it was Cap who called in the copy from records.'

'Great, Nancy. That's another world-shattering mystery solved. Don't rub it in when the boss gets back, though. He's in a bad enough mood as it is.'

'My lips are sealed, kiddo. I want to get home just a little bit late, rather than the usual late late, tonight.'

'Don't we all, Nancy. Thanks a lot. I'll get down to records and collect the updates and then get back into the battle.'

'No need, they're on their way up. Coffee?'

'Nancy, you're a life-saver,' Michelle gasped and sat down in one of the admiral's guest chairs.

'It's funny, isn't it,' Nancy said, as she poured out the coffee, 'you would think that the Deputy Director of the CIA would be organised and very security-conscious. I tell you, the Russkies would have been marching up Pennsylvania Avenue years ago if it wasn't for good old "all-American gals" like me who keep the fabric of the nation ticking over and all the little secrets in their little secret places. Cream?'

'No thanks, I have a cholesterol count of seven and growing.'

'Ouch. Eat more garlic . . . it works! The admiral is the same. Too much red meat, but you can't teach an old dog new tricks. He does everything the same way he did from the early days in the service.'

'I have sympathy with him in that respect,' Michelle replied. 'I don't believe in change for change's sake. Even in the security business.'

A messenger came into the room. 'Notes for the gorgeous Nancy,' he quipped.

'That's for me,' Michelle hailed, with a dramatic sweep of her arm. 'Thanks for the coffee, Nancy. See you later.'

As she entered the corridor, she turned left towards her own office, entered, picked up a mobile phone out of her desk drawer and dialled Yani Bar-David in Tel Aviv.

'Hi, bro. Get the money?'

'Not yet, sis. How are you doing?'

'You won't believe it but I locked myself out of the master bedroom today, you remember, the one with the security lock, because the last owner kept his gun cabinet in bedroom wardrobe?'

'Yeah, I remember. What's the problem?'

'I used to keep the entry code in the knife drawer in the kitchen, in case it was accidentally locked, but I'm dammed if I can find it.'

'Get a locksmith to have a look at it, sis.'

'I've already spoken to one of our experts in locks here. He reckons that it works on one of the original code systems, but the combinations of possibilities are many millions. I've given him the name and birthday of the last owner – they're some of the more common combinations that people use as code keys. He says the computer can run all the options in less than two hours. I should know by noon today. I'll call you later to let you know if I'm sleeping in the bedroom or the hall. Let me know if the money doesn't arrive today, I'm worried it's gotten lost.'

'OK, sis, speak to you later.'

Michelle put the phone back into its drawer, its coded message complete. She went to the ladies room, freshened up and returned to the Ops meeting.

Yani Bar-David called Sharon at home.

At around the same time, Samir Jamayal called Don Falcone at home. He wasn't available. He hadn't been available for two whole days. Major Valentine Nelson, on the other hand, was not only available but landing in his Puma helicopter on Jamayal's front lawn.

And Stuart? Stuart was moving out across the river shallows towards the target.

9

Rendezvous

As the small convoy continued north-east, the savannah slowly gave way to taller and thicker vegetation. They were almost paralleling the river, which, along with the tributaries from the west, created a fertile and watered enclave across the northern territories. The plan was to stop about three kilometres before the target and let Maclazowitz out to walk point. The others would follow 15 minutes later in two groups, 200 metres apart. In fact, they stopped about four kilometers out from the target, in a copse of tall trees and thick undergrowth.

'OK guys, this is it,' Stuart said, to everyone. 'Last equipment checks and then we're on our way. Chet?'

'Yeah.'

'You ready?'

'Always ready, Trap.'

'OK, move out then, and keep loose.'

Maclazowitz waved and ambled off, his long legs covering distance quickly in their usually deceptive manner. As well as the rifle, he carried a muffled Uzi and a Beretta 92F 9 mm pistol. The latter held a 15-round magazine, but Maclazowitz always carried an extra round in the chamber, for luck. Some automatics would be considered unsafe in this configuration, but the Beretta had been declared one of the safest automatics on the market by the US Army no less, after exhaustive tests on two occasions.

The air was still, so the wind gave him no advantage. His

route was to take him through the large village – a town really – which had been the source of the human feedstock that had worked the Jamayal mine when it was producing bauxite for the aluminium smelters of the western world. He came upon the access road when expected, its dual ruts paying homage to the countless journeys the 16-wheelers from Detroit had made over the years, on their treks from the mines to the harbour at Freeman. He shadowed the road from an old *game* track to the south. The road appeared empty, but he crouched and waited at a point that gave him good vision both up and down the scar.

'Broadsword? Hawk,' he said quietly into his earpiece microphone.

'Yo, Hawk!' came the reply from Stuart.

'Made the road – seems clear. Wait, I see something.'

Coming from the direction of the mine was what looked to be a small group of local people. Maclazowitz pulled out his Zeiss binoculars. As the images came into focus, he could see that the group was actually a lot larger than he'd first thought. People continued to appear from around a distant corner in the road, which hadn't been evident to the naked eye. They were at least 500 meters away, so he risked a call.

'Broadsword, we've a group of twenty plus with carts and animals coming your way. Don't cross the road till I call.'

'Got you, Hawk,' came the clipped reply from Stuart, who was leading the group which would hit the road first.

Rider was leading the second party, and everyone heard him click his comms set on and off twice, to acknowledge that he'd copied the transmission and its intent.

It took a good ten minutes for the slowly moving column of Africans to get within clear sight with the naked eye. Something was scratching away at the back of Maclazowitz's brain. It wasn't a question of danger; something just wasn't right. He turned to stone and watched. He was good at turning to stone.

Almost half the column had passed by before it struck him. The majority of the people were thin and gaunt. This was not unusual in Africa and certainly not Sierra Laputu, but the carts that accompanied them were full of food. Fresh food, tinned food, boxed food. The cattle weren't the accustomed thin, raking beasts that scratched a living from the African savannah. They weren't fat Jersey milk cows, but they didn't look half bad. The anomaly was, that apparently starving people were making no attempt to eat the food that was overflowing, by African standards, right by their sides.

Chet Maclazowitz's family had been starved and gassed by the Nazis. The contradiction in front of him was ringing warning bells deep down in every cell of his body.

'Broadsword, I've got starving people with lots of food. Come in under condition red. Something's far wrong!'

'Roger, Hawk. Coming in now. Both teams your side of the road. ETA ten.

'Broadsword, Hawk. Tell the goatskinner to stay back. I've got a bad feeling about this.'

'Hawk, Broadsword. He's been at the back door since we launched. You concentrate on your own fishing trip.'

Maclazowitz didn't answer. He just watched the last of the column disappearing into the distance. None of them had spoken a word as they passed by.

By the time both teams had hit the road and regrouped together, the column had completely passed by. Stuart called his point man.

'OK Hawk, we're here. We avoided your party, so hit the bricks. Hawk? This is Broadsword, wake up!'

'I'm going, *I'm going.*'

Stuart swore under his breath. 'What the fuck's the matter with Chet? Starving people carrying food? Christ, if he throws a wobbly we're all VSF.'

'VSF?' queried Sandys, by his side.

'Very seriously fucked.'

Skinner appeared by Stuart's side. 'Funny bunch, that lot, Trap. Piles of food and looking like something from an Oxfam advert.'

'You saw them?'

'Yeah, I hit the road about three hundred metres down the line. Got a bit lost if you must know, and there they were, just like Chet said.'

'Starving people with food?'

'Yep.'

'OK, let's keep loose and watch out for the unexpected. Wait a minute! *Got a bit lost?* Stuart repeated, as he turned back to Skinner.

'Only a bit, Trap. I'm here, aren't I?'

'So it would appear. Hit the back door.'

'Broadsword, this is Hawk. Repeat please,' Maclazowitz called.

'Christ!' Stuart snapped. 'Is nobody paying attention? Everyone, clear the air, front and centre. Move out!'

The cocktail of mercenaries spread out and melted into the woodwork. All except Skinner. He hung back as ordered. He hated the rear unless they were on the run. They needed him then, he thought; him and Chet. Between the two of them they could waste a company of tenderfoots before they knew what had hit them. 'Funny about those Blacks,' he said, to the undergrowth, 'thin as beanpoles and hauling a banquet. *Africa ...* you never knew what to expect – gods, spirits, ghouls and butchery.'

A large multicoloured caterpillar crawled past Skinner through the rotting vegetation at his feet. He sliced it in half with a Tanto and waited until it had stopped thrashing its life away, before moving off after the assault team. None of the others understood the ecstasy of killing, he thought. All except Chet. He'd seen that look in his eye once or twice before. Yeah, Chet understood. He was fucking good as well.

Maclazowitz had a creepy feeling up the back of his neck as he crossed the road 200 metres ahead of the assault group. When he reached the corner from which the native column had first appeared, the road ahead was clear ... clear, that is, except for a 12-foot-high security fence and gate, topped by the West's most efficient razor wire.

'Trap! We got tall wire and a guarded checkpoint right across the line at two hundred,' Maclazowitz whispered into his radio.

Stuart noticed that call signs had been forgotten, but replied as normal. 'How old does the wire look?'

'Wait one,' Maclazowitz answered, lifting the camouflaged

ten-by-fifties to his eyes. 'It's shiny and the posts are newly stripped. Uniforms are new . . . no insignia. Couple of regular boy scouts, packing AKs. No wheels in sight and no buildings, just a sun shelter, on my side.'

'Hold your position and report any changes,' Stuart replied

The group were all together now and it was Carter who spoke first. 'No reports of this in the briefing?'

'No, but the intelligence photos I saw were good enough to show a fence, and from what Chet says it's a new one,' Stuart replied.

'Regular satellite photo passes might not have shown the fence, but they would certainly have shown the fence makers,' Van der Merwe cut in.

'Yeah, you're right,' Stuart agreed. 'And it wasn't put up overnight.'

'So, what have we got?' Sandys asked. 'Let's take stock.'

'What we've got is a big question mark over our intelligence package, which means we've got to gather our own. Skinner!'

'Here, Trap,'

'Go and join Chet. Cross the wire and *rece* the mine complex. Don't leave any litter around unless you have to. Understood?' Stuart ordered.

'No problem,' Skinner replied, with a smirk. 'On my way.'

'Hawk?'

'Come on!' the Confederate accent replied.

'The goatskinner's coming to join you for a look see. Don't hang around once he arrives. In and stay in – got it?' Stuart relayed.

'Yeah, in and stay in. See you at the party.'

Maclazowitz lifted his glasses again and raked the wire, studying its make-up. If there were no landmines there wouldn't be a problem. He swept the lenses back to the guard post and listened for Skinner. It was a game they played.

Samir Jamayal also liked to play games, but this one was being played by someone else's rules.

The chopper had arrived early, preventing him from his quest to reach Falcone on the telephone – a quest that had borne no fruit for several days. The Sicilian was either avoiding him or camping out on the moon.

Nelson had hardly spoken a word to him except to wish him a polite, but terse, good morning. Puma choppers were noisy, but this one was equipped with headsets and passenger cabin intercom. The silence was obviously part of the game – a game which was taking him deep upcountry, alone. He hadn't been alone, *really* alone, for a long time. Men of power are never *really* alone, except within themselves.

They flew low. There was no traffic control. The rain was heavy, but falling straight down, with no wind to turn it into a driving battering ram.

It was Jamayal's practice to spend as much of the rainy season as possible out of the country, travelling the world. His business interests encompassed every region and religious enclave around the globe.

A rich country with a poor population, Sierra Laputu had excellent connections to London, Amsterdam and Beirut, allowing him easily to make onward connections to the Middle East, Far East and the Americas.

Being a man of great riches, he often flew in private helicopters from airports to business destinations and exclusive functions. He would have given a million dollars to have been on one of those flights now, to Ascot, the Monaco Grand Prix, or the powerboat world championships in Hong Kong. He closed his eyes, pretending to sleep. For now, he'd have to play this dangerous game.

The rain was thinner by the time they reached the burnt-out wreck of the Hercules transport.

'Time for a little fresh air and a stretch of the legs, Mr Jamayal,' Nelson smiled, as the Puma rocked back slightly in its final few feet of decent.

The accompanying young soldiers dropped out of the Puma first, followed by Jamayal and finally Nelson. The pilot and co-pilot remained in the aircraft, but didn't shut her down; the rotors continuing their air-slapping tango through the falling silver water droplets.

They walked towards the remains of the aircraft, which lay

like a gutted chicken, its wings hardly touched by the fire.

'So, what do you think?' Nelson asked.

'Don't ask me,' Jamayal answered. 'I'm not an air-crash investigator. The plane crash-landed and caught fire?'

'Let us have a closer look, my friend,' Nelson smiled and indicated for Jamayal to proceed first.

Nelson's apparent pleasant demeanour hadn't escaped Jamayal's attention, but the Fox was used to running on the edge and his instincts were at fever pitch.

The only indication of any cargo was the skeletal remains of several vehicles.

'Burnt-out trucks. Must have been an army transport of some kind,' Jamayal said.

'So it would seem, but my men report that there is no evidence of human remains. Don't you find that strange?' Nelson asked.

'No bodies? So they got out before the fire took hold!'

'Quite possibly, but it is there that we have our dilemma. Who were *they* and what was their mission?' Nelson asked.

'God only knows, if you don't, Major. There are so many different groups and nationalities roaming our countryside. This could belong to any one of them.'

'Perhaps. Shall we continue our journey?' Nelson waved his six young soldiers back to the aircraft.

They ran across the damp savannah and jumped easily into the belly of the Puma. Jamayal and Nelson followed at a quick walk, their rain capes rustling in unison around their ankles.

As the chopper lifted off the ground, the smell of wet and sweating humanity began to fill the aircraft, but the windows didn't have time to steam up. They had only been in the air a few minutes when the pilot started a landing procedure again.

This time there could be no doubt about what had happened around the landing site. Bodies were swelling everywhere and the wrecks of two helicopters could be seen quite clearly.

'What we have here are the remains of a company of the pan-African peace-keeping force,' Nelson said in a balanced monotone, as he surveyed the scene before him. Soldiers were picking their way through the battle site, collecting any useful equipment and loading it onto assembled vehicles.

'Who did it?' Jamayal asked.

'Africa is full of mysteries, as you know,' Nelson answered, 'but fortunately this one has solved itself.' They had been walking towards the edge of the waterhole. At their feet were the remains of Landau's partially burnt body.

'He's white!' Jamayal said, stating the obvious from behind a handkerchief which was failing to protect his senses from the rancid stench of death all around him.

'Yes, he's white; a man who has been wounded and then shot in the head. He is also the carrier of some rather interesting body tattoos which tell us he was British, inspite of the burning.'

'A mercenary?'

'A mercenary,' Nelson confirmed.

'There are mercenaries all over Africa, indeed the world,' Jamayal offered.

'Yes, yes, of course,' Nelson replied, 'but this one appears to be alone. He is not an officer adviser; the tattoos tell us that. He appears to be a plain boot soldier. What does that tell us?'

'I haven't a clue.' Jamayal shrugged.

'It means, Mr Jamayal, that more than likely he was not alone and that he was shot in the head by his accomplices in this carnage, after being wounded.'

'So he couldn't talk?' Jamayal asked.

'You begin to understand,' Nelson replied. 'So he couldn't talk. Surely that tells you something?'

'Major – President Nelson, or whatever you're calling yourself today, I'm impatient with this game you play. What d'you want from me and what is the tourist show for?'

'So, you become tired, do you, Jamayal? Well, let me wake you up,' Nelson spat, as he poked Samir Jamayal so hard that the bruise would still be visible two weeks later. 'What we have got, I think, is a group of mercenaries travelling light and fast to some unknown objective. Anyone who gets in their way is dead. I mean soldiers, women, children and multimillionaires. This man was shot by his own people. Not to save him from torture and a guaranteed slow and excruciatingly painful death, but to prevent him giving away the purpose of his – their – mission. So I have to ask myself who has the money and the motive for launching a raid of this kind in Sierra Laputu, and then I have to ask myself who in the country knows him best of all. To these questions, I find the most logical answers arc Mokomo and Jamayal. Still with me?'

'Oh, I'm with you all right. This is all a load of bullshit to put the frighteners on me to up the bribes you want to negotiate. So what's the anti? A million, two million, ten million a year? What's the price this year for a businessman to stay alive in SL?'

'You claim you know nothing of this,' Nelson asked, sweeping the area with his arm.

'Give me a break. There's some war or other going on for a thousand miles in any direction from where we stand. Stop shitting me and let's get the hell out of here. I'm a busy man.'

Samir Jamayal had turned the tables and gained the initiative in the game. To emphasise it he turned on his heel without invitation and strode back to the Puma. Nelson stared after him until he was conscious of his men staring at *him.* He stood up straight and followed Jamayal, barking orders as he went.

No one spoke as the Puma returned to Freeman. When they arrived, the pilot feathered the rotor blades and the heavy machine landed delicately in the garden of the Jamayal mansion.

'I believe it's not too late for afternoon tea, Major. Would you like to be *my* guest? It's the very least I can offer after such an interesting trip.'

'Be careful, my friend,' Nelson replied. 'A fox in Beirut has only one enemy, and that is man. In Africa there are many animals that can feed on the fox. Never forget, Mr Samir Jamayal, that I am one such animal.'

The chopper screamed and rose quickly from the garden. The two men stared at each other until they were out of sight.

Jamayal knew he was running out of time, but Nelson had done him one favour at least. Now he knew that the Stuart assault group was still running, but without Falcone he couldn't spring the trap. He ran into the house, brushing the awaiting servants aside. The east coast of the States was just waking up. He would try Falcone again.

Around the time that the telephone rang at the Falcone estate, a combined phone and fax machine rang in Michelle Christie's apartment and an A4 sheet of paper appeared from the slit in its front. It had 50 numbers on it. No signature or addressee appeared, just the numbers, which ranged from four to six digits. She grabbed the sheet and left for her office. She was running behind schedule.

Stuart was also running behind schedule and losing more time with every hour, but he wouldn't move until he heard from Maclazowitz and Skinner.

'Five minutes ago you scratched yourself on some saluki thorn,' Maclazowitz said over his shoulder, as Skinner crept through the undergrowth behind him.

Skinner touched the laceration on his right cheek and smiled. 'Good, big fella, good, but did you know I'd been watching you for ten minutes before I came the last 50 metres?'

'Bullshit,' Maclazowitz smiled.

'Well, I've given several people the shits over the years, but never a bull, lovey! Shall we go, or are you planning on spending the night here? Trap's like a bear with a sore paw. Every time we turn a corner we're walking into some kind of unplanned shit or other.'

'Well, the wire is quite new and there's too much ground cover to indicate underground nasties. It looks just like those wires they've got up on the Zambian border to segregate the bush from the domestic cattle herds. You know, the thousand-mile-long wire of misery that's accidentally trapping thousands of migrating wildebeest and other species as they try to follow their ancestral trails.'

'Yeah, I remember the wire. We had to cross it three years ago on the way home. This is the wrong kind of area for a cattle wire though, ain't it?' Skinner asked.

'Bang on, little buddy; and cattle wire don't have razors on the top, so this wire is to stop people and people wires are often live.'

'Never did fancy frying, Chet.' Skinner grimaced.

'Not that kind of power on this one, I think. Just a few volts to let people know the wire has been touched,' Maclazowitz said to himself, as much as to Skinner.

'No, all kinds of beasts would set it off, Chet,' Skinner answered.

'So, what do you reckon?'

'It's just a fence.'

'Sure?' Maclazowitz ansked, raising an eyebrow.

'My honour, I think?'

'You're dammed right, buddy. We'll watch your back,' Maclazowitz smiled, patting the silenced Uzi around his neck.

Skinner could crawl across the ground at an alarming rate. He reached the wire in just a few seconds and had a slither hole cut in less than a minute. He didn't wait for, or look at Maclazowitz. He just went through and into cover.

Seeing Skinner through safely, the big man crouched low and ran to the opening. It took him a little longer to get through, because of the extra equipment he was carrying, but as he picked up his rifle and ran to Skinner's position, he noticed a well-worn Jeep track on their side of the wire.

'See the patrol tracks,' Skinner asked?

'Yep.'

'Close the hole?'

'Close the hole,' agreed Maclazowitz.

Skinner slid back to the hole and bent the wire so that only a detailed inspection would identify the cut. He was back beside his partner within a minute.

'OK, Chet. Head 'em up, move 'em out,' he laughed quietly, quoting a famous line from an old sixties TV Western series. The two men melted into the undergrowth.

Michelle Christie almost melted with tension, as the nineteenth number on the A4 sheet faxed by Yani Bar-David, accessed Carlton Hess's security window in the records computer. Her hunch had been right and Nancy's innocent slip had led them to the right track. Hess's password was the number he'd probably used for years. He was a creature of habit – a strange quirk for an intelligence specialist.

The Mossad code-breakers had searched out every combination of personal numbers they could think of, from birthdays to service numbers. The fax had held the best 50 options from the multitude of possibilities.

She keyed in the file code and there it was: *Operation Masada.* The level of secrecy code attached to it hit her immediately. It allowed for the Head and Deputy Head of the CIA, the Secretary of State and the President. It had the narrowest of access, but Mark Cappricci had been able to call it up.

'There's a bag of worms loose here, girl,' she said under her breath, as she punched the print button and waited. The file heading indicated 16 pages. The laser printer was an old one, but it would deliver the total file within two minutes.

Fifteen minutes later the last page ground its way out of Yani Bar-David's fax in Tel Aviv. His protégée had done well. All that was left to do now was get her home.

Getting people home was also Chris Marker's business. Right now it was Stuart and his men who were the potential cargo. While Michelle Christie waited for orders from Tel Aviv, Marker was attempting to fulfil his.

He'd gone to the less than respectable shipping market to find a small vessel in the area of Freeman which could reach Palm Island, just to the south of the harbour, within the allotted timeframe.

It hadn't been easy and it wasn't going to be cheap, but a Russian oilfield support vessel had been found, en route to Europe from Gabon. The captain would accept the large amount of hard currency on offer to do the job with no questions asked. The only stipulation was that payment had to be in cash and it had to be made on the boat before the cargo was accepted on board. This meant only one thing: Chris Marker, Vasco, had to hand-carry the cash to the vessel himself. This in itself was a hazardous mission in Africa, but his main worry was the timeframe, as he would have to fly to Geneva first, in order to withdraw the funds. Any delay at the UBS bank there would render his rendezvous time in Sierra Laputu compromised. Having very little choice, he just threw the dice and set off.

Swiss Air were on time leaving Terminal 4 at London Heathrow for Geneva. He thought this must be a good omen, because he couldn't remember the last time he'd been on a flight from LHR which had taken off on time.

The seat next to him in club class was empty, as were several others in the front section of the aircraft. He lifted the armrest between the two seats, ordered a large single malt whisky and spread out.

The aircraft was cruising at around 37,000 feet. The sky was blue and very bright. Marker slipped a pair of Cartier sunglasses from out of his jacket's top pocket and slid them over his nose. The soothing darkness, combined with the warmth of the whisky and lack of sleep, stimulated a sudden flood of overwhelming tiredness throughout his body. He decided he must try to catch some sleep, however shallow it might be. Once the money was in his possession, sleep would be out of the question. He took the last of the whisky, slackened off his seat belt and pushed the seat back a few more inches. Sleep washed over him in just a few seconds. Twenty minutes later he awoke with a start, a second sense telling him he'd started to snore. The meal had been served. A black coffee and another whisky would have to substitute until they landed.

Back in tourist class, Louis Rodriquez Gomez watched Marker from behind his own light prescription graded sunglasses, which provided relief from the sun within the top half of their lenses, but merging into an almost clear lens at the bottom of the designer glass; typical glasses for a typical South American, to any casual observer.

In fact, Gomez was from the Domenican Republic, on the island of Hispaniola in the Caribbean. For Marker, he was a messenger from the Angel of Death, who had been stalking him and waiting in the wings, to balance the books for Marker's role in closing down one of the world's largest marine fraud

111

syndicates some five years ago. Six men had been instrumental in sending Gomez to prison in the United States, for life plus 40 years. Money had arranged his escape. Five of the men were dead. The sixth was within feet of him. Chris Marker was going to die in Geneva and he, Gomez, was going to return to his ranch on the Colombian–Venezuelan border. When he'd killed the last of them, Marker, his face would have great strength and his name would be feared around the world. No one would ever cross Louis Rodriquez Gomez again.

The Mafia *guinea*, had been true to his word and the money Gomez had paid. All six had been at the place, time and loca tion advised by the Family minion they had used as a messenger. Marker didn't know it, but he was on his last business trip, whatever that might be. Don't sleep, Vasco da Gama, Gomez mused to himself. Soon you will be sleeping the long sleep of the dead.

Thirty minutes later the A3000 Airbus banked and descended into Geneva airport. Gomez hung back and let most of the passengers disembark from the forward doors. He knew Marker had a bag in the hold, so he was able to take his time and easily keep from being noticed.

As he reached the baggage area he just noticed Marker exiting from the men's lavatory and heading for the luggage carousel. Passengers were engaging in the usual pushing and jostling to retrieve baggage; a little like pigs at a trough. Gomez walked through the hall and into Customs and Immigration control. His passport was false, but it was a very good one prepared by the legendary Carl Shultz, still resident in the old town region of East Berlin.

'How long will you be staying in the country, Mr Mendez,' the Immigration officer asked, as he glanced back and forth from the passport photograph to Gomez.

'Less than five days, I hope, but bankers are bankers,' he shrugged.

'Yes, you would think our money was their money sometimes.'

'But the world can't function without them, señor.'

'Enjoy your stay in Switzerland. Try the restaurants on the

lake. You may bump into your banker eating there and speed up your trip,' the official offered, smiling at his own humour.

'I will, I will. Thanks for the tip,' Gomez answered, accepting his passport back from the smug officer. Proceeding out of the concourse into the arrivals lounge, anyone close to him may have heard him spit 'Asshole!' under his breath.

Marker collected his soft holdall and followed the same route out to the arrivals area that his would-be assassin had just completed. Gomez was already sitting inside his taxi when Marker emerged from the building, to slip quickly into a similar vehicle to the rear. As the Mercedes slipped by Gomez, the Latin American looked up at the driver and said, 'That's my amigo, señor. Please follow him. I didn't know he was in town and I would like to speak with him.'

'I can call the other driver through the radio if you wish,' his own driver answered.

'It's not necessary. I would like to surprise him.'

Gomez sat back in his seat and his driver settled down in the traffic, keeping the other taxi in sight. Friend indeed! Who did this guy think he was kidding? Still, it was none of his business, as long as the fare was paid.

It was clouding over and the sky gave the lake a grey and unwelcome look. Marker's driver was one of those talkative types, who wanted to know everything about you during a journey which only lasted 20 minutes. Marker made all the usual polite noises and smiled on cue, but it was a mild relief to arrive outside the Intercontinental and divest himself of his new friend. As he entered the five-star hotel, Gomez was paying off his own taxi and telling the doorman he'd no baggage.

When you're tailing a man, 20 seconds can be a very long time, but in the reception of a large hotel there is only one stop for an arrival. While Marker was checking in at reception, Gomez went through to the coffee shop and sat down. After ten minutes, he left his seat and an untouched expresso coffee and made his way out to one of the two public phones in the business centre, to the right of the reception lounge. He telephoned the hotel reception desk. It took only ten or fifteen seconds to ascertain that his business colleague, Mr Marker, had arrived and was in room 211. He was booked in for two nights. Gomez replaced the receiver and then immediately made a second call to a number that the guinea had given him. The call finished, he returned to the reception lounge, seated himself at a 45-degree angle to the lifts and waited.

In 211, Marker called the bank before unpacking and hitting the shower. His appointment was for three o'clock, so he'd time to bathe and eat. If all went well, he could catch the afternoon flight to Paris and then the evening UTA flight to Sierra Laputu, where he was booked into the Tumani Palms Hotel for two weeks as a diamond trader, under his own name. Part of the money he was carrying would be his visa . . . Africa was Africa.

Gomez only had to wait 35 minutes for his Geneva connection to arrive. He was a stout man, with very Germanic features. In his hand, he carried a newspaper and a thin, soft black leather document case with a zip along its top and side openings. The two men greeted each other as if they were acquaintances rather than friends and talked about this and that for a further 15 minutes. Their meeting completed, they went through a pleasant departure routine and the stout man left, his document case by the side of Gomez's armchair. The Dominican sat for a further five minutes. Then, picking up the case, he entered the lift for the second floor and room 211.

As the lift reached its destination and the doors opened, the room number indicator arrows on the opposite wall directed Gomez to his left. He was dressed in blue jeans covering the tops of cowboy boots, and a light summer jacket. A regular briefcase would have looked out of place, but the document case fitted the picture well as he strolled, with the slightly bowed legs characteristic of his race, down the well-appointed corridor.

When he reached the door of room 211, he instantly noticed that it was locked in the open position, preventing it closing the last half-inch. He could hear that the TV was switched on and the shower was running in the bathroom. Gomez slipped inside, entered the body of the bedroom fully and sat down in one of the two armchairs.

A British comedy that he recognised, dubbed into German, was playing on a satellite channel. Unzipping the document case he extracted its only contents, a silenced .32 calibre Smith & Wesson revolver with no markings or serial numbers; a sanitised *piece*. He sat and waited, both feet on the ground, with the document case across his knees and the gun in his left hand, relaxed on the case. The shower stopped and the noise of Marker stepping out of the bath could be heard above the out of sync chatter on the TV. The bathroom door opened and a naked Marker, rubbing his hair with a towel, appeared in the room. Their eyes met, and Marker turned to stone.

'*Hola*, Señor Vasco. It is so nice to make your acquaintance again, after all this time. Unfortunately for you, our visit must be short – and alas, our very last one. Please sit on the edge of the bed ... and do move slowly, señor. I do not wish to harm you. I just want my money returned. You do have it, don't you? You and that *bastardo* Stuart.'

Marker didn't move. 'How the hell did you get out, Louis? And how on earth did you find me?'

'Ahh, my friend. You spent two years leading me into your clever trap, using many people in many countries. Do not assume that you're the only one with connections. It is really quite simple. I took out a contract to find you. The information I received was correct and here we are having our little reunion. Now please, on the bed!' Gomez waved the gun slightly towards the farthest of the twin beds in the room. 'You received over one million American dollars before we knew you were working with the Feds and the rest of those gringos from Treasury and the Agency. That crazy motherfucker Stuart acted as your banker, and where are you today? *Bank City!* Believe me, If you don't come across with the green stuff, you'll be sleeping with Christopher Columbus tonight – your names sake. Not on my island, señor, but here, with these fucking gnomes. Now sit on the bed!'

Gomez pulled the hammer back on the revolver and pointed the silencer at Marker's stomach. At that moment there was a knock on the door. 'Room service, sir,' a female voice called.

'I ordered food,' Marker whispered to Gomez, with an

appealing frown burning into his forehead. 'That's why the door was unlatched.'

'Get rid of her,' Gomez replied softly, slipping the gun half-way back into the case.

It was too late. Hearing the TV and seeing the door wasn't locked, Astrid Jensen stepped into the room. She was carrying a large stainless-steel tray with an array of drinks, food, pots and utensils, topped by a single red carnation in a small thin glass vase.

'On the desk, please,' Marker beckoned, as she approached him.

He looked across at Gomez. The Dominican was sitting rigid and stiff and Marker could imagine the whiteness of his knuckles as he gripped the partially concealed weapon on his knee.

As the girl passed Marker, who hadn't changed his position except to cover himself with the towel as the girl entered, he snatched the tray from the startled waitress and in the same movement hurled its cargo at Gomez. The girl screamed and Gomez leapt to his feet, discarding the case completely and raising the weapon in the direction of Marker and the girl. Marker continued to move without hesitating, lunging towards Gomez, with the heavy tray directed towards his antagonist's head, in a half-dive, half-punching motion.

The gun spat its quiet oblivion twice, as the two men careered over the top of the armchair, and Marker felt a stinging whip-lash across his right side. In the background, he was vaguely aware of the girl's screams over the sound of the TV laughter. Gomez's head hit the triple-laminated glass of the veranda doors and he was instantly knocked senseless. A similar fate awaited Marker a split second later, but the cushion of Gomez's body reduced the momentum and the subsequent crack his head received resulted in great pain, but not the sinking depths of unconsciousness.

The moment was over. Blood pumping in his ears and trick-ling down his nose, Marker struggled to his feet. Astrid Jensen was dead. It had been the eleventh day of her very first job.

The phone rang.

'Yes,' Marker answered, in a daze.

'Herr Marker?' a voice requested.

'Marker? Yes, this is Marker.'

'Ah, Herr Marker, this is Ingrid Saltzenburger, Herr Bonhoff's assistant at the bank.'

'Oh, the bank,' Marker half responded, vaguely watching the blood of life running freely from the body of the girl. 'What can I do for you?'

'Herr Bonhoff has become available two hours earlier than expected and has asked if you wish to see him within the next 30 minutes. You indicated you were on a tight schedule.'

'Tight schedule? Yes, tight schedule. What time did you say?'

'Well, If you would like to come over, now? Herr Marker, are you there?'

'There? Yes, sorry. Come over now? Yes, I can come over now. I mean, in a few minutes, ten minutes, no, ahh, twenty minutes. Is that OK?'

'Twenty minutes will be fine. Please forgive me, but are you all right?'

'All right?' Marker almost whispered. 'Yes, I'm all right. See you soon.'

The noise of the telephone dropping back into its cradle sounded like a thunderclap to Marker. Its finality shook him back to reality. He knew that Stuart would have shot Gomez as he slept, but Stuart was Stuart and he, Chris Marker, was first and foremost a businessman. He stared at the picture before him for only a few seconds. There was only one thing to do – get the hell out of there!

Quickly, he threw clothes into his bag and dressed in the items that remained strewn around the bedroom from when he'd undressed . . . a thousand years ago.

As he left the room, he wiped the door handles on both sides. The forensic boys would note this, and someone might assume that foul play had been planned by persons unknown. It was just a small curved ball, but anything that delayed action was a bonus. Lastly, he left the door open on the latch, just as he'd done for room service, took the lift down to reception and then a taxi to the UBS Bank on Rue St James. On the way, he wiped and threw the room keys out of the window; another curved ball. Now, he just needed two things, the money and a plane. If the room's secret was discovered after he was in the skies, the implications could be dealt with in a more considered light. He just didn't have the time to suffer any delays.

He was shown into Bonhoff's office immediately on arrival.

'Mr Marker, how nice to see you again. It has been such a long time. Five years at least.'

'Eight in October,' Marker smiled, his composure having returned almost to a normal level during the car ride. 'The funds are ready?'

'But of course. Can I offer you a drink while your case is prepared?'

'Scotch on the rocks, please. Single malt if you have it.' Marker sighed as he slumped into one of the stylish armchairs on his side of Bonhoff's desk.

'Ah yes, of course, I remember now. Large Scotch on the rocks. A favourite drink of your associate also, I recall.'

'Good for the heart, but bad for the temper. A character changer with love from the Highlands,' Marker mused.

Bonhoff passed the drink over to him, taking a sherry for himself. Before they had time to raise the glasses to their lips, Ingrid Saltzenburger knocked and entered the room, without waiting for a reply.

'Herr Marker,' she nodded, placing a briefcase on the coffee table. 'The funds you requested. Would you like to check them?'

'I'm sure that if you've supervised the counting and packing, there can be no mistakes.' Marker smiled at the vision of an Alpine schoolteacher before him, tweeds and all.

The feigned compliment bounced off her armour-plating like a wooden arrow. 'As you wish, Herr Marker. Please could you sign the receipt.'

Marker took the pink sheet of paper from her, after taking his first life-saving pull on the whisky. It showed a sum of $500,000, a small amount in terms of the transactions the bank had closed out for Stuart, or Marker in the past. The first $50,000, in small bills, would go to the vessel master, who would never have to work again, his salary in Russia being the equivalent of $8 per day. The remainder would be held for contingency requirements until the operation was over and was provided in $1,000 bills, for ease of concealment.

'Many thanks, my dear,' he smiled again, returning her pen, but holding onto it one second longer than necessary, as she tried to take it back.

'Herr Marker,' she nodded once more, without even a crack showing in her armour, and left the room, closing the door very quietly behind her.

'Bucketful of laughs, but very efficient, I'm sure.' Marker grinned at Bonhoff.

'Reformed alcoholic, actually.' Bonhoff smiled in return. There was no warmth in his reply. It was a rebuke, and both men knew it.

'I'm sorry,' Marker began, but Bonhoff held up his hand in friendly dismissal.

'Please . . . May I top up your drink?

'I would love to, but time waits for no man and I must be on my way.'

'Then let me show you out. You have a car waiting?'

'Yes, if he hasn't been moved on by the police. I know how touchy they are about vehicles loitering around outside banks!'

The two men left the office, passing Ingrid Saltzenburger typing at her desk. She didn't look up.

The men shook hands and Marker got back into the cab. 'Airport, please,' he directed.

The driver nodded and pulled his Mercedes out into the traffic.

As Marker sat back in the rear seat and closed his eyes, Louis Gomez was just opening his, to see the body of Astrid Jensen in front of him.

In Africa, Chet Maclazowitz was only using one eye.

'All quiet on the western front,' Maclazowitz almost whispered, without removing his eye from the rifle's scope. 'Native village at what must have been the entrance to the workings, run-down buildings, thin and gaunt people.'

'The usual,' Skinner said, echoing the big man's thoughts.

'Seems like it,' Maclazowitz agreed, rolling onto his back and sliding back down the shallow incline he'd been using. 'Fucked if I know what's going on, Shag. Nothing seems to click.' The big man pulled off his bush hat and wiped his face again.

'Well, there's one thing for sure,' Skinner offered. 'That elephant wire isn't to keep anyone away from this place. This complex hasn't been used for years and the locals have only parked there because it saves them from clearing the bush themselves. Any guns around?'

'Nothing. D'you know what it reminds me of? Remember that leper colony in Sri Lanka? Well, it's like that, without the bandages. Know what I mean? Kind of . . .'

'What you getting at?'

'It's like dead, but not dead . . . dying, but alive.'

'Well, that's very poetic, Chet, but one thing's for damned sure – if that's supposed to be where the target is, *we've* been shafted.'

'Broadsword, this is Hawk. You copy? Broadsword, the Hawk. Do you read me?'

'Too far out?' Skinner asked, knowing the answer already. 'What do you reckon?'

'You go back, get into range, then bring 'em on in.'

'You staying here?'

'Yep.'

'You won't get lonely, will you?' Skinner mocked, as he melted back into the undergrowth.

Ten minutes after Skinner's light sounds had become silent, Maclazowitz pushed himself back up on to the bank. He could count 23 native houses and the remains of eight larger mine buildings. Dirt roads led in and out of the area, but there was no evidence of any vehicles, and the ruts had collapsed in several places, indicating only light traffic, if any, over the last few months.

'Oh, fuck it,' he said to himself, sliding the sniper's rifle back in to its camouflaged slip and slinging it across his shoulders. 'It's about time someone found out what the hell is going on around here.'

Securing his equipment around him, he took up the silenced Uzi, rolled over the bank into the undergrowth below and headed for the village.

Skinner made his way all the way back to the wire before he tried to make contact. He would have had to return there anyway, to check its status and lead the others through.

'Still with us then?' Stuart replied, when Skinner's East-End tones hit the air.

'Roger on that! Hawk's in the nest. You hit the wire half a mile north of your position and then call in. I'll hold your hand from there.'

'On our way! Over and out. OK you guys, move out. Steve, you give Petey a spell with the fifty – we don't want him melting on us at a critical moment.'

'I'm OK,' Van der Merwe cut in. 'You guys look after yourself. Petey's in good shape.'

'Suit yourself. Let's go! If you're not hauling, you can ride point, Steve.'

'OK,' Rider agreed, smiling at Van der Merwe as he took the weight of the 50-calibre machine-gun. 'Professionals first, donkeys to the rear,' he joked. Then he was gone.

'Does Sandhurst ever provide soldiers, or just comedians?' Van der Merwe said, with his piratical smile, as he passed Stuart.

'Sometimes both, Petey . . . sometimes.'

They both knew that Steve Rider had been top of his class at Sandhurst, with a high-flying career ahead of him. A question mark over how his seemingly deranged SAS commanding officer had died, on a covert mission, had sidelined him into, first of all, resignation from the British Army and secondly, desertion from the Legion. A sporadic cobweb of appearances on the freelance market had followed, but his reputation under fire had grown – as had his price. Steve Rider was good at what he did, but he was a loner. Unlike most mercenaries, he was distant, except for the odd humorous crack which showed a glimpse of the man he'd once been.

It took the group around 35 minutes to reach the wire. Rider and Skinner had already made contact when Stuart and the rest of them caught up with their lead man.

'Skinner's at two o'clock,' Rider informed Stuart, as soon as he drew up alongside him, 'but we've got company.'

A lumbering old army truck was bouncing its way down the tracks on Skinner's side of the wire. There was a pop hole in the roof of the cab and a soldier with the requisite AK47 was lolling out of it. A routine patrol. Nothing special.

The assault group sank into cover and waited for it to pass. It took another 15 minutes for it to disappear and make crossing the open ground possible . . . another delay.

Back at the old mine complex, Maclazowitz was circling the area just inside the treeline. He stopped regularly to sweep the target with his binoculars. A hundred metres to his right was an old water tower, which could have been the reason for the villagers choosing to live in the old mine area. He decided to head for the tower and make a new nest there.

As he lowered his glasses, a twig snapped behind him. Spinning quickly and attaining a hold on the Uzi as he turned, he was confronted by two small and bedraggled children. Their eyes were sunken pools within the tight skin of starvation, but what was left of any life in them was focused down the hole in the barrel of Maclazowitz's gun.

'It's OK, it's OK,' Maclazowitz whispered, letting the gun fall to his side on its webbing sling and holding both his hands up in front of him.

The elder was a boy, about six or seven years old, and the smaller and younger, a girl who couldn't have been much older than three. They just stared at him. They didn't cry or call out, they just stared.

'Chet,' Maclazowitz said quietly, patting his chest. 'Chet,' he repeated with a big smile, taking a small step towards them. The boy was like lightning. As soon as Maclazowitz moved towards them, he let go of the girl's hand and was past the big man in a second, shouting unintelligible warnings towards the village just 150 metres behind him.

'Shit,' Maclazowitz let out, pulling the Uzi into his right hand and grabbing the startled girl with the other. 'That's torn it.'

He picked the remaining child up in crook of his left arm and retreated far enough into the bush so that he could see out, but an observer couldn't see in. The little girl still made no sound, just stared at him with a trusting innocence. Five minutes turned into ten and still nothing happened, but just as he was about to move position, a group of natives appeared at the edge of the compound. At first there was just a few, but slowly the group grew and spread out in front of him. To the left of the front group was a thin, emaciated woman. The boy held her hand and was pointing directly to where Maclazowitz was crouched. Even as the crowd grew, he didn't get any feelings of hostility. No one was carrying a weapon of any kind, not even a stick. It appeared that their only concern was finding the girl. He made a snap decision. Standing up, he let the girl go and started to walk into the camp.

'Crazy, Chet. This is fucking crazy, baby,' he said, more for the company than the certain knowledge.

The little girl took hold of his hand and walked in with him. 'Ched,' she echoed incorrectly, patting her chest. 'Ched!'

'Whatever you say, kid. I'm in your hands now.'

Chet Maclazowitz etched a wide smile on his face and continued towards the gathering. His right thumb clicked the Uzi's safety catch to the off position. Stuart had said no litter. One hostile move and this place is going to look like a city dump, he thought.

In Black Africa, a white soldier usually meant death, abuse, torture and rape, to the ordinary villager. They were to be feared and run from.

None of these emotions registered on the faces of the villagers who blocked Maclazowitz's path. In fact, when he finally reached them, the group parted and accompanied him into the body of the village. Everyone he saw was gaunt and thin. Visions of the newsreels of the Nazi concentration camps came back to him vividly. The faces held that same deep resignation of impending doom, carved for ever in the minds of all those who had seen them.

He was funnelled towards a relatively large hut in the centre of the compound, built on the side of what once must have been an administration block of some kind. At the entrance was an old man. Compared to many of the younger followers, he looked quite healthy.

'*Bonjour, monsieur,*' the old man said.

'Hi, yourself,' Maclazowitz replied, in as friendly a manner as the current circumstances would allow.

'Oh, American?' the old man said, with a quick switch.

'Close enough. Who are you?'

'Dr Charles Talumbatu, at your service. Please come in.'

'A doctor?'

'Don't be afraid. There is nothing here to harm you. Come in, come in.'

He tried to let go of the little girl's hand, but she clung on like glue. 'OK, missy, time to go back to momma.'

'Ched,' she called, with a crushing smile.

'There is no momma, I'm afraid,' the Doctor replied. 'The sickness took her last week.'

'Sickness? I thought you said there was no danger here.'

'There isn't,' he replied, as they entered the building, 'as long as you're careful with any bleeding and refrain from unprotected sexual relations.'

Realisation began to hit Maclazowitz. 'It's not HIV, is it? *AIDS!* Not the whole village, surely?'

'And many others. Whole communities live with it, as if it's a biblical plague which has descended from the heavens to punish them. There are many Christians in this country, you know – probably the only legacy the British left that has had any lasting value.'

'But why doesn't somebody do something?' Chet asked, as he sat down on a hand carved chair.

'A good question, soldier. But unfortunately, like all good questions of that kind, the answer is neither short nor terribly pleasant, and from your apparel and the toys you carry, I would guess that time is something you don't necessarily have a great deal of.'

'That's a fact!'

'Are you alone? Are you running from someone?'

The yawning gap that had appeared in Chet's training and

instinct closed like a heavy trapdoor. 'Alone? Yes I'm alone. I managed to survive a helicopter crash several miles away. I'm a member of the pan-African peacekeeping force and I'm trying to get back to my unit. Do you have an MF or HF radio here, to make contact with my headquarters, or a nearby mobile unit?'

'I regret no.' The doctor smiled knowingly. 'We have no contact with the outside world other than by road. You must wait for a supply run, or an unscheduled visit by an army patrol.

'How often do these army patrols come through?' Chet asked.

'We can never tell, but their visits are not welcomed by us. At the very least they steal our food. At the worst, rape, or . . .' The doctor's sentence tailed off, leaving the meaning hanging in the air. 'Well, I'm sure you're conversant with the ways of the military, or shall we say those who *dress* like the military, in this war-torn land.'

'It wouldn't do much good to deny it.'

'Or serve any purpose,' the doctor replied. 'Can I offer you some food? It's not very elegant, I'm afraid, but we have enough to share with guests.'

'I haven't had hot food for some time. That would be real welcome, but I must continue to try to get back to my unit.'

'It's quite safe, you know – the food. You can't catch the virus from the food.'

'I didn't mean to . . .'

Maclazowitz didn't have time to finish. A commotion outside distracted both men, and the doctor walked slowly towards the door. Maclazowitz sank back into the room, checking possible exits as he reslung his rifle and cocked the Uzi.

'It would appear that your luck is in, soldier. More of your kind – soldiers – are entering the village.'

'Which direction are they coming from?' Maclazowitz asked, as he slid along a wall to one of the holes that served as a window in the wood and mud building.

'From *every* direction, it would seem,' the doctor replied.

'And it's a fucking good job we're the good guys,' Stuart said from the back of the room, his AK levelled at the doctor. 'In another man's army you'd be on a charge for dereliction of duty. What's going on?'

'Don't shoot him, Trap. Tell the guys not to shoot anybody. They're frendlies! The village is clean!'

'They've seen us, Chet. Move away from the window.'

'For God's sake, Trapper, don't shoot him. He's a doctor.'

'So was Crippen. Move away! I shan't tell you again.'

'These people can tell us what the hell's going on around here. The doctor's an educated man – he speaks good English. Trapper, it makes sense!'

'I'm beginning to wonder if anything makes sense around here,' Stuart countered, lowering the weapon and releasing the tension in the room. 'Get outside and get the guys under cover, fed and watered; then back here sharpish and give me a full briefing on what you've been up to. And you, Doctor whatever your name is – '

'Talumbatu, Doctor Charles Tal—'

'*Doctor* will do. Come over here and sit down. I want to know everything about you, the village, the area . . . the whole nine yards.'

'There is really nothing much to tell.'

'Just start. I'll tell you when to stop.'

It was more than an hour later before Stuart was satisfied that the group were safe and the village was no threat. The troops had searched the area thoroughly, but what they'd found was only what they'd seen on arrival. Sentries were posted and Stuart was in conference with Van der Merwe and Sandys.

'Well, I think we should pull out and hitch a ride with Vasco,' Van der Merwe repeated for the third time.

'Sounds good to me, Trap,' John Sandys confirmed. 'We're hovering around the edge of a big black hole and we're lucky not to have fallen down it already.'

'Two did,' Rider said, coming in from the night's orchestral chorus and his rounds of the village perimeter with Maclazowitz.

'Three,' Stuart growled.

'Right, sorry, three. I meant two here . . . I haven't forgotten Shanks.'

126

Stuart got up and paced the room. 'OK, let's go over it again. There has to be an explanation for all this shit. It's got to be right under our noses. The target, the reason and the curved balls. A lot of money has been spent to get us here. The intelligence is shit, but why?'

'They want us to fail and the world to know we did?' Van der Merwe offered.

'Fail at what?' Rider chipped in.

'The mission, of course,' Van der Merwe replied, his famous lack of patience rearing its head.

'What mission?' Stuart asked quietly.

'Well, if you don't know, how the hell are we supposed to, Trapper, for God's sake!'

'Cool it, Petey. *Think*. If they want us to fail, the reason for sending us here is irrelevant. It's only our presence here illegally, getting caught, or wasted, that counts. It's part of a much bigger picture.'

'We've got the money,' Van der Merwe insisted. 'If we've been screwed by the client, the contract's void. Let's get our asses out of here.'

'*I* have the contract with the client, Pete.' Stuart turned on Van der Merwe. '*You* have a contract with me. *I'll* tell you when that contract is completed, and don't you forget it.'

'Hey, you guys, slow down. I can hear you clear across the compound,' Chet Maclazowitz's slow deep drawl interjected, as he climbed up the outside steps and entered the room.

As Stuart turned and stared at him strangely, the room fell silent. When Stuart was angered, or his authority was challenged, he was very dangerous. He spoke more quietly than usual and the predator in him oozed to the surface.

'What did you say?' Stuart said, calmly and quietly.

'Hey, I didn't mean anything, Trap. I just–'

'No, no, Chet. What was it you said? *Compound?* You said compound, not village, not town or camp. You said compound. That's it! Get that doctor back in here. If he's an angel, I'm the fucking Pope!'

10

Honourable Men

The motor yacht *Salamander* rocked easily at her moorings in the secluded but beautiful Friendship Bay, off the south-west coast of West Guinea. She was one of the largest private yachts in the world, and those in the know in the yacht-chartering market indicated, confidentially, that she'd been chartered for a month by a famous Turkish arms dealer to celebrate his fortieth wedding anniversary with friends and clients from all around the world. Built in 1931, she'd just completed a three year rebuilding programme and radiated the elegance of her years, combined with the sophistication of nineties equipment and facilities.

She could accommodate 34 guests in 17 elegant suites, a number of them having separate sitting rooms and two marble and gold bathrooms. The main reception suite and many of the private suites sported original furniture and blending antique accessories. There was a library, various drawing rooms, a gymnasium, sauna, dining saloons and bars to complement the Black Sea Lounge, which served as the main dining room, at the bottom of a set of unique double spiral staircases which swept throughout her five accommodation, entertainment, recreation and pool decks.

A helicopter landing area lay empty at her stern, 446 feet from her bowsprit's heel. Her standard crew was over 50 in number and the paperwork showed she was attracting a charter rate in excess of $230,000 per week.

'Simply magnificent, Nasir,' Falcone said politely to his apparent host, Nasir Ataturk Savarona. 'Her refit has brought her back to the elegance of her youth. It is many months since I last stepped on her decks, but she remains the pride and joy of my life.'

'It has been an honour to have had the responsibility to supervise her rebirth, my don.' Savarona deferred to the original builder and actual owner of the *Salamander*. 'Is it not fitting that she is the host to these new beginnings for our families and their generations to come?'

'Fitting?' Falcone sighed, raising his hands slightly from his side. 'Perhaps more than you know, old friend. Come, let us join our – *your* – guests. The time has come to launch a *new* ship . . . onto a sea of gold.'

'As you say, Caesar, a sea of gold. I pray that we have navigated the rocky channels without foundering on unknown rocks.'

'Life's voyage is littered with unknown rocks, Nasir. If the channel is blocked by them, they must be removed.'

'And our guests?'

'Yes, all are rocks of some kind. We must watch carefully and be on guard for any that may appear to be slipping across our course and into the channel ahead.'

'Shall I go on?'

'Yes, Nasir. That would be best on this occasion. I will wait for a few minutes before following.'

The aging Turk left the yacht's owner alone in his stateroom, leaning lightly on a walking cane that sported a golden handle cast in the form of a diving falcon. Falcone walked with the gait of a tired old man towards a telephone by the entrance to his bedroom. Lowering himself down onto the chaise longue beside the telephone's table, he let out a grating sigh which underpinned exhaustion with pain. Lifting the handset, he dialled a familiar number, lengthened by the access code for the satellite link that would bridge the 44,000 miles through near space to New York. The announcement on the telephone answering machine was short and to the point, just like its owner. He replaced the handset without leaving a message.

The call was not scheduled, so his young nephew, five times removed, could be forgiven for not being there. He would be there later . . . after the meeting.

He rose and straightened his curled frame, leaning the walking stick against the telephone table and commanding the pain in his legs and hips to retreat into the caverns of his mind. He shed ten years from his face and walked out into the yacht's top-deck concourse. Mario, as always, was near at hand. As the king of all that was corrupt and evil in the civilised world appeared from his room, the old retainer slipped in to step just in front and to one side of his sovereign.

'OK?' Mario asked.

'OK,' Falcone replied; and then in Sicilian, 'Watch them all, even the Turk.'

'Especially the Turk, if you ask me!' Mario answered. 'It was a sad day when we stopped killing these greasy Arabs and started doing business with them.'

'He's not an Arab, they are not greasy and I didn't ask your opinion.'

'They're all the same to me. You can count the number of white faces on this boat on–'

'Yacht,' Falcone corrected.

'Yacht, boat, ship – it's all the same to me.'

'That is why I own this yacht, and you, my old school friend, do not know the difference.'

'I might not *know* the difference, but I've *made* the difference on more than one occasion throughout these long years for you,' Mario smiled, with just a slight turn of his head.

'So you have, old friend,' Falcone agreed, patting him on his shoulder as they started to descend the spiral staircase. 'And we enter the arena together once more, hey?'

'Good afternoon, gentlemen, welcome, welcome. Mario, more champagne for my guests,' Falcone urged, as the gathering came into view; the Sicilian language instantly gave way to his heavily accented Bronx American-Italian. His old village school friend, and associate in countless murders transformed himself like a chameleon back into the servant's mould from which he rarely broke free, in public or in private.

130

The large table could be set for 50 people, with carver chairs in attendance at each cover. Seventeen places were set, but not for a meal. The trappings of a conference adorned the table, except for the obvious lack of writing materials. Spring water, fruit juices and a liberal attendance of chilled champagne were scattered uniformly on silken table mats, and trays of hors d'oeuvres were circulated by starched stewards.

In the Black Sea Saloon, guests were standing in small groups, making small talk about family, friends and the multiplicities of corruption in its most sophisticated and barbaric forms. As Falcone entered, the room fell silent. A few nodded and an English lord even smiled, but none made a move towards the table, until Falcone had settled at its head.

'Gentlemen,' Falcone began, 'we come close to the last days and hours of our labours. Soon we will have control of the President of the United States, his administration, policies and longevity in office, including his ability to be re-elected in the months to come. Unlike the last time, this man will listen to our needs. His past CIA activities are buried within the sealed and timed archives representative of the so called democracies to repress the truths of democracy itself; but we now have the key. The last US President we had to have removed. This new man is weaker. He will acquiesce to our control, as long as it is wielded within a velvet glove which also protects him, his ego and, in the finality of things, will bury his past and protect his liberty. You have all played your parts – chairmen of multi-national corporations, bankers, politicians, national presidents, members of my Family from all the corners of the earth- . . . Europe- . . . Asia; Pauli here, for example, who is following his father's footsteps in Laos. Now the time has come to pull the trigger; to press the button that will complete our years of labour. Yes, it is true that we have been fortunate in our recent discovery, but it has been the years of planning and restructur-ing of the organisation into its new, apparent legitimacy that has made it possible to react to an opportunity with global implications when it arose. Let us now review the current status, to ensure that all are clear in their duties once we leave this

131

place. President Mokomo, what is our news from the target zone?'

'Don Falcone, gentlemen, friends. First may I thank you for your support during my recent, ah, inconvenience. I will look forward to extending my hospitality to you all once the project is complete and the peasants have been returned to their huts.' The large man smiled to all around the table and raised his right hand in a regal salute.

Pauli Cintenzo, the family capo from Laos, stared at the deposed President and played with the diamond ring on his left little finger.

'I'm sure we all look forward to that,' he smiled, 'but for the time being, we have much to do in a short time and I have been awake many hours during my hasty trip to be here on time.'

'You will understand,' Falcone chipped in expertly, 'that Pauli and others have had to react instantly once it was clear that the Stuart group were going to make it to the target zone. You and I, Mr President, have had time to sleep and collect our thoughts.'

'Of course,' Mokomo smiled. 'Let us get right down to business. The Stuart party have indeed reached the target zone, but only to the abandoned mine complex.'

'How far is that from the original crash site?' the chairman of a worldwide news network asked.

'They are five kilometres south of the original crash and their apparent target,' Mokomo answered.

'And that's within the existing compound?'

'Yes, the compound stops approximately one kilometre north of the site. When the local population began to be affected by the wasting disease all those years ago, no reason could be found. It was only with Don Falcone's assistance that the extent of the plane's significance was accidentally discovered and any interest taken in the wreckage and its contents.'

'The site is completely safe?'

'Medical experts, recommended by a representative of the World Bank, made extensive tests in the area earlier this year. The radiation levels are of no consequence, since the source

132

was removed and sold, through the goodwill of our friend from Laos, to the North Koreans,' Mokomo confirmed.

'So what is the status at the site now?' the English lord asked.

'At the crash site, or with Stuart group?' The ex-President gave him a hard look. He was used to being listened to, not being questioned by white men.

'Please tell us about *both* and about our operatives on the ground,' the news mogul offered in a calming tone, catching Don Falcone's eye for a fleeting second.

'My pleasure,' Mokomo smiled. 'The crash site is clean. It has the broken remains of the Masada weapon on board and a replica of the containment crucible which housed the nuclear source . . . unsuccessfully. The virus was designed to become harmless in just a few hours and is therefore safe. The latter leaked a small amount of radiation over the years before it was removed, but years of rains, mud and nature have helped to continually reduce its direct and residual effect on the site. Its monumental effect on the history of the world occurred at the point and time of impact and the immediate seconds after the plane crashed.'

'Is it not incredible that such a blink of an eye could have such a shattering effect on an unsuspecting world,' Falcone sighed, as the ex-President paused to mop his ample forehead with a dazzlingly white handkerchief.

'Incredible,' the English lord echoed.

'Posted and hidden all around the site are native watchers,' Mokomo continued, 'and, within thirty minutes' hard driving to the north-west, a crack company of North Vietnamese-born regulars, again courtesy of Mr Cintenzo, are ready to neutralise the Stuart group and close the trap effectively, without local forces being involved. Before you ask, Stuart and his little band are currently stood down, under their own initiative, within the compound at the old mine complex.'

'What happened to the World Bank personnel and their recommended medical and scientific team that visited the site?'

'Dead,' Mokomo replied, without looking at the newsman.

'All this seems very satisfactory,' the English lord commented almost aimlessly. 'How are we keeping tabs on all this, ahem, on the ground stuff?'

'My personal assistant is with the Vietnamese and his brother is in control of the compound.'

'Forgive me for interrupting,' a Republican senator from the eastern seaboard of the United States cut in. ' How are you – we – able to have these people on the ground in such numbers without being in control of the country? I understand that the situation on the ground is confused, with many different countries participating in the war, or the peacekeeping effort, but I would have thought a company of *VC* would have been noticed by someone.'

'Our Vietnamese friends walked in from the north, via Mozambique and Bamako in Mali, after hitching a lift through the sand into West Guinea's walking country. They're good at walking, you'll recall, Senator.'

The American remained silent but lifted his eyebrows as a sign to continue.

'All their direct helpers were removed, after their usefulness was complete – with the knowledge and co-operation of the country officials involved.'

'That sounds more like it,' the senator sneered.

'Incredible,' the English lord said again.

'Please continue,' Falcone urged the ex President, in his best conciliatory manner.

'Communications are, and have been for some time, to and through this vessel. All involved now await our – Don Falcone's – signal to commence the operation to scoop up Stuart's group and then present our ultimatum to the White House. We are ready gentleman . . . Are you?'

There was a smattering of polite clapping.

'Where's Jamayal?' the senator asked. The clapping stopped.

Falcone rose to his feet and raised his hands to the gathering for a second or two, before dropping them with light slaps to his sides. 'Samir Jamayal has been a key player in the success of this business opportunity. He continues to be so and is operating under my direct instructions at this time. He is to ensure that should anything go wrong in the next few days, the organisation is protected from implication, or direct action against it and those around this table. You must allow me to keep his duties to myself for a little while longer.'

No one spoke, but their looks deferred to the old man's wishes. It wasn't as if they had any choice anyway.

Just a relatively few nautical miles away in Freeman, Samir Jamayal would have been surprised to learn of his key role in the don's planning for the future. He'd still been unable to make contact with him and was a very worried man.

Ten nautical miles to the north of Jamayal, Chris Marker's aircraft was dancing its last few steps before landing in the inadequate lights of Bpungi airport, the gateway to the resource-rich hinterland of Sierra Laputu.

11

Pits and Pendulums

Marker obediently fastened his seat belt and returned the seat back to its upright position. The UTA flight had been very comfortable and the leather seats in first class large and soft. An overindulgence in free champagne and the airline's particularly good Glengoyne Scotch whisky had drained the tension of the last two days from his tired body. Sleep during the flight, between drinks, had been easy.

A smattering of French, followed by its English equivalent, flowed from the cabin intercom. He wondered why English spoken by Frenchwomen always sounded more sexy than by any other nationality; perhaps with the exception of Russian women.

His daydreaming was brought to a halt by the jolt of landing, followed quickly by the roar of reverse thrust and the aircraft's strain to brake on a somewhat lumpy runway. As the large bird rolled to a stop at its designated parking spot, Marker noticed a couple of choppers and some small jet fighters lined up on the side of the apron, all covered by dust sheets and air intake protectors. Outside, the sky was blue and the vegetation green. As the aircraft's doors swung open, the smell of West Africa filled the cabin, followed almost instantly by the heavy raft of heat that accompanied you wherever you went in this corner of the continent.

Putting his shoes back on, he retrieved a light jacket from the empty seats on the next row and his briefcase from the overhead locker. In the hold, he had a suit carrier which strained at its zips; around his chest was a light linen money vest containing the cash. He put on his sunglasses as he stepped out into the light, smiled to the pretty UTA cabin attendant and descended onto the sand-dusted apron.

"Ave a nice stay, monsieur,' she beamed after him.

'Let's hope so, my dear,' Marker replied over his shoulder.

The airport building in front of him looked like a second-rate, badly maintained warehouse. There was a crushing mass of black faces at the entrance to the building and on the balcony above it. The rainbows of colour from their clothes were heavily dampened by the presence of a large number of camouflaged soldiers milling around within the civilian ranks, the green and brown shades of their jungle colours diluting the happy cascade of greeting, so often the trade mark of an African welcome.

The Russian vessel's shipping agent was to be in the arrivals area of the terminal to greet him and transport him to the vessel, which was across the estuary in Freeman itself, undergoing repairs.

As he entered the mêlée, he could see a rope divider behind which several locals stood holding up pieces of card and paper with names on them. One of these cards had the name *MARKA* written on it. Marker pushed his way towards the small youth waving it and asked, 'Marker? Chris Marker? For the tug *Petetchkin?*'

'Yes, yes,' the boy smiled, 'Mr Marka for the *Petetchkin*. Please go to the end of the rope walkway and collect your bag. I will be waiting for you after you have cleared Customs and Immigration. The bags will be only a short time. Give your baggage ticket to one of the boys and he will bring it off the trolleys. I am John.' Then he melted back into the swirling crowd.

Before Marker could reply, a boy in a grubby yellow coverall with the sleeves cut out was at his side.

'Ticket, sah. Ticket, sah,' he insisted, holding out his hand for the stub off Marker's flight wallet.

Marker gave it to him, and the boy launched himself into a

scrummage of similar yellow coveralls, all pushing for a front place at the entrance to where the baggage train was to arrive.

Sweat was already running down Marker's back. He undid his tie, rolled it up and slipped it into his jacket pocket. Looking around, as he joined the Immigration desk queue, the soldiers struck him as being very young. Very young and armed. The badge of Africa, the AK47 rifle, was everywhere to be seen. Its many versions festooned the building and the route to the outside.

'Passport,' a blue-uniformed Immigration official demanded, with the sullen look common to many of his ilk around the world.

'I have no visa – I'm passing through to join and sail with a ship from Freeman today,' Marker offered.

'You have seaman's papers?' the official requested.

'No, I'm not a member of the crew, I'm the charterer's representative. The ship's agent's runner is here to meet me and take me straight through to the vessel. Surely this is normal procedure.'

'Normal procedure in normal times, Mr ahh, Marker. Unfortunately, these are not normal times and I must get clearance from the army commander of the airport to let you pass through without a visa.'

'Oh, I see,' Marker replied. 'Will this take long? Obviously, I don't wish to delay the ship.'

'You are the charterer. I'm sure they will wait for you. What is the vessel's name, please?'

' The *Petetchkin*. The anchor-handling tug *Petetchkin*.'

'So, you are in the oil business, Mr Marker?'

'The ship business. This sometimes means the oil business,' Marker smiled, with new respect for his knowledgeable questioner, who turned and spoke in an unintelligible dialect to a young sentry.

'Please follow the soldier. There will only be a slight delay.'

'Thank you,' Marker replied, holding out his hand for his passport.

'You must have this stamped, after the commander has decided what we must do. I will hold onto it until you return,' the official smiled. 'Please have patience. These are difficult times and we are all under martial law. There are many new procedures. Next please!'

Marker followed the young soldier. They weaved their way through the crowd towards the southern end of the terminal. As they progressed, Marker noticed his bag being claimed by the boy in yellow. He was just going to alert his guide when an equally young soldier approached the porter, spoke harshly to him and claimed Marker's bag. The guide took them to a dirty white-painted door and knocked. Someone shouted something from within. The soldier entered, threw up a crisp salute to the officer in front of him and stood to attention.

After a short, clipped conversation, the young guide turned back to Marker and signalled for him to approach and enter the room.

'Thank you,' he said to the soldier, as he went into the hot and musty office. Behind a large table sat the epitome of African manhood. Even in his seated position the officer was clearly very tall, as well as strikingly well built and handsome. When he spoke he was articulate and reflected an education fulfilled overseas.

'Please sit down. I will not keep you long. Have you your passport?'

'No, I'm sorry,' replied Marker. 'They kept it at Immigration.'

The officer rattled off an order to the young soldier, who once more clicked to attention, saluted and turned to leave. Marker assumed he was returning to retrieve the passport. This was in fact the case, but as he turned to leave, Marker's bag appeared at the door with the other soldier and the accompanying boy in yellow, eager not to miss his tip. A great deal of agitated conversation ensued between the officer, the two soldiers, the boy and the Immigration officer, who now also appeared at the door with a more senior colleague. It was as if Marker didn't exist.

'You have some maps in your luggage?' the officer asked quietly.

'Maps?' replied Marker. 'Not maps, charts! They're nautical

charts for the ship. The master requested I bring some charts of the area, because they weren't in his chart folio and the local coastline is treacherous.'

A further round of animated discourse ensued between the representatives of the army and the civilian authorities, ending with a deep sigh from the airport Commander.

'I am sorry, but we must detain you for a little longer. Under new laws, it is not permissible for anyone, other than the army, to own or carry maps of any kind without prior authorisation from the army.'

'So *keep* the charts,' Marker offered.

'It is not as simple as that, I'm afraid. Please, come with me. You must go through a security check. You, your baggage and your clothes.'

The waistcoat under Marker's shirt weighed heavily on his already soaking shoulders. His mind raced as he was led into a small room off the office. There were no windows in this room. The only furniture was a long, thin, high table with a heavy wooden top. Marker was accompanied into the small space by the commander, the two soldiers and three new players dressed in civilian clothes.

'Please take off your clothes and lay them on the table,' the commander instructed.

The blood was thumping in Marker's temples, but he was resigned to the situation. There was nothing he could do or say that was going to prevent the discovery of the waistcoat and its contents. As soon as he started to unbutton his shirt, the audience descended into a cacophony of excited gibbering. The valuable garment was spirited out of the room by two of the civilians and the mood within the small room visibly became more hostile as Marker continued to strip. He stopped when he got down to his underpants.

'Everything!' the commander ordered.

Marker slipped his briefs down his legs and slowly stepped out of them. Never in his life had he felt so vulnerable.

'So,' said the commander, almost to himself, 'you will wait here. I will return in a short time.' With that, he rattled off a string of instructions. Marker's clothes were gathered up by the soldiers and the entourage left the room. There was a noticeable click as they locked him in alone, amid the heat and dust of the airless room. He stood naked, staring at the door. A large beetle scuttled under it and stopped in the middle of the room, turned around and scuttled out again. Freedom was a subjective thing. Suddenly, the lights went out.

'Jesus Christ,' Marker muttered, as he backed carefully up to the wall opposite the door. Animal instinct told him to keep his back to the wall. All he could see was a small pinpoint of light in the door, which he assumed was the key-hole.

The minutes passed . . . He was drenched in sweat, his mouth like sawdust, and he was convinced that at any moment a group of bad guys was going to burst through the door and give him a beating, or worse. Suddenly, a key turned in the lock. Marker braced himself for the inevitable. A young soldier poked his head into the room, followed by several curious faces.

'Sorry! Power cut. It's normal,' he said in heavily accented English.

'Oh,' Marker said, in mild shock. It was all he could think to say. In any event, he wouldn't have had time to say much more because the door was closed and locked as quick as it had been opened.

'Jesus Christ,' Marker muttered again, his nakedness seeming like a beacon in the drowning darkness enveloping him.

Fear is an unusual animal. It often only manifests itself as panic, or hysteria, when the possibility exists to change or get out of the situation which has created the fear. If a situation can't be changed, fear will still remain, but can be coated with a veneer of calm resignation – as in Marker's case.

It was another 15 minutes before the door opened again. A thin man, in partial army uniform, entered the room, along with two soldiers. One of them was his original guide; the second an ugly, older soldier with a broken nose and a deep scar from the edge of his left eye, across his cheek and viciously across his mouth and lips, ending in a deep indentation at the base of his chin. The face was slightly lopsided. His eyes said nothing.

The thin man carried a small leather bag, from which he produced a old pair of latex gloves.

141

'Please turn around and bend down,' he said, as he started to wrestle the gloves onto his fine, artistic hands.

'Why? What's going on?' Marker started to ask.

At the first sign of less than instant compliance, the thin man made a short sound and the soldiers grabbed Marker and bent him over. The ugly soldier grabbed Marker's genitals to encourage composure, maintaining just enough pressure to render him helpless, but not in agony. A searing pain followed the degradation, as the thin man buried two fingers deep into Marker's rectum, followed by a further two from his other hand. The manner of the search that followed was designed to be painful and remembered long after its conclusion. Marker cried out, more than once.

After the search was complete, he was once more left in the darkened room alone. He was wretched, naked and dirty. Rectal fluid ran in a small trickle down the inside of his leg and the room's grime clung to his soaking body like a second skin. He sank to the floor with his back to the wall, his stomach churning and his intestines screaming against the violation. Champagne, whisky and first-class food arched from his mouth involuntarily, slapping against the concrete floor, burning his dry mouth and rendering the room's atmosphere rancid and foul.

After what seemed an age, a soldier opened the door and placed Marker's clothes on the floor.

"Dress, please,' he said. 'I leave door open small, for de light.'

A shaft of daylight witnessed the pitiful scene within the room. Marker stirred himself and pulled the pile of clothes to the side of the door, enabling him to see what he was doing without being visible from outside. The clothes sat uncomfortably on the sticky layer of body grime, but the action of getting dressed gave him some dignity, dulling the pain and clearing a small path for the brain to consider constructive thought.

He was just brushing off his jacket when the lights came back on again.

A soldier poked his head around the corner of the door, wearing a broad smile across his face. 'Good!' he laughed, like a small boy. 'Good, lights!' he repeated.

'Yeah, lights,' Marker found himself replying. 'Very good, lights!'

The child warrior was just about to say something else, when he was brushed aside by the commander and his fawning entourage.

'Mr Marker, we need to spend some time satisfying ourselves of your credentials. You are carrying three passports, two British and one Swiss, plus a considerable amount of money in American dollars.'

'I can explain everything. It's really quite simple,' Marker began.

'I'm pleased to hear it, but you would be wasting your time trying to explain it to me. Military Intelligence and the Chief of Police in Freeman wish to interview you.'

'So I will be going to Freeman now?' Marker asked.

'No,' the commander shrugged. 'Until you have full clearance you will remain in Bpungi. The officials will come here tomorrow. So, if would come with me, we will organise some suitable accommodation for you. Oh yes, don't worry about your ship – it won't leave with out you. We have arrested it until all things are clearly understood. Now, follow me, please.'

Marker fell in behind the commander, to be quickly flanked by a group of four soldiers. The group attracted only mild interest as they passed through and out of the terminal. This seemed to give more confidence to Marker. It was as if he and his situation were an unimportant hiccup in the terminal's day. Just another white man who hadn't got his paperwork in order to satisfy the new regime and their new regulations . . . perhaps.

Outside the entrance to the airport was a line of four-wheel-drive Japanese vehicles. Marker was directed towards the rear right-hand door of the second one.

'Please sit in the middle of the rear seat,' the commander requested pleasantly.

Marker obeyed. He was instantly flanked on either side by an AK-carrying soldier. A similarly equipped youth sat in the right hand front passenger seat, and an officer of some kind slipped into the driver's seat. All the windows were down and the commander leaned through the right front window to talk

143

to the driver. The local dialect was heavy and fast and Marker could distinguish very few words until, with a lightning switch, the commander turned to him and spoke once more in the very best English.

'Do not be afraid. You are a guest of the Provisional Ruling Council, the PRC, and your needs will be provided for by the government. These are very difficult times. We do not know who is our friend, or who is our enemy; only that our enemy has great wealth and can pay for a counter-coup, out of the loose change in his pocket.'

The tall officer reached through the window and took Marker's hand in the classic African handshake: three movements – hand, hand and thumb and then hand once more. The action took Marker by surprise. The officer smiled, gave instructions to his junior officer at the wheel and stepped back from the vehicle.

It pulled away, the middle one of a convoy of three. The one in front and the one at the rear were crammed with armed soldiers. I'm some guest all right, Marker thought.

They ran down a small stretch of tarmac road from the airport building, onto the main dirt road out of Bpungi to the south; but just when Marker thought they were at the beginning of a journey of some duration, they pulled off the road onto a side track which sported a decrepit sign on which Marker could just still make out the faded words *Bpungi Airport Hotel.*

The total journey from the terminal to the front of the hotel had taken less than five minutes. As soon as they stopped, the soldiers piled out of the convoy. Marker was beckoned out by the officer.

'My name is Major Bintu. I have been assigned to ensure that your stay at the Bpungi Airport Hotel is as comfortable as can be expected in these difficult times.'

'Everybody keeps saying that,' Marker commented. '*In these difficult times.*'

'Then it must be true, Mr Marker, mustn't it?'

'It certainly must, Major. Lead on, I'm literally in your hands.'

The hotel reception was run down, like everything else he'd seen in the country so far, and there were soldiers everywhere.

Bintu spoke to the pretty girl behind the reception desk and she handed him a key with a large wooden room number tag. 'Room 24, Mr Marker. Please stay in the room for your own security. These *are* difficult times and the hotel has been partly taken over as a barracks. Your meal will be brought up to you and I will see you in the morning. If you order anything, just sign your name and mark the bill *PRC*. Have a restful night. Hopefully, everything will be in order after you have met our officials tomorrow.' He spoke sharply to a young soldier, who signalled Marker to follow him up the stairs to the first floor.

Room 24 was a standard twin room with en suite facilities. Much to his surprise, everything worked and the sheets smelled freshly washed. The soldier left the key on the fitted dressing table and left without saying a word.

'Well,' Marker said to his reflection in the mirror, 'this is another fine mess you've got me into, Stanley.'

The joke broke the tension in the steel band that had been slowly tightening around his head as the day had gone on.

'Unpack, shower, bed,' he continued to himself. Then the lights went out. As the air-conditioner's fan slowed into silence, Marker slumped onto the nearest bed. 'Shit,' he whispered, 'shit, shit, shit!'

Marker's despair was as deep as Sharon's elation. 'Can this really be true, Yani?' the old man asked of his rising star.

'There can be no doubt about it. The HIV virus and its consequence, AIDS, were man-made, the result of bad management and a freak combination of accidental circumstances in the mid-sixties.'

'No green monkeys then?'

'Green Berets, maybe, but certainly no green monkeys,' Bar-David confirmed with a beaming smile.

'My God! It's incredible. Attempted genocide in the 1960's causes an epidemic of Old Testament proportions two decades later. All from the hands of the most powerful nation on the planet. The Americans chose the name for this abomination in the same corrupted context that the Masada weapon itself was conceived. Those ancient warriors who died on the three-

145

stepped mountain of Masada died with courage and purpose; with a spirit that has become the steel in the resolve that is Israel. Masada was like the British Dunkirk, in some ways: a defeat turned into a victory. Right finally defeating evil. I can't believe it! After all these years of our uneasy alliance with America, we find that these self-righteous allies are capable of making plans more akin to those associated to the *Gestapo*, than those the world has come to expect from the so called model of democracy.'

'Perhaps,' Yani began, 'your feelings are being distorted by the past. This is an incredible opportunity for us to gain many debts from your Bear. The past is the past ... we must play the game that's on the board now, not taint our judgement with the poisoned wine of past US betrayal and manipulation. The US is our ally, but only we can turn the ruins of Masada into the seeds of a twentieth-century promised land.'

'A passionate plea, Yani. You should have been a politician. But what is your actual point?' Sharon asked.

'We must take control of this situation. The Americans have always known what the truth was, but now a curved ball has arrived in the form of the Sierra Laputu ex-government and possibly even the current new incumbents. It's a race to collect irrefutable evidence of the Americans' folly. He who wins the race can wield previously unthinkable influence over the White House, possibly for years. Don't forget, this US President was there, in the thick of it, when the concept *and* the implementation of the Masada weapon was authorised. He had to know. He simply had to know!'

'Don't assume knowledge, Yani – only confirm it. I've told you this before. But your thinking has merit. This *race*, as you call it, is an important one and I agree we should enter it, as soon as I have spoken to others and won their agreement. The implications are outside even the authorised cloak of the Mossad,' Sharon sighed.

'Time is of the essence. If someone like Stuart gets wind of the total picture, not even your desert eagle will be a match for the tiger which will have been let loose. Power, conscience, cause, publicity is nothing to a man like that, only the size of the pay cheque. He above all must be stopped. He is a wild

146

card, a loose gun. He must be found and neutralised as soon as possible, or the quiet ripples of secret diplomacy and the immense power and influence capable of travelling down its course could be shattered. There has never been an opportunity like this for Israel to control the Americans. We must grab it now, and then afterwards we can turn our attention once more to our reluctant neighbours and finally drive the Arab from our country and our lives. Finally, the solution to Israel's war of a thousand years!'

'A solution?' Sharon asked. 'A final solution?'

'Yes, Sharon. The final solution.'

The room fell silent. The old man stared unmovingly at the centre of his desk. The young man was almost panting with the emotion of his excitement, his words echoing through every fibre of the hallowed office. Then, slowly, his words rebounded back off the cedarwood panels. Their implication grew and became heavy within the deepening silence between the two men. Three words, that was all, just three words. Spoken first by Himmler, but universally credited to Hitler, the words *the final solution* were burned and tattooed into the very soul of every Jew throughout the world, just as the number tattoos of the death camps could never be erased from the spirit, even if the skin was surgically cleansed.

Bar-David sank into the seat opposite the hawklike predator before him. 'I didn't mean–'

'Stop,' Sharon cut in.

'But we.'

'I said stop,' Sharon repeated. 'I know what you meant. You only speak the forbidden secret within every Israeli's heart. What you miss is the responsibility that was given to us by our God during the Holocaust. Yes, we must be strong, we must protect our people, we are surrounded. We *are* strong, we *do* and *can* protect our people, we *are* a nation. And we *must, show* mercy. God and our history have chosen us to be the conscience of the world. The final solution must be, *peace.*'

The young man was lost for words. In front of him was the man most revered in Israel for being the epitome of the warrior of the desert. He, more than any individual within a country of front-line soldiers, had planned and executed the obliteration of the enemies of his country. Now he talked of peace, when all around, old and new enemies waited only for the slightest sign of weakness to pounce and claim the land of Moses for themselves.

The old man was saddened. A lifetime of war had tempered his fires. Even now, he wouldn't waiver for a second to order the most extreme of measures against any individual or nation that threatened the survival of Israel. The passion of his young colleague was both life and death for the country. He, Sharon, was at the end of his spiral of influence. His wars had been simple. The enemy had been clear to define – the Arabs, the British, the Arabs, some Muslims, occasionally the Chinese, the Arabs, the Russians, the UN, . . . the Arabs.

In front of him now was a man of the future. Was this future to be tempered by the experiences of the past? Did it understand the intricacies of international diplomacy. Did it want to? Did it care? Was there an end to it all? Could this opportunity be turned into an ending rather than an escalation? He needed to be alone, to think . . . to consult.

'Yani, leave me. We have much to consider. Have an outline operational plan available for me by noon tomorrow. I have much consultation to engage in throughout the night. This load is a very heavy one. Be strong, but consider all implications before you formulate each section of your approach. Remember, no "final solution" has ever worked. God does not will it and neither does Allah!'

'Yes, sir.' The young man turned to leave.

'Wait.' Sharon sighed, looking up from his desk and pinching the bridge of his nose between a sun-mottled finger and thumb. The thumbnail was almost completely black, a victim of inept shelf-fitting for a wife who seemed to spend all her time rebuilding every house they had ever bought or built. 'What of the girl?'

'The girl?'

'Yes, the girl at Langley . . . Michelle Christie, code-named Miriam, isn't she?'

Yani knew that Sharon not only knew the current code names

of all his operatives, but every code name of every operative the State of Israel had ever trained or placed in the field. 'Miriam, yes, it's Miriam,' he replied. 'We're trying to get her out today.'

'Trying? Do we have a problem?' the old man said, replacing his half-moon glasses on the bridge of a nose made red by the recent rubbing.

'Not exactly a problem; more a delay. We've temporarily lost contact with her, but I'm sure she's just keeping a low profile while she makes arrangements to leave without arousing suspicion.'

'Is there a contact schedule?'

'No, sir. Her deep cover called for random access in both directions.'

'Give her twenty-four hours to make contact and then start looking. I want her home within forty-eight hours and an operation mounted while she's in the air.'

'Where can I contact you?' the young man asked.

'Here, Yani. I'll sleep in my ready-room until the game is over. Get her out. Get the Masada evidence out. Keep Stuart out . . . and above all, keep *Israel* out of any dealings with any of – of – all this,' he finished with an almost offhand sweep of his arm.

'So, sir. Here at noon tomorrow?' the young man confirmed.

'Noon,' Sharon nodded, with a dismissing wave, turning to walk towards a door to the right of his desk. It was made of heavy cedar, imported from the Lebanon. Behind it was a small bedroom in the style of a four-star hotel room: a double bed, small wardrobe, adequate bathroom, small desk and the inevitable Corby trouser press. The hours and nights Sharon had spent in this room added up to too many years to think about.

He suddenly felt very tired, but sleep would not wash over him. He would lie in the dark on the bed. There was always an angle, a trick, a way to use intellect as well as, or rather than, violence.

Michelle Christie was also searching for a trick, an angle; anything that could get her out of the building for an apparently

149

legitimate 24 hours. If she ran she could never return, and she wanted to return, badly.

'Excuse me, is this all a bit boring for you, Miss Christie?' Hess enquired of the attractive woman on the other side of the small conference table.

'I'm sorry,' she replied. 'I was just thinking.'

'Admirable, admirable, but I would be grateful if you could address yourself to listening to these latest intelligence reports, and then put your thinking cap on. A thought without facts is a spurious one, not a focused one. Cap, continue pleaoc.'

Mark Cappricci was also sitting on the opposite side of the table to Hess, who was slowly rocking back and forth in his chair as he listened to the latest information his agents had collated. Nancy, his PA, was fussing with coffee and lukewarm pizza on a side table that had served as their running buffet for the last 36 hours.

'Stuart still has to be close to the target site, or we'd have picked up something somewhere,' Cappricci began.

'Perhaps they're dead,' Michelle offered.

'Not dead, not captured,' Hess replied. 'If they were either of those we'd definitely have heard something. It's my guess that Stuart has gone to ground. He's out there planning and scheming.'

'But planning what?' Cappricci asked, in a voice laden with desperation.

'His own agenda, Cap. He's a loose gun now. Everyone else is a bad guy. We have to get under his skin; think like him, plot like him, work out what he thinks his needs are. What's going to be driving that son of a bitch right now; back against the wall, an unknown prize just a stone's throw away from him? What does he want, now?'

'To get away. To escape,' Michelle replied, as though it was obvious. 'I would, anyway. The only thing I'd want to do would be to get out of there, collect my money and melt back into the murky world I'd come from.'

'But you're not him, my dear. His instincts are different. His crippled codes of life are different. Think like an animal, not

150

a human being. What does a cornered animal do, a frightened animal, an animal that has teeth?'

'It attacks,' Cappricci answered for her. 'It attacks indiscriminately and viciously until it's free, clear and sated.'

'Add revenge and greed to that and what have we got, people?'

There was silence in the room, the size of their problem only just seeping through the arrogance of assumed, retrievable control. Each one of them was coming to the same conclusion, from different angles and with different emotions.

Hess thought of another soldier betrayed by *the system*, and the implications of the widening of the threat to the Presidency.

Cappricci thought of the webs within which he'd allowed his life to become irretrievably entangled.

Michelle thought of the man. The strength and the predator within him. His eyes.

'We have to remove him and his men from the game,' Cappricci answered for them all. 'We have to do it quickly and completely.'

'Damage if we do?' Hess asked.

'We have to assume that some form of blackmail from *somewhere* is going to happen, no matter what we do. The President will have to be informed.'

'I don't think so, Cap,' Hess replied. 'The last thing we want to do right now is formally advise the President that we're fucking around with a bunch of video nasties with guns, and not doing it very well.'

'But he knows, anyway,' Michelle chipped in.

'No he doesn't, formally.'

'I thought it was our job to protect the interests of the President by verifiable deniability,' Michelle questioned.

'Quite right, Miss Christie, but it's also our job to protect the interests of the Agency.'

'Above those of the Presidency?' she retorted.

'Leave that choice to me, if you don't mind,' Hess snapped. 'You two put your expensive talents into how we neutralise the Stuart threat and the possibilities of neutralising the Masada information.'

151

'It's a bit like chess,' Nancy Carmichael interrupted, as she placed a tray of coffee and almost cold pizza on the table between them.

The room fell silent. Nancy was always around where Hess could be found, but she was part of the furniture. Normally, she never spoke unless she was spoken to.

'I used to play a lot of chess when Geoff was alive, but I never had the inclination after he passed on. What was it he used to say?...*One board, two colours, two games to one end.* I always thought there was a poet locked away in that rugged exterior of his. He was always coming out with little sayings like that. He never wrote them down, though. Pity, really! D'you want me to pour the coffee or can you manage that yourselves? I've a lot of work to do next door and my lunch is going cold just the same as yours is.' She turned and left the room.

'That, Cap, is the answer.' Hess smiled.

'Chess is the answer?' Michelle cut in.

'No, Miss Christie. *Chess* is not the answer, but the vision and interpretation of that ancient game by a long-dead small-town cop *is*. Think about it. Most people see the game as a single game with two players, when in fact it's just the opposite. Each player looks at the same pieces on the same board, but they see two different games. Each game is designed towards the same ending, but the routes, the plans and the tricks to get there are very different. Two games on one board . . . to the same end.'

'I still don't quite see the connection,' Cappricci said frustratedly. 'Chess . . . boards . . . games? We play games all the time. It's our job. We change tactics, allegiances, promises. What's the bottom line to your thinking?'

''Same game, same players, same ground, but a different goal, Cap.'

'But how,' Michelle asked. 'Time has to be short before this thing breaks. What can we do to turn the situation around?'

'We use the same situation, the same evidence, the same players to turn the same threat against those who are undoubtedly about to play the Masada card against us. Masada is their king to our pawn, but remember, pawns can turn into queens. All they have to do is to reach the other end of the board, the target. Once they're there, they can turn round and attack from behind.'

'OK,' Cappricci conceded, 'we turn the tables. But with what, with whom and in what timeframe?'

'With what? With diplomacy. With whom? With an old man in Scotland, Stuart and the press. And when? Now, Cap. *Now!*'

'I'm lost,' Cappricci admitted.

'I'm intrigued,' Michelle Christie added.

'Well, I'll put you both out of your misery while we travel to the airport. Nancy!' he shouted into his phone console. 'Get Miss Christie on the next Concorde to Heathrow and Cap on the next one to Paris. I want a car downstairs now and the *widow* to call me there. This is all a Priority One. We're on our way down now.'

Stuart's priorities were a little different from those of Carlton Hess. His men were tired and irritable. Steve Rider's interrogation of Doctor Talumbatu, with the assistance of Skinner, hadn't exactly complied with the principles of the Geneva Convention, nor taken allowance for a weak heart. However, before his unfortunate death, they had been able to identify that while he *was* a doctor, he was not a doctor of medicine but a PhD in chemical engineering and he'd only been at the camp for less than two weeks. Most important of all was the discovery that he'd known they were coming. He had known the word Masada, but his untimely exit had prevented them gaining any further clarity for the real reason behind his or the native presence there.

'You always have to go too far, don't you, Skinner?' Van der Merwe accused, as he paced up and down the shack.

'Fuck off, Petey. I only tickled him a little. It was his ticker. How was I supposed to know he was going to croak on us?'

'Petey, it was an accident. We needed him alive not dead,' Rider cut in.

'Leave it,' Stuart ordered. 'What's done is done. At least we got something out of him. Listen, If he was waiting for us, then he clearly has help at hand. We haven't found a radio, but one could be hidden anywhere. We could search for a month of

153

Sundays and still not find it. Whether he did or he didn't, one thing's for sure, help isn't far away – and my guess is that the answer to all this is at the same location as that help.'

'So we hunt?' Chet Maclazowitz asked.

'We hunt,' Stuart confirmed, smiling at the big man.

'But which direction?' Van der Merwe pointed out.

'That depends on Chet,' Stuart replied instantly.

'Why me?'

'The wire.'

'The wire? What about the wire?' Steve Rider asked.

'Chet,' Stuart continued, 'I didn't see the gate at the compound's entrance. On the radio you said there was just a lean-to and a gate with a couple of gooks lounging around.' Was the gate in the middle of the wire's line, or was it at a corner of the wire, Chet? We all hit the wire to the north of the gate. Which direction did the wire go after the gate? To the south, the north – which direction?'

'It ran along the road, to the south of the road, parallel to the road,' Maclazowitz answered.

'Then the gate is at the southern end of the compound.' Stuart smiled. 'We don't know what this wire's for, but we do know that whatever it's guarding is to the north of that gate. We've cut in too far north to cover the whole area, but the odds are we're still south of the target zone and its protectors.'

'So we go north,' Chet stated, rather than asked.

'We go north,' Stuart confirmed, 'and we go now.'

'Sounds good to me,' Skinner mumbled. 'Anything's better than sitting around here waiting for something to happen.'

'OK, let's go then. Chet, we're going to have to take pot luck, so I think the best thing for you to do is head north-east. Steve, you head north-west as a second point man. That way we've a better chance of actually bumping into something in this large area. We'll follow you in twenty minutes, right up the middle.'

Outside the shack, the other mercenaries were cleaning their weapons and making a half-hearted effort to keep watch. Children sat around the men, staring, smiling and sometimes fighting the ten-second battles that small children fight, anywhere

154

in the world. As Stuart and the others came out of the shack, a little girl ran up to Maclazowitz.

'Ched,' she called, patting her chest.

'Hey! Howya doin',' the big American laughed. 'I keep telling you, I'm Chet and you're somebody else.'

'Ched,' she agreed, patting her own chest and holding up her hand for Maclazowitz to take it as they walked. The big man chuckled. It was clear, from the reaction of the other children, that his accidental relationship with the pretty little girl had given her some kind of status in the village children's hierarchy.

'OK baby, I'm going to have to leave you now. Chet's got to take little walk to search for some bad guys.'

'Ched!'

'Yeah, that's right, baby. You-all go find your momma and be a good girl.' He looked around for the young woman who he'd rightly or wrongly assumed was the girl's parent. 'Hey, momma,' he called, catching sight of her shadowing their progress across the village compound, 'come get Diana Ross here. Chet's got to go and I don't want little britches to go following me into the bush.' The young woman didn't understand a word that Chet said, but a beckoning hand is part of the universal language, and *that* she understood.

'Come on, Chet,' Stuart shouted across the compound. 'Haul ass!'

'I'm going, I'm going. Just give me a minute to say goodbye to the relations.

The young black woman reached Maclazowitz and picked up the child. 'Luck,' she said, smiling and retreating at the same time.

'Hey, wait!' Maclazowitz called after her. 'Can you speak English?'

'Luck,' she called again, in the middle of an urgent exchange with the child.

'Ched,' the little girl shouted, with a soul crushing smile. 'Lut! Ched!'

He watched them returning to their world, and for a fleeting second his was blanked out.

'Christ Almighty,' he said to himself, shaking his head, 'got to get out of this business . . . OK, the Hawk's on his way, *Keamosaby*,' he called into his comms set.

'About time,' Stuart replied, from the other end of the village. 'Clock's ticking. We're on the blocks.'

The key turned in the lock and the clockwork actions and reactions of the combat soldier, clicked into gear. They fanned out, with little instruction required from Stuart, Maclazowitz and Rider covering the front door and the inevitable Shag Skinner lurking ominously across their rear.

Not long after the group pulled out, the rain started to fall. It was like a warm shower that needed just a little more heat to feel that the exercise of showering had been worthwhile.

The men's capes had been made by a small English company, in a small town in the Pennines. They specialised in equipment for mountain expeditions, but their lightweight capes had become famous during the Vietnam war. Even the Special Services had carried them, because the construction was uniquely light and dispersed the moisture so quickly and completely.

Chet Maclazowitz had been in that war, but he wore no cape. A sniper used every tool in his cupboard when he was in the nest; but on the move, he had to be light, free and flexible. The cape was for grunts, not for professionals. Many a Vietnam veteran would disagree with that definition, but few would do it to Chester Maclazowitz's face. He didn't give a damn anyway. He could smell the kill again. Each muscle, fibre and the thinnest cilium on his body was aching for the moment the quarry was found. He didn't know it, but he wasn't going to have to wait long.

As he stalked across his designated quadrant, he was heading directly towards the Masada plane's original crash site and the VC who were supposed to be picketed several miles to the north-east. But, true to form, they had obeyed their own masters and infiltrated to the south, to gain any further advantage that hadn't been negotiated with their Mafia paymasters.

On the other flank, Steve Rider kept fanning out on his designated course. It led him into open ground. His radio was only working intermittently, but he hadn't realised it. The

156

sporadic conversation in his left ear had lulled him into a false sense of security. He thought the guys were acting in a really professional manner, keeping chit-chat down to a minimum. In reality he was only receiving 30 per cent of the transmitted traffic. He was becoming isolated and alone, just like on that other operation, years before.

The remainder of the group followed at the appropriate time, keeping a silent routine unless absolutely necessary. They had only been moving for just over an hour when Maclazowitz called in.

'Broadsword? The Hawk.'

'Come back, Hawk,' Stuart replied.

'I've walked straight on to an old aircraft crash site.'

'What's it look like?'

'There's been recent activity all around the area. Hard to tell how many or how long ago, without moving in across a perfect killing zone.'

'Stay put and talk us in. Any high landmarks nearby that we can home-in on? We have cover, but there's lots of sky in view.'

'Not really, but I think you won't go far wrong if you keep the sun at your back.'

'On our way. Don't get spotted.'

'Yo!' Maclazowitz confirmed.

'Rider, comeback,' Stuart transmitted. 'Steve, talk to me!'

There was no answer. Steve Rider was continuing on his route away from the group, his radio silent and his situation getting more dangerous with each step.

'Rider, come in,' Stuart tried again. 'Shit! OK, guys, move in. We'll check on Rider later. Chet's the priority, just now.'

'I'm touched,' Maclazowitz whispered, as he surveyed the target site again.

'I'll go for Steve,' Skinner offered.

'Later,' Stuart repeated. 'Let's confirm the site's all clear first.'

It was then that Maclazowitz saw the first movement. 'Bad guys,' he whispered into his radio.

The following group stopped in their tracks and waited. Pete

157

Van der Merwe was 20 metres ahead of the line, carrying the 50-calibre machine-gun. He slid down the side of a tree onto his haunches, with the trunk at his back, braced the weapon, and began a slow sighting sweep of the immediate area. Skinner turned and scanned their rear.

John Sandys had a rivulet of sweat running down the side of his nose. Under normal circumstances, it would have caused an automatic reaction to wipe it away and relieve the tickling sensation, but the tension of the moment and the adrenaline flush it triggered dulled all sensations except vision and hearing. He didn't move a muscle, other than the tiny ones that allowed his eyeballs to swivel slowly from side to side.

'I got me lots of company and they ain't black.' Maclazowitz's voice interrupted the tension. '*Chinks!* We got Chinks or something similar, right across the path.'

'Chinese?' Stuart queried, his voice taking on an unfamiliar edge. 'What's their status?'

'Wired up and switched on. They're in full assault mode and coming right down the pipe. Trapper! these guys are fucking *regulars* not riff-raff! I see twenty-plus and they're still walking into view. Hold on!' He swept the on-coming force with his glasses until he hit on a officer, straining every blood vessel in his tired eyes. Realisation hit him. *Jesus, VC!* We've got *Vietnamese*, in full combat kit! There's something very fucking naughty going on around here. If these guys don't stop at the crashed plane they'll be on me in, oh, ten minutes. What's the plan?'

'Hold!' Stuart replied, his mind racing. 'Stay put, Chet. They'll stop at the plane.'

'How d'you know that, for Christ sakes!' Maclazowitz replied in a stage whisper. 'My ass is hanging out here. These guy's aren't a bunch of pissed-off blacks, Trapper. They're fucking nuts! You know they are.'

'They'll stop,' Stuart snapped. 'You hold your fucking position, Chet. I mean it! You hold, get down in your nest and stay put.'

The radio fell silent. None of the other mercenaries spoke. They just waited for Stuart to give the next order. Maclazowitz wasn't far away, but they didn't know exactly *where* and he was unable to talk them in. Stuart was staring at the ground where he crouched; then, looking up, he signalled Pete Van der Merwe to proceed. As one, the group rose and began to stalk through the medium bush in front of them.

At the same time, Steve Rider called in, but nobody heard him except a native soldier, who was one of the sporadic ring of Sierra Laputu conscripts who had been ordered to circle the crash site at a distance of one mile. The actual circle had changed radically in shape as the days had gone by, and now it resembled a random picket rather than a security ring. It was the first bit of luck the group had encountered since they had landed, but they remained blissfully unaware of it, except for Rider. He smelt the man before he actually saw him. The sentry had been smoking when he'd heard Rider's voice. Extinguishing the cheap home-made cigarette hadn't dispelled the lingering and tell-tale odour.

'Halt! Who is going dah?' the young conscript called out.

Rider actually smiled. It sounded so ridiculous under the current circumstances; like a cry from and old British Ealing Studios B movie.

'Just me,' Rider replied quietly, his silenced 9 mm pistol popping three times quietly. The second shot hit the juvenile square in the throat, turning his cry for life into a premature death rattle. Rider bent down to check him out. In a mindless spasm of the primeval instinct to survive, the young black youth buried his bush knife into Rider's groin. The soldier died before the rush of pain exploded in the Englishman's brain, but the damage was done.

Rider crumpled into a heap on top of his latest corpse, teeth grating as his desperate breath hissed out from between lips that wanted to scream out to the heavens. He rolled over and stared at the sky, instantly screwing his eyes up against the searing sun, which added a background flare to the explosions of light that cascaded across his retina, as every spasm of pain let loose its fiery bolts.

The blade had entered his inner thigh, four inches below the groin itself, skirted the artery by fractions of a hair's breadth and lodged in the inside of the hip joint. He gritted his teeth

159

and yanked the unwelcome intrusion from his body. Blood flowed easily from the wound, but there was no tell-tale pumping from damaged arteries.

The small range of field dressings in his pack were ample to deal with the first aid of minor and major wounds. He selected size by instinct and training and tightly bound the wound, after slitting his combat fatigues enough to accommodate the dressing and its bindings. Pain was not an issue at this early stage. Nerve ends were dulled by the trauma and the rivers of adrenaline that were rushing to the rescue, inevitably in vain.

The ground around Rider was covered with the blood of the two men, attracting a myriad of ground-locked insects and their flying cousins. A further death rattle expelled itself from the lifeless form of the young black soldier. Rider coughed in answer and tried to rise.

'Jesus Christ!' he cried out, as the wounded leg protested against the weight it was demanded to carry. 'Rider to Broadsword?' he called in vain into the completely defunk radio. 'Rider to Hawk?' he tried again. 'Chet! Come in, for Christ sake!'

Tearing the useless headset from its wiring, he started a torturous journey towards the general direction of the main party. The leg began the throbbing which would increase into a wet searing at every move of his body.

'Looks like you've done it this time old son,' he whispered under his breath.

Chet Maclazowitz was thinking the same thing, as the size of the opposing force became apparent.

'Trapper, they've *stopped!*' he whispered into the radio.

'Yeah. Pretty, aren't they,' Stuart replied.

'Where are you?' Maclazowitz asked, relief unusually obvious in his voice.

'East of you. Directly in line with the nose of the wreck. Got some VC between us, but they're starting to make camp.'

'Wait for dark?'

'Roger,' replied Stuart. 'But try to get a more secure nest and a bead on the officer while we wait.'

'Then what?' Maclazowitz asked, echoing the thoughts of the rest of the diminishing party.

'I'll tell you when I know,' Stuart responded.

No one answered. They just bedded down in the best cover they could find, 200 metres from the nearest picket.

Michelle Christie hadn't had time to bed down, or even sit down, until she collapsed into the contoured seat of the Anglo-French Concorde aircraft. It was a British Airways version and looked quite petite alongside the towering fleets of Boeing 747s lined up at their gates and lumbering about on the tarmac.

Champagne was always welcome. She managed two glasses, before the aircraft's four Rolls Royce engines poured out their incredible thrust from within the square-sectioned engine combings, which grew from the undersides of the delta wings swept low beneath its arrow-shaft fuselage.

She couldn't believe her fortune. Hess had ordered her out of the country with a first class ticket to safety; but even so, she was unsure of how best to proceed or what she wanted to proceed to. Sense told her that she should hop onto the next flight out of London Heathrow to Tel Aviv. Her heart told her to wait and find a way to remain under cover and beyond suspicion.

An attractive stewardess, with the almost regulation British Airways blond tint in her hair, broke into her thoughts as the menus were handed out for the meal to come.

'Would you like a warm towel to freshen up with?' she asked with a smile.

'Thanks,' Michelle smiled back. 'What time, UK time, will we land?' she asked.

'We should be at the terminal about 0830 hours.'

'Thanks again,' Michelle smiled, passing back the quickly cooling towel and returning to her dilemma.

The task Hess had given her might seem quite simple, to some. She was to leak a story to one of the British tabloid newspapers, using false documents, indicating that evidence had been found of a long-standing chemical weapons factory hidden away in the Sierra Laputu bush, funded by the Chinese or the North Koreans to supply various dubious or terrorist

161

states around the world, in their continual struggles in their fight against Western imperialism.

The evidence would indicate that the facility was believed to be located in one of the country's many disused mine complexes and would suggest that there were only minimal safety precautions, continually exposing the workers to serious illness and often death. There would be further hints that this information had only come to light since the recent *coup d'état*.

Having fulfilled that task, she was to fly to Scotland to find Urquart. Hess was convinced that the first person Stuart would contact would be his old and trusted retainer. She was to stay with the old man until something broke and then communicate Stuart's known whereabouts to Hess immediately.

She wondered how Cappricci was getting on. His flight had left before hers, but his onward destination was not as pleasant. He was to transfer to a UTA flight to Freeman and await further orders from Hess. Being on site, he could react more quickly to the unfolding events. He would, however, not make contact with the American Embassy, but stay in a hotel as a businessman on a trading visit to meet with the Jamayal organisation.

Both Michelle Christie and Mark Cappricci couldn't believe their luck. Each had been sent in directions and to locations that suited the needs of the Agency, their own individual needs and the potential needs of their *real* masters.

As she settled back to enjoy her flight, she flicked carelessly through the *Times*. A picture of a good-looking man, under the headline, *Well Known City Broker Wanted For Questioning*, caught her eye. Apparently there had been a struggle between at least three people in a Geneva hotel and a young waitress had been shot. Two separate blood groups had been identified and the fingerprints of a well-respected London shipbroker called Christopher Marker. His picture smiled out from the page. Something rang a bell in the far reaches of her mind, but she couldn't put her finger on it.

12

'One Board, Two Colours, Two Games'

'So,' Major Nelson asked. 'Have you ever seen this man before?'

'No,' Samir Jamayal answered, in as bland a manner as he could muster. 'I have no idea who this man could be. Is he under arrest?'

'At the moment, yes,' Nelson answered.

'And the bruising on his face?'

'An unfortunate fall as he was disembarking from the aircraft. The airline should be reprimanded,' Nelson smiled.

The two men were sitting at a table on the open-sided covered porch of the crumbling Bpungi Airport Hotel's dining area. The rain was falling like a solid wall of shimmering lights, enhancing the heady smell of the soaking vegetation which surrounded the buildings at every turn. Birds took shelter in the bushes and wide-leafed plants. All manner of lizards scuttled about between their hiding places, with a great sense of urgency.

A few soldiers lolled on chairs at some of the other tables and a couple of local civilians talked over a fruit drink and a Star beer.

Marker was at the other end of the porch, unaware that he was undergoing an identification exercise. He assumed that the well-dressed Middle Eastern-looking man with Nelson was just another official come to interrogate him or discuss him . . .

The last 48 hours hadn't gone well with Marker. When the lights in his room went out, before he'd even had time to unpack, he heard some female shouting in the corridor. On opening his room door, he noticed the flicker of candlelight under the doors of some of the other rooms in the corridor. As his eyes became more accustomed to the dark, he saw that there was also a candlelit hue coming from the area of the stairs which led down to the open-plan reception, dining and bar area. He decided to go down and try to purloin some candles for his own room.

The middle of the first floor corridor was the landing for the stairs that led from the reception to the bedroom areas. From this landing, the remaining sections of the hotel's ground floor could be viewed. Soldiers were everywhere, laughing, joking, sleeping and messing about with the female camp followers who festoon any mobilised West African army's barracks.

At the bar were three white men. Marker went down the stairs and approached them.

'Good evening,' he said, flashing his famous disarming smile.

The men nodded, and the nearest one turned and smiled. 'Would you like a beer? Bit of a bugger about the lights. Afraid it happens all the time. The generator is on its last legs, just like the rest of the bloody country.'

'Thanks,' said Marker. 'What d'you all do here? You're English, aren't you?

'Australian actually, but we moved to Britain when I was only seven. I'm Joss Ireland. This is Pierre Costcona and the ugly guy at the end is Jean-Pierre Guston. They're pilots with Air Gambia and I'm the ground wallah that looks after them. Cheers!' he finished with a flourish, and downed half the glass of Star beer that the barman had just poured him.

'Cheers,' replied Marker, to all of them.

'What do you do yourself?' Ireland asked.

'I'm in the marine business . . . ships.' Marker took a pull at his beer.

'On your way to Freeman then?'

'Well, yes, but there's been a bit of a hiccup.'

'That's normal. Don't worry about it

164

'Well I don't know about normal,' Marker answered. 'My entry to the country was somewhat unorthodox.'

Marker recounted the events of the day to his small audience, but just before he was about to finish and return to his room with some candles he'd liberated from the bar, there was a loud shout from the hotel entrance. Bintu stood there with a small entourage.

'Mr Marker! You were instructed to remain in your room. Return there immediately!'

'The lights went out. I was just getting some candles.'

Bintu shouted some instructions and three soldiers doubled towards Marker. He was manhandled up the stairs and unceremoniously pushed into his blackened room. The door was slammed and locked from the outside. Marker stood in the dark, breathing heavily. 'Holy shit,' he said, staring into the creeping darkness, 'holy shit!'

Downstairs, Joss Ireland was already attacking his next beer. 'Well, I don't know what he's been up to, but he's in better shape than old Bill Shanks, whatever he's done. Come on, you guys, I thought this was a wake for an old and sadly missed colleague and drinking partner! *Bill Shanks*,' he toasted, his glass spilling some of its contents down his arm.

'*Bill Shanks*,' the Air Gambia flyers echoed and emptied their glasses in one.

'More beer!' Ireland called to the bored barman.

In the darkness, Marker felt his way to the louvred windows. They were in two sections, with separate lever controls for each side. He pulled the first small lever he found, and the horizontal glass partitions flapped open to reveal a fine wire mosquito mesh on the outside. The downstairs hotel lights formed a background hue which silhouetted the window's form and cast a ghostly shadow on the wall above the bed.

Instantly, the insects of the night seemed to know that the glass partitions had opened, and they milled around the aging mesh, searching and probing, with the instincts of a millennium long passed, for any minute failings in the imperfect protection that man had constructed against their insatiable thirst for his blood.

165

A Taiwanese air-conditioning unit intruded through the outside wall, just above the top of the window line. Its inactivity, due to the power cut, accentuated the damp staleness of the room.

Somewhere in the room, a six-legged winged foot soldier was sporadically strafing the hot spot in the dark that Marker created. In the morning, he would start to scratch the first of many assaults that this foot soldier and his scouts perpetrated against his pampered skin.

Suddenly, the lights came on. The air-conditioning unit rattled into action and the assault troops buzzed temporarily into retreat.

Marker stripped and went into the bathroom. It was designed on the standard Western hotel room's facilities; grimy, but operational. He was surprised to discover the pleasing efficiency of the bath's shower tap – good pressure, hot and cold water. There was even soap in the soapdish and towels on the rack above the bath. Perhaps things weren't going to be as bad as he'd first thought !

He showered, the dirt, sweat and grime of the journey and its unexpected ending peeling off him like layers of a knight's chain mail. As he dried himself on the rough and overwashed towels, the effect of the day's events and the single Star beer he'd managed in the bar washed over him in an avalanche of exhaustion. The room was becoming cool, so he threw on a pair of loose sports shorts and left the blankets on the bed as he crawled under the covers. Sleep was almost instantaneous.

At just after four o'clock in the morning, the door of his room flew open and Major Nelson strode in, accompanied by Cassa and two guards. Bintu was hovering in the background, but even in Marker's shocked awakening, it was clear to him that the new arrivals were something special. The thickset man had a UK passport in his hand.

'You're Christopher Marker?'

'Yes', Marker replied, trying to push himself into consciousness as quickly as possible.

'Why do you bring strategic maps into our country?'

'Well, you see –'

166

'Who are you working for?'

'I'm in the shipping business and–'

'Why do you carry two passports?' Nelson rattled on, at an increasingly swift pace.

'I have to travel to both Muslim countries and Israel, so I –'

'You must come with us, Mr Marker. Leave your things here.'

'Now wait a minute,' Marker began, as he started to get out of the bed.

Nelson then said something unintelligible to his guards, spun on his heels and left as quickly as he'd arrived.

'You dress!' the smaller of the soldiers said.

'Now you just wait a minute,' Marker objected, pointing at the man.' I've a right to know what is happening and where you're taking me. I am a Briti—'

The second soldier's AK47 rifle butt dug deep into Marker's kidney area and cut him off in mid-sentence. He collapsed in a heap on the floor, the world spinning and the incapacitating pain making breathing impossible. In that moment he thought he was going to die. Then a second blow caused him to pass out.

Marker's first impression, after he'd been scythed down, was that he was drowning in a slowly spinning whirlpool of black, putrid water. Something was wrong with his side and he couldn't swim properly; a pity, because he was a good swimmer. The water was warm, but his lungs were screaming to suck in life-giving air . . . Then there was a light above him.

He struggled with his working arm and leg to kick for the brightness. If he pushed just a little more, he might be able to reach for it in time. Clawing hands seemed to drag at his feet, slowing his progress to safety, but the pool of light was getting bigger and brighter, closer and more attainable. Suddenly, he could breathe. The womblike encapsulation dissolved and his disabled limbs came back to life with a rush of pain. He opened his eyes . . .

Focus was not good and small coloured lights were dancing across his retinas. Wherever he was, it was fairly dark and incredibly hot. A sickly, rotting smell invaded his nostrils with a faint hint of recollection. The bright pool of light was still above him, but its edges were sharper and more defined. He was aware of human sounds, somewhere in the distance. The dull edges of his vision began to retract into focused, meaningful shapes. The bright light transformed slowly into a high window, with bars as its only decoration. He attempted to rise.

'Jesus Christ!' he shouted out loud, as incredible pain shot through his damaged side; his hands automatically reaching for the offending area.

He managed to sit up and swing his legs over the side of the wooden bed pallet he'd been lying on. His exploring hands could find no cut or signs of bleeding, but the whole of his left side, from just below his armpit to just over his hip, was badly swollen, tender and discoloured. In the murky light it was hard to tell the extent of the discolouration, but whatever damage had been done would take time to mend. Any attempt to spin in either direction brought on an instant lance of sharp pain on the surface of the damaged area and a more worrying, duller explosion beneath.

Deep within man's soul is an animal. In some, it is deeper than others, but even in the most civilised of the species, life threatening situations open up a Pandora's box of instinctive and uncharacteristic behaviour.

At the St John's Club, in the heart of the City of London's marine community, Marker would have been spending his lunchtime entangled in the prospects of a remarkably good Chablis and a possible charter or insurance fixture. At noon, in Sierra Laputu's infamous Freeman military prison, he was scanning his surroundings, recording strengths, accepting weaknesses, like a fox cornered in a pheasant pen by an over-enthusiastic gun dog.

The room, if you could call it that, was about 15 feet in length and 8 feet in width. The proverbial cat couldn't be swung within its walls. High in the narrow outside wall's width was the window. It was just a hole formed by a lack of bricks, with iron bars set in the untidy mortar of its lintels. Marker noticed that the bars were quite thick, but that their width was irregular, implying many years of painting on top of rust, scale, dirt and previous coatings, without any cleaning of the bars

168

before each application. The floor was earth, compacted over almost two centuries into a layer of natural concrete. In one of the outside wall corners there was a small drainage hole. On the inside wall a too-large iron door, containing the classic viewing and feeding holes popular with the imperial powers of a bygone age.

'Welcome to the Ritz.' Marker stifled a hysterical laugh. As he moved to make himself more comfortable, he felt a grating in his back and side.

'Well,' he continued, straining to hold back the cough that was building up below his diaphragm, 'that's at least one rib fucked, buddy! We'd better get our shit together before the Borgias come back.'

The comfort of speaking out loud was a therapy to Marker, not an adverse indication of his state of mind, but this was not apparent to him, or to his captors, who were observing and listening to him from their observation point through the apparently oversized colonial door.

He decided to test his body to the limit. Only then would he really know how to handle the trials to come. The guards observed him with a growing respect, as the injured man stretched, twisted and stressed his body to, and past, the limits of excruciating pain in preparation for the interrogation he suspected was to come.

During this testing of his resources, whilst bending to try to touch his toes, he noticed a small flash of light in the middle of the top half of the steel door. He stretched slowly back to an upright posture and slowly walked towards the door. The speck of light went out.

'Got you,' he whispered to himself.

The knowledge that he was under observation gave Marker strength. He was clearly deemed important enough to merit it, which meant that what vestige of international law remained inside the country might more easily be used to his advantage. If he had been perceived as a nobody, then his body would probably already be rotting in the African bush.

It was clear from the taste around his pallet that he'd been violently sick during the period of his drifting consciousness.

Both nausea and a desperate need to relieve himself washed over him simultaneously. He steadied himself on the wall opposite the pallet and forced the bile to return to his stomach. Its burning punched some more adrenaline into his flagging system and gave him the strength to make for the hole in the rock-hard earth. As his bladder discharged itself in an urgent and steaming torrent, Marker's worst fears were realised. The combination of his bladder's painful relief, his assault injuries and the murky light couldn't hide the faint hue of red in the darkening green of his urine. 'Forty–love,' he said to himself and the potential audience. 'Marker to *serve*.'

After the steamy torrent was finished, he struggled back to the pallet to lie down on his right side and rest. He still was only clad in the loose sports shorts he'd gone to bed in, but he was thankful for that small mercy. The heat was so oppressive that undressing in his present state would have caused intense pain.

During the next couple of hours, the small observation port in the cell door clicked open and shut many times, but Marker was unaware of the intrusion as ragged sleep of exhaustion criss-crossed his consciousness.

At six o'clock, just as the sun was dying in the west, the cell door opened quietly and Bintu entered alone. The door shut equally quietly behind him.

'Mr Marker, ' the African said, in a whisper. 'Mr Marker, are you awake?'

Marker heard him, but took time to gather his wits and tense his body against the possibility of a physical onslaught.

'Mr. Marker, it is I, Bintu. Can you hear me?'

The calmness and formality of the question put Marker further on his guard, particularly as his damaged side was directly next to the officer. He groaned and started to turn over to be able to see his visitor.

'Mr Marker, be careful. You have hurt yourself. Let me help you.'

'Bloody careless of me, wasn't it, Bintu, old lad?' Marker replied, turning with a suddenness that made the officer take half a step back and caused Marker so much pain that he almost couldn't hide it.

Bintu feigned apology. 'Most unfortunate accident, Mr Marker. The soldiers involved have been disciplined.'

Marker had expected to be beaten more, but instead, this previously aggressive officer was deferring to him in the most bizarre of circumstances and surroundings.

'What's this, Bintu – the good cop, bad cop routine?'

The comparison appeared to be lost on the man. 'I'm sorry?' Bintu asked.

'Forget it,' Marker answered quickly, sitting up fully on his pallet. 'Where am I, why am I here and when I am getting out?'

'You're in the Victoria Military Prison in Freeman. You're here for your own safety. These are difficult times and–'

'I've heard that last line already, Bintu. Try another.'

'You're to go before the Military Council on charges of spying.'

'What!' Marker raged, regretting the action instantly, as pain lanced deep into his side. 'How do they make that out?'

'That is not for me to answer. I have been sent from Bpungi to bring your clothes and to advise you of the procedures in these matters.'

'Procedures? If I'm going to be charged with something, I want to see the British Ambassador. *He* can advise me of "procedures".'

'Regrettably, in cases of security, which you are, international law allows for a period of seven days before you're required to be given access to your embassy. Here you British have a high commission, not an embassy.'

'Is that right?' Maker said, controlling a cough to its mildest form of attack. 'Then tell me, Bintu, how would a simple foot soldier like you know about the intricacies of international law?'

The sneer was not lost on Bintu, nor its implication. 'Before the coup, I was a lawyer, Mr Marker. Edinburgh-trained, actually.'

'I don't care if you were trained in Billy Smart's fucking Circus! I'll say nothing, nor sign anything until I've seen a representative of the British Government.'

'That may prove difficult, Mr Marker, but I will pass your sentiments on. Is there anything else you need? A meal is due quite soon and washing facilities will be made available.'

'You said you had my clothes?'

'They will be brought to you before your – ah – appearance. You may be questioned again before that time, but this is just a matter of procedure, you know – good cop, bad cop stuff!'

Marker stared at the man, who smiled and turned to leave. 'So send in the good cop, Bintu,' Marker replied wryly.

'But Mr Marker,' Bintu said, in mock horror, 'I've already been.'

The heavy door shut with a finality that left Marker in a sea of desperation. He'd been fairly fit when he landed, but he wasn't trained for this kind of thing. The only thing he knew about prisoners and interrogation was what he'd seen in movies and read in books. In the event, he didn't have time to think about it.

The door flew open and three guards rushed in. They grabbed Marker without any consideration for his wounds, or the screams that their handling caused, and dragged him down a bleak corridor to another room.

From within a red haze of pain, Marker could see that the room had several pieces of equipment in it, but pain prevented him from taking anything in. The preparation he'd gone through in his cell was a complete waste of time. Searing pain clouded every inch of his being.

He was aware of being lifted up vertically and bonds of some kind attached to his wrists. He was hauled up by these bonds until his toes just cleared the ground, and then his shorts were ripped off.

There was a vague sense of spinning, as he tried to rationalise the pain with the murky edge of consciousness. The room . . . the men . . . the equipment . . . the spinning . . . the pain . . .

He vomited all down himself. The guards laughed. Tears came to his eyes and a mixture of acidic vomit and mucus trickled from his nostrils. A guard approached him. 'So, Mr White Spy, you don't think the people and the Provisional Ruling Council should be running this country, hey? You think that murderous fat bastard Mokomo is a better ruler? How much did he pay you? How much did your masters get to organise a counter-coup? What are you – CIA, SIS? Come on, Mr Clever Hero, who's paying the bill?'

Marker couldn't have answered if he'd wanted to. The pain in his side was now at the outer limits, each movement in his swing causing the broken ribs on his left side to grate and click, edges popping apart and scraping past each other.

When the home-made electric cattle prod was placed between his buttocks, the pain in his side erupted into an explosive convulsion that caused every orifice in his body to discharge anything that was available for release. His screams could be heard hundreds of metres away from the underground chamber first designed to punish unruly slaves before they were transported to Havana and the Americas beyond. The searing shocks felt as if they were burning his anus and melting through the sack of his scrotum. Just when he thought the attack had subsided, the prod was engaged on his injured side and onwards onto both nipples. The only part of his delicate senses that hadn't been abused was his penis, which hung limp and pathetic between swelling inner thighs.

As quickly as the attack had started, it finished. Cold water was thrown over him and his wounds. The guards left, pleased with their game and the effeminate screams that they'd wrung out of the white man.

Marker hung in a fantasy world. Every sense in his body was sending frenzied information to his brain, overloading it with conflicting information. Thresholds of pain that had never even been contemplated had been reached and surpassed. As always, numbness followed pain. When it subsided, the pain would return tenfold, but for now, the body's defences cut off the nerve levels until the brain could receive and rationalise the bombardment it had been soaking up. He thought his arms were aching. The spinning was annoying. Where was he? Why was he here?

He hung there for what seemed like infinity, time becoming an invalid reference for his circumstances and the stresses rebounding through his body.

Whether it was his bonds or his joints that were stretching, he sensed that his toes were just able to touch the floor and control the nauseating, uncontrolled movement that the tether's axis point created. The distraction of having some control, however small, of anything at all became the centre of his being, as he searched for a grip on the dirt floor.

It seemed an eternity, but less than an hour after the most serious assault, a different group of soldiers entered the room, cut him down and removed him back to his cell and the luxury of the wooden pallet. He was vaguely aware of the move and the sounds that accompanied it; of someone tending to his wounds and washing down his naked body. Hands forced him to drink some fluids and shortly afterwards, the drug it contained enveloped him in deep sleep.

When he awoke he was back in his room at Bpungi, transferred unknowingly by Nelson's Puma helicopter. There was a woman nurse in the room and he could feel wrappings of some kind between his legs and around his waist. As soon as she noticed that his eyes were open she left the room. Five minutes later, Nelson entered.

'How are you, Mr Marker? Well, I hope?'

Marker just stared at him from blood-shot eyes that were encased within pools of dark skin, surrounded by a face that had the colour of sour milk. The whole situation was surreal.

'My guards tell me that you had an unfortunate accident on your way to Freeman – a car crash. You are very fortunate. The medical facilities are not what they might be in the country, but a military ambulance happened to be passing by and we managed to rescue you. The driver of your Landcruiser was killed, I'm afraid. We have, of course, made your high commission aware of your situation and the fact that you are safe and well, if not a little bruised.

So that was it! Marker thought. The official version – or was it still just mind games? He hesitated before he spoke. 'I could be better. I keep seeing you. Who are you?' he asked.

'That's unimportant,' Nelson answered, dismissing the question. 'I'm here to ensure that you're comfortable and that your immediate needs are being attended to. The doctor tells me that once the sleeping draught has fully worn off, you will be surprised at your mobility. You have three broken ribs, but we have strapped you up and it's important that you become mobile as soon as possible, for your own good. I will come again this evening to see how you're getting on. Perhaps you will feel like getting up then.'

With that, Nelson smiled, turned on his heel and left the room. The door was locked from the outside.

Marker stared after him, in a state of abject shock. It was as though the last hours had been played out on a non existent stage. *Get up?* he thought, I can't even *move!*

But, that evening, Marker did get up, and was surprised at his mobility. The cattle-prod treatment had left him extremely sore where it had been applied, but he could walk, and some attempt to treat and dress the shocked areas had been made during his lack of consciousness.

At lunchtime the next day, Marker was required to leave the comparative comfort of his room and take lunch on the veranda downstairs. Sitting was painful but possible. The only food he'd had since his arrest was one plate of rice and groundnuts – standard army rations.

He hadn't realised how hungry he was. His body had been in overdrive trying to repair the multiple damage that had been inflicted on him in such a short time. Much to his surprise, he was presented with a brief menu and asked if he would like a beer. When the anonymous thick-set officer and an aquiline nosed Middle-Eastern-looking man also sat down to eat, without looking at him, the impression of a staged set piece had been overwhelming.

'So,' Nelson repeated to Samir Jamayal, 'you have no idea who this man could be?'

'Why would I possibly have any idea who the man is? Who is he and what has he done?'

'He is a spy for the old Mokomo regime. Our security people at the airport caught him attempting to enter the country with special maps and charts. We believe he was here to perform a reconnaissance of the beaches and other strategic areas, to plan an assault of some kind from the sea. They probably plan to land mercenaries at a remote location as a spearhead to insurgency. This approach is a pretty standard procedure in Africa, but we are on the alert, and any attempt to destabilise the PRC will be crushed, even if unfortunate mistakes are made.'

'What will happen to him?' Jamayal asked, knowing the answer.

'He will continue to be questioned until we have confirmed who actually sent him. Then, he will be charged and put on trial. We are fair and just people. At this point in time, we are anxious to be seen to be doing the correct thing in the eyes of the rest of the world, and particularly in the eyes of our people.'

'So, you're going to shoot him?'

'Of course . . . after the due process.' Nelson smiled.

'Very democratic.' Jamayal smiled back. 'And extremely convenient timing. The people will see that the new government has everything under control, and the financial might of Mokomo will be demonstrated as not strong enough to strangle the new beginning at birth.'

'Yes,' Nelson replied, breaking into another bread roll, 'timing is the essence of life.'

And bad timing is its death, Jamayal thought. Bad timing and isolation. He still hadn't been able to get in touch with Falcone and time was slipping by. He just had to find him soon.

Getting in touch with Don Falcone was also the first priority on Mark Cappricci's mind, as his UTA flight landed at Albertville in West Guinea, its only stop before Bpungi.

It was raining quiet hard. The rush of warm, humid air that hit the forward cabin, as the door was swung open for disembarking passengers, was a startling contrast to the environmentally controlled atmosphere during the four-hour flight from Charles de Gaul airport. A dozen or so people gathered their belongings. Mostly they were native African, with a smattering of British and French ex-patriates. He noticed a Spanish-looking passenger and thought that he might be a seaman

176

joining one of the ships plying their trade up and down the coast. Gomez would have been pleased, had he known that his choice of dress had worked so well, at least on Cappricci.

It took less than 30 minutes for the aircraft to be ready for its short hop from Albertville to Bpungi. The DC9 powered up and swung back onto the glistening apron, taxiing somewhat quicker than would be normal at a busy European airport.

The runway approach lights flicked by as they trundled to the end of the tarmac. The pilot swung the aircraft round to line her up for take-off, but didn't stop. The Pratt and Whitley engines roared into screaming life before the turn was complete and she lunged forward into an urgent sprint that catapulted her into the streaming clouds. Before they passed into the cloud-base and a clearer night sky, Cappricci noticed a large, brightly lit vessel also heading south-east, in the direction of Freeman's huge natural harbour.

The vessel could have been anything, as far as Cappricci was concerned, but as she disappeared below the clouds the *Salamander* was just attaining half-ahead, at the beginning of a leisurely passage to a pre-planned anchorage off Palm Island. The distinguished guests had departed by helicopter before she weighed anchor and Falcone stood alone on the starboard bridge-wing, contemplating the most recent past, the Syndicate's plans for the future and the very personal ones that only he, Don Falcone, *boss of bosses*, had formulated.

Within what seemed no time at all, the UTA DC9 was descending once more into the rain, to make a circle in from the north and land at Bpungi. Cappricci packed up the contents of his complimentary first-class toilet kit and straightened the back of his blue leather seat.

It was quite bumpy as they made their run in, the grumbling cloud layer providing an uneven roadway to the ground. The landing itself was clean and smooth, the seasoned pilot correcting trim and speed with practised ease as he slid the large metal bird into the airport's landing gateway.

They pulled up very close to the airport terminal, so the

prospect of getting soaked diminished from Cappricci's thoughts, to be replaced by the apprehension of arriving in an unstable country that he hadn't visited before. He'd got used to sending others on missions like this.

The airport building was just as Marker had found it, but Cappricci negotiated the perils of its guardians more successfully; one of the small black youths grabbed his bag and struggled with it to a rather dubious-looking taxi. He gave the youth five dollars, and immediately there was a rapid dialogue between the boy and the driver. Cappricci's taxi ride had just doubled in price.

'Where you go?' the driver asked, over his shoulder.

'Tumani Palms Hotel, Freeman,' Cappricci answered.

'Hovercraft,' the man replied.

'Hovercraft? No, Freeman. The Tumani Palms Hotel,' Cappricci repeated.

'Yes, Freeman, by the hovercraft. I take you.'

'OK, you're the boss,' Cappricci agreed, not knowing the local routine, 'but we do go to Freeman?'

'Yes, yes, very quick. Take all day by car.'

The old Nissan taxi, its interior in remarkably good condition for its age and location, set off down the short patch of tarmac road that led from the airport onto the main dirt road that ran through the Bpungi area and onwards to the north beach of the estuary.

They passed through a small market area, with every manner of goods for sale in small quantities. Men, women and children were milling around the stalls and shacks. Cappricci noticed that there was a general air of good humour amongst the groupings. Perhaps the coup had been for the better, after all.

It wasn't long before Cappricci could see glimpses of the ocean and the estuary inlet peeping through the high palms that threw up a modest canopy over the groundnut fields.

The taxi pulled off the road and onto a well-used, tyre-tracked passage to the beach. As the tree-lined canopy fell back, the spectacular view of the massive estuary, deserted beaches and the distant skyline of Freeman on the southern coastline sprang into view. The taxi stopped.

'Hovercraft coming soon,' the driver chirped, pointing to a small mud-brick building which had a large outdoor thatched sunroof protecting a few seats and benches.

Cappricci paid the man in dollars, causing a smile to explode on the driver's face. No 'Yankee go home' here, he thought.

'Five minutes, hovercraft coming,' the man laughed, getting back into the car and returning up the track.

Cappricci picked up his bulging suit carrier and made for the hovercraft station some 30 metres to the west. The wind was blowing about force five from the east, offshore, picking up any sand that was kicked up by his shoes and whisking it away in a small flurry. Three locals were lolling around the shade provided by the sunroof, and as Cappricci reached them they smiled and then continued their unintelligible conversation, interspersing it with much gesticulating and laughing.

Across the bay a faint, high-pitched engine note could be heard. Cappricci scanned the horizon and could just see the intermittent flashing of the hovercraft's bow wave. At the moment he spotted it, a small minibus shot down the track and onto the beach. Down its side could be seen part of the familiar logo of the Royal Dutch Airlines, KLM, inadequately masked by the logo of Middle East Airlines. Eight or nine passengers disembarked and waited for the driver to offload their baggage. By the time this had been completed, the hovercraft itself was clearly in sight and rapidly approaching the shoreline. Similar blue markings associated with the KLM company could now be seen on the speeding machine, but it was unclear who was actually operating the service.

The local people stood back from the front of the sun porch, experience telling them that the hovercraft would be on the beach in seconds, blowing sand in every direction, covering the inexperienced and new travellers with a fine mist of annoying dust. Cappricci was its first victim.

'Marvellous,' he said out loud, as the mechanical dragon spun round and settled down onto its skirts. A dozen passengers got off the craft, to make way for the passengers off the bus, and Cappricci.

The hovercraft was an old version, with one pilot and double seats down each side for 24 passengers and space for their luggage. The heat and the sand that had found its way down his neck contrived to make the journey across the estuary itchy as well as bumpy. All the passengers except one were white business types who looked as though the foremost thought in their minds was a shower and a change of clothes.

The southern shore rushed towards them and 20 minutes after boarding at Bpungi, they were stepping ashore beneath the Tumani Palms Hotel. Runners picked up the bags and hotel guests were ushered into the complimentary transport.

Inside the building, the comfort of the hotel contrasted with the crushing deprivation in evidence only a few miles inland. Cappricci decided he would unpack, shower and then call Hess at Langley – he would be in the office within an hour. Then he would call Falcone on the satellite number he'd been given.

Three hours later, he still hadn't been able to get a line to the States and the satellite link number just made a click in his earpiece. The people at the US Legation had gone home for the day. The whole world stops if the phones don't work properly, he thought. Might as well go downstairs for a beer and some chow.

It wasn't exactly chow that Michelle Christie was sitting down to, in one of London's fashionable restaurants just off the Broadgate, in London's banking district.

Her guest, an obese, sweating man, was one of the managing partners of the Austin-Marks News Agency. John Austin had consumed two large whiskies whilst choosing and ordering the largest and most expensive combination of courses on the menu. He had a small white patch of glue-like spittle at the corner of each side of his mouth, which he wiped away every few minutes with a large grubby handkerchief.

'What can I do you for then, sweetheart?' he leered.

As they ate, Michelle went through the story that Hess had developed, changing her attitude to Austin as she progressed. She was impressed by the depth of his knowledge of the intelligence community, past and present, as well as the manner of its workings.

180

'Well, I think we can do the business on a story like that, particularly with the paperwork being available.' Austin chuckled heavily through his large frame. 'But why bring it to *me?*'

'You're an American and you've worked for us in the past.' Michelle smiled sweetly back. She noticed his belly button winking out from between two buttons of his straining shirt and suppressed a giggle.

'Yeah, but not for the love of Uncle Sam – strictly for cash.'

'Ten thousand, under the table, should keep you in Scotch for a long time, Mr Austin – even with your appetite.'

'Oh, nasty! The lady has claws.'

'If you don't deliver the goods as required, someone else may have to visit you with somewhat larger talons than I have.'

'Hey, truce. We're on the same side! Did anyone ever tell you that you were a very attractive woman?'

'No, it's a complete surprise to me. When did you notice?'

'Seriously,' Austin continued, 'a girl like you could earn a lot of money, on the side, in London. Have you ever considered doing any photo shoots – top-quality, of course?'

'I think our business is concluded for now, Mr Austin,' Michelle announced in a cold, clipped voice.

Before Austin could answer, the waiter appeared at the side of the table.

'Will there be anything else, sir?' he asked politely.

'I'll have another large Scotch, thanks,' Austin bellowed.

'And for madam?'

'Nothing thank you, just the bill please,' she smiled.

'Aw, come on, honey, loosen up, have a brandy on Uncle Sam and let's get to know each other a bit better.'

'Enjoy your indulgence, Mr Austin.' Michelle smiled through partially clenched teeth. 'Your money will be in the account tomorrow, and I expect to see some action within seven days.'

With that, she retrieved her handbag from under her seat, rose and left Austin chuckling to himself, eyeing every movement of her body as she stepped out towards the head waiter's desk. After a brief conversation with the small Italian, she turned and smiled to Austin and gave him a big wave. He returned it instinctively, if not a little nonplussed; then she was gone, whisking down the steps to catch a cab.

Austin knocked back the remaining Scotch and made movements to leave.

'Thank you, sir,' an instant waiter said at his side, presenting the bill.

Austin stared at it for two seconds too long and then produced a corporate American Express card.

'Thank you, sir.'

'Don't bother, there's no tip,' Austin growled.

'Madam said tha–'

'Madam's a cow. Nice tits, though. Tuff shit for both of us.'

The waiter stared after the lumbering newsman. Elephants never forget, he thought. Neither do waiters.

There was never any problem getting a cab in the Broadgate area, especially when you looked like Michelle Christie and were dressed in a hunting-pink suit, with matching shoes. A taxi painted like a newspaper pulled up as soon as she reached the curve.

'Where to, luv?' the smiling driver chirped.

'Heathrow . . . terminal one, please.'

'Just the ticket, LHR then home for tea. Got any bags?'

'Go past the Regency Hotel at Queen's Gate on your way. My bags are with the porter,' she said, getting into the back of the taxi.

'Right. I'll go through the park. It'll be quicker this time of day. Going anywhere exotic?'

'Scotland,'

'Never mind, luv. But watch those Jocks, they're buggers for the ladies when they've had a drink.'

'I'm banking on it,' Michelle laughed over the diesel's throb.

The throb of the *Salamander*'s twin 6,000 bhp diesels sang a different song in the still of the African evening. Falcone, Mario and the crew were the only people on board, except for one other special guest.

Mario led him up the companionway to the starboard boat-deck, where Falcone was relaxing in a cushioned recliner, taking in the muted warmth of the evening sun with some champagne and goat's cheese; an unusual mixture stemming from a poor and distant upbringing and a less distant acquired pleasure.

Opening the heavy weather door, which had a gleaming brass porthole, Mario led the guest out into the balmy air. He then returned through it, closed it and proceeded to the navigating bridge to watch over his master from a discreet distance.

'Come, come, Alpha, don't stand on ceremony. Join me in a glass of wine and some cheese. We don't have much time – the helicopter that will take you back ashore has other duties tonight.'

'Thank you, Don Falcone, it would be an honour to share some wine with you,' Alpha replied, his nervousness spreading before him. Mario had smelt it the instant Alpha had stepped onto the *Salamander*'s heledeck. He could smell fear at a hundred metres.

'Come, sit with me and tell me how our plans progress.'

Alpha sat on the film-director-style deckchair that stood waiting for the interviewee, on the opposite side of a small table separating it from Falcone's recliner. The old man made great theatre of pouring a second glass of the wine, wiping its outside with a silken cloth so that no drips fell on Alpha's clothes.

'So, my young friend, are we on course?'

'The act will take place during this very night. The assassin has been his lover for almost six months. He suspects nothing and *she* will be shot while evading escape.'

'This is good, my young friend. As planned, Jamayal has become an unstable, grumbling volcano. As a major international businessman, his death will be the spark, the beginning of a roller coaster that will create not a *city*, owned and built by the Families like Vegas, but a *country* . . . our country. I have planned this event for half my lifetime. Once, years ago, I was this close before, but two punk reporters blew the whole scam when they caused that other, corrupt, President to chicken out. I have to admit it, I misread him. I thought his ego would force him to *tough* it out, but his resignation destroyed all my plans. The information that we had created, developed and collected all those years ago was more than enough to black-mail *that* President into endorsing the puppet government I was going to install in the State House in Freeman. Now we have a second chance. No two-bit reporters are going to spoil my plans this time.'

Falcone wiped the back of his neck with a large blue silk handkerchief, turned to Alpha and continued. 'Mokomo is a crook, but he was and is unacceptable in the outside world – to investors, bankers, Western governments. He grew fat and greedy by starving his people and always asking for more. No use to me, or my plans.

My virgining ideas to remove him were superseded by the coup. We have re-grouped and our position could not be stronger. This time, *this time*, we have an unbeatable hand. The Masada weapon's existence is the lever that can, without doubt, ruin this current President, if *we* will it. We have access to the paperwork, but that fool Mokomo's greed caused the Ameri-cans to launch a spoiling mission, just as the coup was taking hold and our window of opportunity opened. So far, only a handful of people know of this American action. It must be our route to attaining the irrefutable proof that the paperwork gives witness to: the final nail in this President's coffin and our control over him. Our initiative tonight will be the beginning of our two pronged attack. It will light the fuse of outrage that will start the ball rolling towards demands that the UN step in and take a larger and larger position in the country, defusing any pretence of power that this PRC rabble hang on to and creating a back-up and cover for our overall strategy, from any revelations that the public discovery of the weapon and its consequence could cause to divert our course.'

'If we fail to attain the weapon, we use the supposed excesses of the PRC to attract world attention and the involvement of the UN organisations that we control,' Alpha contributed.

'Barbarism,' Falcone almost whispered, 'barbarism attrib-uted to the PRC, combined with our capturing the physical evidence of the weapon's existence, puts us in a win, win situ-ation, as my young grandson puts it. If one route fails, the other remains to be taken. Neither must fail, however. The

184

weapon gives me the President of the United States of America. Outrage only gives me the UN and a longer road to my goal.'

'Yes,' Alpha interrupted, his excitement overriding all caution, 'and with me managing your affairs in the country, we can build the future you have been dreaming of for so long.'

'But first Jamayal,' Falcone continued, ignoring his guest. 'his father will also die in London tonight, with evidence of PRC involvement left behind, along with some chosen bankers, lawyers and a ex British ex-high commissioner of the country, just for luck . . . The international community will call for and rally behind the UN. Troops, aid, money and investment will follow. Through the Jamayal Group's controlling shares in all the country's natural resources and trading industries, this money will be desperate to align itself beside the new management of the group – our group. *Clean* money will flood in, to mix with the billions of dollars of dirty money that we invest. Can you not see it, Alpha? The dirty profit, from a poxed, red-neck hooker in Baton Rouge, will become a clean ten bucks in a hospital in Freeman or a bauxite mine in the interior. Dirty money and clean money will mix like never before, to give starving people food and work, hospitals light and the best equipment money can buy. The spectacular beaches will be full of wealthy tourists staying at five-star hotels and gambling on a strip that will make Vegas look like a bingo parlour. Industry will grow; the Family thrive.'

The old man rose from the recliner, out of breath but looking 20 years younger and walked to the ship's rail. 'It will be *my* country, the *Family's* country. We will build it and defend it; the biggest money-laundering operation in the world, supported by the world and partially financed by the World Bank. The Jews wanted a Jewish state, so they took it. I want safety and wealth for the future of my Family. Can you see the picture, Alpha? A golden, prosperous country, where all the people have their needs, run by a moderate, educated, multiracial government, owned by the Mafia!'

Falcone started to laugh. *'Mafialand?* They can chase us out of Italy, Sicily, the United States and anywhere else, but from our own country? Only by *war*,' he decreed, snapping the

185

wineglass's stem in his powerful hand. 'Control, Alpha. Through our network of operations, we will be in control of a majority slice of the world's finances within ten years, including the Japanese. The legitimate governments of the world won't even know it has happened to them.'

The old man stooped against the rail, white exhaustion flooding over him. Even in his excitement, he hadn't shouted his dream like the madman Alpha believed he was, but stated it as if it was already a fact, in his distinctive deep Bronx-Italian accent. The only physical signs of emotion during the *speech* had been the tight crumpling of the silken cloth with which he had wiped Alpha's glass and the unfortunate accident with the wineglass.

As he watched Falcone, Alpha felt a cloak of intense evil descend around the old man as he sucked in the reviving sea air. This man really was the most dangerous man in the world, he thought. He was glad he was working *for* him, not against him.

The mood was broken by Mario entering the deck area again. 'My don,' he said quietly.

'Ah, Mario,' Falcone responded with a smile, 'you're quite right, time is marching on. Alpha, you must forgive me, Mario reminds me of other business . . . duties. I just felt it was important that I informed you personally of your valued contribution to our project and that we have complete faith that you will not let us down in the future.'

The transformation back to a grandfather figure rather than a godfather figure took Alpha completely by surprise. After a pause, he approached the old man and took his hand for the customary kiss.

'Tonight has been a great honour, Don Falcone. Your confidence in me will not be misplaced. I will never let you down.'

'I know,' Falcone agreed.

With that, Alpha bent over to kiss an outstretched, liver-mark blotched hand. As he rose from the ritual, Mario slipped a wire garrotte around the young man's neck and squeezed off his life, as easily as a knife cuts through a peeled melon.

Falcone said nothing, just finished off the glass of wine that

Alpha hadn't touched, and returned to the recliner. He didn't sit.

Mario easily walked Alpha's dying body to the ship's rail and slipped it into the ocean. The immaculate wooden deck hadn't been soiled by the young man's blood, but a stain appeared on the old tennis shirt that Mario had changed into on his way down from the bridge. It was an old shirt and it had recently attained a bolognaise sauce mark that the laundry just couldn't get out. The shirt followed the body into the water and was lost in the fluorescent wash that minute plankton give out to the world as a ship passes by in the seas of the tropical night . . . night which had quickly rushed in as if to hide the abomination that had recently occurred.

Mario turned to join his master. The two old men walked together towards the boat deck door. They spoke of a light supper and the wine they should take with it.

The *Salamander* was left to her lonely quest, steaming up and down a charted line, 15 nautical miles off the northern tip of Palm Island. The skies had cleared, to reveal the glory of the tropical heavens, magnificent without the masking effect of man made light from the land. The Milky Way was painted across the sky like a five-lane highway. Bright and clear, the constellation of *Cygnus* was flying down it, to a destination light years away.

Chet Maclazowitz glanced at Cygnus during his continual and routine panning of the killing ground in front of him. The moon was rising, leaving a silver edged night light on the brush and the encampment in the distance. A jackal barked in the middle distance, to be answered by the cry of a frustrated night-jar.

Just to his right he saw a movement and clicked on his night-sight. One of the VC mercenaries was wandering around the edge of the medium-height brush that lay between the crash site clearing and the deeper brushland where the remains of the assault group were concealed. He wasn't particularly doing anything, just ambling about on a boring night picket duty. On looking a bit more carefully, he could see that the man was actually making progress into waist-high undergrowth, quite close to the area where Maclazowitz had pegged Pete Van der Merwe, on the flank of the main group. He kept on going.

Maclazowitz closed on Van der Merwe's position with his scope and then swept back to the soldier. *Stop*, he willed. *If you need a shit, do it there.* He swung back to Van der Merwe. Clearly Petey had seen him and was crouched like a spring, with a killing knife in his hand. The VC was 20 metres from the blade of a knife when he stopped, staring directly at Van der Merwe's position. Suddenly, without warning he called out.

'Shit,' Maclazowitz spat, just before the sniper's rifle kicked, burying a round in the Vietnamese's head. Then, all hell broke loose.

Pete Van de Merwe raked, and continued to rake, the campsite area ahead of him, with the 50-calibre. Stuart shouted, but nobody heard, and before they could blink an eye, the assault group were confronted with a sea of advancing VC mercenaries firing in every direction except to their rear. Grenades were hurled indiscriminately in salvo after salvo by Stuart and the men around him, then suddenly and unexpectedly Maclazowitz watched them charge forward towards the onslaught.

In the green light of the nightscope, he could see Stuart and Sandys running across the line of advance, throwing grenades behind and towards the VC as they ran. In the dark, the explosions tended to draw the enemy fire away from the running men, and their progress was only hampered by the odd loose trooper who was unsure of his direction . . . just before he died.

Pete Van der Merwe stayed with the 50-calibre until he was completely out of ammunition. Then he picked up his AK and followed in the direction of Stuart and Sandys. A firefight on his right indicated that the others were well engaged, but his instinct to follow his leader overtook reason. The decoy tactics being used by Stuart and Sandys worked fine for them, but anyone following behind ran slap bang into the fire that they had diverted from themselves. Van der Merwe found himself showered with all manner of fire and quickly veered off to the right, launching himself into the comparative darkness of the camp area that he'd only just finished emptying his 50-calibre into. As he jumped over the fourth or fifth body, the burst of AK47 fire that killed him ripped into his back, exactly where the protection of the bullet proof vest he'd removed for comfort during the night would have saved him. The 7.62 rounds shattered his spine and sent a supersonic shrapnel burst through his lungs, heart, ribs and chest, exploding from the front of his body in a moonlit cocktail of hot offal. He thought someone had kicked him hard in the back, but died before a scream could be formed or another thought formulated. He landed heavily on one of his previous victims.

Maclazowitz saw the kill and the killer. His first shot missed, but the second lifted the lightweight VC off his feet and left him, along with Van der Merwe, for the jackals. He swung his scope left and right and just caught a glimpse of Stuart and Sandys as they disappeared out of view to his left. There was silence to his right. Instinct told him it was time to go.

Unceremoniously and easily, he dropped three more of the enemy and then made an orderly retreat from the nest, slowly moving back and to the left; he would track Stuart in the daylight and meet up with him later in the day – if he was still alive.

Maclazowitz thought of Pete Van der Merwe for a second, then he became a ghost, there but not there.

Stuart and Sandys ran and ran, until the tracer around them started to thin out. Then they slipped beneath a large fallen tree and took stock.

'What've we got?' Stuart wheezed, kneeling with his hands in the mud and his head down, trying to suck in much needed air.

'Unless someone is right on our tail and dropped as soon as we did, we could be in the clear,' Sandys replied, through equally strained lungs.

'Wait or go?'

'I'd prefer to go. No sign of any of the other guys.'

'OK, hit the road. I'll watch the back door for the next leg,' Stuart ordered.

The two men took deep breaths and launched themselves back into the night. The moon was in front of them and disabled their night vision for a few seconds if their eyes strayed too close to it. The same went for the pursuers, and although they would never know it, Stuart and Sandys only survived that night because looking at the moon caused one of the enemy to take a couple of seconds longer than normal to readjust his night vision to full focus.

Yani Bar-David was also adjusting focus, but on an overhead projector in Sharon's briefing room.

'Operation Ascension,' the young man announced. 'Two long-range C130s, with mid-air refuelling capabilities, have been arranged from our friends in South Africa, as have all the support logistics for a three-thousand-mile journey and penetration. They are two of the aircraft we sold them last year and will have no markings. The route will take us out across Namibia, where we will hit the Atlantic Ocean just south of Cape Fria, before any complications on the Angolan border can occur. The next landfall is Sierra Laputu, with Ascension Island being the bail-out landing point, if anything goes wrong.'

'The British will love that!' Sharon interjected.

'With Stuart involved, the British are going to keep as low a profile as possible, if anything breaks.'

'And when we get there?'

'We are taking Mony Severs of the Gourdan Company with us. The company's turnover is about 3 billion US dollars and Mony, as you know, is a senior executive with the company, as well as a reserve colonel of the Special Forces and very very fit.'

'He has volunteered?'

'Yes. The cover story is that he has been taken hostage in the country by Hizbollah sympathisers, while on a very low-profile business trip for both one of the group's military equipment manufacturers and also one of their cement and building material companies.'

'Bit thin, Yani. I think there's little doubt we would go in and get him if he was close by and we knew where he was, but publicly, one man would never warrant a three-thousand-mile

Entebbe-type operation, unless there was clearly something else at the back of it.'

'We've had a break,' Bar-David continued 'Miriam has been sent to Europe by Hess, to break a false story that chemical weapons materials are being manufactured in the country for export. The story will break while we are in the air and we can quell any diplomatic challenges by confirming, unofficially, that it was actually Mony who discovered the existence of the facility, thus causing his detention – allegedly by Hizbollah factions in the Freeman Lebanese community, but actually by the PRC, who are still floundering about, not knowing who is friend or foe.'

'OK, that's complicated enough to pass for a sound bite on CNN and leave enough confusion to regroup, if required.' Sharon smiled, getting up to pour himself a strong black coffee from a glass pot on a low cupboard by his desk. 'So, we've got there, we've got an excuse to play with . . . what happens then?'

'Our own access within the Americans' camp has provided us with detailed satellite photographs of the crash site area. We can land and take off very close to the target, even at night.'

'What about Stuart? If *we* can do it, surely the odds are that he has already done it.'

'For some reason, probably lack of trust, he changed his access plans and is walking in.'

'I'm not surprised; dropping in a C130, isn't conducive to covert operations, unless you're in and out in a very short period of time.'

'We've actually got more than that now.' Yani smiled, indicating to Sharon that he had saved the best until last. 'The satellite surveillance has shown that there's been one hell of a firefight around the site during the last twelve hours. Stuart is probably dead or captured by the PRC army, who must have been guarding the area in force. Bodies can be picked out by the photo enhancers – a lot of them – so we are assuming that Stuart's group came under fire from a much superior force.'

'In that case, we have one problem out of the way. What about the Masada weapon? What if it's not there?' Sharon growled.

191

'If it's there, if it's not there, it doesn't matter. All the Americans have to know is that *we* were there! and we either have it, or have proof of its existence.'

Sharon rocked back in his chair and sipped the hot coffee. 'OK, run me through the full military briefing and then *go!* I'll do the necessary at this end.'

'An *El Al* 747 in Swissair livery has been in the air, on the sea route towards Johannesburg, for six hours. On board are a hundred and fifty men and their equipment, on a training exercise . . .'

Sharon had watched the 747 take off during the night. Mony Severs, his wife's cousin, had been one of Mossad's best agents in Iran for some eight years. The air force commander in charge of the Civilian Covert Air Group had had his orders signed by Sharon, underneath the signature of Yani Bar-David, and the Prime Minister had approved Yani's plan before the young man had even formally presented it. Sharon would let Yani find out for himself that nothing happened in Israel without Sharon's tentacles being touched. For now, the adrenaline was running in the young man, he felt good . . . so why not let him?

Major Dani Cohen also felt good. He was a combat soldier and the army was his profession, not something you did for a month a year as a reservist. When he got the green light from Bar-David, the 747 was just entering the airspace over the Comoro Islands at the entrance to the Mozambique Channel. He started to brief the men for the fifth time. When they hit South Africa, they needed to be in the air again within three hours to have the best chance of arriving at the target zone just before dawn the next day following.

Mony Severs, an expert on West Africa, would also run with the mission, as a ranking officer not as a bystander, but still under the operational command of Dani Cohen.

13

Masada

As she drove up to Castle Stuart, Michelle Christie was taken aback by the raw beauty of the countryside that surrounded Stuart's heritage.

Silas Urquart was at the front door before she'd paid off the taxicab, his aging eyes twinkling at the feline image that descended from the vehicle. An old black Labrador followed him out, gave one condescending half-hearted bark and then accepted her as a long standing member of the family by branding her calf with its wet nose.

'Nice dog, Mr Urquart,' she beamed.

Urquart smiled in return. 'Not much of a guard dog, though. He'd show a burglar around the castle if he bribed him with a piece of milk chocolate. You'd be Miss Christie then.'

'Oh, yes, please forgive my manners. The dog '

'Not at all, young lady. Let me help you with your bag. But as I told you on the telephone, I'm not sure how I can help you. I haven't heard from the Major for some time.'

They made their way up the stone stairway to the kitchen, where the Aga was ready and willing to provide steaming hot water for a cup of tea.

'Earl Grey?' Urquart asked.

'Who is?' Michelle replied.

'No, lassie, the tea. Would Earl Grey tea be in order?'

She felt a complete fool. The surroundings of the castle had taken over her subconscious for a second. 'Oh yes, of course, the tea! I'll just have what you're having.'

'The Earl Grey it is then.' Urquart sighed, just perceptively, implying a minute sense of resignedness to the presence of an American heathen who hadn't truly grasped the finer points of living and had to be tolerated.

They mumbled about the castle, the history and the antiques while the tea brewed. After a little while, Silas daintily poured the steaming aromatic liquid into bone-china cups and sat down. Just as he was about to enjoy his first sip, Michelle threw a killing smile across at him and said,' Where the fuck is he, Silas?'

He nearly spat the hot liquid across the room, but managed to control his spasm to a scalding dribble down the front of his open necked shirt.

'The last I heard, he wasn't doing too well. He indicated that there was perhaps a little confusion as to who was on whose side, if you get my meaning.'

'Oh, I get your meaning all right, Silas. It's directly because of that problem that I've been sent here to sit with you until we get some kind of contact, in order that I can give him any assistance he may need.'

'Then we'd better get you organised into a room and consider dinner and a shopping list for tomorrow. I wasn't expecting company until the laird and the family come up in two weeks' time.'

He led her up to the eastwing of the ancient building, via a steep granite spiral staircase which had a rope handrail threaded through solid brass wall rings.

'God, isn't this dangerous?' she commented.

'Only if you're drunk, miss.'

'Or wearing high heels,' she laughed, as she followed him into a turret bedroom.

'I'll let you settle in. Dinner will be about seven thirty. We'll eat in the study – it's more cosy.'

'Thank you, Silas, it's a beautiful room.'

In fact, the room was almost round, with stone walls covered in tapestries and pictures of ancient Highlanders with moderately pronounceable names – and, of course, the ever-present Stuarts.

The bed was a high four-poster, with its mattress almost at waist level. She tried it out and sank into its voluminous depths. That night, she would sleep the sleep of the almost dead in comfort she'd never experienced, even in the best five star hotels.

A world away, Stuart was actually sleeping in the cover of green brush around one of the Seti River tributaries, while Sandys took his turn to keep watch.

'Trap, it's getting light,' Sandys said softly.

Stuart opened bloodshot eyes and nodded. 'Anything happening?'

'Nah, just animals, birds and crawling things.'

'Got any water?'

'Only from the creek.'

'Have to do – I'll risk the shits.' He drank sparingly. 'What d'you reckon about the rest of the guys?'

'I saw no one,' Sandys answered.

'I reckon Chet will have made it, but what about the rest?'

'Bought it?'

'Reckon so.'

'Petey?'

'Yeah, him and that fucking fifty-cal. I bet Chet had that gook bang on. If Petey had just waited a few seconds more we would have been in the clear.'

'Give him a break – the VC called out.'

'Only to tell his mate that he was going to have a crap.'

'I forgot, you speak some of that gook lingo, from training their rangers.'

'Petey obviously didn't. When I heard him cock the fifty, I nearly shot him myself. No, I reckon Petey paid the price for his fuck-up ... and the rest of them as well. What about Steve?'

'Well he *could* be OK, wherever he is,' Stuart remarked. 'He must have heard the commotion, so he's probably walking straight into the wrong camp just about now.'

'What's the plan then, boss? We need to try to regroup in some way and then get the hell out of this country, in my view.'

Stuart splashed water onto his stubble-surrounded face. 'Let's give Chet time to find us, if he's alive. He'll start tracking as soon as the sun gets up, which is just about now,' he said, looking up at the sky. 'Six hours, or there-about, if we don't have to move on. We'll check the immediate area and pick the best spot to wait. What's the food situation?'

'Zilch,' Sandys answered.

'Well, we can pass the time putting a few snares out. We might catch something to eat raw which'll keep us going.'

Keeping going was all that Steve Rider could think of. The wounded leg was swollen and raw, but the bleeding wasn't heavy and its moderate flow was actually cleaning the cut as he walked.

The noise of the firefight had been at least a mile away when it slowed and stopped. As the morning hue started to show, he slowly began to make his way in the direction of the diminishing sounds.

He'd travelled for 30 minutes before the familiar smell reached him. Carnage on a significant level has a particular smell: the mixture of blood, sweat, spilled intestine, faeces, semen and urine, all combining to permeate into the natural smell of the undergrowth and signal the proximity of an abomination against man and any of his gods.

Suddenly, he saw movement and dropped, his leg screaming complaints that the automatic rush of adrenaline struggled to mask.

There was a large clearing ahead and he could see the odd soldier meandering around the area, checking bodies, identifications and collecting equipment. Something was strange about the picture, but he couldn't quite place it; the pain in his leg was seriously intervening in his thought processes. There was a noise behind him, but he couldn't turn quick enough to challenge it.

'Stay cool, baby. It's just an old homeboy,' Chet Maclazowitz

196

said quietly. 'What happened to you, been having your period?' He smiled, nodding towards Rider's bloody crotch.

'Knife,' Rider answered, adjusting his position.

'Deep?'

'Yeah, but everything's still there. Got any antibiotics on you?'

'Sure, but stay low, they're still cleaning house and I don't want to have to leave you.'

Maclazowitz crawled around Rider's left-hand side and broke open a medi-pack. 'I'll give you a shot of morphine as well as the pills. Here, take two of these now.' He changed Rider's dressing and jabbed him with a disposable morphine capsule, which had an integral needle for use and discard in the field.

'How's it look?'

'Seen worse,' replied Maclazowitz. 'It's not going bad yet. Smells OK. I'll pop some stitches in as well. It can't do any harm, can it?'

'Where's the rest of them?'

'Lying out there somewhere. Trap and John made it, I think.'

'So we were expected. Must have been a large force?'

'VC,' Maclazowitz answered, as he finished tidying up the dressing.

'That's it! I knew there was something odd about the whole mission, but it just didn't click. Hasn't done yet, actually, but at least we can identify a bloody great big curved ball. What the hell are they doing here?'

'Same as us, I guess. Just earning a buck.'

'Petey?'

'Definitely gone . . . I saw him cut down.'

'Why didn't you all pull back?' Rider queried.

'A fuck-up, plain and simple. Time enough later for explanations. Right now we've got to get the hell out of here.'

'How come your still hanging around, anyway?'

'Figured you and your ugly Limey ass would turn up, if you were still breathing, 'specially after all that racket. Was your radio down?'

'Yeah, cheap shit.'

'OK, let's go. We'll skirt round to the east and then head

197

north-east to cut the guys' trail. We need to move now, before the *spore* is lost. You up to it?'

'No problem,' Rider smiled. 'The funny juice has got to me. Lets go. Oh yes, and thanks.'

'Your turn next time. Take some of my camouflage webbing and melt into the background behind me. We're going real slow and real easy, so keep your eyes open and watch my signs. Step where I step, if you can. Silent running until I speak.'

They moved away very slowly, keeping the enemy camp and the aircraft wreckage in view; putting distance between themselves and the immediate danger. For now, Steve Rider could cope with the journey ahead. Having Chet with him had given him a belief that perhaps all was not lost, after all.

Samir Jamayal was also moving slowly. The olive-skinned French-Canadian beauty, who had been his lover for nine months and jet-setted around the beautiful people spots of the world non-stop with him, was kneeling on all fours across the satin and linen sheets of the rounded bed. He was entering both moist caverns alternately from behind, enjoying the expert muscle control that she practised with consummate skill.

She could tell when he was at the edge of the male explosion and held him there until he retreated off the precipice and could be brought through the valley of pleasure to the edge once more. As he withdrew to enter the second moist rose again, she turned and pulled him down on top of her, wrapping her legs tightly around his body, high up around his waist.

After he entered her, she contracted her vagina muscles and sucked him deep into the velvet purse. He moaned, burying his face into the nape of her neck. The tell-tale tingling began in his penal muscle and he knew that this time he couldn't hold back. She felt the urgency in his movements change and the pressure in his fingers increase. As the primeval ejaculation racked his body, she expertly drove a nine-inch Italian stiletto through his right eardrum and deep into his brain. His eyes bulged and he defecated, but the ejaculation automatically continued to reach for the instinctive heights, demanded of the male species of every mammal.

198

She held onto him as the death throes convulsed through his body, bringing herself to her own corrupt climax, but never letting go of the stainless-steel blade's carved bone handle; twisting it and straining on it, in time with her own convulsions. When it was over, she rolled him over onto his left side to reduce the flow of blood from the wound, which in any event was minimal and mixed with the fluid that surrounded the brain.

Leaving the knife in place, she covered the body with the expensive bed-clothes and began her standard routine of showering and dressing, paying particular attention to her make-up and hair. By the time she'd finished, Jamayal's blood pressure had fallen and equalised. She took a handful of toilet paper and withdrew the stiletto, wiping it as it came clear. A small amount of red fluid followed it, but the time for a gusher of blood was past and the scene could be made to look calm and void of trauma quite easily.

She collected her bag and dropped the weapon into it, having one last quick look around the room before she left. The Beirut Fox was in a deep sleep, after making love to his girlfriend. No one would disturb him for hours. She, of course, would be heartbroken when she heard the news, but the money would help. It had been a long hard job. Nine months of continuous attention to detail and being forced to perform the sexual acts that her lesbianism hated, always in hotel rooms, never at his homes.

It was as if he'd lived in two worlds, one from the East and one from the West. He'd showered her with gifts of jewellery, and the most exclusive clothes available to womanhood, but men of power treat their women like possessions. It's a mutual deal in the exclusive hierarchy. He buys, she looks good and screws. When one stops, the other stops. It's easier when it is just a job, rather than a profession.

The KLM flight she was booked on to Amsterdam would leave Bpungi at 6 p.m. She would make it easily, long before Jamayal was found in Room 172 at the Tumani Palms, the room with the *do not disturb* sign on the door. No one would even think of banging on the door until at least noon the next day.

199

Cappricci noticed the attractive lady sweeping through the hotel reception area, and along with others strained his neck to get a better look.

He was returning from the US legation, where there was still no news or instructions from Hess. When he collected his key from the porter, the smiling boy gave him a message on a piece of paper. It said, *Timber Wharf 8, 2300 hrs.* He folded the paper, said his thank-yous to the boy and went up to his room. Falcone, at last!

The old wharves in Freeman Harbour had once been one of the bustling centres for exports to the world's engine room, as the British Empire had been known. Raw materials, precious metals and stones – and of course the slaves that were needed to stoke the fires of that empire – in great numbers and cheaply.

When America decided to leave the empire, nothing much changed except the prices. Now, the quays were visited only infrequently, controlled by the remnants of the Mokomo regime and the new empire of Samir Jamayal, soon to be announced regrettably deceased.

Cappricci took a taxi to the harbour area, because officially there was still a curfew.

'It's OK, no problem,' the driver had told him. 'I am policeman during the day. No problem!'

The tops of the quays were pitted and needed much refurbishment, so the cab driver often had to take a circuitous route along a once straight journey down the wharf to quay number 8. You could just see the number 7 painted on a crumbling warehouse, so Cappricci told the driver to stop.

'That's OK, I'll walk from here. Will you wait?'

'No problem, I wait for you. Not moving from here at all. I just wait for you.'

Cappricci didn't pay him. He thought it might encourage the driver to actually wait rather than just to promise to. He walked towards the east, assuming the direction rather than actually knowing that the quay numbering system rose from the seaward end towards the land, west to east.

After a couple of minutes, he heard the idling throb of

an engine and walked closer to the edge of the quay. Sitting alongside a vertical quay service ladder was a large sleek motor launch with a covered cabin. A uniformed man was at the stern and another was almost at the top of the service ladder, coming ashore. He and Cappricci reached the top of the ladder together.

'Mr Cappricci?'

'Yeah,'

'We both seem to have good timing. May I help you aboard?'

Now he was closer, he could read the name on the stern of the launch. *Salamander 1*, it read, in swirling gold letters with blue shadows.

'The *Salamander*?' he asked automatically.

'Don Falcone's compliments. We have come close inshore, to make your journey short and pleasant. '

'Oh, the taxi driver. I haven't paid him.'

'Don't worry, sir. He's been well paid. He will have waited for you to come out of the hotel for at least one hour.'

Cappricci turned round and looked back the way he'd walked. The taxi was gone. 'Oh, that's, ahm, very efficient . . . Let's go then.'

'Just so,' the deck officer agreed politely, and the two men made their way down the ladder and onto the hand crafted launch.

Cappricci dropped onto the deck and made his way into a comfortable cabin which was set half a deck below the vessel's bridge and accessible from it.

The helmsman bent down to look at him and nodded a courtesy, then swung the wheel hard to port on a signal from the officer on the bow, throttled up the twin Volvo Pentas and powered the launch off the fendered quay. She heeled to starboard as he directed her towards the open sea, levelling out as he eased his helm.

Salamander 1 cut through the relative calm of the huge estuary, taking a good 20 minutes to feel the residual lop of the Atlantic swell. A gibbous moon lit up the skyline and threw a ghostly hue across the native fishing canoes that speckled the entrance to one of the world's largest natural harbours. Palm

201

Island could be seen like a large black iceberg on the starry horizon to the south-west, and in between the dancing lights of the mother-ship winked a beckoning welcome.

Spray occasionally splashed up against the bridge windows, but the view was hardly restricted. Cappricci thought how much larger the *Salamander* looked in real life, at sea, than in the pictures he'd seen before.

'Beautiful, eh?' the officer confirmed rather than asked.

'Sure is,' Cappricci agreed. 'Many people on board just now?'

'The crew and the owner, plus Mr Mario – that's all.'

'Hence the VIP treatment?'

'All guests aboard *Salamander* are treated as VIPs, sir,' he replied with a mock bow.

'Of course,' Cappricci chuckled, feeling far from easy.

The mother vessel seemed to get huge very quickly and the launch eased down on the power. A smattering of VHF radio traffic announced their pending arrival and granted permission to come alongside.

A stainless steel accommodation ladder, fit for a queen, eased down the side of the vessel on surprisingly quiet hydraulics. Cappricci stepped off the launch onto the ladder's platform, timing his movement to coincide with the top of a complementary swell.

'Bravo, Mark, Bravo,' Mario hailed him from the top of the accommodation ladder. 'Once a sailor, always a sailor!'

'Prefer the big boats though,' Cappricci answered, as the two men embraced and kissed each other on the cheek.

'Come,' Mario continued. 'The don is sleeping. Let us have a drink and some pasta, and catch up on our news.'

'Sounds good to me. How are the family? What news from the old country?' The old man put his arm around the young man and they ambled down the *twenties*-style alleyway to the forward cocktail lounge. The bulkheads were covered in fine wooden veneer, with art deco marquetry figures. A mirror behind the bar was beautifully engraved with the entwined bodies of naked lovers.

'So, Marky, what can I get you?'

'Scotch is fine.'

'Ah yes, you were never a wine man, were you?'

'Always a great disappointment to me,' a strong, but grating voice pronounced from the other side of the private saloon.

Both men at the bar turned in unison. Don Falcone stood at the entrance to the plush room. He was like a vision from another lifetime: leather carpet slippers, dress trousers, a quilted smoking jacket and his famous cane.

'It has been a long time, Mark. How is your mother? I have not seen her since your father died.'

'She's well, Don Falcone. The Family's assistance has been a great comfort to her.'

'I must make a greater effort to see her, my time has been preoccupied in these last months.'

'I know she would be honoured, Don Falcone, but she is happy.'

'Good . . . good. Now to business.' The old man's face turned from mock concern to granite. He lowered himself into a comfortable armchair. Mario fussed around him to make sure he was comfortable, plumping cushions and placing a small table with spring water in easy reach.

'Thank you, Mario. Mark, you want something to eat?' Cappricci signalled he didn't. 'So, the game comes to its climax. We have started to clean up the loose ends. Let us consider the players. The Jamayal Group have lost their head, or will have done before this night is out. The Americans have trapped themselves into a position where their only defence is to act publicly, countercharge and denial being their only currently viable weapons. Their surrogate, Stuart, has been engaged and is probable also dead at this time.'

'His body wasn't found at the crash site,' Mario interrupted, but with deference.

'That is so, but our friends only had a two-year-old photograph of him. Enough bodies and equipment have been found to discount Stuart's group as players, practically or publicly. Your attractive colleague is wasting her time in Scotland, and I have chosen a successor to that punk Mokomo.'

'May I ask who?' Cappricci questioned.

'Yes.' The don smiled. 'You may . . . particularly as he is the reason you are here.'

Cappricci looked at Mario, who was sitting behind and to the right of Falcone. The old assassin smiled and raised his eyebrows.

'What can I do, Don Falcone? I thought that my task was only to gather the intelligence you needed to construct and execute your plans.'

'Indeed, that *was* your task, Mark. You have fulfilled your duties admirably, but you must know that you can never return to the States again as Mark Cappricci. In time yes, as someone else, but now I need you here, the Family needs you here. We are all connected in some way. What one of us does affects the whole. What is good for the whole, is good for the individual. It has been so for centuries and will continue to be so. You are part of a great Family, its strategy for the future and, now, its critical implementation.'

When Falcone finished, no one spoke. The old man took a sip of water and wiped the edge of his mouth with a fine handkerchief. Suddenly he coughed. Mario reacted instantly, but before he could get to his feet, Falcone raised his hand to signal that he was all right.

'Mark, this man I have chosen is named Cassa. He is a right hand man of the Provisional President, Major Valentine Nelson. He is young and idealistic; and will be acceptable to the outside world when the pending chaos has been quelled. All the countries in the world who want to take a major influence in the region will see him as malleable to their influence.'

'Have we contact with him?' Cappricci asked.

'Yes, we have made contact with him. Our agent has indicated that with the help of the CIA, Mokomo insurgents are planning a quick and early counter-coup. They already have people in the country and believe Jamayal is implicated.'

'Who is our agent and who does Cassa think we are? They seem to be well informed.' Cappricci asked, trying desperately to tie together the threads and ideas that were swirling around in his mind.

'Our agent is, ah, out of the country. Cassa thinks *we* are from the diamond cartel in London. Their presumption of the CIA being involved is an instinctive reaction in this region, not a measure of actual knowledge of the operation you and Hess have launched,' Falcone answered, shifting in his chair as a sign of mild impatience at the continuous interruptions.

'What interest do they perceive the cartel have in helping the PRC? If anything, their interests would lie with a corrupt Mokomo regime who will do anything for a buck,' Cappricci asked, failing to hide his mounting frustration by following the question with a distracting pull at the generous shot of whisky Mario had poured him.

Falcone rose from the chair. 'Mark, Mark, Mark, be still. This is not a quick scam that a couple of greasers from the east side are trying to pull! This is a multibillion-dollar operation, cloaking the whole of the Western world and a significant part of the East. It has been waiting in the wings for the right opportunity and the right location. An idea only wins or fails due to the timing of its presentation. We have the idea, the will, the funds, the access, the control and the timing. I will make it happen.' He walked to the bar and rested his cane against one of the leather stools. 'Mario, a brandy please. Fuck the doctors!'

'Don Falcone, forgive me,' Cappricci replied. 'My frustration is only a reflection of my wish to understand and to help to the best of my ability. I do not mean to be disrespectful.'

'Respect? That word has kept this organisation in the dark ages for too long. I do not crave respect, Mark, only obedience.'

'You have it,' Cappricci answered quickly.

'I know,' the old man smiled. 'Understand, these PRC children trust no one bearing gifts. What they will trust is someone declaring self-interest, a self-interest that is mutually beneficial. A hungry man does not begrudge paying for food. A starving man will kill for it! Hatton Garden in London is run by the Jews. The diamond business is run by the Jews, worldwide. The States? it has an incredible Jewish lobby. Their tentacles, like ours, encompass the world.'

'And their, *our*, supposed interest in supporting the PRC?' Cappricci risked.

'Simple economics. Profit margins will be higher with

Mokomo gone. They don't want him back. Their contacts in the States run throughout the infrastructure of the country and its government, including all the security services. How can I put it? A word in Hebrew here, a word in Hebrew there. Look at yourself! If you haven't rubbed shoulders with an agent from Mossad within your own organisation, I would be most surprised. As the Family have *you*, the Jews will have their own network of information-gathering. Nelson and his frightened boy scouts will want to believe that the Jewish lobby has accessed intelligence information which could be mutually beneficial. They are expecting contact from this lobby. You are it.'

'What's the MO?' Cappricci asked.

'Mario?' Falcone gestured, remaining standing at the bar as his companion re-filled the large balloon glass.

'You will return to the hotel tonight,' Mario began. 'Tomorrow, Cassa will come to you there. Remain in your room. When he comes you will tell him that a highly trained group of mercenaries, working for Mokomo but paid by the CIA, are already in the country. They are in two separate groups; one has landed inland and has already had skirmishes with various forces in the hinterland. PRC intelligence will be able to confirm this, but they will not know their intentions.'

'I haven't worked that out yet either,' Cappricci echoed.

'Their supposed role is to cause uncertainty and make the population think that perhaps the new order will be worse. In order to achieve this insecurity they are reported to be engaged in raids on villages, vulnerable army units, supporters of both sides. Massacres of women and children . . . hit and run guerrilla tactics . . . The rumours will run rife. Can't you imagine the panic? Mokomo has returned and is wiping all before him. Anyone associated with the PRC will be rounded up and they and their families will be butchered.'

The quiet assassin had become a tactician, a general. Was he simply reiterating Falcone's plan, or was he a much bigger player in the game than Cappricci and many others had imagined?

'What about this second team? What are they supposed to be doing?' Cappricci asked.

206

'The first team is the Stuart group, of course. The second doesn't exist, but the belief that they do will put them on guard everywhere. The whole country will fall deeper into a state of emergency.'

'I will be asked about the second group though.'

'Yes,' answered Falcone, 'and you will tell them that your information is that this group has broken up into smaller groups, in order to carry out the reconnaissance of potential landing beaches for the main assault group, which is already on the water and approaching the country. Every small incident near the coast will be put down to them. The PRC will be spending all their time looking for ghosts, while *we* enact the final play.'

'Which is?' Cappricci questioned.

'Which is . . . for the good of the Family. You will return to the *Salamander* once your mission is complete. Then, you can join us in the final act. Now go, Mark. Time is our only enemy.'

Falcone walked towards the door, a large brandy in one hand, but no cane. Mario followed with the missing symbol.

Mark Cappricci took a deep breath as the room threw up a deafening emptiness. He turned around and looked at his reflection in the ornate mirror. The man he was looking at was confused, frightened and trapped.

For years he'd worked in a grey world which had taught him to expect the unexpected, but even in that world there were certainties, conventions and controls. Now, all this grey was plunged into the blackness of complete confusion. Who was running what? Who worked for whom? Whose side was anyone on? Were there any sides, or was is just a cocktail of conflicting ideas, created to enhance the master control of the big picture by one or two massive and intertwined commercial organisations who were never voted for, or in?

'We are ready, sir,' the *Salamader 1's* officer called quietly from the double glass doors that formed the entrance to the replica-strewn room.

'Oh, right . . . thanks,' Cappricci answered vaguely, downing his Scotch and turning towards the man. 'Lead on,' he said with false sparkle and a twinkling smile. The officer smiled back, spun on a blindingly white uniform heel and led the way out of the bar and back down the alleyway to the boat deck's watertight door.

'It's started to rain, I'm afraid, sir,' he said. 'I do have an umbrella, though, for the accommodation ladder.'

'Don't bother yourself. I'm hardly dressed for a royal reception.'

'As you wish, sir. This way please.' The officer pushed the heavy weather door open and led the way out onto the boat deck. The immaculate wooden planking was as shiny as polished glass, but the accommodation ladder was only a dozen steps away and neither man was significantly damp by the time they reached the sanctity of the launch's cabin. The helmsman powered the boat away from the ship with his practised skill and within three minutes from leaving the bar, Cappricci was bumping his way towards the shore.

The recent squall had left the sea a little choppy. The white horses, flashing in the moonlight on top of the rolling Atlantic swell, picked the *Salamander 1* up by the stern with gentle ease and offered her forward like a master surfer on a lee shore. The motion of the launch made Cappricci a little queasy and he was grateful for the quelling effect of the approaching beaches and the estuary's shelter.

As they approached the lights of the timber wharf, Cappricci went out on to the deck to get some air. He heard some crackling communication on the VHF as he left the cabin, and as he steadied himself on the launch's starboard rail he noticed two lights flash from the quay.

The jovial taxi driver was waiting for him as he attained the top of the quay's ladder. Cappricci turned around to look after the launch, which had spun to port immediately his feet had left the deck. The white wake was already disappearing in the background lights of the limited harbour illumination, but he could see the officer on the stern give a short wave, before proceeding below deck.

'You see, I tell you no problem, OK?' the driver chirped, breaking the tension Mark had felt ever since he'd stepped onto the launch on the outward journey. 'Back to hotel?'

'Sure, back to hotel. I need a drink!'

For the first time, Cappricci felt at a loss. His loose family connections with the Mafia had always been known at the Agency, in fact, in some circles it had been seen as an advantage. The Family had helped him on the odd occasion, but the requests he'd made were nothing compared to the level of return favours that they had requested when the Masada operation became an issue again. He was caught up in a situation of which he now had no control. Both the Agency and the Family could hang him out to dry . . . More importantly, they could find him just about anywhere in the world.

He stared out of the taxi window as his thoughts raced back and forward over the recent and the distant past. Evidence of the army was everywhere – young men in groups, some with girls – but the general feeling of Freeman was comfortable. He was very tired and looked forward to a shower and an air-conditioned room. He was in the kind of limbo that people fall into when there is nothing they can do about the situation they are in . . . except wait for events to turn the next page.

As the taxi swept round the corner before the Tumani Palms Hotel, the next page fell open. Army personnel and vehicles were straddled around the entrance to the hotel; not a situation you would expect at four-thirty in the morning. All the vehicles had their headlights on and there was an urgency about the people's movements. The taxi pulled up and Cappricci got out. Again the driver didn't wait to get paid, but the look on his face as he quickly pulled away from the scene was less than happy.

Cappricci smiled at everyone as he passed through the milling, closely attentive soldiers and fought his way through to the reception. When the porter saw him, he stared to gesticulate and talk very rapidly to an officer on his side of the counter. Everyone in earshot immediately looked towards Cappricci, and the officer lifted the desk flap to approach him.

'Are you the American, Cappricci ?' Cassa said, in his best English.

'Yes,' replied the startled Cappricci. 'What's the problem?'

'Please, can you tell me where you have been tonight?'

'Well,' he replied, trained mind clicking into gear. 'I went

209

for a walk, earlier last evening, and was approached by a young lady . . . You know how these things happen.'

'Where?' Cassa asked impatiently.

'Well, I think it was quite close to the harbour.'

'You're aware that there is a curfew at twenty-three thirty hours for civilians?'

'Well no, I only just arrived, really.'

'The regulations are clearly stated in your room. Can you read?'

'Well, of cour–'

'Come, we go to your room,' Cassa ordered, and he and a large chattering entourage led the way to the stairs.

When they got to his corridor, Cappricci could see a lot of activity in and around the doorway of a nearby room.

'What's going on?' he asked, to no avail.

Cassa swept into Cappricci's room. 'Please sit,' he ordered, pointing to the fitted wall-desk's chair.

'One of Sierra Laputu's prominent citizens has been murdered in that other room. We are questioning everyone in the hotel to disqualify them from suspicion. Can you prove, in any way, where you were tonight?'

'Well, ah, I'm not sure, let me think.'

'While you think, where is your passport?'

'In my briefcase.' He stared to rise, but Cassa held up his hand and shouted an order to a soldier. The briefcase was delivered to Cassa in seconds and he stared to search it. 'You were saying, Mr Cappricci? Your movements?'

'Well, the porter may have seen me leave, but apart from that I was in a couple of bars – you know, just cruising around, looking at the place.'

'Very good,' Cassa smiled. 'The porter did see you, as did others, but they say that you got into a taxi and asked for the harbour area. Not exactly a walk?'

'Well yeah, OK. I didn't realise the seriousness of the situation downstairs and I didn't freely want to admit that I went into town looking for a girl.'

'So tonight you went *looking* for a prostitute; a hooker, you call them in America?'

'Yes, I admit it. I hope I wasn't breaking any local laws?'

'Hah,' Cassa replied, shaking his head. 'That will be for the court to decide. A hooker, you say? Well, I think that perhaps I have been doing the hooking tonight, and I think I may have hooked a big fish.' Cassa turned to a well-dressed civilian and rattled an order, passing both the briefcase and Cappricci's passport to him. 'Mr Mark Cappricci,' the man read from the passport 'I arrest you on suspicion of the murder of Mr Samir Mohammed Abduhla Jamayal. Please come with me.' He indicated that Cappricci should rise and follow him.

Four armed soldiers fell in around him and the group proceeded quickly downstairs. He was bundled into a Japanese jeep of some kind and it pulled away immediately, followed by two more crammed with soldiers.

Cappricci didn't speak, he just stared ahead, trying to lock onto something that made some sense inside his mind; something that could be used as a foil to what was happening to him. There must be some kind of law here. Perhaps the civilian-looking guy had been a policeman and the army were only involved at a certain level. This country had been part of the British Empire ... The Brits might have made a mess of handing the empire back to the people they had stolen it from, but usually the structure, the administration and the concept of the law remained etched in their systems in some kind of fashion. A few calls to the legation later in the day and the diplomats would sort it out, he thought.

'Where are we going?' he asked anyone who might be listening.

'Bpungi,' replied the soldier squeezed in on his right-hand side.

Cappricci didn't answer the man. Why Bpungi? he thought. It was on the other side of the estuary. The only thing there was the airport. A glimmer of hope shot into Cappricci's mind. He was just a suspect, really. He'd broken the law regarding the curfew. Perhaps they were taking him to Bpungi so that when it was all sorted out, they could put him on a plane as an undesirable. The argument wasn't convincing, but it made him feel a little better. His main concern was that Bpungi was

211

on the wrong side of a large patch of water. Access to the American Legation was suddenly becoming more difficult.

Forty minutes later, they pulled up to the ferry point on the Freeman side of the estuary. The first ferry didn't go until eight-thirty.

'We wait for the ferry,' the soldier on his right said. 'About two hours. You can sleep.'

'Thanks,' Cappricci answered automatically, spreading out a little in the new space that was created as the soldier and his silent companion on his left disembarked from the jeep.

He didn't expect to sleep, but now and again he found himself achieving a light doze. During one of his wakenings, he wondered what this man Cassa was going to do or think, once he found out that he'd unwittingly arrested the contact he was waiting for. Falcone's plan was foundering at the outset. Who could have known that Jamayal would be taken out in the same hotel and on the same floor. A growing horror started to creep up his spine. Who could have known? One man could have known. Falcone could have known! What was it the old man had said? *'We have started to clean up the loose ends'* Was *he*, Mark Cappricci, a loose end, or was all this an unhappy coincidence? Was the game so frightening, the prize so great, that everyone involved in its conception and implementation had to be removed as soon as their function was complete? Surely not? It wasn't the way the Family operated with its own people and he, Mark Cappricci, was one of them ... wasn't he?

Cappricci's doubts grew and ballooned as the dawn came in and the odd local started to arrive for the first ferry. About eight o'clock, some movement could be seen on the vessel and soon the main engines were started up, heralded by two plumes of thick black smoke, which quickly turned into light grey smoke and then thinned out to a shimmering exhaust haze as the engineer tweaked their settings and the engines heated up.

Heating up was the last thing that Stuart and Sandys needed. They had stayed by the creek much longer than they had planned, or was safe.

212

'Perhaps Chet didn't make it,' John Sandys said, saying what they both were thinking.

'He'll have been travelling real slow in the dark, even with the moon. He won't risk the chance of giving himself away by trying to race it.'

'The light's been in for a good hour now. We can't wait for ever.'

'No point in moving until we know where we're going,' Stuart shrugged.

'I was coming to that.'

'Well, that's why I've been waiting, really. If Chet makes it, we've got another head, another skill and more immediate options. There's no immediate problem, let's give him some more time and think about how *we* get out of the country. That's the big one. If we can agree on the *where*, we can work out how to get to the *gate*.'

'Well, you know what my views are before you ask,' Sandys retorted. 'We can't *walk* out of here and I can't see us rowing a boat to a friendly country. The only way is for me to fly us out.'

'Where to?'

'Well, you'd better think more about what direction rather than where to. It's going to depend on what size of aircraft we can steal and how much fuel it's got on board as we lift off. Remember Angola?'

'Yeah,' replied Stuart, 'but we took a pile of hits in the fuel tanks as well. You managed, though!'

'Oh, I managed all right. But I tell you, there's no way on hell's earth that I can walk in from seven hundred miles again at my age, after ditching or not.'

Sandys threw the killing knife he'd been playing with into the sand, as if to emphasise the point, stood up and stretched. There was a bit of frustration, or even desperation in the action, and Stuart noticed it.

'John, I don't intend to die out here, you know. There's just no point in doing something just for doing something's sake. We must plan.'

'Well, plan yourself out of *this!*' Sandys whispered, dropping to the ground and grabbing his weapon.

Stuart stayed where he was, in the cover of a greying, dead

213

and sun-bleached tree which at one time had stretched its roots out towards the moving water.

Sandys made signs with his right hand. Stuart read them and then changed position to look for the single line of troops and to try to assess their numbers and direction. At first he couldn't see anything, and then he noticed the top of a bush hat, bobbing up and down on top of the elephant grass which contoured both banks of the narrow waterway. The tree gave him good cover so he raised himself higher to get a better look.

Suddenly, both Stuart and Sandys froze as the noise of an automatic weapon's action being cocked thundered into their brains.

'Don't move,' the middle-aged black professional said, in very good English, from just ten metres behind them. 'Drop the hardware, gents, and then hit the dirt, face down. The boys'll be here in a jiffy.'

Stuart obeyed – Sandys was already lying flat on the ground. They heard movement around them and watched as boots scuffled around their prone shapes, stripping them of their weapons. When the task was done the voice returned.

'OK, boys, on yer feet. Let's have a look at you.'

Stuart and Sandys rose simultaneously and looked round at their captor. The big black face beamed back at them. ''Allo, fellas, what the fuck are you two doing here?'

'*Robo?*' they both said in unison.

'The one and only,' the big black sergeant smiled. 'You two wouldn't be the big bad terrorists that every man and his dog in the country are looking for, would you?'

'What are you doing here?' Sandys got in before Stuart.

'Me? Oh, that's an easy one. Pan-African peacekeeper, that's me,' the cockney mercenary replied, tapping the shoulder flash on his tunic's left shoulder. 'It's a good game, Johnny. You and the Major here should of got into this game a long time ago. Money's good, risk minimal and the chow comes in from Ghana. Been here a year past, last month.'

'The rest of them?' Stuart nodded at the approaching line.

'Nigerians and Ghanaians mostly, plus a Tamil fucking Tiger that lost his way. Brilliant, ain't it?'

'What about the officers?'

'Come on, Trap. Officers don't walk in Africa! Me and the three degrees here were out on the other side of the water when we heard you two rabbiting on. *I'm it!* No officers. But don't try it on. I'm here to do a job, and right now it's to hand a group of bad guys over to the PRC, if I find them.'

'*If* you find them,' Stuart replied.

'Oh, I've found them all right. Dead lucky as well. We only got dropped off two hours ago. The whole fucking region was put on alert after that mess you left behind last night. Just think yourself lucky an old mucker found you and not anyone whose totally pissed off with you. Kill ratio of between four and five to one to you last night, if my calculations aren't too far out. I should of guessed! What's going on? Who's with you?'

'Fuck off, Robo,' Stuart replied. 'If you're going to play it straight down the line, you might as well get on with it. Don't come crying to me the next time you're out of work, though.'

'I had a good teacher, Trap. *If you sign a contract you stick with it* – that's what you drummed into us in South Africa. Anyway, I'm not the enemy, just in the middle.'

'*Bullshit,*' Sandys cut in. 'We saved your arse on that last job we did together.'

'Yeah, that's right. It was nearer eight hundred miles we had to cover, you know, not seven hundred. You guys broke the rules today, chatting away like two old ladies in the pub. We heard you and you got caught. Come on, let's go. We've only got five miles to walk today.'

'Which way are we going?' Stuart asked.

'Don't worry, we're not going back the way you came. I don't fancy my chances negotiating your safety with a bunch of prickly gooks.'

'I'm overwhelmed,' Sandys sneered. He'd never liked Sam Robinson. He'd always thought there was something not just quite right with the man. Couldn't put his finger on it, though . . . Just a feeling.

'You will be, if either of you two start to try anything,' Robinson threatened.

'Hey, cool it, you two,' Stuart said, with practised affability.

'Five miles is a long way for an old man like me. Your claptrap is tiring me out already. Hey, Robo, can I get a shit before we go?'

'Don't see why not. Go down in the rushes if you're shy. This big fella here will come and give you a hand.'

Sandys stood and waited, troops milling around him as they arrived from the line. Robinson got involved in giving instructions to the other NCOs in the party and Stuart walked the few metres to the privacy of elephant grass with his companion. As he reached the edge of the grass, he noticed Sandys' knife still sitting where he'd thrown it, buried up to its hilt in the sand. It hadn't been noticed. He turned round to his attendant, who was hovering about ten steps behind him, half listening to the conversations building up as the rest of the soldiers came in, half keeping an eye on Stuart. He clearly didn't think there was any threat from Stuart or Sandys, as they were outnumbered many times over.

'Hey,' Stuart called. 'Get some grass?' He pointed, showing the actions of wiping his back side. The attendant nodded. As Stuart bent down to pull grass out of the tuft next to the commando knife, he palmed it and slipped it up his tunic sleeve. While he completed his natural urge, he buttoned down both sleeves, so as not to draw attention to the hidden weapon that was now held in place by the fastening of the left cuff.

'Come on, Major Stuart,' Robinson called. 'I didn't realise I'd given you that much of a scare!'

Some of the soldiers understood the joke and laughed. Stuart took his time and made certain that the retrieved weapon wouldn't break free or make his arm look unnatural.

'I'm coming. Keep your hair on. Oh sorry, Robo, forgot you were bald.'

'Get that smart arse out of those rushes and get moving,' Robinson shouted to everyone within hearing.

Stuart fell in behind Sandys, and the line snaked out again, retracing its steps to the vehicles.

Chet Maclazowitz watched them move off, through his Zeiss binoculars, from a slight rise in the savannah to the east.

'*And then there were two,*' he quoted from the old poem.

216

'So, what next?' Steve Rider asked.

'Follow them at a safe distance. We can do it in the open, if we just keep the last man in sight with the glasses and watch our tails. The boss really messed up this time. I could almost hear the clowns that picked them up from over here.'

'Any signs of injury?' Rider asked, his own predicament in the forefront of his mind.

'Both walking OK, and they haven't got any kind of restraints on them.'

'What kind of speed are they making?'

'Faster than we've been. You want another shot?'

'Not yet,' Rider answered. 'Wouldn't want to run out of morphine just when I need it most. The bleeding seems to be under control anyway, as long as I don't stretch too far.'

'Let's go then. Sunday school outing in the country!'

'Piece of cake?'

'Definitely, old chap,' Chet mimicked. *'Piece of cake!'*

'Lead on, then, before I change my mind.'

The big American slid out of cover and walked across the open country. Steve Rider followed at 20 metres, steeling himself for a long day's walk in the sun. If he'd known they only had about five miles to go, he might have had a lighter step . . .

It was lots of very *heavy* steps that Chris Marker heard in the corridor outside his room, as Mark Cappricci was bundled into the one next door. There was a brief interchange inside the room, which he couldn't make out. The door was closed and locked; more loud voices, and then silence again.

He took the glass from the bathroom and practised the age-old technique of eavesdropping, but all he could hear was movement, as the new 'guest' checked out his surroundings. He'd just taken his ear from the wall, when the lock in his own door started to turn.

Marker expected one of the usual guards or inquisitors to appear in the doorway, but instead there was a tall, elegant man, dressed in a dark blue silky African suit buttoned up to a collar which was in the lapelless style common in both Africa and Asia.

'Mr Marker, my name is Kimo. I wondered if you would like to join me for lunch downstairs?' The voice was quiet and refined, reflecting the bearing, confidence and manners of an educated man who was assured of his position and status. Maker was taken completely off guard.

'Lunch? Ah, yes, that would be a very pleasant change.'

'Good. I'm so pleased. Shall we go now? Perhaps we could have a beer before we eat. I think we should lock your room while we are gone, just in case.'

'Yes,' replied Marker, in a partial daze. 'It would be safer.'

'Come then. After you, Mr Marker.'

'Thank you.'

'My pleasure,' Kimo answered, holding the door like the perfect host.

As they entered the corridor, Marker could see that there was a bored armed guard at each end. He went ahead of his new host, down the wide stairs and into the large and airy reception, lounge and bar. The floor was made of stone, giving the whole area a feeling of coolness. When he reached the bar area, which also led to the dining room and the open terrace beyond, he stopped and waited for a prompt. Kimo indicated that he should carry straight on through to the terrace. Normally there were about a dozen tables of varying sizes laid up on the open area, but today only one was prepared. Unusually, it had a tablecloth and a full spread of napkins, cruets and cutlery. He sat down without being asked. Kimo followed, after he had had a quiet word with one of the restaurant staff.

'They don't seem to be very busy today,' Marker commented.

'No,' Kimo answered. 'I told them that I would like a little privacy.'

'Then you must be an important man.'

'That's very kind of you, but I am just a simple policeman.'

'Not the army then?'

'No, no, the army classes have got more than enough to do right now, to spend time having a pleasant lunch with an educated and interesting man like yourself.'

'The army not being full of educated and interesting men?' Marker asked.

218

'Something like that . . . Shall we order?'

'You mean we don't have to eat rice and groundnuts today?'

'An extremely healthy staple diet, but I rather think some seabass with a mixture of vegetables would be appealing. Would you like to join me? I brought the fish with me in a cool box.'

'Certainly would,' Marker replied, flashing his best smile at his unusual host. 'And how can I help you, Mr Kimo? You haven't driven miles with pleasant offerings out of the goodness of your heart, surely?'

'Actually, Kimo is my first name. May I call you Chris?'

'I'm sorry. Yes of course.'

The waiter approached and placed a large basket of mixed breads in the middle of the table. He took the order and then left, and proceeded to call out instructions as he passed from the terrace into the dining room proper.

'I have been speaking with your High Commissioner, Mrs Leadbetter. Amusing name, isn't it? She feels that there has been a terrible misunderstanding, that you're a well-known shipbroker, and as the ship's agent in Freeman has confirmed that you were indeed on your way to the *Petetchkin*, we should release you into her custody until all charges are formally dropped . . . If they are. How do you feel about that?'

Marker's heart was thumping. He didn't know what kind of emotions he should reveal to his likeable host. He was just going to speak when the waiter arrived with two bowls of mixed salad.

'An appetiser.' Kimo smiled, and both men started to pick at the locally grown produce. 'You were about to say?'

'The High Commissioner would seem to have a very good point. What do *you* think, Kimo?'

The black man put down his fork and dabbed the edge of his mouth with his napkin. 'Mr Marker, I don't know if you're guilty or innocent of the charges the army have brought against you. Something of what you have said is verifiable, but here we have martial law, and currently a nationwide security alert. Unusual visitors with unusual stories and documents in their bags are a worry to us.'

'Is that why you torture them at the slightest chance?'

There was a look of genuine surprise in the eyes of Marker's host, before they quickly glazed over again to present their normal, practised, calm and considered exterior.

'I know nothing of torture, Mr Marker. It is not, ah, civilised behaviour.'

'Would you like to see its results?' Marker asked, aware that the power play at the table was shifting emphasis.

'The army did mention that you had had an accident when you arrived. Leaving the plane, wasn't it?'

Marker slammed his fork down on the table. 'An accident?' he shouted. 'Oh sure! That's how I got these marks around my wrists and a fucking cattle prod up my arse.'

Soldiers appeared from nowhere, but the policeman raised his hand to stop any action.

'I think it would be wise to lower your voice and resume your seat, Chris. The fish will be ready soon and this excitement will give you indigestion. These are difficult times, but solutions can be found for problems, if people talk. Please, sit.'

Marker looked around him and realised how close he'd come to another beating. He slowly sat down and watched as the soldiers sank into the back-ground, this time not disappearing, but keeping a discreet distance that still signalled the potential for instant menace.

'They tortured me and laughed,' Marker said calmly.

'Then they are criminals under Sierra Laputu law. You can make a statement and identify your attackers. We are a civilised people, coming out of a dark era. Do not judge us all by the excesses of a few.'

'You don't like the army being in charge, do you?'

'I have a BSc Hons in chemical engineering from the United States and an MA from Oxford. The best job I can get in my home country is that of policeman. Don't you find something wrong with that? The army is full of people who need to be fed, led by officers trained in places as far away as China and Peru. You will note that I don't quote democracies as our previous leader's first choice as a training ground for his army. We in the police are generally the intellectuals of our

220

martial groups. We have nothing in common with butchers and thugs.'

'Then let me go!'

'To Mrs Leadbetter?'

'Home, preferably. Her, as a second choice.'

'Do you really think that's wise?' Kimo said, getting up to retrieve some papers from an adjacent table. 'I need to wash my hands, before the fish. Why not leaf through the news while I'm gone. I don't suppose you've had much chance to read the English press over the last few days.' He left the room with the feline grace of a cheetah.

Marker picked up a three-day-old copy of *The Times* and flicked through its well-fingered pages. On page three, *his* face leapt out of the paper. The story was almost word-for-word what Michelle Christie had read on the flight to Heathrow. It was repeated in the copy of the *Telegraph* that accompanied *The Times*. As he finished reading it for the second time, the fish arrived.

'Thank you,' Marker said to the waiter, putting the papers down on the floor beneath his chair. He didn't begin to eat, initially waiting for his host to return, but when no meal arrived for him and there seemed to be no sign of him returning from the bathroom, he signalled to the waiter. 'Ah, where is Mr Kimo?'

'Not here. Gone Freeman. He say that you to eat anything, drink anything, take a walk and then back to room. One other man here soon. Fish very good.'

'I'm sure it is.' Maker shrugged, tucking into the fish that was still warm due to the 36-degree temperature out on the terrace. 'Could I have a cold beer?' he called across to the waiter, who nodded and went to fetch it.

As he downed an enormous swig of the cool drink, he felt rather calm, he thought, for a man who was under arrest as a spy in an African war zone, wanted as a prime suspect for murder in Switzerland and presumably still being pursued by a maniacal Latin who wanted to kill him. He supposed it was because right now his options appeared to be a big fat zero. The fish was good though. 'Another beer please,' he called. It was brought over by a small young man in cheap jeans and a tee shirt.

'I am Daniel, from the Bpungi station. I am here to be with you.'

'Are you a policeman?' Marker asked.

'I am a detective constable. My parents are dead in the border wars and my wife is having a baby. If I can tell you anything, I will . . . if you can help me feed my family,' the young man blurted out.

'Well hi, Daniel! That was a hell of an opening mouthful, if ever I heard one.'

'They know you're not a spy. They will let you go home, but your bruises must heal first. Kimo is the head of the Secret Police – like your Special Branch. He is the only senior officer to retain his rank and position under the PRC that he held under Mokomo. He is very dangerous. He told me to talk to you like a friend and write everything down.'

'Woahhhh there, *Silver!* Take a breath. Have some bread or a beer.'

'If you can help me with money, I will help you. You're not a criminal.'

Marker had a thousand dollars in American Express Travellers Cheques sewn into the inside lining of his suit. They were for emergencies and about three months old.

'What do you make . . . Daniel?'

'I am not a craftsman, I am a policeman,' he replied with a worried look on his face.

'No, no, you misunderstand. How much *money* do you make, in US dollars, or UK pounds?'

The young policeman looked up to the ceiling and did a quick calculation. 'Twenty pounds.'

'Twenty pounds a week?' Marker asked in disbelief.

'No, no, absolutely not. I am not a Kimo! Please believe me, I am not rich like Kimo, I am just a constable having twenty pounds for one month, from which I send just over half to my wife.'

Marker paused, as he quickly calculated what this man, with a rare steady job, had to live on. 'Where's your wife?'

'She is in our village in the interior, maybe three days' travel, with the rains.'

'Kimo asked you to spy on me. Maybe you're very clever and all this is just to put me off my guard?'

'I have seen the papers. It is almost certain that they will send you home when you heal.'

'We've gone from certain to almost certain. Daniel, I *can* help your family, but I must be sure I can trust you.'

'You can, you can. I am a Christian, you can trust me.'

'That's an interesting concept, Daniel, but I must be sure.'

'What can I do?'

'I want lots of exercise time, good food – not that barracks shit. Plus I want to know everything about my new neighbour upstairs. For this, I will give you fifty dollars tomorrow and fifty dollars in two days' time.'

'You promise?'

'If the information is good,' Marker said, holding out his hand. The constable grabbed it and gave him the classic African handshake – hand, then hand and thumb followed by hand again.

'Tomorrow. I will have this for you tomorrow. I am a Christian. You can trust me.'

'There are a few ghosts who could take issue with that last one, but let's leave that to history,' Marker replied with a heavy dose of irony. 'When's the baby due?'

'In about six weeks, sir.'

'Hey, waiter . . . two beers!'

'Sir, I am on duty. I cannot drink,' the young constable explained.

'Oh dear, what a pity. Never mind, I'll have to have it.'

By the time Marker was locked up back in his room, he'd fed well, had a mild alcoholic glow and had had an hour walking and sitting around what had once been a well kept garden and swimming pool area. Now the plants and fixtures were wild or crumbling, with small lizards peeping out from the cracks and holes that over a decade of decay had sculptured out of the backdrop.

He showered and went to bed. Sleep came quickly and lasted

for over nine hours. It was a sleep punctuated by wild and interconnected dreams, filled with snapshots of a million incidents and faces that had passed through his life. One theme recurred, in all the different facets and locations of the dreams Gomez kept turning up to ruin the good dreams and be the instigator of the bad ones. One minute he was here in Africa, and the next he was outside Marker's Eaton Place apartment in London. No matter what Marker tried to do in his dreams, he couldn't shake him off.

Steve Rider was also having trouble shaking something off; the pain in his leg. They had covered about three miles, at the faster pace required to keep up with the Pan-African Peace Corps patrol that had Stuart and Sandys in custody.

The leg was throbbing and swelling within the confines of the dressing. He'd started to drop further behind Maclazowitz and was waiting for the next time the big American looked round, to signal him to stop for another morphine shot.

As things turned out, he didn't have to wait. The tell-tale sound of a helicopter jumped out of the background noise and quickly appeared to the west of the group. It was a Puma.

Circling only once, the pilot whipped its nose up and landed with practised speed and ease. The large sliding fuselage doors were locked back on both sides, and as the pilot reduced the power a crewman appeared and waved to the front of the line, which was not fully visible from Maclazowitz and Rider's positions.

'Now look at that, boys,' Robo chuckled, up ahead. 'Nothing but the best for the famous Hollywood team of Stuart and Sandys. A Rolls Royce of the air to carry you to the Freeman Ritz for tea and cucumber sandwiches!'

'You wouldn't know which knife and fork to use, Robo,' Sandys returned, scathingly.

'Tch, tch,' Robinson replied, wagging his finger. 'Why don't you and his highness here shut the fuck up and get your arses up and over and into the bird. Move it!' The last instruction was accompanied by a short, but recognisable, change in the emphasis of his weapon's aim.

224

Sandys got in first and slid across the bare floor to the rear of the compartment.

'Now you, *Major*,' Robinson sneered.

Stuart climbed slowly into the aircraft and sat facing Sandys, at the door. Five soldiers followed them in and took their own positions on the deck. The crewman said something to Robinson that was lost in the rotor noise, then jumped into the aircraft and the pilot pulled her out of the savannah and into a steep, curling climb to the west. Stuart's eyes never left those of the cockney, as they rose and left him and the rest of his platoon behind, until they were at such a distance that eyes could no longer be differentiated. Stuart was on the low side of the aircraft's banked turn and he noticed that two of the corps platoon appeared to be patrolling quite a way back from the rest. Very good, Robo, he thought. Watching the back door, just like I taught you.

'What could you see?' Steve Rider asked.

'They've picked the guys up, with a few guards.'

'Shit! What the hell do we do now?'

'No change. All the men would have gone with the chopper if they'd have come in by air. They must have some rolling stock somewhere, and that's our best bet to getting out of here. We're on our own now. Our only chance is to get to Freeman and slide out somehow.'

'Well, I'm not going to be doing any more sliding anywhere unless you give me another shot, big fella.'

'OK, but if you start singing I'll have to shoot you,' Maclazo- witz joked. 'Sounds quite an attractive option right now,' Rider smiled up at him.

The joking helped, but both men knew their situation was desperate. By the time Maclazowitz had given Rider another injection and rechecked the wound, the patrol ahead had made another hundred metres on them.

Rider gritted his teeth and raised his rate of step. The mor- phine had taken hold again, but the effort precluded even the thought of attempting speech.

The corps patrol were easy to follow. They were relaxed,

having completed their assignment with a feather in their caps. When they finally reached their vehicles, Robo announced that they would camp there for the night, rest up and start the day long journey back to the main camp in the morning. No need to overdo it, he thought. Another day, another dollar.

Maclazowitz and Rider heard the patrol making camp before they could see anything. One of the vehicles had been started up for some reason and moved around. From the engine it sounded like a big diesel and shortly after its noise interrupted the natural sounds, a distinctive exhaust smell wafted over the duo.

'Wonder how many vehicles they've got?' Rider whispered.

'Only one way to find out,' Maclazowitz whispered back. 'Here, look after this gear. I'll crawl in and take a peek.'

Chet Maclazowitz passed all his equipment, except the silenced Uzi and two spare clips of ammunition, over to Steve Rider.

'There won't be any pickets. They're too secure in their minds and busy on their feet to think it's necessary,' Rider offered.

'Yep, reckon so. Keep the coffee warm!' With that, he snaked off towards the downwind side of the camp.

Steve Rider pulled Chet's sniper rifle out of its slip cover and popped a magazine into it. He thought there were about nine or ten men left, but the size of a platoon like this could be anything. He put the scope to his eye and acquired the top of a truck above the savannah grasses. Not an ideal place to set up, but there wasn't much choice in the vicinity and Chet knew where he was. No sense going through the pain of crawling somewhere else just to have Chet return and find him gone.

The cover that Maclazowitz was using was about waist high and ended some 70 metres short of the camp. He crawled right up to five metres from the edge and turned to stone. There was quite a lot of activity. It appeared that the vehicle had been moved to make more of a circle with the other ones, around a fire that was being built for lighting later in the centre of the circle. He counted 12 men, including an officer. There was something familiar about the man's walk, so he pulled out his binoculars and had another look. Well, well, he thought, *Sammy Robinson.* Bad pennies always turn up where you least expect them ... and an officer now, it looks like! This discovery changed Maclazowitz's mind. As far as he was concerned, Sam Robinson couldn't lead a bag full of groceries. What Stuart and Sandys were doing – or not doing – to let someone like Robo get the drop on them was beyond him. He crawled further around to his right, to put the first vehicle between himself and the camp, got up onto his haunches and slowly rose to half height, checking all around him for any stragglers. He was on his own, so he calmly walked towards the truck. When he reached it, he slowly cocked the Uzi and pulled a grenade from his tunic. Hope Steve's awake, he thought, and then stepped around the front of the vehicle. Nine of the twelve were directly in front of him at about fifteen metres.

'Good evening gentlemen,' he said, lobbing the grenade at their feet. He waited the one second it took them to react and then slipped back behind the truck. The grenade exploded two seconds later, killing four of them outright and wounding all the rest except one, who was so badly shocked by the blast he might as well have been hit. Two more appeared around the back of a second truck, and the Uzi spat their deaths. There was no sign of Robinson anywhere, so Chet held his cover position by the first truck, quickly looked round its front, sprayed the writhing bodies at the grenade site with 9 mm fire and then sprang towards the back of the second vehicle. As he covered the gap between the two green diesels, something moving caught his eye, past and beyond the grenade victims. It was a running man. Robinson was careering across the savannah, away from the danger zone. His beret was missing and he carried only his AK.

Suddenly he stopped in his tracks, rose slightly from the ground and fell back the way he'd come. The unsilenced crack of Chet's rifle echoed across the plain, followed by an eerie silence.

Nothing moved. The savannah slowly reacted to the silence and started to get back to normal business. Tiny birds started

227

to flit between the grasses and small land animals scuttled away from the noisy area. One of the bodies moaned, but Chet stayed where he was. Two minutes later he saw Steve Rider walking in, swamped by his own and Chet's equipment. The big American came out from behind the truck and walked towards his companion. He heard the moan again, but it came from outside the camp. Robinson!

'Watch yourself,' Chet called out.

Rider lifted his hand to show he'd heard the warning and approached the area where he'd dropped the man, pistol in his hand.

Maclazowitz saw Rider stop, cock the weapon and point it towards the ground. He was only 15 metres away now and could see the look on Rider's face as he looked up towards him.

'Before you say anything, *I know*,' he called to Rider.

'*Sammy Robinson!*' Rider exclaimed.

'You always were useless at a distance, Rider,' Robinson spat, through clenched teeth.

'You missed?' Maclazowitz asked, mockingly.

'I didn't miss. He's bleeding like a stuck pig.'

'Why don't you two bastards cut the bullshit and help me, instead of letting me bleed to death? You've shot half my bloody shoulder off as it is.'

'Hardly, Robo. You always were a whiner,' Rider laughed. 'A well aimed round to the upper right torso, three inches above the nipple. The speed your arms were moving, it might even have got a deflection straight through, off the shoulder blade, or it might even have pulped it. What do'you reckon, Robo? Big exit wound in the back? You treacherous bastard.'

'Hey, chill out, partner,' Maclazowitz cut in. 'He's just doing a paying job like you and me. Just happens to be being paid by the other side, that's all.'

'This time!' Rider snapped.

'Oh, I get it,' Robinson half grimaced, half laughed. 'You guys are off the bosses' team?'

'This bastard is used to running, Chet. Aren't you, Robo? Four of the best men in Three Para bought it because this little worm turned tail and ran, leaving their flank wide open. The CO got it as well.'

'Down south?'

'That's right, Chet. This fucker ran, *they* were wasted and I got it in the neck.'

'Why you?'

'I was this *turd's* officer. When he got back to safety he blabbed a story that Hans Christian Anderson would of been proud of . . . How I panicked and shouted all sorts of conflicting orders, causing a hole in the advance and setting the boss up for a fall. There were no witnesses to his run except me – and the whole regiment was looking for someone to blame for the CO's demise.'

'Tough shit.'

'Yeah, but every dog has his day, and today's mine. Patch him up, Chet. This lowlife is coming with us, for a while. Get up, you bastard!' Rider kicked Robinson hard on the leg, probably causing himself more pain than he dispensed to his enemy.

'Well,' said Maclazowitz, 'whether we take him, shoot him or just leave him, the noise we just made may have carried to our oriental friends. We should choose a vehicle and leave, pronto.'

'OK, you check the motors out. I'll escort our guide to his feet and follow on directly. Oh yes! The next time you get an overwhelming urge to be a gung-ho Yank, give me a bit of warning, will you?'

Maclazowitz relieved Rider of his equipment and turned back to the vehicles; two trucks and a Land Rover.

Rider prodded Robinson with his AK. 'Up you get. If you want treatment, get over to those trucks and we'll sort something out, but believe one thing . . . if you make just the slightest wrong move I'll stick a nine mill in your gut and leave you to be eaten alive by the vultures!'

'You always were a bastard,' Robinson almost spat out.

'That's right, Robo, but with me it was an accident of birth. Now you . . . you're a self-made man.'

Maclazowitz heard the exchange as he walked towards the vehicles and chuckled, shaking his head. The two trucks were old Toyotas and he jumped up into the second one to see if there was anything worth taking with them. There was box of Chinese made 7.62 ammunition for the AKs and the like, some cold rations, water and a small pack of medical supplies. Transferring over to the first truck, which had taken quite a blast from grenade fragments on the one side, he found another body. Careless, Chet thought. I could have been popped from behind if grenade fragments hadn't passed through the truck's canvas cover and given this good old boy a shock.

There was a similar stash of equipment in this truck, with an extra box of ammunition.

'How are you doing?' Rider called, from outside.

'Clearly these guys didn't expect to be gone long, or their main camp wasn't far,' Maclazowitz replied. The thought worried him. This country was getting a bit too complicated and crowded for his liking.

Stuart was having similar thoughts, as they touched down at Bpungi airport. The game was a completely new one now. Mercenaries were usually beaten and shot if they were caught in Africa, unless there was a special reason. The only bargaining chip they had was the Masada weapon and its use as a political tool. The problem with that was that he didn't know to what extent the situation was, or was not known by the new government. *Out of the assault group, only he still knew the real reason for the raid.*

'Tell them the truth when they question you,' he said to Sandys, as he jumped out of the chopper next to him.

'No talking,' a guard shouted, and pushed them apart.

John Sandys just raised his eyebrows and continued to walk towards the two Landcruisers that were sitting on the apron waiting for them.

Fifteen minutes later they were locked up, in separate rooms, at the Bpungi Hotel. It was swarming with troops, with each floor having several permanent guards.

Stuart was pushed into a room and the door was locked. As with Marker before him, the quality of the surroundings was a great surprise. As soon as the noisy lock finished clicking, he looked around for a safe place to hide the knife. There was a spare pillow and a blanket in the musty wardrobe. He opened the flap at the end of the pillow cover and made a small incision in the pillow itself, sliding the knife into the stuffing. It went in fairly easily and was held firm by the material. Even a maid making up the room would probably fail to discover it.

The door to the balcony was locked, but through the louvred windows he could see part of a terrace, with tables and chairs, some of them taken up by soldiers eating a casual meal. To the right of this and in front of him was a garden with overgrown paths and rotting wooden benches, and when his view was at full stretch, he could just see the concrete surround and a small corner of what looked to have been a swimming pool, in more affluent days. A wall between his balcony and the next one prevented him seeing any further.

The lock in the door started to turn again and he walked back into the middle of the room. Cassa walked in, with two guards and a man with a camera. More guards could be seen in the corridor.

'Sit in the chair,' Cassa ordered.

Stuart smiled and sat down. Immediately, the cameraman checked his light reading and then fired off half a dozen snapshots of his head and shoulders. Then, as quickly as they had come they were gone again. He sat looking at the closed door. There's a curved ball in here somewhere, he thought. Nobody's even tried to search me yet.

He went into the bathroom and looked into the mirror. A tired face looked back at him: dark patches underneath his eyes just showing through the embedded tan and greying whiskers powdering the darkened skin. An overwhelming weakness came over him and he had to snap himself out of it with a tremendous effort. If his body was really that tired, he had to concentrate on rejuvenation for the trials yet to come. First, a shower and a sleep. Anything could happen at any time. He might not get another chance.

'What chance d'you think we've got?' Rider said to Maclazowitz, out of Robinson's hearing.

'None without a plan of some kind. We've won some ammo and rations, but we might have announced our presence if anyone else in this crowded countryside was listening. Robo's wound isn't as bad as it could have been, so I suppose he's an asset right now, seeing as how you missed and only wounded him.'

'Intelligence?'

'Yep. He won't know much, but he knows a darned sight more than either of us do.'

'What d'you reckon, then?' Rider asked. 'You're the only fit guy around. Anything we do hinges on your capabilities.'

'Well, that's a comfort,' Maclazowitz laughed. 'Look, there's a full map folio in the Land Rover. Why don't we put a couple of rounds into the truck fuel tanks, load up the Rover with the stores and head for the nearest border?'

'It's too far, Chet. I'd never make it, or if I did they'd be cutting large chunks off me when I got there. Don't fancy that, somehow.'

'Well, we've only got three directions. East to the war zone, west to West Guinea or head for the coast and see what happens.'

'I wonder if Robo knows where they've taken the guys?'

'Let's ask him,' Maclazowitz agreed, 'but let me do it.'

'OK, I'll have a good look at the maps and see if anything else occurs to me.'

As Rider turned to go to the Rover, he thought he heard a noise in the distance and turned back to Maclazowitz.

'Heard it,' Chet said, grabbing his Uzi and scanning the horizon.

'Aircraft?'

'Yeah, big one as well. Sounds like a Herc.'

'It is,' Rider confirmed. 'Look!'

Coming in low and fast from the south was the familiar shape of a C-130 Hercules. About a mile before it got to them it banked slightly to starboard and then, after a few seconds, flipped over to port to commence a sweeping turn.

'Can't be looking for us,' Rider said. 'They haven't got any Hercs.' He looked round at Maclazowitz. The big man was straining through his binoculars at the aircraft.

'There's not even a small registration mark on that sucker, Steve.'

'What about the second one?'

'The second one! Where the fu—?' He lowered the glasses. 'Jesus, I see her!'

'Chet! They've got mid-air refuelling probes sticking out in front and up-to-date undercarriage strut supports. That means one thing – those guys aren't from this neck of the woods.'

'Who the hell could they be then?'

'It's probably your lot come to sweep up the mess,' Rider said excitedly, the combination of morphine and adrenaline pushing a glowing cocktail around his body.'

'Americans?' Maclazowitz mused. 'Wait a minute, one of those babies is coming in for a plains landing, right over the top of us.'

'Well, I hope they have better luck than we did. Wait a minute – that's it!'

'What you talking about?'

'Quickly, get out of your tunic and switch it for a Pan-African Peace Corps uniform top. Whoever they are, this is our passport out of this bear trap.'

Their conversation was partially drowned by the first Hercules as it roared overhead, its strengthened undercarriage already down.

'That's the one good thing about working in Africa,' Maclazowitz shouted, 'I can always find clothes big enough to fit me. What about Robo?'

'Oh yes,' Rider shouted back. 'I'll go and see how he is. You got everything you need?'

'Just about. I'll be with you in a minute.'

Steve Rider walked around the back of the second Toyota to where Sam Robinson was resting.

'What the bloody hell's going on?' Robinson asked, pointing at the Hercules as it dropped onto the Savannah plain a quarter of a mile to the north east of them.

'What's happening?' Rider echoed. 'Some ghosts came out of hell and dealt you a losing hand. Read 'em and weep!'

Rider's Beretta kicked twice into Robinson's stomach. The

man screamed and clutched the area around the two small holes that hid the shredded contents of his torso. He looked up at Rider and tried to formulate words.

'Don't bother, asshole. I've heard it all before. I just wanted to see the pain in your eyes. This is for the guys you left in the shit, not for *here*.'

With that, Rider placed a round square into Robinson's face and turned to go back to the Land Rover, where Maclazowitz was finishing getting ready. As he turned, he saw that the American was standing about 15 metres behind him and had witnessed everything.

'Not a word, Chet. *Not a fucking word!*'

Maclazowitz shrugged, lifted both hands in the universal sign of submission and let Rider storm by him.

'You drive,' Rider snapped.

'Where to, *boss?*' Maclazowitz queried.

'Right there,' Rider answered, pointing at the Hercules, as it turned to face in the opposite direction to its approach. It stopped just to the right of its successful landing site, acting as a marker and leaving room for its companion, which was already on approach with wheels down. 'And dump that silenced Uzi and the rifle. From now on we're just a couple of picked-on foot soldiers who've survived an attack from an unknown force. Got it?'

'Way ahead of you, baby.' Maclazowitz gunned the Land Rover towards the parked aircraft as the second one screamed overhead.

'Put the headlights on, Chet. We're the good guys, we want these turkeys to see us, not shoot us.'

The light brown savannah dust thrown up by the aircraft covered the Land Rover as they sped across the plain to meet the new arrivals. Men and vehicles could been seen pouring out of the first aircraft.

'They've got armoured troop carriers with twin fifties on the front,' Chet called across to Rider as the distance was reeled in.

'I'll tell you something else they've got as well,' Rider shouted back.

'What's that?'
'White faces.'
'Jesus, it must be a Delta Force company!'
'Could be, Chet.'
'If it is, we're home free.

The co-pilot of the first Israeli Hercules saw the Land Rover approaching. He clicked on his air-to-ground radio. 'Dani, we have a single Jeep approaching.'
'OK,' Dani Cohen replied. 'My men will have picked it up. We're just about empty back here. How's number two doing?'
'Coming down the ramp now.'
'OK, shut down and keep loose.'
Before Rider and Maclazowitz had reached the closest aircraft, the whole Israeli force was unloaded from it and on its way towards them.
'All right, Chet, stop. Leave the talking to me.'
Maclazowitz pulled the Land Rover to a halt and Rider stepped out, leaving his weapon behind. Dani, a captain and an NCO got out of the lead Jeep. The NCO carried a standard Uzi and discreetly held it at the ready.
'Are you Americans?' Rider asked, knowing that all the tiny bits of information his senses were picking up were ringing warning bells in his ears.
The captain had been born in Yonkers. 'Yeah, how're ya doing? What unit are you guys from?
Rider went into his story about how they were training officers with the PAC and that their unit had been suddenly put on alert to look for some insurgents in this area. Suddenly, their group had been attacked while they were making camp. The two of them had been patrolling the outlying area when it happened and by the time they got back to the camp a full firefight was in progress. He was wounded and his companion got him out. All this had happened last night.
To Rider's surprise, there followed a rapid exchange in Hebrew and then Dani Cohen turned to them.
'This officer will take you to medical attention. Your colleague must come with us. Do you have maps?'

235

'Israelis?' Rider said, unable to hide his shock.

'Hardly the PLO,' the man replied. 'Maps?'

'In the Rover,' Rider offered.

'Good.'

Dani Cohen turned to his own men and rattled off some more orders in Hebrew. The NCO passed him a mobile radio and a similar conversation took place.

'Chet,' Rider said, returning the two steps back to the Rover.

'Heard it all, Steve, heard it all. Go get yourself patched up. I'll see what this here major wants me to do for him.'

The captain took Maclazowitz's place behind the wheel and drove off with Rider towards the aircraft.

'Please come with me,' Dani told Maclazowitz, pointing to his Jeep. 'What is your name and rank?'

'The name is Chester Maclazowitz, ah, Major. My friends call me Chet,' he answered, thinking that it would help relations if he gave himself the same rank as his new associate.

'Then, Major Chet, I need two things from you immediately. Where were you attacked and have you any knowledge of an old aircraft crash site in the area, near a disused mine complex?'

'Attacked? Oh yeah, right. We were attacked just a couple miles back the way we came. We'd just got back from hiding to see if there was anything we could do for the CO and his men. You know what it's like fighting in the dark. Everything goes mad and then each side waits for daylight to pick up the pieces.'

'And was there anything to be done?'

'All dead – those who were left behind and didn't hightail it off into the bush.'

'So some of your men could still be in the vicinity?' Dani probed.

'Maybe one or two. Ah, we hadn't got around to a body count when you kind of dropped in.'

'And the crash site?'

Maclazowitz's mind was racing. It was obvious why they were here, but if they walked into the VC without warning, his own chances of getting out of this godforsaken country would be diminished. The VC were weakened considerably, though, as long as they hadn't received re-inforcements. The whole picture was blurred now. He wished Stuart was there.

'There's a secure area about ten clicks to the south-west. Pan African Corps forces aren't allowed into the zone, so I can't tell you what's in it, only that its guarded quite well.'

'Guarded by who?'

'Local army, I guess.'

'Sierra Laputu forces?' Dani tried to confirm.

'I guess.'

'Any armour?'

'No, just regular trucks and small transports . . . infantry.'

Dani rattled more Hebrew down the radio. There was a grouping of replies and minor conversations from more than one voice, then, all but the guarding force for the aircraft and the runway, pulled away at medium speed in formation.

'Where are we going?' Maclazowitz asked, knowing the answer.

'To your secure zone, Major Chet.'

'Forgive me for asking, but why?'

'I forgive you,' Dani answered, giving Maclazowitz a wicked smile that was almost childlike.

'My weapon is in the Land Rover.'

'Maclazowitz?' Dani questioned, ignoring his comment. 'Sounds like a Jewish name. Are you Jewish, Major Chet?'

'On my mother's side,' he answered.

'Then for your mother you can borrow this.' From out of the front shelf of the Jeep, Dani Cohen pulled out a webbing pistol belt and holster and dropped it into Maclazowitz's lap. He picked it up, undid the flap and took out a large automatic pistol.

'Jesus!' he exclaimed; slipping the 0.50 calibre Desert Eagle semi-automatic pistol back into its holster. 'That's one big *mother.*'

'There are two spare clips on the belt,' Dani added.

'*They're in,*' Yani Bar-David said to Sharon, as he put down the telephone.

'They're late,' Sharon answered, without looking up.

'Unforeseen technical delays with one of the aircraft and bad weather en route.'

'It will be dark by now?'

'They landed in the last of the daylight, at dusk,' Yani confirmed. 'The timing has actually worked to our advantage.'

'They've picked up a possible guide, from the remnants of a Pan-African Peace Corps unit which may have unwittingly got mixed up in the firefight at the crash site. He wasn't able to give any indication of possible opposition or their strength,' he continued, 'due to some sort of protocol that decrees that PAC forces are not allowed into this particular secure zone.'

'Do we know if any of that is registered with the UN? The PAC operate with a loose mandate from them, even though no non-African states are participating.'

'The UN involvement is purely humanitarian, I believe.'

'Yeah, money for food, turned into weapons and tribal genocide.' Sharon sighed. 'The universal formula . . . Carry on.'

'We should be approaching the crash site and this secure zone at any time now. There is a much heavier level of tree cover in that particular area, but it posses no hindrance to our tracked and untracked vehicles. The size of our force and its technical capability will outstrip anything we expect to find in the area.'

'Let's go down to the operations room. I need to stretch my legs, and the coffee has gone stale.'

Yani Bar-David picked up his file from the desk and opened the door for his superior. Sharon took off his glasses, folded them with care and slipped them into his shirt pocket.

'What news on Miriam?' he asked.

'She's still in Scotland, but with the strong possibility that Stuart and his group are all dead, I suppose there's no sense in keeping her there,' Yani offered.

'Is she at risk there?'

'Minimal, if any at all.'

'I mean from the Americans.'

'So do I, sir,' Yani answered, with a slight smile.

'Then leave her there. It will only be a matter of hours until this whole thing is over, for us. The politicians will be chopping and hacking at it for years.'

The operations room was in the basement. In reality it was a bunker designed to take a nuclear blast, crammed with communications equipment and intelligence archives. It also had the best coffee machine in the building, which dispensed regular cappuccino and expresso of an almost acceptable quality. Attention increased as Sharon walked into the room and made his way immediately to the machine. He demanded a large expresso from it, but the section was empty.

'Is it *impossible* to get a decent cup of coffee in this place?' he called out loudly, throwing his hands in the air.

An olive-skinned, dark-haired girl in uniform got up from her seat and approached him.

'May I get you something, sir?'

'I want a large, strong expresso. I don't mind getting it myself. It's just that I get angry when the last person to use the machine doesn't refill the dammed thing.'

'Would you like sugar in it,' she soothed.

'Yes, sugar . . . two please, thank you.' He sat down at the operations table with a thump. 'What's new then. How are we doing?'

A middle-aged colonel with a headset on lifted his hand as if to indicate that he was listening to something.

'Is he on the direct link?' Sharon asked quietly.

'Yes,' Yani answered back. 'We can monitor all communications and cut in if we wish to.'

The colonel pushed one of his earpieces back off his ear, so that he could listen to both the action and the conversation within the room. 'They encountered resistance the moment they approached the site. Mostly small arms, but there was an attempt to rocket one of the armoured troop carriers. It failed.'

'And now?' Sharon asked quietly.

'Still going on. It sounds as though they are just mopping up, though.'

'Anyone been into the plane?'

'Dani's in there now, but I haven't heard anything. D'you want me to call?'

'No. If they're still engaged, let's keep out of their hair for a little while longer ... Ah, the coffee, and some sticky cakes! What are you trying to do, my dear, get me shot by my wife?'

The girl smiled at him and resumed her place at her communications consul. She had a master's degree in electronics and was a career officer – as all the operations room staff were.

'That's Dani now. D'you want to cut in?' the colonel asked. Sharon nodded.

'Dani, this is Sharon. Do we have it?'

'We have it ... Just as described.'

'Both items?' Sharon pushed.

'Both items!'

'Any casualties?'

'Three wounded, no dead. We're all coming home.'

There was a small cheer in the operations room.

'When?' Sharon asked in a clipped voice, not wasting airtime.

'ETA in the air is one hour, the cherry-picker is lifting the cargo out of a new hole in the side of the aircraft now.'

'Anything we can do?'

'Everything is running smoothly. Oh, there is just one thing for you. The area was guarded by an outfit from the Far East, dressed like Viet Cong!'

Sharon was silent.

'Eagle Base, come back. Did you receive?'

'All received and understood, Dani,' Sharon answered. 'Come home quickly and safely. Out.' He passed the headset back to the colonel, who had just demolished one of the sticky cakes.

'You'll die of a heart attack, you know,' Sharon said with mock concern to the old friend who had worked in the operations room for so many years he was part of the furniture. 'Let me know if anything goes wrong, Eli.'

The colonel nodded, putting the headset back on and stealing another cake.

'So, Yani, are the arrangements for the cargo transfer in South Africa in order?'

'No problem. The nose of the 747 will be open on arrival

240

and the cherry-picker hydraulic lift will do two quick runs from the C-130, over a distance of less than seventy metres. The cover story remains good.'

'Evidence for the UN?'

'Of a chemical warfare plant that now is destroyed.'

'And what of our man Mony, whom we have gone to rescue?'

'Found and rescued at the plant before its destruction.'

Sharon rose slowly, had a last sip of his coffee and started to walk towards the door. 'You know, it will never cease to amaze me what absolute humbug the governments of the world churn out to the people and the media – and have it accepted. It is almost as if there are two worlds. The *real* one, that we read of in the newspapers and see on the news networks and the *actual* one, which operates within a world cartel of governments' self-interest and the big-business lobby. It's a bit like being part of a large crime syndicate: one face legitimate and the other as corrupt as any Mafia godfather's. Sometimes, even I wonder who are the good guys and who are the bad.'

'We're the good guys,' Yani answered, pushing the button for the lift doors to remain open until Sharon reached them.

'Of course we are, Yani; of course we are. Oh yes, thanks for the coffee,' he called over his shoulder. The girl smiled back at him.

When they got back to Sharon's office, Yani noticed that new filter coffee had been made up in a glass jug on his low bookcase. Sharon poured a cup automatically into a clay mug that one of his grandchildren had made for him the previous year.

'You know, I use this cup because there's a flaw in it. If I fill it more than half full, it causes a small leak down the side and a mess on the desk. In this way, I can cut down my coffee intake and help to keep my doctor happy.'

'D'you have a limit?'

'Yes – zero.'

'No coffee at all?' Yani asked in surprise, especially as he knew the amount of coffee Sharon took.

'No coffee, no whisky, no sticky cakes. You know, there was the story about the two guys who couldn't eat pork or drink alcohol because of their religion. One day, a Christian friend of theirs caught one of them drinking Scotch and eating a bacon sandwich and the other just drinking. He said to the friend who was just drinking, "I see that *you* drink, and your friend drinks and also eats pork. Is that because you're more religious than he is?" The young man looked up at his Christian friend and said, "More religious? No, no, I just don't like pork." So you see, Yani, I am an old man. I have had a life of accomplishments and seen dreams come true. I happen to like coffee, whisky and, once in a while, a sticky cake. Now, what else can we do from this end?'

'I was wondering if there is anything else we can use Miriam for, before we bring her home.'

'I don't think so, Yani. She has done all that has been asked of her. The role of a sleeping agent is the hardest of all. Did you know that over fifty per cent of them never reactivate? They get so involved with their new life that it becomes their real life and they don't want to leave it. The Russians were absolutely un-bending when this happened to one of their agents. They would risk lots of other operatives just to assassinate the traitor to their cause and set an example. The West usually just let them go, expecting a high wastage factor.'

'And us? What do we do?' Yani asked.

'Oh, just the same as usual. We do what I say.'

'Yes, sir.'

'Extend Miriam's exile for a further forty-eight hours. That business about the Chinese or Vietnamese was quite unexpected. I want you to look into that urgently and get what intelligence you can. Also, if those stragglers they picked up from the PAC are white training officers, we might be able to gain some intelligence on what has happened to Stuart. They're all mercenaries of one kind or another, and that little club is a tight one.'

'Where are we?' Steve Rider asked, as he came out of the anaesthetic.

'On a freedom bird,' Chet Maclazowitz said quietly into his ear.

'On one of the Hercs?' Rider asked, his memory clicking back into gear as the chemicals dispersed in his body.

'Right on,' Maclazowitz smiled, 'and if I'm not mistaken, looking at the hue before the rising sun, we're headed south.'

'South Africa?'

'Looks like it. We could be on a plane to the UK in no time.'

'But weren't they Israelis?'

'That's right. I haven't got a handle on that situation at all yet, but they're being real nice and the doctor has done a fantastic job on your leg. The back quarter of this plane is a field hospital that has even got a goddamned X-ray machine.'

'Were they after the same thing as us?'

'Well, Steve, they took two pieces of junk from the crashed Herc, after giving it a quick sweep with one of those gamma ray detector things – you know, the click-click machines?'

'Yeah.'

'So I guess they were after the same thing. I'll tell you what, though – it would have been a complete waste of time. They had to use a small hydraulic mobile crane to get the stuff out. It's all in the lead Herc. He's just ahead and to our right. I saw him in the morning sky.'

'Has our story stood up?'

'So far. They even apologised for bringing us along. They said it was due to operational security and that we would be released as soon as possible.'

'So you haven't actually been told, or heard, that the destination is South Africa. You're just guessing?'

'Well yes, but there's a lot of water underneath us and it's been there for most of the journey so far.'

'So, your friend is awake,' a voice chipped in from behind them. A middle-aged man with a full head of short grey hair stood just behind and to Maclazowitz's left. It was the doctor who had cut, cleaned and sewn up Rider's leg.

'You were lucky, young man,' he said in a mid-European accent. 'Your friend's tending and our timely arrival have probably saved your leg from amputation.'

'Probably?' Rider queried urgently.

'Almost certainly,' the doctor corrected. 'Two or three days' rest and you will be walking about on crutches or sticks. In a month it will be all a bad dream.'

'Thanks, ' Rider smiled.

'Thank you friend. The manner in which he recognised that the wound had to be closed and then went about it was textbook.'

'He's a trained paramedic,' Rider confirmed.

'Yes, I know, he told me.'

'I'll bet he did.' Rider laughed, and they all joined in.

'It was also handy that you had your blood group and name on a medical band around you ankle,' the doctor added. 'Well, I've got a few more minor ailments to check on, so I'll see you later.'

The doctor squeezed past and made his way to the next bed, which was locked against the bulkhead a few metres down the aircraft, past a large item strapped in under a tarpaulin. Maclazowitz and Rider stared at each other. They had completely forgotten the ankle bands that all the group had carried in case of emergency treatment. On these kind of operations you usually only have to worry about treatment if you fall into friendly hands. For Rider it had worked, but now they knew who he was, and Chet had no inclination to upset anyone on this journey.

'Just play it by ear,' Maclazowitz said.

'Get me a drink, will you, big fella. My tongue could be used to sharpen one of Shag Skinner's knives.' He remembered as soon as he'd said it. 'Sorry, I didn't think.'

'Neither did he, a lot,' Maclazowitz answered, turning away to find some water.

'He was a moaning old faggot, anyway. He didn't make it – we did.'

14

Risks and Rewards

'I agree with you, Cassa.' Nelson nodded. 'Mokomo, his factions or even someone else is attempting to destabilise us, before we have even got going. Mokomo was to be expected. He has many followers in the country; just about everyone who was not poor and starving.'

'These people are mostly based in Freeman. We could round them all up for questioning,' Cassa answered.

'Yes, we could do that, but the eyes of the world are on us and we will be judged on our actions *now* for years to come. Also, many of these Mokomo supporters are exactly the people we have to convince that life under our government will enhance their prospects as well as those of the rest of the people.'

'But it must be Mokomo, who else would have any interest in the country?'

'This I do not know, but let us examine what we do know. In our hands we have two mercenaries. One of these men is famous not only in Africa, where I believe there are several death sentences passed upon him in his absence, but all over the world. At this time we have not questioned them, so we do not know why they are here, or what excuse they will give for their being here.'

'They must have been sent by that tyrant Mokomo,' Cassa insisted.

'Maybe, maybe, but they arrived very quickly. Mercenary

operations take a long time to put together, they will have had no problem with finance, but they needed equipment, transport, documents . . . the right men for the job. For example, this other man is a pilot. He can fly just about anything that can get into the air, and we believe that at one time it is possible that he had a very good job as the personal pilot to President Marcos of the Philippines. These are *special* men. They do not contract second rate jobs. They are expensive and skilled.'

'They can't be all that good,' Cassa mocked. 'We caught them easily.'

'Well, we certainly have them in custody, but I believe it was a coming together with a PAC patrol that caught them out, after we put out your alert . . . apparently from this mysterious contact of yours, whom you never actually met, but who now appears to be involved in some way in the murder of Samir Jamayal. Don't you find that there are too many coincidences happening?'

'I understand what you say, Major, but why would this man Capricki–'

'I think it is Italian, pronounced Ca-pree-chi,' Nelson corrected.

'So, why would this *Cappricci* make contact and tell a story about insurgents entering the country to mount a Mokomo counter-coup and then murder, or be involved in the murder of one of Mokomo's old allies . . . particularly when it appears that his story has some foundation?'

'What of this other man, Marker? What do you make of him?' Nelson asked.

'We have expected Mokomo to do something, from the moment we saw him disappearing over the water in his helicopter. The officers at the airport have been given strict instructions to detain and question anyone, particularly non-blacks, who are entering the country for the first time. The man was carrying maps with coloured circles printed around the defence deployments we placed on the coast within the first forty-eight hours of the coup. They were right to arrest him.'

'But not to beat him!' Nelson rasped unforgivingly.

246

'These are difficult times, we –'

'Enough.' Nelson stopped him in mid-sentence. 'What do we do with him now?'

'Kimo has spoken with him and still wants to keep him here. Officially he is in the hands of the police, not the army.'

'We are the law, until a government is elected,' Nelson cut in. 'Has this Marker changed his story?'

'No, he remains firm that he was here just to join a ship, and that the charts were for the vessel. He says that you can buy these charts in any marine shop in the UK and that many vessels on the world's oceans will have similar charts.'

'Have you checked this?'

'No, but Kimo has. The markings around our new defence points are actually markings to show a ship where coastal radio beacons are, for their navigation purposes.'

'So, do you think he is telling the truth?'

'I don't know. I'm unsure,' Cassa admitted.

'Where is the ship he is supposed to have been meeting?'

'It remains in the harbour, arrested until investigations are complete.'

Nelson sighed. 'So we have many grains of rice in the bowl . . . OK, we have much work to do. The one thing that is for certain is that when you boil a bowl of rice too much, the grains stick together. I have a feeling that if we start to boil this bowl of rice we will find that they were all together in the first place. Make arrangements for us to go to Bpungi, together with Kimo and the Chief of Police, tomorrow at dawn.'

'Yes, sir!' Cassa replied, saluting as Nelson got out of his chair and left the room. Once Nelson was well gone, Cassa closed the door and picked up the telephone. Soon he heard Kimo's refined voice at the other end.

'*Mr President* has called for us,' Cassa said, in a mocking tone down the telephone.

'I suggest you get hold of one of yesterday's Western newspapers, before you say anything else on the telephone, you idiot. Any one will do, but *The Times* seems to carry the best account.'

'Of what?'

'Well, this issue came in on today's KLM flight, so it is actually today's. I knew it was a mistake to call in all our high commissioners immediately the coup was confirmed – our outside intelligence is useless without them,' Kimo said out loud, to himself rather than Cassa.

'Kimo, of what?'

'Get a newspaper, you stupid idiot! Everyone on the coastal belt will be on the telephone before you can bat an eyelid.'

Kimo slammed the telephone down and Cassa was left talking to a slight crackle. He spun round in the chair and shouted for his attendant corporal to go and collect every newspaper he could get his hands on. Then he remembered the CNN link in the presidential suit upstairs. It didn't always work, because they didn't have comprehensive satellite coverage, so he hoped he would be lucky.

This time he was, the face of a blonde female newscaster with strangely staring eyes, came into view. She was rambling on about the financial markets, which were of no interest to Cassa, but her eyes held a strange fascination for him. He couldn't quite work out what was strange about them, until he realised he could see the *whole* of her pupils, with the white bits round the edges. In most people, the eyelids covered a small section of the Iris, softening the staring look. The attractive lady on the screen was most unusual.

Suddenly an insert picture of ex-President Mokomo appeared just over her left shoulder and Cassa turned the sound level higher.

'. . . in exile in West Guinea, strongly denied that Sierra Laputu had ever had anything to do with the manufacture or selling of materials which could be used in chemical weapons of mass destruction. There were no links between him, the country and any Middle East state. He further said that this story was probably being put around by the, as he put it, *criminal* rebel government currently in temporary power, to attempt to discredit him and his twenty years service to the country . . .'

The insert then changed to a picture of the President of The United States at a press briefing in the White House regarding the situation in the Middle East. A reporter chipped in and asked him for a comment on the reports from Sierra Laputu. He replied that he was having his security advisers look into the reports and would not like to comment at this time until there had been a full investigation as to the truth of the allegations about Sierra Laputu was available. He believed that this was something that should come under the umbrella of the United Nations.

The staring lady then went on to a sports item. Cassa switched the TV off.

'Castle Stuart,' Urquart answered. 'Oh, yes, sir, the young lady has just returned from walking the dog. I'll call her immediately.' He put the call on hold and rang the extension to Michelle Christie's room.

'Hallo,'

'Ahm, it's Admiral Hess on the line for you, miss.'

'Oh, thanks, Silas.' There was a pause, a click and then she immediately recognised the Admiral's voice.

'Michelle?'

'Yes, sir.'

'Well, I just want you to know that you've done a fantastic job. The story is all over every part of the media. The new SL government is up in arms. Mokomo is denying it so heavily that people are beginning to believe he actually did it. Even the President has been able to get a timely sound bite out of it, with a very concerned look on his face.'

'Yes, I saw the papers. We can only get Scottish and English papers up here, but even the local paper carried an inch on it, mixed up within the births, deaths and the Inverness Rotary Club's cheese and wine night.'

'Have you heard from Stuart?'

'Nothing.'

'Then he must have bought it. Snoopy in the sky has shown lots of happenings around the zone of interest, including heavy vehicles. Stuart couldn't have coped with the volume.'

She was conscious that he was talking around the subject, because of the open line, but anyone who had the slightest

249

idea about the operation could have understood with ease what he meant.

'So, what do you want me to do now, sir.'

'You might as well make your way home, young lady. There's still going to be the need for someone to monitor the public relations side of this baby, until we're in the clear. It's Thursday now, why don't you walk the dog for a couple more days and I'll see you in my office first thing Monday morning.'

'Whatever you say, sir. But I think I would rather walk in a big city. The country's fine in small doses, but I'm a bright lights girl at heart.'

'Whatever you like. It's on the company, as long as you don't go crazy.'

'Thanks.'

'See you Monday.'

She held the phone to her ear for an extra couple of seconds, until she heard the tell tale click of Urquart carefully replacing his receiver. A few seconds later the sounds of the Labrador at her door heralded Urquart's polite knock.

'Come on in, Silas. I'm decent,' she called. The door opened and the man for all seasons, as Stuart described him, took two steps into the room. The dog came straight up to her, had a good smell at her dressing gown and then flopped heavily on the Persian rug at the foot of the bed.

'The Major has been written off before, you know,' Silas said, to her surprise.

'You've been eavesdropping, Silas,' she announced, with mock shock.

'Of course, miss. It's my job.'

'And a very good job you do as well,' she continued.

'Yes, miss. Thank you, miss. I know.'

Michelle put her head back and laughed out loud, as she continued to brush her hair.

'The Major, miss?'

'I really don't know. We thought that the first place he would get in touch with would be here. He hasn't, has he, Silas?' she asked, suddenly wondering if the old fox, the *widow* had outwitted her again in the cause of his master.

'Actually no, miss.'

'Well, thank God for small mercies. I would hate to think you'd been holding out on me.'

'He isn't due to, ahm, *yet*,' Urquart continued, with an almost sheepish grin.

The brushing went down from a brisk sweep to a slow crawl and Michelle slowly spun round on the vanity stool and looked Urquart square in the eyes.

'Excuse me?' she said, dropping the heavy brush onto the glass-covered dresser with a loud bang. *'He isn't due to?'*

'No, miss. He isn't due to make contact until midnight the day after tomorrow.'

'Keep going, Silas. Don't give up on me now!'

'Well, it's like this. We have a complicated contact schedule that we operate all year round, whether he is working or not. That way we keep in touch and I know if there's anything wrong that might warrant me calling someone for help.'

'Calling someone for help? Who for God's sake, the Lone Ranger or International Mercenary Rescue, perhaps?'

'Well, it would depend on the circumstances, miss, but there are a lot of influential people who owe the Major a great deal, confidentially speaking, of course.'

'I'll bet there are,' Michelle answered, as full realisation dawned on her for the first time. Stuart probably knew more damaging secrets about heads of state and big business than any other single man on the planet or close to it. That's why he lived in strange out-of-the-way places, continually moving around with just one single anchor point – Silas Urquart and Castle Stuart. Even then, if this haven was compromised, the complicated procedures that had grown up between these two men would tip him off and another set of arrangements would slot into place.

'And what do you have to do if he doesn't check in at the right time, this time?'

'Well, ah, could we cross that bridge when we get to it, so to speak, miss?'

'Silas! – she shouted in frustration, clutching her hair in her hands and appealing to the heavens for help.

251

'I'm sorry, miss, it's, ah, procedure.'

'Yes, Silas, it would be! And once more, Major Thomas Stuart has messed up my plans for a few days off in the big city. Jesus H Christ!'

'Tell me, miss – it's always been a mystery to me – what does the *H* stand for? I've always thought it an amusing turn of phrase bu—'

'Get out, Silas, before I lose my temper.'

'Certainly, miss. Is there anything I can get you?'

'Well, on second thoughts there is. Get me a bottle of the master's best brandy and a glass that sings a song when you flick its edge. I'm going to go to bed with it, watch an old weepy on the box and dream of the sun and the surf.'

'An admirable pastime, miss. Perhaps I could bring you a little supper, later on?'

'Silas, you're a rogue and a rascal and probably a dirty old man, but a little supper later on sounds fine to me.' She gave him a huge smile, which he returned.

'May I confide in you, Mr Marker,' Kimo offered quietly, the next day. 'We do have a small difficulty which may delay your release.' It was more a statement than a question, so Marker didn't answer, he just waited for him to continue. 'You see, there has been a report that a group of terrorist mercenaries have been landed in various parts of the country to assist in the build up of a counter-coup. Some of my colleagues think that you may have something to do with this group and they are currently blocking your case until further investigations have been completed.'

'I thought that my story had been checked out and verified?' Marker asked.

'Well yes, it has, in so far as it goes, but my colleagues have made the point that your story could actually be true, whilst also part of the conspiracy in some way. It is this we have to be satisfied with. Personally, I firmly believe that you're innocent and that your detention is an unfortunate mistake, which in these difficult times is, perhaps, understandable.'

252

'Well, I'm glad someone believes me. Is there anything else I can do to convince your people?'

Kimo smiled and moved position in his chair. 'I don't know, Mr Marker. It would help if we could verify, externally, that your visit here is one of only legitimate business. Is there any way that we can do that?'

'No more than you've already done,' Marker answered.

'That's a pity. Tell me, in your business, have you ever been approached by mercenary groups, or similar organisations, to ship arms and equipment?'

'Oh yes,' Marker confirmed quickly, so as to show instant honesty. 'Just about every time there is a war on somewhere.'

'In that case you must be a busy man.' Kimo smiled. 'The world being what it is today.'

'It's an up and down market. There are lots of people in it.'

'Tell me, have you ever heard of a man called Thomas Stuart?'

The hairs on the back of Marker's neck bristled and he felt his heartbeat quicken. They must know, he thought, or perhaps they were just fishing? He decided, in a split second to give them an answer they were not expecting.

'Trapper Stuart? Oh, yes, he's been an acquaintance of mine for years. In fact, I suppose you could say that I'm the closest thing to a friend that he's got, along with a few others. He doesn't have friends in the normal sense of the word.'

'He hasn't approached you recently?' Kimo asked, visibly put off his stride.

'Recently? No. The last time I spoke to him was at least six, or even nine months ago. He was in South Africa and wanted to know if I knew anyone who would like to buy some diamonds at a cut-price rate. I didn't, so that was that.'

'Unusual friendship,' Kimo observed.

'I suppose it is, but that's what it's like. It doesn't matter if we've spoken yesterday or two years ago, it's always as though it was just yesterday.'

'He is two doors down from you, under arrest!'

Kimo's statement was like a thunderbolt. Marker felt as though he'd been played with like a salmon on a fly rod,

253

worked, teased and then landed at the most opportune moment. The elegant man opposite him just stared into his eyes, without blinking.

'You seem shocked, Mr Marker?'

'Surprised, not shocked.'

'Then I will leave you to consider your surprise, for the time being. We can continue our chat a little later.' He got up to leave the room and then turned as though he'd forgotten something. 'I meant to ask, how is the food now . . . better?'

'The food? Oh yes, thanks. Much better.'

'I'm so pleased.'

Kimo smiied and left the room, but the door wasn't locked. A few seconds later Daniel came in and locked the door behind him.

'They say that today you must have your lunch in your room. You can have some exercise later.'

'Never mind that. What information d'you have for me?'

'Much has been happening. There are four of you now. I have their names, but you must not write them down or I may get into big trouble.'

'No problem, go on.'

'There is an American called by a name that is spelt C-a-p-p-r-i-c-c-i. He pronounces it *Capreechy* and is in the room next to you. Next to him is a very famous mercenary soldier that everyone is talking about, called Stuart, and next to him is one of his men called Sandys. The soldiers have been captured after a great battle which was won by the PRC, to repel a counter coup by the forces of Mokomo. Many were killed on both sides, but our army was victorious.'

'And the American?'

'He is suspected of having something to do with the murder of one of our prominent citizens.'

'Then why is he here, rather than Freeman?'

'This I don't know,' Daniel apologised.

'Well, you're going to have to do better than that, Daniel. Our deal was to do with the American. It's all very interesting to learn about how your war, or whatever it is, is going, but that's not what I asked you to find out.'

254

'I will be able to find out more, because I am detailed to represent the police here for all the prisoners that are being held by the army.'

'That's good then, Daniel. It looks as though I am going to be able to help you and your family, after all.'

'Thank you, thank you. I will tell the boy to bring up your food.'

Stuart *here*, Marker puzzled, when Daniel had left the room. He wondered what had gone wrong. The very fact that Stuart had called him in indicated that he'd suspected some kind of unplanned danger. John Sandys, whom Marker also knew, was here as well. Had everyone else been killed, or had the others been sent to another prison or detention centre? One thing was for sure, he had to continue to disassociate himself from Stuart and the operation, no matter what the others said. He was glad that he'd admitted he knew Stuart, because no matter what Stuart and Sandys said, or were made to say, Marker's version of events would always hold the possibility of being a true version. All he had to do was to stick to his story, if he changed it he was dead . . . literally.

'So, Major Stuart,' Kimo continued, 'you were sent here by the Americans to retrieve a special weapon that was lost in a crashed aircraft. Why didn't the Americans just pick up the phone and ask for it back?'

'They did,' Stuart answered. 'Mokomo said sure, if you dash me several million into my personal account in Switzerland.'

'Cheap at the price, I would have thought?'

'Probably, but there was no guarantee that they would get the weapon once they'd paid. The potential for years of blackmail was enormous. Then the coup happened and the ensuing confusion opened a gateway to pop in and get it, with nobody the wiser.'

'It all sounds a little fantastic to me,' Kimo announced. 'Is it not the case that actually you and your group were part of, if not in fact leading, Mokomo's counter-coup operations, and it was only when you came up against an unexpected superior force of the PAC that your plans were thwarted?'

'The PAC?' Stuart laughed. 'Is that what they told you? Give me a break. You guys don't have a clue what's going on in your own country. You've got the Yanks sending us in, VC regulars parading around the place and PAC troops firing at anything that moves. That's without taking into consideration your neighbours who are still knocking at your door to the east. You're all fucked up!'

'Well, thank you for your observations, Major.'

'Listen, why don't we get this farce over with? Put me up against a wall and shoot me. That's what you're going to do anyway, isn't it?'

'No, actually. But we have had representations from other countries with whom we are friendly who would very much like the opportunity to question you and then shoot you, or throw you into some stinking hole for the rest of your life.' Kimo smiled. 'What I am going to do now is to have a word with your colleague. We have, by the way, sent a helicopter to inspect the region you were picked up from for the signs of your oriental attackers.'

As the door locked once more, Stuart moved from the chair and lay down on the bed. He felt his only hope was to try to gain time by throwing as much unexpected information at them as possible. This was a young and new government. They would check and double-check everything, because *their* lives were also on the line. If Mokomo ever got back, they were dead. John Sandys would tell a similar story, and they wouldn't know what to do, or believe, because the Yanks would deny everything, as usual.

The lock in the door turned again. 'I thought you might like to read a western newspaper,' Kimo offered, as he dropped a large batch of papers onto the table that passed as a desk.

'Thanks, I'll start to worry when you offer me a hearty break-fast,' Stuart laughed.

'One of those is available every day, Major. You just have to ask.' He turned to leave.

'Kimo, does the embassy know we're here?'

'I believe procedures have been followed.'

'When do we get access then?'

'You will be informed. Read the papers,' Kimo emphasised. 'I'm sure you will find them interesting.'

He turned and left the room. His meaning was not lost on Stuart, who waited until the door was closed and locked before he jumped up to see what Kimo had been getting at. It didn't take long for the full impact of the claims and counter-claims to sink in. The Americans were off the hook no matter what happened, what was said or how long the diplomatic and public wrangling went on. He was now a *threat* to them, not an *ally* – if ever he'd been one. The confusion in the minds of his jailers would still last for several days and he would have to encourage it. In reality, however, he only had one option left. He had to escape, or die trying.

Nelson, Cassa and Kimo sat at one of the tables on the Bpungi Hotel terrace. They had eaten well and Cassa and Kimo had both had a Star beer with their meal. Nelson had stuck to spring water, but had eaten enough chicken and vegetables for two men.

'So, basically, gentlemen, everything that the infamous Major Stuart has told us is the truth?' Nelson asked, between mouthfuls.

'As much as we can check, anyway,' Kimo answered. 'Cassa here is extremely worried about what he found at this crash site, though. Either Stuart hasn't told us everything or he doesn't know everything.'

Nelson reached for some fruit. 'Explain,' he instructed.

'There has been a pitched battle at this place, on our soil, and we haven't had anything to do with it. There were bodies everywhere, mostly Chinese or Vietnamese, as Stuart claimed. Two or three whites. On top of this, there has been a lot of heavy vehicle activity around the site. Something has been taken from the plane, which is years old, from a newly blown hole in the side.'

'Then let us find all these vehicles. Send up all the available air force to search,' Nelson ordered. He missed the look that passed between Cassa and Kimo.

'We wouldn't find anything, ah, sir,' Cassa replied quickly.

257

'Why? Have we no planes? Have we no helicopters?' Nelson asked expansively, waving his hands in the air.

'Yes we do, sir . . . but so did they.'

'This *they*, have planes as well. How do you know this, Cassa?'

'The heavy vehicle tracks led us to an area a few miles away, where it was obvious that an aircraft had landed and taken off. A big aircraft.'

'It must have been our neighbouring scum,' Nelson stated. 'They have a greater air force than we have, but the border war is an infantry war. Why should they penetrate so far and risk losing their airborne assets?'

'This is possible,' Kimo soothed, 'but we have absolutely no idea why there should be *oriental* forces on our soil.'

'Mercenaries!' Nelson confirmed to himself.

'This again is possible, but the question *why* still isn't answered. Mr. President, we have a significant and dangerous situation going on in our territory. It had to have been mounted by another country. Something that somebody wanted very badly has been taken from us. Something that has been here for a long time.' Kimo added.

Nelson looked puzzled. 'What are you getting at?' he asked again.

'If the crash happened a long time ago, Mokomo probably knew about it. It looks to me as though he has paid a third party, maybe even West Guinea, to collect this valuable item at the earliest possible time after he departed.'

'You mean that these reports about a counter-coup could just be a cover to allow him time to come and get his prize – this old weapon that Stuart talks about?'

'I think the story about the weapon is rubbish, but certainly it's something of great value. The coup rumours could actually have been started by someone who didn't want *Mokomo* to get it.'

'You mean, to put us on alert and foil any operation Mokomo might mount to extract this so-called prize?' Nelson said proudly. The mantle of President was fitting him well, he thought, as he reached for the last bread roll in the basket in front of him.

'There are too many ifs and buts,' Cassa cut in. 'It doesn't matter anyway, because whatever it was, it's gone now.'

'This is a very complicated situation,' Nelson pronounced, stating what was clearly the obvious. 'Which way shall we proceed? This business about a chemical weapons plant is taking up a lot of my time.'

'It has to be connected,' Kimo said, lines of frustration lining his forehead. He felt he had all the pieces of a jigsaw in his hands, but couldn't put them together to make a full picture. The men upstairs were the key, he was sure. He would have to put more pressure on them, much more ... 'If we don't find out what is, or has been happening, this administration and the future of the PRC could easily be at considerable risk. We have to use more severe methods on our guests.'

'I'm not in favour of torture. I'm a man of faith,' Nelson replied.

'Then your reign as President isn't going to last very long,' Kimo spat. 'Listen, two minutes ago you were a major in the bush. Fate has dealt you a card, but the rest of the hand is being dealt by others. Information is security, just in the same way as a gun is, but usually it's more important. We have to get more information from these men. They are murderers, liars and here illegally. No one is going to bat an eyelid if they disappear off the face of the earth. Stuart is even expecting it.'

Nelson looked shocked. No one had spoken to him in that tone for some time. He looked back and forth from Kimo to Cassa and then back again.

'Very well, gentlemen. Do what you have to. Get your information, but I want no association with your methods. I'm going back to Freeman now. If you want a ride you had better be ready in five minutes.' With that, Nelson got up and left the terrace. Kimo and Cassa stayed at the table in silence, until he was out of earshot.

'Believe me, Cassa, that man will turn into another Mokomo, given half a chance.'

'The title has gone to his head, but he has no real power without the council on which both you and I sit,' Cassa scoffed. 'Do you really believe we could be at risk?'

'Without a doubt. I just don't know from whom. It's as though we were a tool of some greater purpose. If I could just find out what it is, I might be able to turn it to our advantage. You go back to Freeman with the ever popular Nelson and I will return with the prisoners. Let's see what the Victoria Barracks can prise from them.'

The two men smiled at each other, but neither knew why, it was just a natural reaction. Cassa collected his entourage and followed Nelson to the airport. The people on the way had recognised Nelson and waved enthusiastically. By the time Cassa passed, their enthusiasm was still high and he also got many waves and shouts of joy. If they only knew it had all been a crazy accident, he thought.

Daniel visited the four prisoners one by one, to tell them that they were going to Freeman in one hour, by the hovercraft. Cappricci thought he was going on his own, Marker wondered if he was going on his own and Stuart and Sandys expected that they would go together. All of them were surprised, to say the least, when they were all ushered by a milling bunch of soldiers into the corridor and down to the reception area. No one knew what the others had said and so there was an uncomfortable silence while they watched the comedy of Kimo having to check them out of the hotel and sign for their accounts.

It was Sandys who broke the silence. 'Still in one piece then, Trap?'

'Looks like it. Still, we were better off jawing by that stream, weren't we?'

'Yes, I suppose we were,' Sandys answered, searching Stuart's face for a meaning to the odd comment.

'Yeah, playing in the sand can get you in big trouble – you never know what's beneath the surface. There can be glass, and you can cut yourself. That right, Chris?' he said, suddenly turning to Marker.

'Howdy,' Marker said with a beaming smile.

'Howdy yourself,' Stuart smiled, purposely avoiding any eye contact with Cappricci. 'What the hell are you doing here?'

'Misunderstanding. And you?'

'Misinterpretation,' Stuart replied with an ironic smirk.

Kimo let them speak, without letting on he was interested in their conversation. He felt it had the structure of a stage-managed scene, but wasn't totally sure.

Cappricci, on the other hand, was completely sure. Stuart had been trying to tell Sandys something, but as yet he hadn't picked it up. A few other things were also clicking into place. Sandys' presence explained what had happened to Hartman, or what had happened after Hartman. This other man was a mystery, he wasn't part of the team, but Stuart clearly knew him very well. He remembered that Hess had warned him about Stuart's tentacles. Perhaps he was looking at one? He chose to remain silent.

'This way, gentlemen,' Kimo directed, and they were escorted out of the hotel to the waiting convoy of Landcruisers.

'Come on, John. Get your toothbrush. We don't want you leaving any more kit behind, do we?' Stuart called, like a Scout-master on a camping trip. Sandys knew Stuart was up to some-thing, but he couldn't grasp the association that Stuart was trying to get across to him.

The ex-KLM hovercraft had been laid on especially for the transfer of the prisoners and was waiting at the beach station for them when the small convoy arrived by the sea, its wing-like bow door open.

Everyone except the drivers got out of the vehicles. There were some rapid and loud exchanges between Kimo and a soldier who had his sergeant's stripes pinned on his uniform with a safety pin, and the four men were hustled into the machine. Besides Kimo, there were seven young soldiers, with each prisoner placed between two guards. Stuart was sat between Kimo and the sergeant, at the front of the cabin.

The resting goose roared into life, sending strong vibrations through its hull and fuselage. The ugly black skirts billowed into life, and she rose up to her operating height, spinning round to face the sea as she did so. The pilot increased the propeller revs and she launched onto a slightly skewed course towards the far coast of the huge estuary.

261

Stuart was staring at John Sandys without blinking. When he caught his eye. the deep granite hue in Stuart's face instantly rang warning bells in Sandys head and he became hyper attentive. Everyone else was looking around, not paying too much attention. Both of Stuart's tunic sleeves were rolled down and buttoned. Slowly and almost aimlessly, he unbuttoned the cuff of his right sleeve and began to roll it up. He made a point of making the folds tidy, in the normal military manner, and then changed his attention to the left cuff. In a flash, as soon as he'd flipped open the cuff button, the razor-sharp Tanto knife was in his hand and then, in the same movement, at Kimo's throat.

'Don't do anything that would damage your health, Kimo – and tell the rest of these goons to be sensible or you will bleed to death for them.'

'You will never get away with this,' Kimo spluttered out of his shock. 'There's nowhere for you to go.'

'Tell them,' Stuart urged, just nicking the skin on the underside of Kimo's Adam's apple, to stave off any knee-jerk reaction from the confused guards.

Kimo shouted a frightened instruction over the loud roar of the hovercraft's turbo prop. Stuart nodded to Sandys and he instantly disarmed the guard to his left; the soldier almost offered the weapon to him.

'And the rest of them, Kimo,' Stuart threatened, applying a fraction more pressure through the blade.

Another unintelligible order was coughed out by the terrified Secret Police Chief, and a clatter of falling AK47s quickly followed.

'OK fellas, take your pick. Johnny, go and relieve our pilot of his duties. This thing is half boat, half plane, so you should be able to handle it.'

'Piece of cake,' Sandys shouted back, and made his way up to the front of the machine to where the pilot, still blissfully unaware of the turn of events behind him, was enjoying the speed of his machine and his skilled control of it. When Sandys tapped his shoulder with the barrel of his AK, the pilot almost relieved himself where he sat.

'Slow down, Fangio.' Sandys smiled. 'It's time for a pit stop, and if you say one little word into that microphone, I'll cut your frigging tongue off. *Savvy?*'

The Indian pilot nodded and pulled the throttle back. The turbo's screaming fell back to an uncomfortable throb, which caused increased, uncoordinated vibration in the hull.

While Sandys was familiarising himself with the simple controls and instruments, Stuart and Cappricci were completing a search of the guards.

'Hell of way to run an army,' Cappricci called. 'They've only got one clip each for their AKs and those are the ones mounted.'

'I don't know what you're doing here, Cap,' Stuart called, 'or what the hell has been going on, but believe me, you've got some heavy explaining to do when and if we get clear. Until then you're under my orders.'

'Hey, OK! I can explai—'

'Later, I said. John, how are you doing?'

'Just getting this skirt thing sorted out, then I'm up and running – aren't I, Gunga Din?' he said to the pilot.

'Chris,' Stuart called to the dumbstruck Marker. 'See if you can get that central emergency exit door open, while we keep our eyes on matey here and his little band of Black Berets.'

Marker got up and pulled and twisted at the door's rusting red handle. Finally it moved and the door fell outwards.

'John?' Stuart called again.

'In the seat, Trapper,' Sandys shouted back.

'Send the pilot back here and try to keep her as slow as possible.'

This was easier said than done. The controls could be translated from aircraft and boat, but the skill of fine handling only came after much practice. The hovercraft started to dance into a slow, mild spin which Sandys had great difficulty in controlling; finally settling for a slow slide sideways across the water.

There were four 20-man containerised life-rafts on the hovercraft's roof. Stuart had Marker cut one loose and it fell into the sea with a heavy splash. When he pulled the release cord, which should have activated a compressed gas canister to open the container and blow up the rubber raft inside, nothing happened.

'Shit,' Marker cursed.

'Forget it! Get another one,' Stuart ordered, 'and you lot get ready for a swim.'

'Where can you go?' Kimo cut in. 'It is only a matter of time before you have to come ashore. You will be in custody before nightfall.'

Stuart took absolutely no notice of him. The second raft burst into life and he turned to the uniformed soldiers. 'Over the side!' Nobody moved. 'Over the fucking side, or die where you stand. It makes no difference to me!'

Almost together, the youths climbed out onto the fuselage and in ones and twos leaped into the warm sea. Ironically, Sandys' inability to control the hovercraft's slight sliding motion had created a calm lee for the swimmers, who instantly began thrashing front-crawl strokes towards the raft, which was receding in the distance at a moderate speed. The pilot jumped next. Stuart turned to Kimo. 'Out you go, you slimy faggot. What's the matter, can't Kimo swim?'

The African stared long and hard at Stuart. Hatred spewed from his very being. Slowly, in a dignified manner, he climbed out of the cabin and stood on the edge of the rubber skirt.

'I will be seeing you again, Major Stuart,' he called as he turned back to look at him.

'Only in hell, you bastard,' Stuart shouted back over the noise of the propeller, 'only in hell.' Then, almost as an after-thought, and to the complete shock of his companions, he released a short burst from his AK and blew Kimo off the fuselage and into the sparkling water. The African died while his body was in the air, a strange look of surprise on his face.

'Jesus,' Cappricci gasped, watching the red cloud of Kimo's blood spreading as they crabbed away from his body.

'Don't expect any help from *Him*, Cap,' Stuart said, with a stony face. 'Chris, pull that door shut.'

Marker obeyed, giving Cappricci a worried look. 'Seems like

we should introduce ourselves,' he said. 'Chris Marker, shipping.'

'Mark Cappricci, US Government.'

'What happens now?' Marker asked.

'Don't know. Suppose we hightail it out of here and hope we can reach somewhere that's friendly.'

Up in the cockpit, Sandys had asked Stuart the same question.

'We're free, that's the main thing. There was only a one-way ticket to a bullet if we reached Freeman.'

'No arguments with that, Trap but this contraption isn't the most inconspicuous of vehicles, and it's noisy as hell.'

'How much fuel have we got?'

'It's quite full, but I've no idea what the consumption is, or the range.'

'You mean you didn't ask the pilot?'

'Well, you didn't actually confide your pending little performance back there to anyone. It all happened so fast. What was the shooting all about?'

'Kimo couldn't swim, so I saved him from drowning.'

'That was good of you, but you still haven't answered my question. Where to?'

'Just head out to sea, keeping the coast in sight while we have a powwow and see if anyone's got any bright ideas. Chris might still have got a boat for us.'

'OK, out to sea it is.'

Sandys pushed the throttle lever to the end of its travel and the propeller returned to its high-pitched scream. Stuart dropped back down into the passenger cabin and the expectant faces it contained.

'It's no use looking at me like that. I haven't got any magic formulas. You guys will have to put your thinking caps on as well. Chris, what's the status on the boat you were trying to get hold of? As *you're* here I presume *it* is . . . somewhere.'

'It's alongside in Freeman. Because I was picked up at the airport it never got to its stand-off position, off Palm Island.'

'That's a pity. We could have transferred at sea and disappeared as planned.'

'As planned?' Cappricci asked.

'Look, we haven't got time to tell each other our life stories and what we're all doing here at the same time, in the same place. We can and will have a reckoning once we've worked out what to do. This bunch of toy soldiers must have some kind of navy, even if it's only a gunboat or two. We could have company sooner than we think.'

'Yeah,' Cappricci agreed. 'We must be overdue at our destination by now, and anyone with a pair of binoculars could have seen us stop in the middle of the bay.'

'Why don't we just run this baby along the coast towards Liberia or Ghana until the fuel is about to give out, park her on a beach and then get home from Monrovia or Takoradi somehow?' Marker suggested. 'Mokomo's in West Guinea, so we can't go that way.'

'It's an option, Chris,' Stuart agreed. 'Anyone else got any bright ideas?'

There was silence in the cabin, except for the ever present roar of the engine. The occupants looked at one another and then suddenly Cappricci said, 'The *Salamander!*'

'The what?' Stuart asked.

'The yacht, the *Salamander* – Falcone's yacht.'

'Falcone's yacht? What's it got to do with anything?' Stuart asked again.

'I don't know everything, but Falcone's hand has been in the background of everything that has been happening here, and he's here, on his yacht.'

'Cap,' Stuart sighed, 'I think we'd better forget what I said about not having time to explain the whys and wherefores of how we all got to be here. We're not going to understand a damned thing unless we do. You first, but make it quick.'

It took 20 minutes of rapid-fire explanations, questions and answers, before the small group started to have a partially clear idea of what their current situation was and who had caused it.

Marker was flabbergasted at the whole thing. Cappricci still wasn't quite sure whose side anyone was on. John Sandys really didn't care, and Stuart? Stuart just sat and weighed the options for survival. Other things and accounts could be settled another day and in another place.

'Can we get on board this *Salamander*, d'you think, Cap – or would the don suspect a rat the moment we approached?'

'I don't know. I suppose it depends on the story we tell him over the radio. There's only the crew and Mario on board. They'll have arms, without a doubt, and there's only four of us.'

'Three and a half, if you're thinking about fighting,' Marker cut in.

'Is she anchored?' Stuart asked.

'Slow steaming when I was on board,' Cappricci confirmed.

'Hang on a minute, let me have a word with Johnny. Is the accommodation ladder one of those heavy posh ones that sits at an angle down the side of the ship?'

'Yes, it's a permanent one that's lowered up and down by a hydraulic winch.'

Stuart went back up to the cockpit and the rest of them watched him and Sandys having an animated conversation.

'This Don Falcone character seems to be a bit of a megalomaniac,' Marker said to Cappricci.

'It's worse than that. You know, the more I think about it the more I think he's verging on being mentally unstable. It's all those years of corrupt power. Almost total power to do anything he wants, anywhere in the world.'

'Without being voted in as well,' Marker said, in a lighter mood.

'Oh, he was voted in all right, a very long time ago. He just hasn't had another election since.'

'Right, Cap,' Stuart called, jumping back down into the cabin. 'John reckons he could hold us alongside a vessel that was slow steaming and put us onboard if there was a ladder down. We'd probably do quite a bit of damage because he's no expert on this contraption, but it would be a one-way trip in any event.'

'What's the story going to be?'

'Silence,' Stuart answered.

'Silence?'

'Yep. If the main accommodation ladder is down the side of the ship, at say a forty-five degree angle, we can drive up, trap the ladder with the side of the rubber skirt and just step aboard. It's a risk, but I reckon we could actually be on board while the crew are still wondering what's going on. You could call them on the radio as we go alongside, just to add to the confusion. Ask for the don or Mario.'

'They'll hear us long before we get there.'

'Can't do anything about that. Well, what d'you all think? Chris?'

'Sounds feasible. People have been boarding ships without invitations for hundreds of years.'

'Cap?'

'Have you thought what you're going to do when you get on board?'

'No, I knew you would have that angle covered.'

'Oh, sure.'

'Well?'

'Better the devil you know than one you don't know. I never did fancy my chances in the bush. The Liberians and the Ghanaians would probably have been about as friendly as our recently departed friends, especially with you in tow. You've probably got a price on your head in every country on this coast.'

'Funny you should say that,' Stuart replied, turning to go back to John Sandys. 'Oh yes, where is this *Salamander?* Which direction for John?'

'I don't think he's going to need directions,' Chris Marker interrupted. 'Look!'

They all turned round and looked out of the cabin window. Just to port of the hovercraft's heading, Marker's trained eyes had picked up a familiar shape.

'Looks like a yacht to me. A big one,' he confirmed.

'That's her,' Cappricci added.

'Right,' Stuart said. 'Pick a weapon and collect spare clips from the others. It's time to go on a cruise.'

'Trapper!' Sandys shouted.

'We've seen it, John,' Stuart called back. 'Put your foot down, before we change our minds, back here.'

Sandys waved his hand and pointed the noisy machine towards the white hulled motor yacht on his horizon, about six miles away.

'Trap,' Marker said softly. 'If we get out of this, don't call me, I'll call you . . . OK?'

'Don't be a whiner.' Stuart laughed, the adrenaline pumping again. 'You're getting a free boat ride, aren't you?'

'Where to, though? That's the point.'

'Anywhere you like, Chris. Anywhere you like.' Stuart snapped the AK's action closed and mounted a full magazine. 'Right, when we get there, I'll go first. You come straight after me, Chris, followed by you, Cap. John reckons he can get back quick enough before she starts to veer off. If he can't, he'll wait until we have control and we can pick him up some other way. Any questions?' Nobody spoke. 'There's just one more thing. If you see so much as a kitchen knife, *waste* everything that moves. It's you or them remember, and Mario's a fucking psycho.'

'You know these people?' Marker asked.

'Nobody knows these people, Chris. They come from another planet. They just run this one.'

'Ten minutes,' Sandys shouted.

'OK, everybody clear?'

'As mud,' Marker answered.

'Then that'll have to do. Kick that door out again, Chris – and when I go, you follow me like glue. Cap, you go and announce yourself and ask to speak to Falcone. As soon as they acknowledge, get back down here ready for the off.'

Cappricci nodded and went forward. Marker struggled with the emergency door again. Stuart slung a spare AK over his back for Sandys and then stood in the doorway, enjoying the eddy of the wind-rush that blew into the cabin.

'You'll be OK, Chris,' he said quietly to Marker, ducking his head back into the hovercraft. 'Just stick by me and obey my orders, instantly.'

Marker smiled back at Stuart, thankful for the attempt at

269

reassurance and surprised as ever at the complexity of this man who could be a cold-blooded killer one minute and a father figure the next.

15

Winners and Losers

The President of The United States read the report in full himself, rather than have a briefing. Carlton Hess sat impassively in the chair opposite him, drinking fresh orange juice.

'So you think we're out of the woods on this one, Carlton?' the President asked, closing the file and dropping it on the table between them.

'One can never be one hundred per cent sure, but the woods are real thick and we've only left false trails.'

'Just as long as we don't find ourselves on a false one. What's the worst downside in your view?'

Hess ran his hands through the thick greying hair. The whole damned thing was a downside. The fact that Masada had been conceived at all was crazy . . . but those had been crazy times.

'I suppose the worst thing that could happen is that our files could be connected to the actual weapon.'

'I know that, Carlton. That's why you've gone to all this trouble to retrieve it, and put up a massive smokescreen – after you failed to retrieve it.'

'Yes, but as you know, the retrieval operation had several upsides, even if retrieval wasn't possible. It, in itself, was an available smokescreen. I had all the options covered,' Hess replied defensively.

'Who's got it then?' the President asked pointedly.

'Masada?'

'Yep!'

'We don't know.'

'We don't know?' the President repeated. 'Do we have a hint? I thought you said you had all the options covered?'

'Only in the context of the operation that *we* launched.' Hess was struggling. 'There has been a major incursion at the Masada site and an engagement far in excess of that resulting from an attack, or a defensive action by *our* assault party.'

'D'you think this Mokomo character could have mounted such an operation?'

'There have been confused reports of a counter-coup attempt, inland and on the coast, but we felt that these could be linked to our operations and the subject of local paranoia by the PRC. He easily has the funds available, but on balance we think it unlikely.'

'So?' the President asked again, eyebrows arching.

Hess wriggled in his seat, downing the orange juice in an unconscious reactive defence mechanism. 'We are continuing to examine all the options at this time.'

'That's a long-winded way of telling me that we don't have our eyes on the ball, Carlton.'

'The situation down there is very confused at this time and we don't have any means of clear verification, other than our own satellite sweeps. Everything else is second-hand, right now. If it was a fairly big outside operation, there are two clear possibilities. They either came in from a neighbouring country, or the operation was a massive one that came in from a long way away. The latter is highly unlikely and the former will get swallowed up in the misinformation campaign that is in progress. As I said, we're examining all the likely antagonists and their motives.'

'Well, keep doing that, Carlton. But I have a feeling that we aren't going to have to wait long to find out who picked up our piece of junk from down there. Someone is longing to tell us that they know the USA launched the AIDS scourge on the world. Yes, it was an accident, but that's irrelevant. What isn't irrelevant is how they knew what it was and where it was, and why suddenly now?'

'What are you suggesting, sir.'

272

'Come on, Carlton! This is an inside job and you know it. Someone with access to the Masada file and probably directly involved in the most recent operation has to be working for someone else.'

'I have every faith in my people, Mr President. I –'

'Baloney, Carlton! Reel 'em in and put 'em through the mill,' he added in an exaggerated Texan drawl. 'There can't be many . . . Who've we got?'

'Well, there's Mark Cappricci, Michelle Christie, the records supervisor, Admiral Grant, myself and anyone *you* have confided in, sir. No one else has information on the details of the operation's target or its background.'

'The team that developed the weapon are all still living, bar one, and I've spoken to them personally,' the President said into space. 'I would discount all the *old* protagonists. They could have done something years ago. No, I'm sure that it's someone who only learnt about the weapon and its devastating consequences within the last month. That means he, she or they are on your team. On that basis, I'd get Cappricci and Christie in this afternoon and grill 'em.'

'Ahm, that won't actually be possible, sir. They're both still out of the country at the moment – working on the operation,' he added hastily.

The President laughed sarcastically. 'Well, you won't have to worry who crapped on you. Just wait to see which one doesn't come back.'

'But, Mr President, I –'

'Reel 'em in, Carlton. Now! I want a report every morning until we've tied this down. Got it?'

'Yes, Mr President,' Hess deferred. He wanted to make some comment about who had actually authorised the original operation in the first place, but it didn't seem to be quite the time.

'Good, Carlton. Good.'

As Hess left the Oval Office, a million options raced through his mind. Cap? Michelle? Stuart? What about Stuart? Where was that man? Was he dead? He hoped so. What if he wasn't? He hadn't even mentioned that possibility to the President. Stuart knew about the weapon and about the radioactive

273

source, but he didn't know about the consequences . . . or did he? No, Hess thought, he must be dead.

'Go, go, go!' Stuart shouted, as he leapt out of the hovercraft's starboard side emergency exit, closely followed by Marker. As he did so, he looked up at the faces on the bridge wing, smiled and waved. One of them half-heartedly waved back, not knowing really why – it was just an automatic reaction.

The accommodation ladder was about a metre wide, made of high-quality aluminium, with three pristine white ropes running up the outboard side, underneath the handrail. There was a good-sized boat landing stage at the bottom and this smashed into the hovercraft's rubber skirt, trapping the whole ladder against the craft. The top of the skirt was about two metres above the landing and Stuart jumped easily down onto the fourth step.

'Come on, Chris, I've got you,' he shouted, as Marker hesitated for a second and then mirrored the short jump.

Just as Cappricci was about to follow, the hovercraft veered back off the ladder again. Not far, it was the energy reaction to the first contact by the rubber skirt, bouncing the smaller craft off the white hull of the *Salamander*. Cappricci didn't wait as she swung back in again and Sandys corrected the sheer from the cockpit; he leapt as soon as the skirt made firm contact with the ladder.

Only Sandys was left. He held her steady on course and then flipped in the automatic pilot. As soon as he saw she'd taken it, he clicked a five-degree course alteration into the system, towards the yacht, and ran for the door.

It took five seconds before the command to the controls was actioned by the autopilot, and by the time Sandys reached the edge of the skirt, the hovercraft had just started to push her bow into the *Salamander*'s port side. The accommodation ladder began to complain more loudly, and two of the handrail stanchions snapped off as he jumped. The bottom part of the landing stage and its handrails collpased, causing Sandys to fall down the steps and tumble onto the landing. As he struggled to his feet, he was thrown all over the place by the interaction

274

of the skirt and the super-yacht's side; the top of the skirt was now well above his head. Slowly he tried to climb the bucking accommodation ladder, but he kept slipping on the heaving steps as the hovercraft tried to turn into the yacht. On the *Salamander*'s bridge, the master saw what was happening and ordered the helmsman to come ten degrees to starboard. As the yacht obeyed the command, the stress on the action between the two vessels started to ease and the hovercraft appeared to parallel the larger vessel's course. The pressure of the skirt on the accommodation ladder eased and the bucking reduced. Sandys reacted like a racehorse and flung himself up the crumbling aluminium structure. As he reached halfway, the hovercraft crashed back into the yacht and the landing smashed completely, falling down into the sea and tearing a large hole in the skirt, allowing a massive uprush of air up the ladder. From the speed he arrived next to Stuart on the boat deck, it was as though Sandys had been blown up the ladder.

'Permission to come aboard?' he shouted over the screaming of the hovercraft's engine.

'Looks like we are anyway.' Stuart smiled, looking up at the bridge to see Cappricci's worried face straining over the bridge wing taft rail for a second.

The *Salamander* suddenly started to come further and further to starboard, her engines slowing to dead slow ahead, allowing the hovercraft to slide along her port side, leaving a nasty black rubber scar down the beautiful white finish of her shiny hull. As the smaller craft got halfway past the *Salamander*'s bow, she started to clear the yacht, struggling to follow Sandys' preset course. The scratching, blowing and the scraping receded until only the hovercraft's engine and propeller noise could be heard. An unarmed crewman appeared and indicated that Stuart, Sandys and Marker should follow Cappricci up the port side boat deck companionway to the bridge.

As Stuart got to the top of the bridge stairs and stepped out onto the bridge wing, he was met by Cappricci, who gave him a quick nod and a wink, to indicate that so far everything was OK. Behind him, Mario came out onto the bridge wing from the bridge itself.

'Thomas, Thomas, you always were one for spectacular entrances. Are you all right? And your friends?'

'We're OK, Mario. It was nice of you to come all this way, just to be around in case we needed picking up.'

'I've given them a quick background, Trapper,' Cappricci cut in quickly. 'We can go through it all in better detail once we all calm down. I for one could do with a drink.'

'Look, fellas,' Mario offered, 'the don was sleeping when you, ah, shall we say rang the door bell? I've put his mind at ease and he will get up and join us in a little while. Why don't you go below, get a shower, get cleaned up? We'll have some food and a drink, relax a little and then you can tell us all about your problems and we can see how we can help. Hey! What'ya say? Good?'

'Sounds good to me, Mario,' Stuart confirmed, acting up to the false hospitality.

'That's great, Tommy.' Mario smiled, knowing Stuart hated the abbreviation of his name. 'You guys just follow the steward here down to the guest accommodation and he'll show you to some cabins.'

The four men smiled, and followed the steward as instructed. As he left the bridge, Marker looked over his shoulder. The hovercraft was heeling badly to starboard, careering along all by itself, towards what must have been Palm Island.

When the steward had shown them to separate cabins, Stuart thanked him and followed Cappricci into his.

'What gives?' he asked.

'How well d'you know the don and Mario?' Cappricci asked, feeling insecure again.

'We've met now and again over the years. Now what's the deal here?'

'I've told Mario that we were all set up and double-crossed by the CIA. We were all in the same prison and were being transferred together. The rest as it happened.'

'OK, good enough. It's even the truth. All we have to do is get off this boat in a friendly port and that's that. They never even mentioned our weapons, so that's good as well. D'you think they'll let me make a ship-to-shore phone call?'

276

'Don't see why not.'
'OK, see you at the bunfight.'

'It looks like he lost the fight this time, Silas,' Michelle said quietly to Urquart, who was peeling potatoes over the kitchen sink.

'There's still a few minutes left until eleven hundred hours, miss,' he replied with a kind smile. 'The Major does try to be as punctual as possible under these kind of circumstances, but I have known him be an hour late.'

'An hour?' Michelle replied in mock horror. 'Not our Major Stuart!'

'Yes, it was quite interesting, actually. We, in the UK, had just gone on to summer time that day. He just forgot.'

'Where was he?'

'Working undercover in Tunis, if I recall correctly, miss. I could be mistaken though.'

That'll be the day, Michelle thought, her concentration suddenly broken by the ringing of the telephone. Urquart didn't move for what seemed an age. He put the peeling knife down and rinsed his hands under the cold tap, picked up a hand towel and walked over to the wall mounted phone on the other side of the room, wiping his hands as he went.

'Castle Stuart,' Urquart answered in his usual unhurried tones. There was a pause as he listened. 'Yes, could you hold? Very good, sir. Miss? It's for you.'

'Me? I thought it was . . .'

'Just so, miss, but it's for you. Admiral Hess?'

'Oh, right. Thanks, Silas,' Michelle replied, getting up quickly and joining Urquart by the telephone. The old man started to leave the room.

'You might as well stay, Silas. It's easier to eavesdrop from in here.'

'Only a one-sided conversation that way, miss.' Urquart replied as he passed into the old game larder to pick up the ancient Bakelite telephone that had been in there for over 50 years.

'Michelle?' Hess's voice echoed down the line, indicating a satellite link.

'Yes, sir,' came the automatic reply.

'The shit's hit the fan and I need you back here pronto! . . . Any news on Stuart?'

'Ah, no, no news. What's happened?'

'Can't tell you on this line – the *widow* will be listening or recording us. Hi, Silas, wherever you are! Get back here on the first available flight, OK?'

'Well yes, of course.' The phone had gone dead as she spoke. She returned the handset to its cradle and ran her fingers through her hair. So, she thought, the time has come. Was the call genuine, or does he know? It didn't matter really, she couldn't return to the States now, no matter what happened. *Israel.* She must go to Israel immediately. A new life . . . perhaps a new identity?

There was a cough behind her. 'You will be leaving Castle Stuart, miss?' Urquart asked.

'Leaving?' she replied, as if startled. 'Oh yes, leaving. As soon as I can make arrangements, Silas.'

'If I can be of assistance, miss? The travel agent?'

'Thank you, Silas, but I have an open return back home, via Heathrow. All I need to do is get ready and then pack.'

'A light lunch then?'

'Sounds good. I'll go get a shower and then get organised.'

'Very good, miss. The Aga has been on all day so there will be lots of hot water.'

Cappricci let the shower's hot water beat down on the top of his head. The steaming heat penetrated every pore of his body, but couldn't wash away the fear and uncertainty for the future. He had no plans and could trust no one. Deep down, he was almost sure that Falcone had set him up as part of his tidying up exercise.

Stuart was completely unpredictable and could turn on him at any moment. He clearly would suspect Cappricci in some form or other, and his own relationship with Falcone was unclear. The man Marker was harmless, but would support Stuart if the crunch came. And Hess? Well, he must wonder what the hell was going on and where everyone was, but did he suspect him . . . and how could he find out? Perhaps he should make a call to see what the score was? He couldn't tell him where he was, but that could be got around easily. At least he would be perceived to be following procedure, when he could.

He was conscious that time was passing and looked at the steel-grey face of his Ebelle watch. Thirty minutes had passed. He cleared his mind and switched the flow of water off. Stepping out of the shower, he wrapped a thick towel around his waist and walked through into the bedroom of his suite. A glass clinked in the main room, next door. Cappricci peered round the bedroom door. Mario was sitting in a large armchair, a large glass of red burgundy in his hand.

'Drink?' the old Sicilian asked.

'I'll get dressed first, Mario,' Cappricci answered. 'What's going on? I nearly got a one way ticket this time.'

'We don't know yet, but Jamayal got whacked. We're looking into it.'

'What was he doing in the hotel?' Cappricci called from the bedroom, struggling with a sock.

'Screwing, by all accounts. One too many. It looks like the work of a professional.'

'A woman?'

'Or an accomplice.'

Cappricci remembered the attractive woman he'd seen leaving the hotel, but didn't say anything; it might be nothing.

'So what happens now, Mario?'

'Markie, Markie. You're one of us, you're not one of these others. We have had a setback, yes – but all great ventures have them . . . they are to be expected. The question is, what do we do about Stuart and this man Marker?'

'Stuart's a mercenary. He's been paid; the job's over for him. He'll go back under a stone until someone else calls,' Cappricci suggested.

'Maybe, maybe.. Ordinarily I would agree with you, but Stuart is a special kind of man. His mission has failed, he has lost men. There is the thing with this Shanks, and he will feel betrayed.'

279

Cappricci joined Mario in the main room. 'But we *didn't* betray him – circumstances changed.'

'Ah, events!' Mario replied. 'But will Stuart be as, ah, understanding?'

'Why don't you ask him?'

'Now that you mention it, this is precisely what the don has suggested that *you* do. It is *you* that sent him on the mission originally. Your own *apparent* difficulties will protect you from instant retribution until he is sure, or has had time to investigate who he thinks is responsible for compromising his group. It is important that we know what he is thinking.'

'So you want *me* to speak to him?'

'When you can. Of course, not immediately, or he may suspect something. In a quiet moment, when you're alone, perhaps?'

'You're right, it won't be easy. I'd just let him fade away if I were you.'

'But if we can convince him to join us, a man like that could be of great use in the early days,' Mario suggested, as if trying to win Cappricci round by a recently considered view.

'And if I can't persuade him?'

'Much is at stake. He and his friend cannot leave the *Salamander* alive, of course.'

'He's armed.'

'So are we.'

Cappricci looked sceptical. 'What with, Mario? The crew on this ship are no match for a man like that with his back against the wall.'

'There are more subtle ways to remove a boil than to lance it, Mark. Believe me, if he has to be removed, there will be little or no loss of life on our side.'

'Very well, Mario, I will speak to him when I can.' Nothing needs to be rushed, the other parts of our plan are progressing well. There is confusion and mistrust within the PRC. This chemical plant story is sweeping around the world at all levels, from the odd sound bite to fully fledged debates in the House of Representatives. The politics of a strategic move like this are complex, but are like a snowball running down a hill. All we have to do now is to control the direction and the momentum. Greedy politicians will do the rest for us.'

'What's the White House saying about it all?' Cappricci asked. 'There must be a barrel of claims and counter claims going on.'

'We have the BBC and CNN on satellite upstairs – you can see for yourself after we have eaten. Things go well, but we must decide what to do with Stuart soon.'

When Cappricci and Mario entered the saloon lounge, Stuart had just preceded them.

'Get through OK?' Marker asked.

'Yeah, he's had a visitor,' Stuart replied.

'Who's that?' Cappricci asked from behind him.

Stuart turned round and almost smiled at Cappricci. 'You mean you don't know, Cap?' he replied from behind hooded eyelids.

'I didn't hear the first part of the conversation. Is it important?'

'Well, your Admiral Hess must think so. He's had the Christie woman camping out in Silas's backyard for a few days, just in case I made contact.'

'So Hess will know we are alive and well, then?' Cappricci asked, confused signals returning to his thoughts.

'Thankfully no,' Stuart replied. 'The lady got called back to the States urgently by Hess and she missed my call by a few minutes.'

'So no one knows we are here except your man?' Cappricci asked again.

'Oh, I wouldn't go as far as to say that, Cap.' Stuart smiled, warning bells ringing in his head. 'Anyway, what does it matter now? We're amongst friends and soon this lot will be just a bad dream. God, I'm starving!'

'Forgive me, old friend,' the voice of Don Falcone grated from the open double doors. 'My hospitality has been lacking.'

'Not at all,' Stuart deferred. 'It is my recent eating habits that have been deficient, not your hospitality.'

There was a ripple of smiles and light laughter in the room, to enhance the drama that was playing to a private house.

'It is just that I can tell you that our other dinner guest is almost here and that we can proceed through to the dining room if you wish. I have ordered some chilled champagne, to bring you all back into civilisation.'

Cappricci, Sandys, Marker and Stuart glanced quickly at one another, before Sandys once more broke in to prevent an awkward silence.

'Sounds good to me. Let's get in there before the other guests arrive and drink it all!'

'Have no fear, Mr Sandys,' Mario cut in. 'You may drink all you need. There are large stocks on board and it's *guest* not guests.'

'And who would that be?' Stuart asked, losing patience with the game.

'Please, Major, allow an old man a little pleasure. It's a surprise. Let's not spoil it. All I will say is that he will be making a less dramatic and expensive entrance than you and your colleges did.'

As he finished speaking, they were aware of a slight course change and an invading noise. Within seconds, the familiar slapping of a helicopter's rotor blades vibrated down from the helideck.

Mario waved the way through to the dining room, with the courtesy of a trained maître d' and the small group of tired men channelled through the doors, engrossed in their own thoughts. Stuart hung back a little and walked through with Falcone. The old man held his arm.

'I was sorry to hear about your man Shanks, Thomas,' Falcone almost whispered.

'Any ideas?' Stuart replied, without looking at him.

'I guaranteed your passage through Europe and this was not respected. We continue to look into it and you will be the first to know.'

'I'm obliged.'

'It is the way of things. We do this as much for ourselves as for you.'

That's a fact, Stuart thought, and if you don't know *already* who whacked Shanks, I'll drink the champagne *and* eat the bottle!

'Perhaps we should ask Cap about it. He's got a lot of questions to answer. We might as well start with that.'

'Later, old friend. We have other business first.'

The group were standing around a small table at the end of the dining room when Stuart and the Falcone arrived, a couple of minutes later. All had glasses and Mario was continuing to play host, but before he could pour out a drink for Stuart, steps could be heard down the alleyway. All turned to look at the double doors.

A junior ship's officer came through the doors and then stopped, waiting for his charge to pass by him into the room. The man wore crisp clean and pressed jungle fatigues, a beret with gold-coloured parachute wings and at his waist a new leather belt and holster. In it was what looked like a stainless-steel revolver with a wooden handle in the Smith and Wesson style – probably a .357. Stuart decided.

'Ah, my friend,' Falcone called out, 'come in, come in! I believe you know everyone here?'

'Cassa!' Marker said out loud, without thinking.

'Mr Marker.' Cassa nodded, tipping a swagger cane to his beret as a greeting to the others. 'I find you in somewhat different circumstances than last we met?'

'That's an understatement,' Marker replied, sinking his glass of champagne.

'Please, gentlemen,' Falcone interrupted, 'the past is the past, but I believe we can now have common goals.'

Stewards appeared at the service door. 'Ah, the meal is here,' Mario announced, 'let us sit . . . eat!'

'Yes,' Falcone added, 'sit, eat – we have much to discuss and there is limited time.'

The seven men sat at one end of the large table. For over an hour they ate well: a fish soup, a quail dish and a chocolate sweet which would have graced the best restaurants in the world. Once more, Falcone described his dream, adding the potential places that they all could take within it. All except Cassa. His fate was cast in stone and already in progress. He described the initiative that had been taken, immediately the theft of the hovercraft and the escape of the prisoners had been discovered. *President* Nelson had been blamed and implicated in the escape. Cassa and four other young officers of the council had sent guards to arrest him. Unfortunately, he'd resisted arrest and one of the young guards had overreacted and wounded Nelson. A group of Nelson supporters demonstrated violently, and in the short conflagration that followed, Cassa had emerged as leader and saviour. His face had even appeared on the cover of the *Sunday Times* magazine in the UK.

'This seems to have happened very quickly,' Stuart commented, as he sipped a rather good brandy – the only alcohol he had taken. 'This *Sunday Times* thing. How can this have happened in the short time since we escaped? Wait a minute, what day is it?'

'Saturday,' Maker answered, with a grin.

'Seems like a set-up to me,' Sandys confirmed to himself, as he poured another brandy under Stuart's disapproving look.

'It is true that sometimes things are not as they seem,' Don Falcone cut in. 'Look around this table. I am dressed in a thirties smoking jacket; Mario all in black, as usual; four soldiers in track-suits, whilst their fatigues are cleaned; and a country's president in a lowly captain's uniform – drinking expensive liqueurs after a exquisite meal. To a stranger, nothing here would represent what actually exists underneath.'

'And what would that be?' Stuart asked, without deference.

'It is a question of perspective, Thomas,' Falcone answered, as if addressing a child. 'To some we could be described as a group of "cut-throats and defilers of humanity", to quote a past, disgraced President of the United States. Ironic, isn't it? Or, some may describe us as the saviours of a people defiled by a cut-throat tyrant. How would you have us described, Thomas?'

'Me?' Stuart replied. 'Well, I always thought *that* guy was a good president, but what do I know? I'm just a simple soldier trying to make a living.'

'That'll be the day!' Cappricci laughed. 'But for once I agree with you.'

'It is of presidents that we must talk, gentlemen, and of what we can do with them. President Cassa here is a very new one and is going to have a difficult time in the short term. We must make sure that he *appears* to have a difficult time, watching and assisting when required, in order that the financial assistance that *we* provide seems to have been created by his leadership and guidance of the PRC, which will slowly become disbanded, our friend being elected *democratically* as the new hope of a grateful people. The US President, on the other hand, must *go!* He is very bad for us and the clamp-down on our activities and consistent betrayal of our associates in Central America cannot go unpunished. The potential Masada scandal is our tool to create his removal at the next election and make provision for someone more controllable, someone with a past, who can be manipulated without his actually knowing it. The Europeans continue to fight each other. In Central Asia there is only confusion and continual potential strife. The Chinese can always wait a thousand years, but we are making arrangements to have changes in the government of Japan. It is true that we continue to have problems in the old country. This will be addressed, but only radical change in Italy can produce a result that will sustain stability for us. This will take time; meanwhile, we have much work to do here, our new home, *our country!'*

The diners remained in silence as Falcone's words sank in. Was it possible that this old and failing man could wield so much power, control so much of the fabric of the world? A power that many had craved and died for – madmen and kings.'

'But how can you be sure that all this will come to pass?' Cappricci whispered, the silence around the table a yawning gap in the proceedings.

'Of course you have doubts, Mark,' Falcone continued, 'but power is money and money is power. We have major shareholdings in all the prime banks of the world, under a hundred or so legitimate company and personal share-holdings. The Family is enormous and many relations do not know to whom they are related. It has always been so, but my life's work has been to build, spawn and create new cells in far-flung areas of the world, to watch and nurture their growth and prosperity, finally

285

bringing them under the same powerful umbrella. Only I, Caesar Falcone, Don of Dons and the Godfather, have this knowledge. When I die, there will be a new godfather, but he will not be of the world that I have lived in. He has been chosen, but does not know it. He is respectable and respected, a captain of industry and friend of presidents and kings. The circle will be closed and the Family will continue to grow and flourish.'

'And what of us?' Marker asked, echoing the thoughts of the recent boarding party. 'What of an insignificant group of escaped prisoners? Is this the last hearty meal of the condemned men?'

Falcone looked at Mario. Stuart looked at Sandys and Cappricci, and Marker bit his lip, cursing his unguarded question. No one moved.

'You, Mr Marker,' Falcone replied quietly, 'are going to be a fairly rich man, as are all those around this table who are not already. Those who are, will become even more comfortable, and before you ask why, I will tell you. As you asked the question first, I can tell you that you're a wanted man. There is enough evidence available – some provided by me – to send you to prison for the rest of your life for the murder of that unfortunate child in the hotel in Switzerland.'

'But it was –' Marker tried, but Falcone held up his hand.

'Who it was is irrelevant. You can be found guilty of the murder and the rape of the child.'

'Rape!' Marker almost shouted.

'Please,' Mario called in a stage whisper, 'let the don finish speaking. This is disrespectful.'

'Yes, button it, will you, Chris,' Stuart growled. 'I think we've heard enough from you for now.'

'But I –'

'I said shut it!' Stuart ordered, as Sandys quietly poured another brandy. 'And you lay off the booze, Johnny. You might be flying us out of here tonight.'

Falcone's eyebrows rose slightly at the implied but undefined threat, then he continued as though nothing had happened.

'You misunderstand me, Mr Marker. I said could, not would!

You, Thomas, are a wanted man in so many places that your survival over the next few years is somewhat dubious, to say the least. Mark, your career is finished and you could be arrested for treason. However, gentlemen, what actually will happen is that you will be landed at the port of Las Palmas in the Canary Islands, our current destination, in about four days, Mario?' The man in black just nodded. 'On disembarkation you will be given pass books to numbered accounts in different banks around the world. The sums deposited will ensure that you all can slip away into whatever world you now wish to be part of.'

'What's the catch?' Stuart asked.

'Ah, the catch, as you put it, Thomas, is not so much a catch as a welcome.'

'A welcome to where?' Marker cut in, to find everyone scowling at him.

'Not to where,' Falcone smiled, 'more into what. You, Mr Marker, will have become part of a greater cause, a Family of purpose and achievement. You will be left alone but watched. If you betray the Family's trust – my trust – you and anyone close to you, family or friends will pay with their lives.'

With that, Falcone and Mario rose and began to leave the room.

'Mr President, may I talk with you before the helicopter returns you to Freeman?' Falcone asked. The tall black man smiled and joined Falcone as he left the room. The four remaining men remained silent, but they didn't hear Falcone whisper to Mario, as they walked slowly down the alleyway.

'Have you been able to contact Gomez?'

'Yes, my don,' Mario replied.

'Good, good, all goes to plan. President Cassa, this way please, into my stateroom. We have much to talk about in such a little time. I must have this last word with you.

'The last word we had was that the 747 should be landing within two hours at Ben Gurion,' Yani Bar-David answered Sharon.

'What arrangements have been made?'

287

'The cargo will be taken over by the air force and a full examination concluded.'

'What of the two white mercenaries?'

'One is injured, but not badly. The second one is of significant interest because his description fits that of one Chester Maclazowitz, a professional sniper who has an interesting file downstairs. If this is him, we not only have two survivors from the Stuart group, but a man who can fill in some other intelligence blanks for us.'

'Do we think he has worked against us?' Sharon asked.

'There is no evidence of that. Our interest is in those that he has trained in his craft. He himself seems to prefer combat missions rather than assassinations, although there was a suspicion that he was involved in those drug cartel assassinations in Colombia earlier this year. They were taken out at over a thousand metres.'

'And Miriam?'

'She landed on the British Airways flight at five-thirty this morning and is waiting in my office,' Yani answered with a smile.

'So, Yani, everyone is home and the world still sleeps. You have debriefed the girl?'

'Not yet, sir. I thought you might wish to be present.'

'I do, bring her up.'

Michelle was tired, she hadn't slept on the overnight journey, primarily because the film was good and the tension of succeeding without getting caught had been replaced by the tension of uncertainty for the future. Actually, she'd become quite excited. A new life lay ahead of her and a new identity was an easy creation.

When Yani came for her, he had a broad smile on his face. Everyone she'd met gave out warmth and respect. She suddenly realised that *here* she was special, *here* they knew she belonged; only time would need to pass before she knew it.

'Come in, my dear,' Sharon growled, like an old grandfather. 'Would you like some coffee? I made it myself just a few minutes ago.'

The manner in which it was offered made it hard to refuse.

'Thank you, I am rather thirsty, but could I have some water also?'

'Of course, of course. Yani, could you?'

Yani smiled and left the room. The old spymaster took studious care in pouring the strong black liquid into a small thick cup.

'There you are. I guarantee you will not get a better expresso this side of Milan!'

'Thank you, sir,' she replied, trying not to balk at the hot bitter liquid that invaded her mouth and throat.

'Good, huh?' Sharon asked expectantly.

Waiting a few seconds for her vocal chords to recover from the assault, Michelle smiled and put the cup down again. 'Wow! that's a cup of coffee,' she praised, hating it.

'Very good.' The old man smiled, pleased at pleasing a beautiful, if not a little bedraggled, young woman. 'Now, tell me everything, from the beginning. Take your time – we have lots of it and I don't want to tire you and cause you to miss out something important. Afterwards, Yani will go through the whole thing again with you, in greater detail, but for now I need to hear what happened in your own words. Start with your first meeting with Stuart. I'm clear on the proceedings before that.'

Michelle took a deep breath and launched into the events of the last weeks . . . Stuart . . . Cappricci . . . Hess. She noticed that Sharon was very interested in everything she could tell him about Hess, an opposite number in the most powerful country in the world. They had, of course, met, but the man inside the man was what Sharon was probing for. He also asked a lot of questions about the man Maclazowitz, but Michelle was unable to do much more than fill out the profile that she'd been given by Cappricci.

The interview took over two hours, and by the time she'd got to her take-off from Heathrow the previous night, she was drained, and she looked it. Sharon relented.

'You have done well, Miriam – or do you prefer Michelle?' Sharon smiled, turning once more into the grandfather figure. 'Go and get some rest and food. I think we can leave you in

289

peace until tomorrow. Go and see Yani. He will make accommodation arrangements for you. In the morning I think I
am going to talk to this Maclazowitz. I would like you to be
there.'

'Are we nearly there yet?' Rider asked.

'Just flapping our wings to land, old buddy. You'll be in a
proper hospital in no time and doing the hurdles in a couple
of weeks.'

'That's good, Chet. Couldn't do the hurdles before,' Rider
joked as the jolt of landing reminded him that he was overdue
some painkillers.

The Swissair-liveried El Al jet rolled to a stop at a maintenance apron, just in front of a huge hangar that already had
the tail of another 747 poking out into the daylight.

Before the nose-cone cargo door began to open, Dani Cohen
came through the aircraft to speak to Maclazowitz. They talked
briefly and then Maclazowitz went further aft, back to Rider.

'They're going to take you on without me for a little while
... Some kind of interrogation for me. Had to expect that, I
suppose. Don't worry, they say I should be done in a few hours
and then they will talk to us about where we want to go. Five-star
service. Keep your hands off the nurses, they're all black belts
in this country!'

'You look after yourself, big fella,' Rider called after him, as
Maclazowitz turned to follow Cohen down the fuselage to the
rear door. 'I can cope with a few gorgeous Israeli nurses.'

The sun was getting high in the sky and the heat from the
desert wind hit them as they descended the steps.

'Different?' Dani called over his shoulder, as he waved a
hand to the sky.

'Sure is,' Maclazowitz replied. 'It's the difference in humidity. What d'you reckon the temperature is?'

'It will get to the high thirties or even forty degrees today.
Good day for a swim! Here's the Jeep. Let's go.'

Dani spoke to the driver and took over the controls, leaving
the man to make his own way back, somehow.

'Is this your first time in Israel?' Dani asked.

'Yeah, my mom was here once, but I never made it. She's dead now.'

'Then you must make use of your visit. There is much to see, inland and in the ports.'

Maclazowitz didn't answer, he just smiled and looked around as they left the airport checkpoint and headed into the city on the freeway. One hour later he was sitting in Sharon's office, forcing hot black glue down his throat.

'Jesus, that's strong!' he coughed.

'It's supposed to be,' Sharon countered.

'Give me the old filter stuff, or even instant, any day over that. How d'you ever get to sleep?'

'Not often, Mr Maclazowitz, but that's more a function of duty and age. Now, tell me all about your little excursion with our Major Stuart. By the way, is he dead?'

Before Chet could answer, the door opened and a man came in. A couple of seconds later he was followed by an absolutely stunning blonde woman in a white shift dress. Automatically, he rose.

'Howdy,' he said to Yani, and then turned to the woman. 'Mahm,' the Texan nodded, like a scene from an old John Wayne movie.

Michelle Christie held out her hand and Chet shook it lightly. She was surprised at the delicate touch from a man of such obvious strength.

'Mr Maclazowitz, these are two of our intelligence officers who have been following this mission from the outset. Do you mind them being here, or asking questions?'

'Hell no.' Maclazowitz sat down again as Michelle did, not noticing her small nod to Sharon to confirm that this indeed was the man recorded in the CIA's files as Chester Maclazowitz. 'And call me Chet – everyone does.'

'OK, Chet,' Sharon began. 'You are in no danger here, physically or judicially. Just tell us your story and then we will make arrangements for you and your friend – Stephen Rider, isn't it? – to return home, wherever that might be. No embassies have been alerted. You're *not here,* and never will have been. Do you understand?'

291

'Sure!'

'Then please proceed,' Sharon continued, a little impatiently. How could this American not like first-class expresso coffee made by his own hand?

If nothing else, Chet Maclazowitz was a professional. Over the hour it took him to tell his story, very few questions were asked because very few were needed.

It was clear to Sharon that he genuinely didn't know if Stuart had survived, only that he'd been taken. These being the facts, the odds were that Stuart was dead and that chapter was closed. The memory of the possible consequences of the removing of Shanks, with Stuart still roaming around somewhere, had escaped none of Maclazowitz's interrogators. He must be dead. Captured white mercenaries in Africa don't last long!

'. . . and then we landed here,' Maclazowitz finished, reaching for a glass of orange juice that had been filled for him several times during the interview.

'Well, thank you, ah, Chet,' Sharon, said finally. 'I think that's about everything. I suppose you will be concerned about your colleague. We will telephone from here and see what is happening. Ah, Miriam, could you . . . ?

Michelle rose and went towards the door, but Maclazowitz beat her to it.

'After you, mahm,' echoed in the room. Sharon raised his eyebrows and shrugged to Bar-David. As the door closed, they heard the beginning of an unexpected conversation.

'I thought all you Israeli girls were dark-eyed, olive-skinned beauties?'

'Not all of us, Mr Maclazowitz.'

'Hey, you sound American . . .'

Yani sat down in the chair that Maclazowitz had just vacated. 'Our big American seems to be smitten.'

'The bigger they are, the harder they fall,' Sharon quoted, with a smile. 'What d'you think then?'

'Wait until we get the air force report and then call the Americans?'

'Certainly wait for the report, but the call will be in the Prime Minister's hands, no matter how much I would like to phone

Hess and tell him I've got the CIA's little genocide toy and it's come back from the grave to bite his backside! We're covered politically by the chemical warfare bullshit that he put out. Time is on our side, we can consider the right time and the right way to use our new little lever.'

'These two mercenaries . . . They know.'

'There's knowing and proving. They're only interested in going home. But this Maclazowitz, he interests me. You say he's half Jewish?'

'Yes, but his kind are probably half everything.'

'Nevertheless, I want you and the girl to become his friends while he's here. Find out what makes him tick.'

'Oh, I think we know that.'

'What?' Sharon asked.

'*After you, maaaaahhm,*' Yani mimicked.

Sharon laughed. 'You could be right, Yani. Use it. I'm going to try to see the Prime Minister this afternoon.'

'On my way, sir. Is there anything else?'

'Always, but not just at the moment. Meet me here tonight after you have eaten.'

'I feel like a Christian waiting to be eaten by the lions in the arena,' John Sandys announced to the silent gathering, throwing his silk napkin on to the table as he stood up and paced the dining room.

'Well, I'm not one for waiting for miracles,' Stuart replied, 'but right now I don't think there's much more we can do other than keep vigilant and wait.'

'But for what? That's the point,' Cappricci cautioned.

'If we knew that, we wouldn't have to wait,' Stuart replied, joining Sandys on his feet. 'Anyway, I need some fresh air. Let's take a stroll on the boat deck and then hit the sack.' As he spoke, he spun his wrist around above his head with his right hand and cupped an ear with his left, indicating the possibility of microphones in the room.

'Good idea, Trap,' Marker cut in. 'The meal was great, but a bit rich for my stomach. A walk will do me good, especially after all this excitement.'

293

Cappricci and Marker rose together and followed Stuart and Sandys out into the fore and aft alleyway and out onto the starboard-side boat deck.

'Port outer, starboard home!' Marker commented.

'I'm sorry?' questioned Cappricci.

'*Port outer, starboard home* – it's where the word posh comes from. In the days of the British Empire, when lots of people travelled from Britain to India, the wealthy passengers bought specific tickets which always allowed them to have a view of the coastline from their cabins, rather than an uninteresting view of the ocean. In order to guarantee this, they booked cabins which were on the port side of the ship on their outward journey to India, and on the starboard side on the way back to Britain. This cost a premium and on the tickets were the initials POSH. They were *posh* people, with greater wealth. Hence the use today of the word to indicate the upper class side of life, or very nice things. A posh dress, or a posh car.'

'He's full of useless information like that,' Sandys joked, as they joined him and Stuart at the ship's rail.

'It's *information* which is going to save our asses,' Stuart snapped, bringing the gathering to order. 'Four days' steaming. Is that right, Chris?'

'Yeah, subject to weather and that kind of stuff. She must be doing about twelve knots, the way she's riding.'

'What I can't understand is why Falcone would leave these waters, especially now,' Cappricci added. 'It just doesn't make sense.'

'To us,' Stuart pointed out. 'There's so much going on in that guy's master plan, who can tell what his next move will be, or for what reason.'

'It certainly puts Disneyworld into a different context.' Sandys said, the warmth of the brandy mixing with the balmy sea breeze and the gentle roll of the ship, to produce a mellow glow inside his very tired body.

Stuart ignored Sandys' comment. 'Well, it seems to me we have three options. We either steal the chopper and take our chances back on the beach, somewhere; take the ship and go somewhere of our choosing, or play well-behaved passengers, posh or otherwise, and take our chances on the ride!'

'I'd rather take the ride,' Marker offered quickly. 'I'm no soldier, and certainly no hero. Ships I know about. Crawling about in the undergrowth and getting tortured is completely off my agenda, for ever.'

'This could be a lot more than a pleasure cruise, Chris,' Stuart said quietly, understanding what his friend had gone through.

'Don't care, Trap. I'm knackered, hurt, clean again and this lady is heading in the right direction, as far as I'm concerned.'

'Tend to agree,' Sandys followed up. 'It's over, Trap. This is our best option for getting home. If they come for us in the next four days, we'll be ready for them and take it as it comes.'

'Me to,' Cappricci added. The don is complicated. There's a fifty-fifty chance that what he said will happen, will happen. After the last few days, I'd say that fifty-fifty is as good a bet as we're likely to get.'

The three men looked at Stuart. His face was like hewn granite, the sparkle back in his eyes, reflecting the deck lights like mirror images of the spectacular African night sky.

'Right then,' Stuart snapped. 'We do this just as if we were in the field. That way I might be able to get you girls home! During the day we act like tourists, but one of us will always be in reach of a weapon. At night we sleep two to a cabin, one awake all the time. John, you go with Cap, Chris with me. Any questions?'

'What happens if something does happen, if someone comes at us in some way?' Marker asked, concern engraved across his face.

'Chris, all of you, I've already told you: if you see so much as a penknife where you don't expect it, waste everyone you see or come across.'

'Thank you and goodnight,' Sandys announced, turning back towards the accommodation door. 'Come on, sweetie, I'll tuck you in,' he chuckled at Cappricci.

'That must mean you're doing the first watch then,' Cappricci returned.

Marker followed them off the deck, leaving Stuart standing alone at the rail. He turned towards the twinkling lights of the shoreline. In between them and the ship he could see the odd single light, very low down on the surface of the sea.

The centuries-old fishing customs had never changed, only the construction of the nets. Sporadic canoe lights could be seen a lot easier when you had focused on what you were looking for. In fact, there were more and more, the further Stuart looked below the horizon. These fishermen didn't care who ran the country, as long as they had good food, good shelter and a good woman.

'Want to swap?' Stuart asked them. His words were taken up by the wind created by the ship's forward motion and thrown away into her florescent wake.

'It is said that a man who talks to himself has much on his mind.' Falcone's voice drifted into his thoughts.

Stuart turned around slowly, his body coiled like a spring to meet anything that might await him. The effort was wasted. Falcone stood alone, his stance favouring the side that his cane supported.

'I have come to wave goodbye to his excellency.' Falcone explained. 'Mario will see him to the aircraft. Tell me, Thomas, where do *we* stand, we two old friends? Much has gone on between us over the years, but always as a side-line to something else. We have never actually worked together, only extended courtesies to further our other needs. I have always thought that that was a waste of combined talent.'

'I recall we had a similar conversation some years ago,' Stuart answered.

'Ah yes, but your mind was on other things. You had an agenda of your own, steeped in revenge and hatred. You exorcised the cancer but forgot that all operations leave a scar. How many men was it . . . twelve?'

'Twelve men and one woman,' Stuart replied, turning his attention out to sea once more.

'Ah yes, the woman. Has there been another like her since?'

'No.'

'There should have been, Thomas. Keeping people at an

arm's length doesn't solve anything. It just diminishes your ability to judge them, your own quality of perception of them and therefore you miss the point to life itself.'

'*You* preach to me! *You*, a man who has more blood on his hands than the devil himself.'

'Thomas, Thomas. Only one thing separates men like us.'

Stuart asked, turning back to look at the old man. 'And what's that then?'

'Compassion,' Falcone replied softly.

'*Compassion!*' Stuart laughed falsely. 'Now I've heard everything. 'Don Caesar, bloody Falcone has compassion?'

As his words echoed across the boat deck, the whine of Cassa's helicopter starting up deflected his attention for a few moments. The rotors quickly gathered their deafening speed and Mario could be seen ducking back down the helideck accommodation stairs.

'You laugh, Thomas, because you have never understood,' Falcone called, raising his voice above the rotor noise.

'Understood what, Sicilian?'

'How to have compassion for yourself, Thomas . . . *for yourself!*' His words were almost lost in the aircraft's noise as it lifted and swept off to starboard in a theatrical turn back towards the fading lights of Freeman. When Stuart turned away from watching the departure, the old man was walking back towards the beckoning light of the open accommodation door. Turning on his cane, Falcone looked back at the lonely-looking man by the ship's rail, smiled, shrugged and stepped out of sight. Stuart just stared after him. He'd only felt so empty once before, a long, long time ago.

16

Genesis

When they rang the military hospital, Michelle Christie and Chet Maclazowitz were told that Steve Rider was in surgery and wouldn't be ready for visitors until the next day.

Michelle suggested that they went and organised Chet's accommodation, underclothes, a clean uniform and any other bits and pieces he required. She told him that he would be staying in the officers' quarters at the Dov air force base; he could move freely there, but would not be allowed outside alone.

'You going to be my minder?' Maclazowitz asked.

'For the time being,' she replied. 'I also will be staying at Dov.'

'Let's go then, because if I smell like I look, our friendship is going to be a very short one.'

Michelle looked up at the big American and something in his eyes made her smile, then laugh. 'You're right, you stink.'

'Well, thank you for those kind words, little lady. Just lead me to that bathtub. I might even let you scrub my back.'

'I'll take a rain check on that if you don't mind, Mr Maclazowitz,' she laughed. 'Let's see if there are any clothes big enough for you in the stores first. You can get cleaned up afterwards and then we could go and eat. OK?'

'Yes, mahm. I could murder a steak!'

'Well I can't guarantee that, but we'll see what we can do.'

She led him back to the Jeep that Dani Cohen had brought

him in and swung into the driver's seat. It took about 20 minutes in the heavy Tel Aviv traffic to reach the Dov base, which was also used for civilian flights as well as those of the military. It was small and not very grand, running parallel to the ocean, right by the sand dunes. There was security; just a couple of guards at the gate and as they drove alongside the apron, Chet quickly realised that if he wanted to, he could escape from his hosts without much difficulty.

'You have been told you are a guest,'' Michelle said, watching his trained eyes constantly assessing his situation.

'Hey, you got me,' Maclazowitz said, lifting his hands in submission. 'It's just a habit, but tell me one thing: what's a girl like you doing in a place like this? It just doesn't fit, unless you've been just sent here while I'm here. What do you normally do and where do you normally live? If you're in intelligence, this sure as hell ain't your normal abode.'

'*Touché*, Mr –'

'Chet.'

'Chet. You got me this time. I have been assigned here for the period you and your friend are in Israel. The other questions you don't expect me to answer. Anyway, here we are.'

They got out at a wooden complex which smelt of the military as well as looked like it. No one was around, but the area looked well used and lived in. Michelle took him to a room along a short corridor and opened the door. It was a typical, operational junior officer's room, with a steel bed, locker, desk and chairs, a small handbasin and mirror, plus air-conditioning.

'The Tel Aviv Hilton!' Maclazowitz announced with a smile and a slow spin.

'Not quite, but it's just down the road, and if you're a good boy I'll buy you that steak there tonight. You see, you're not in custody, just protective custody!'

'I thought we were going to get some clean kit?'

'In the locker, soldier. I'll be back in one hour. Make sure you're ready.'

'Where are you going?'

'You're not the only one that needs to get cleaned up. I might not stink, but I've had a hell of a day as well and there's not a lot of water at this end of the building.'

'One hour then. Bring your gold card.'

'Key's in the door, on your side.' Then she was gone.

'Wow!' Maclazowitz said out loud to himself, turned to the mirror, saw his reflection and then said, 'Shit!'

Just after the hour was up, Maclazowitz was sitting on the small but comfortable bed, waiting for the knock at the door. He had heard her moving about the building since he got back from the showers and could tell that she had changed her shoes at least, because the heels made a different sound on the corridor's shiny surface. Other people had also been heard, with a few shouts in Hebrew and the odd laugh.

There was a knock on the door. 'You ready?'

'Yeah,' he replied. 'The door's open.'

When she opened the door she had a shock. Chet was clean-shaven and his thick hair, which was still damp, was combed back from his forehead. He wore a white tennis shirt – bought in his size by one of Yani's assistants, along with a few other modest but fairly smart additions – navy blue slacks, white socks and a pair of yachting loafers, the only footwear other than his own boots they had been able to find in his size, in the available time.

God, she thought, a tall, dark, handsome stranger . . . literally!

'Lost your tongue?' he asked.

'No, but *you* seem to have lost a certain odour. D'you want to come and eat?'

'Sure, lady. Do we get to have a beer too?'

'Oh, I think that can be arranged. Well, are you coming? And if you say *yes mahm* just once more, I'm leaving you here!'

'Yes, Michelle. And *please* call me Chet.'

'Yes I know, all your friends do. 'OK, Chet, haul ass!' She spun round and was off down the corridor at speed, but Chet's long legs easily made up the ground without appearing to be making the effort to do so. A taxi waited next to the lonely Jeep, and the evening air was balmy and pleasant to the skin.

Stars were just showing through, but the sun's last hue was still visible in the west.

They both got into the rear of the Japanese-made cab. Chet's size made it impossible for them not to touch in many places. Michelle felt her cheeks flush and was thankful for the semi-darkness. Chet felt like a 16-year-old schoolboy on his first date. The horrors of Sierra Laputu seeming a universe away and easily forgotten. Almost as if it was the most natural thing to do in the world, Chet reached out and held her hand.

'Thought it might break the tension,' he said, in a voice that hid his uncomfortable feelings.

'Sensitive as well, eh?' she said, stress pouring from her body. 'Where the hell did they dig you up from?'

'Texas, mahm, just Texas . . . Michelle.' He squeezed her hand when he said her name and she leant on him just a little more.

Jesus, she thought, pull yourself together, you're acting like a virgin on her first date. What's the matter with you?

'What's the matter with you, Silas?' Hess screamed down the telephone. 'We *know* he's alive. He stole a goddamned hovercraft, for Christ sakes! I'll bet that pirate Sandys is with him as well. He *must* have called. You can't fool me, Silas, I know you two have this blasted system which you follow for weeks until he finally gets in touch, or is found floating face down somewhere. He's alive and he'd called, or I'm a jackass!'

The phone went dead and Urquart replaced the receiver by his bedside. 'Well, Nigger,' he said to the dog, 'that's one very fed-up American.' The dog wagged his tail in agreement and stretched.

'Well?' the President asked, coming into Hess's office. 'Did you talk to the old retainer?'

'He says he hasn't heard.'

'That's not good enough, Carlton. We have to know where that guy is and what he's doing. This whole administration could be hanging on your incompetence.'

'With respect, sir, I –'

'We'll get desperate little of *that*, Carlton, if this lot blows up in our face. There are loose ends everywhere. Speaking of which, what's the story on your two operatives? Are they back yet?'

'Actually no. We're having difficulty tying down arrival times, due to their routes being under their own discretion,' he lied.

'Well, let me know when they get here. I'm anxious to hear what they have to say.'

The telephone rang. 'It's for you, sir,' Hess said, as he passed the handset over to the President.

The President began to drawl on about party funds to his latest campaign manager. Clearly the conversation was going to go on for some time. Hess excused himself and left the room. Outside, the corridor was stuffy and stale, so he went through to Nancy's room, where she always seemed to have a window open no matter what the weather was like. In the summer she said the air-conditioning was bad for you and carried millions of germs. In the winter she blamed the central heating, and if anyone made a comment they would get a lecture about legionnaires' disease and asthma allergy. It was still warm in her room, but the evening breeze had swung round to the west and was filtering through the open glass.

He didn't know what else to do. The satellite photographs were damming. Someone had flown in, left carnage and flown out again, taking the evidence with them. The question was who. Nothing had been heard from any group or state. He didn't really care who it was, as long as he *knew* who it was and the risk could be quantified. Then there was Stuart, still alive and kicking somewhere, he had no doubt. The situation in Sierra Laputu was changing almost by the hour and deep down in his heart he knew that Christie and Cappricci weren't coming back. They must have been working together for years, he thought wrongly. How many operations and agents had been compromised by those two – and particularly Mark Cappricci.

Nancy's telephone rang with a quiet, deep tone. 'Yes,' Hess snapped.

'Oh,' the voice answered, 'I was looking for Nancy, to ask where Admiral Hess was.'

302

'This is Hess. Who are you and what d'you want?'

'Oh, ah, sorry, sir. This is Pendel Jackson at SATRACK. It may be nothing, but I've been looking over the sat shots of Sierra Laputu for a couple of days now and I've noticed something a little unusual. As I say, it may be nothing and the intermittent cloud cover could have masked something, but I just thought it was worth a mention.'

'Well, don't stop now, Jackson. Get on with it!'

'We've all been concentrating on the target site area, but on a couple of tracking shots prior to homing in I noticed that there was a ship in the estuary approach area. I can look back and find evidence of it coming in from the north, steaming up and down for a few days and then starting off to the north again. It just seemed strange.'

'Probably just a cargo ship with a change of orders,' Hess answered in an offhand manner.

'Well, that's just the point, sir. Closer inspection showed it to be a large pleasure craft.'

'What d'you mean, a cruise liner?'

'No, sir. This boat –'

'*Ship!*' Hess cut in impatiently.

'Yes, sir. This ship is without doubt a very large, expensive private yacht. My point is that this isn't exactly a part of the world you would expect such a vessel to be hanging around in. It didn't appear to go into port. It just hung around and then left after a few days.'

'A pick-up?'

'Can't rule it out, sir. But like I said, we had two days in particular where the cloud cover was eighty to a hundred per cent.'

'Could you get a ship's name?'

'No, sir.'

'Jackson, well done. Get a team on those photographs – look for anything that might indicate a pick-up was made. Concentrate on Thursday, and the days before and after.'

'Any particular thing we should be looking for?' Jackson asked, pleased his work seemed to have been of value.

'Anything – anything at all that could indicate the deck

303

equipment has been used. Search for faces, as usual, and get some copies of the photos, including all people and groups, up to me as soon as possible,' Hess replied, with a new crispness in his voice.

He placed the telephone down slowly as his mind started to race. He needed a break. Maybe this was it. If Stuart had organised a back door out of the country, he still could catch him. The circumstantial evidence was thin, but it fitted the timescale for the theft of the hovercraft which had ended up careering up a deserted beach and lodging itself in a group of extremely unforgiving palms. A fire had ensued, but the rains had saved any major environmental damage to the locality, or a spread of flames to other areas.

'The President is going back on to his campaign schedule,' Nancy said from behind him.

'OK, I'm coming. While I see him out, get hold of the duty Operations Controller and get him up to my office. Jackson from SATRACK will be up soon; put him in there as well and tell them to stay there until I return.'

Nancy nodded and stepped aside to let Carlton Hess pass. When he returned to his room there was a note on his desk: *Ask not what your country can do for you, but what you can do for your country.* The almost accurate JFK quote had been scrawled, and underneath was the first letter of the President's Christian name.

What does he think this place has turned into, Hess thought, Twentieth Century Fox?

There was a knock on the door.

'Come in,' Hess called out. Jackson, and a small mousy-looking man with heavy hornrimmed glasses that didn't suit him, came in.

'Jackson, Pendel ... come in. Sit down and let's see what we've got. Photographs?'

The young scientist laid several large photographs on the table opposite Hess's desk. The three men shuffled through them back and forth, inspecting every facet of the frames, occasionally handing round the one available magnifying glass. After half an hour, they were no nearer finding a clue to a sinister meaning for the vessel's purpose than when they started.

Hess returned to his desk and relaxed in the soft chair. 'The bow wave on that lady in the latest photograph shows she's steaming full-away on passage. She's not hanging around, so that makes me even more suspicious. I just feel I'm missing something.'

'Well, you're the sailor in the room, sir,' Jackson said pleasantly, 'and the gangplank, or whatever you call it, can be seen raised and lowered on different days. I'm sure something has been and gone.'

'Could just be stores; putting sick man ashore for repatriation. It's all pretty normal, at sea. Wait a minute! Pass the first and the last pictures over. Steaming into the area and steaming away.'

Jackson obliged and Hess studied the two colour prints avidly with the magnifying glass.

'*That's it!*' he cried suddenly. 'I knew there was something, but I just couldn't put my finger on it. Look, look at the accommodation ladder. A gangplank was good enough for small galleons and sailing ships of old, but a beautiful baby like this has a fancy mechanical accommodation ladder fit for a queen. It is a permanent fixture and often there's one on each side so the ship can berth to port or starboard. When she's at sea, the steps can be closed mechanically flat within their side frames and the whole ladder is then swivelled towards the ship's side at main deck level, then housed in a special recess to make the ladder safe, secure, tidy and flush with the hull for sea passage. Now look here, on the first picture. You see, just aft of the funnel on the boatdecks . . . two long silver-looking lines on each side of the vessel. That's the port and starboard accommodation ladders stowed for sea. Now, on the latest picture, you can see the same line on the starboard side, but there's nothing on the port side. The boat-deck platform appears to be there but the ladder itself is missing.'

'Surely there could be a million reasons for that.' Jackson suggested.

Admiral Hess shook his head. 'No, not really.' They will be

305

made of stainless or galvanised steel. Very little maintenance needed. No, that ladder is *gone*, damaged and lost.'

'But I don't understand,' Jackson added. 'How does that help?'

'It helps, Jackson, because that's just the kind of damage you might expect if a cut-throat and a crazy pilot who thinks he can drive or fly anything try their hand at putting a stolen hovercraft alongside a ship like that. They're soldiers not sailors, and they won't have wanted to get their feet wet – or any gear they had.'

'If you don't mind me saying so, sir, isn't this a bit of a long shot?' Pendel asked.

'Long shot it may be, sonny,' Hess smiled, 'but a long shot by a *good* shot often hits the target. I want every operative in every embassy on the coast to the north of her watching for that vessel. You, Jackson, track and take as many shots of the ship as you can at every opportunity. Get an artist in to make silhouettes – anything – but get me a name and destination, and neither of you leave this building until you have it. My man is on that ship . . . I feel it in my water!'

It took over two days for Jackson to get enough visual shots of the *Salamander* to make a positive identification – and about the same time for her new passengers to begin to relax.

Falcone had been the perfect host and Mario had seen to their every needs, minimal as they had been. They had spent their time sunning themselves on the boat deck and partaking of the vessel's plentiful cuisine and extensive cellars.

'D'you still think we need to keep this watch routine going?' Marker asked Stuart, as he sat down on a deck lounger next to him.

'They know we're doing it, Chris, believe me,' Stuart replied softly. 'Any change in routine would make them suspicious.'

'Well, if you say so,' Marker shrugged. 'It just seems a waste of time to me.'

'I say so,' Stuart replied, swinging his legs off his own lounger. 'Cap on watch now?'

'Yes. He's sitting in his cabin with a loaded rifle by his side, reading a book from the library. Regular cruise, isn't it?'

'Sure, but we get into Las Palmas about this time tomorrow. If anything's going to happen on board it'll be tonight. I'm going to have a wander round. It drives Mario crazy trying to follow me without being seen to follow me. The boat's big enough to disappear for a while, but small enough to bump into each other.'

'Ship,' Marker corrected.

'What? Oh yes, *ship.* Sorry.' Stuart smiled, walking off towards the accommodation.

The air-conditioning caressed him as he closed the outboard door and walked down the alleyway to his cabin. He was convinced that there was some great danger ahead from Falcone. The trick was going to be not to meet it head on, but to bypass it and then make a run for it off the approaching islands. If they could get off safely, under their own control, the game was won. Only the loose ends had to be cleared up. Cappricci was the key to that, he was sure.

He lay down on the large stateroom bed, but sleep was a mile away. The faces of men long since dead, and those recently sacrificed flashed across his mind. Men he had hardly known and men he had almost loved. He saw Yanders de Beer and heard his voice. It wasn't the usual scene from his dreams, but a calming, soothing sound. *'When we get back to Cape Town we're going to have a big party, on me.'* Boy, had they had some parties! Girls, booze, food, more girls . . . In the early days the money had been great. The Yanks funded anybody who would stand up to communism in any godforsaken part of the world. The American people were never aware of 80 per cent of the games that were played and the lives that were ruined or lost. Their freedom of information laws were treated as a joke by Langley, until the very recent past. Even now . . . look at this operation!

Sleep started to close in on him, and he startled himself as a snore erupted quietly from his nose. Tired, so tired. This had to be the last operation. He was getting careless, slow, and always tired.

There was a knock on the cabin door. 'Major Stuart? Are you in there?'

'Yes, what is it?'

'It's Sparks, sir. There's a message for you on the traffic list. D'you want me to patch it down here for you when it comes through?'

'A message? Who from?'

'I didn't ask, sir. It's person to person.'

'Yeah, OK. Patch it down. No, wait a minute, I'll come up.'

'OK, sir. It should be just a couple of minutes.'

'On my way,' Stuart replied, jumping down off the bed. If the call was patched down, anyone on the boat could be listening. If he went to the radio room, only he would get the call. Not even the radio officer could hear it.

When he arrived in the radio room, the radio officer turned round in his seat and smiled. 'Should be any minute now, Portishead Radio is calling the party back now. Strange, this. We normally just use the satellite link. The caller can't have the number.'

An echoing voice called out of the bulkhead speaker. '*Salamander*, this is Portishead Radio. Go ahead, old man.'

The radio officer picked up the handset and replied, automatically cutting off the speaker. A couple of seconds later he turned to Stuart. 'That's it, sir. Would you like me to leave?'

Stuart nodded and took the handset. A familiar voice called at him across the heavens.

'Stuart, this is Hess, d'you copy?'

'Shit!' Stuart said out loud, without pressing the transmit button.

'*Salamander*, this is Hess. Do you read, Stuart?'

'Why Carlton, how nice to hear your voice, after all this time. You clever little rascal!'

'Underestimation is always a fault, Thomas,' Hess replied, conscious of the open airway that he was using on 18 MHz. 'We've got you pegged, and you and I need to talk. Where's your destination? I'll fly out and meet you.'

'Wait one,' Stuart replied, options careering through his mind.

'Standing by,' Hess returned.

They had been found, and that was that. Any hope of sliding

308

into cover and disappearing on arrival at Las Palmas was now
out of the question. Even if he got Falcone to divert, there
would be a welcoming committee of some kind waiting for
them . . . *him.*

'Was it the satellite?' Stuart transmitted.

'Mind your own god-damned business, Thomas, and give me
your destination.'

'It *was* the satellite,' Stuart confirmed to himself as much as
to Hess. 'You got lucky, Carlton. You just got lucky!'

'Lucky or not, you might as well be sitting here in my office.
You're going nowhere until we get things sorted out.'

There was another pause while Stuart thought. 'OK, Carlton,
you win. Las Palmas. We're going to Las Palmas. Should be
there tomorrow night.'

'Don't mess me around, Thomas. We've got you pegged.'

'It's Las Palmas, tomorrow night. *Salamander* out!'

Stuart placed the handset back on the glass-topped table and
left the radio room. As he passed the radio officer's cabin, the
young man looked up and smiled.

'Finished, sir?'

'Yeah,' Stuart replied rudely.

The young man jumped up and quickly went back next door
into the radio room. As Stuart got to the bottom of the first
flight of stairs back down into the accommodation, he heard
him calling, 'Portishead Radio, Portishead Radio, this is *Salamander.* All finished thanks, old man. See you next time!'

There was a reply, but Stuart was out of earshot by that time.
As he passed the forward lounge, Mario emerged in front of
him.

'Tommy, Tommy, there you are. Don Falcone would like to
speak with you. He is here, inside.'

'Fine, lead on,' Stuart answered in a neutral voice.

The old man was sitting at the far end of the lounge. Papers
were strewn on the settee beside him and he had clearly been
scribbling notes on them.

'Ah, my friend, come, sit with me,' Falcone called as he saw
Stuart. 'Have some coffee. It's just been made.'

'Thanks.'

'I hear you have had a phone call, on the main radio?'

'Yeah that's right.'

'May I ask who it was? Did you not call your man Urquart on the satellite link? I am curious to know who knows you are here. I believe you were asked for by name?'

'Yeah, that's right. Worrying, isn't it?'

'Unusual, at least,' Falcone answered in a calm voice.

'It was Cap's boss, Hess. He'd tracked us down on the satellite network. I told him it was just luck, but actually the old wolf must have done a lot of innovative detective work to put two and two together.'

'He asked for you by name?'

'Bluff – chanced his arm and got lucky. If your sparky had said *who* rather than *I'll get him*, we'd probably have been in the clear. Easy mistake. Don't give him a hard time.'

Falcone looked at Mario before continuing. 'What did he want?'

'Me.'

'Just you? He didn't mention anyone else?'

'No, he didn't mention anyone else. I've no doubt that he's scouring every record he can find to discover who owns this little tub, but my guess is that he thinks me and the boys simply hijacked the boat for our getaway from Freeman.'

'And his intentions?'

'Welcome party at the docks tomorrow. Better put some more champagne on ice, Mario. You're going to have visitors.'

Silence echoed in the room as the three men flicked through their own agendas, options and the threats that the news could pose.

'We could land you somewhere else,' Mario suggested.

'Only if we get thick cloud cover this afternoon and you have luck during the night. Even then, he'll have every eye on his payroll in the region spotting for this baby, and she's not exactly low profile.'

'Quite so,' Falcone answered vaguely, deep in thought.

'Look,' Stuart continued, 'Hess is out on a limb. The operation was a disaster. On top of that, some of us got out. He needs to know what *we* know. This little debacle could be all over the world's press, for all we know. He could really be in it.'

'As far as we can tell, your presence in the country was not widely known, or its purpose. The chemical weapons scare has fuelled other reports from other countries and the press have masked the realities by snowballing the story into other ones. I do not believe your position is as compromised as you think,' Falcone offered. 'Our main problem would occur if the Las Palmas, or any other authorities, are involved by Hess. My own position in the recent events could come under question. As you rightly point out, my ownership of the *Salamander* is lost in time. Only my presence on board could cause a compromise. Mario, get a helicopter out here as soon as possible. You, I and our friends are leaving. Admiral Hess has played one card too many. Also, check on flight times and connections from Hess's likely gateway in the States and work out if we can get to shore in advance of his arrival. Thomas, any thoughts?'

'A chopper's only going to give you a leeway of about two to three hours, tops. If he's been clever enough to work out I was here, that bloody great helipad on the stern won't have gone unnoticed. He could have all options covered.'

'Then, old friend, you and your colleagues must go alone. As soon as you've taken off, we will reverse our course and return in the direction we've come.'

'That makes sense. If he gets a handle on us at the airport, or on the island, the boat will become secondary and you can make any number of arrangements before his attention strays back again.'

'So be it,' the old man decreed, looking younger in the face than he had done all trip. 'Thomas, I suggest you advise your men. Mario, stay. We must make plans.'

The old man and his retainer both looked at Stuart without speaking. His presence had clearly become unwelcome, so he rose and left the room, the hairs on the back of his neck prickling. Warning bells were ringing in the back of his brain. This instant action by Falcone was all very well, and he was obviously charged up by it, but one thing was very clear: the easiest way to remove the current problem was to remove Stuart

311

and his men. Only one thing would stop it, if Falcone and Mario realised its implication. The radio call itself was logged at the international maritime radio centre at Portishead near Bristol, in the UK. It proved he had been on board. No, Stuart thought. Those two wouldn't know anything about things like that and probably wouldn't even think to ask the radio officer. No, they were going to be hit and it was going to be tonight. That's what *he* would do, and that's what Mario's advice will be, he was sure.

Up on deck, Marker was still stretched out in the falling sun. Stuart sat alongside him again. 'Don't get up yet, just listen,' he said quietly. 'The CIA are going to be waiting for us when we get to Las Palmas. I don't know if that's going to be good news or bad news, so we have to assume the latter. Falcone's shitting himself and there's a reasonable chance that Mario and the crew will come at us before we get there. We can't trust Cappricci, so not a word about *why*. We'll just tell him to be on guard as a precaution. I'm going down below to let Johnny know what's going on. You come down in about ten minutes. Remember, not a word to Cappricci.'

'When did all this happen? What's going on?'

'Go,' Stuart ordered, cutting the questions off dead.

After Stuart had explained to both Marker and Sandys the full story of the afternoon's events, the men prepared themselves for some kind of attack during the night. It never came. What did come was a strong north-westerly wind, accompanied by heavy intermittent cloudbursts and the crack of tropical lightning.

'Where the hell did this lot come from?' John Sandys growled.

'Over the horizon,' Marked quipped, unaffected by the vessel's movement.

'Well, one thing's for sure, Trap: nothing's taking off or landing in Las Palmas if this lot stretches that far north.'

'It does,' Stuart confirmed. 'We had been making good time, according to the chief officer at five this morning. When he went on watch at 0400 hours, we were only a hundred and twenty miles out from the pilot station. We've been knocked back to about ten knots at the moment so we still should make it there by early evening.'

'What's the plan now?' Marker asked.

'This should put us in the clear, if there aren't any games from the don,' Cappricci offered from his braced position on the fitted settee.

The ship pounded into the next swell, sending shudders down her spine and causing the propellers to cavitate in the mixture of sea and air as her stern lifted clear of the water.

'Jesus,' Sandys started again. 'Who'd do this for a living?'

'Beats getting your ass shot off,' Marker replied. 'Any day!'

'That's a matter of opinion, old lad,' Sandys answered. 'Going up top. I like to look at the horizon when I'm being thrown about like this. It's like flying blind, upside down at night, down here.'

'I'll come with you, John,' Stuart began. 'You guys stay here by the weapons. I doubt anything will happen during the storm. It's too risky, with people falling about all over the place.'

As they left the cabin, a steward fought his way past with a bucket of broken glass from the bar.

'Hope that wasn't the good stuff,' Sandys called after him, but he didn't bother to reply. They struggled to the large bridge, where they found the captain and the third officer, Mario and a lookout. The ship was still in autopilot so no one was at the wheel.

'It's getting worse,' Mario said, from the high pilot's chair that had been stowed in a corner of the wheelhouse area, as they entered the bridge by its aft accommodation stairway.

'What kind of time are we making?' Stuart asked.

'Not bad, considering. The captain tells me that we will soon be getting the shelter effect of the island itself, so we could be at the pilot station at about seven and alongside by eight tonight. You must have a guardian angel, Thomas. This storm has, how do you say? saved your bacon?'

'I thought you were going to turn back.'

'Not in this. The don is sick and nothing will prevent him from getting to some calm water.'

'Seasick?' Sandys asked.

313

'Seasick, yes,' Mario confirmed solemnly. 'Even great men have weaknesses.'

The aft bridge door opened again and the radio officer stuck his head round the opening. 'Just spoken to Las Palmas. The port's closed at the moment. We've been advised to keep coming but keep in touch.'

'I'm not surprised,' the captain replied, without turning round. 'This swell will be running into the harbour mouth and bouncing the ships about on the breakwater, if they haven't let go and run for shelter elsewhere. We have force ten now, with gusts above that.'

'When will we be in the lee?' Sandys half shouted, above the noise of the storm and the crashing of the bow into the on-coming seas.

'We should be getting some benefit within about two hours, but if the port's closed I doubt that it will open again until tomorrow sometime.'

'Then we have to get off another way,' Stuart shouted back.

'Let's cross that bridge if we get to it,' the captain smiled, oblivious to the noise around him. 'This isn't a typhoon, it's only a storm.'

'Well, you could have fooled me,' Sandys shouted. 'I've flown through and over some rough stuff before, but I never realised what it was like to have to sail through it.'

The door burst open this time and the radio officer shouted, 'We've got a mayday about sixty miles off, sir. Small one-hatch, one-hold coaster of two thousand tons. Her hatches have been breached and she's taking water fast. Here's her position.'

The captain took the scrap of paper and struggled with the brass chart dividers to make an estimate of their ability to respond.

'Come round to two-eighty degrees,' he shouted to the third officer, who was hovering over the automatic pilot controls, 'and get a helmsman up here and some more look-outs.'

'Stay where you are,' a cold slate voice was heard over the whine of the radars and the cry of the storm.

Everyone on the bridge turned in the direction of the voice.

Stuart was standing in the aft doorway, which was latched in the open position, on the wheelhouse deck. The radio officer had been pushed into the bridge area and was staring down at the 9 mm pistol that was pointed at his stomach.

'We have responded to a mayday,' the captain stated calmly. 'You probably won't be able to get off when we arrive anyway.'

'I admire your perception, captain, but I must decline your reasoning,' Stuart replied. 'Take this boat to Las Palmas. No tricks, no diversions. Mario, you stay put in that high chair you're in and I won't have to shoot you – *capisci*?'

Mario raised his hands and lowered them in a sign of submission. 'Thomas, what is this?'

'This, Mario, is where I take control and you and the don lose it.'

'What about the distress?' the captain cut in. 'Men are going to die out there!'

'Men may also die here, Captain. I'm sorry. John, get the others, and the weapons, and have them all come to the bridge.'

John Sandys stared at his old friend for five seconds longer than necessary. The looks that passed between them said more than any words. John Sandys would obey, but Stuart was under no illusion about how he felt.

Within five minutes, Marker, Cappricci and Sandys were on the bridge. All were armed but only Sandys knew the actual situation.

'Right,' Stuart shouted. 'Chris, John – you keep an eye on this little lot. Cap, it's make your mind up time. Drop the piece!'

'What d'you mean?' Cappricci asked, looking genuinely surprised as he let the AK slide to the deck.

'You've got three options, Cap: me, Hess or Falcone. You choose *now* and take the consequences. We still have some business to take care of, no matter what happens, but this is for here and now and until we are in the clear. Well?'

Everyone bucked over to starboard as the ship took another swell on the port bow.

'Make your mind up, Cap. I haven't got all day.'

'You mean I'm either with you or dead?'

'You're only dead if you try to stop me. It's your choice. Answer to Hess for your treachery to him, answer to Falcone for your treachery to him or, surprise, surprise, answer to me for your possible treachery. Hell of a choice, baby. Make it now!'

'You're a black bastard, Stuart, but you're the only bastard on your list who hasn't used me, blackmailed me or conned me . . . yet!'

'I'll take that as a vote for Stuart. Pick the gun up and cover the back stairs. Now, gentlemen, we wait!'

'Wait for what?' the captain asked, pure hatred pouring from him.

'The pilot station at Las Palmas, then you can put the blue light on and rush to get your name in print.'

'It will be too late then,' the captain snarled. 'You're sentencing those men out there to death as sure as I'm standing here.'

'They'll have to take their chances,' Stuart answered.

'Do I get this right?' Marker chipped in. 'Is this all about not answering a distress call?'

'On the money, Chris. We haven't got time to divert.'

'Jesus, you are a black bastard, right enough!'

Stuart shrugged. 'Whatever. Just one thing, though, before you get on your high horse. Hey, Sparky, this ship that's in distress – how far away did you say it was?'

'Sixty miles,' the captain cut in.

'I was speaking to our radio expert here. Well, Sparks?'

'Like the captain said, sixty miles.'

'And he told you that, did he, the guy on the other ship?'

'Well, yes.'

'So the guy on the other ship told you he was sixty miles away, did he? Tell me, Sparky,' Stuart snarled, 'how did he know where we were? How did he know we were sixty miles away? Did you have our position? I thought it was the noon positions you kept on that little clipboard by the main radio set. Isn't that right, Chris? Didn't you tell me once that on fancy passenger ships several officers all take the noon position

316

on the bridge wing together, like a ritual, and that the radio officer keeps that position in case of a disaster, as well as a record for the owners?'

'Well yes, but with satellite navigation, he could have a position instantly at any time.'

'Not in the radio shack! Positions need maps, *charts*, to get distances, don't they, Captain? You know, like you did just now when Sparky came rushing in with the terrible news of this sinking ship. By the way, Sparks, what was the name of the ship – you know, the one out there that's sinking? Must have a name, or didn't you have time to think of that after the don called you?'

'But –'

'But nothing! I haven't worked out how someone signalled an alarm to him yet, but this pantomime has gone on long enough. There's no sinking ship out there. At least, not one that *we* know about. This bullshit is just a device to prevent a departure from the boat that would have left us in the clear. John, you take Sparky boy here down and get the old man. If he's seasick I'm Robin Hood. Come on, Sparky, move it! Wait a minute, just one more thing. So as you and the rest of the crew won't be in any doubt about how me and the boys here react to people trying to get us in deep trouble, or worse – Captain, you just resigned.'

The 9 mm kicked and a small hole opened in the captain's startled face. A familiar red haze of blood, bone and brains sprayed across the inside of the port bridge windows and ran down the bulkhead to form small rivers on the deck. The movement of the ship had not compromised his aim.

'One muscle, Mario! Move just one tiny muscle and you'll be lying there with him.'

'*Bastardo!*' Mario shouted.

Suddenly, the ship took a corkscrew dive into the next swell. Stuart lost his balance and was catapulted towards Cappricci. John Sandys was flattened against the starboard bulkhead, and Marker, hanging onto a deck-head pillar that supported the bridge ceiling, was the only one left standing to cover the radio officer, watchman, third officer and Mario. In a flash Mario

317

was on Marker, attempting to wrestle the AK from him. Marker just hung on, as the two of them were thrown off their feet by the ship while they struggled for control of the weapon.

The radio officer took the initiative and leapt on Sandys, but he was met by the pilot's right foot. He cried out as a boot was buried into his solar plexus.

On the other side of the bridge, Mario had just about overcome Marker, when in desperation he pulled the trigger of the automatic weapon. The AK's barrel waved around in the four hands that were holding bits of it, spraying 7.62 calibre death and destruction all around the bridge deck. Rounds smashed into radars, echo sounders, bulkheads and deck-head ceilings. Mario let go with his left hand, which had been gripping the weapon very near the barrel's end. This increased the arc of fire and a scream was heard above the noise as the third officer received two rounds, one in the upper left shoulder and a second in the left hand.

On the floor now, Mario refused to let go of the weapon completely. Marker was in complete disorientation, Sandys was on his knees and Stuart was dazed. Only Mark Cappricci had recovered fully from the confusion, and as the last round discharged itself from Marker's AK, he picked up Stuart's 9 mm pistol from where it had dropped beside him, stood up quickly and shot Mario three times rapidly in the back.

As quickly as it had started, it was over. Only the terrified watchman and Cappricci were left standing. The dead bodies of the captain and Mario rocked in a bizarre rhythm as the ship pitched and rolled. The third officer was slumped in the port-side forward corner of the bridge next to the shattered radar, losing blood rapidly and moaning. The radio officer was curled up next to a pool of his own vomit, and Stuart and Sandys were sitting with their backs to the starboard bulkhead. Cappricci turned to Stuart, with the 9 mm pointing squarely at him. There was a pause of no more than three seconds, but it seemed like three years in the aftermath of the devastation, as the two men stared at each other.

'You dropped this', Cappricci smiled as he clicked on the safety and threw it, very hard, across to Stuart.

Stuart didn't answer, but got up off the deck, helping Sandys to his feet at the same time.

'That was a bloody close one,' Sandys coughed out.

'It's not over yet, either,' Stuart replied. 'There's still twenty plus of a crew down below, weapons and Falcone.'

'Get hold of the chief engineer,' Marker shouted, as he finally managed to extricate himself from underneath Mario's body. 'He's the key now.'

'OK,' Stuart agreed. 'Cap, you and Chris secure the bridge. At least Chris knows what to do up here. John and I will go below and see what we can find. What's the ammunition status?'

'Mine's empty,' Marker replied first, looking around at the incredible destruction that the weapon had reaped in such a short time.

'I've got two spare clips, but we may need them downstairs,' Sandys offered.

'Take the pistol, Chris, and don't forget to take the safety off if you have to use it. On second thoughts, here, it's off now. Just point and squirt if you have to. There's ten rounds left.'

'I've got this clip,' Cappricci patted the one already mounted in his rifle.

'OK, so you've got one up and two spare, John. I've got one up and one spare. Right! Let's go, before we have unwanted visitors.'

Stuart turned and led the way off the bridge and down the wood-panelled companionway staircase that swept in a half-spiral to the next deck, which housed the captain's bedroom and day room. He kept on moving slowly down to the next level, as Sandys quickly checked the rooms out. The stairway continued its spiral off the captain's landing, becoming wider and more opulent as Stuart descended, the original marquetry of a quality that could have graced a Chippendale cabinet. As he approached the mezzanine deck, which served as the area of the ship reserved for the owner, the unmistakable smell of a good cigar wafted out from the open stateroom doors. Holding the AK at hip level, Stuart slipped past the entrance and entered the small hallway that led to the various rooms within the stateroom complex. Falcone was sitting behind a desk in his office, facing the door. The cigar, newly lit, was hanging from his mouth and a very large brandy was slopping about in an equally large balloon glass, fighting the movement of the ship in the storm, but prevented from spilling by the shape of the glass.

'I presume, from the recent burst of noise, that you are here to kill me, Thomas?' the old man said, the tone of his voice cutting through the background noise, even though it wasn't raised in volume. 'I thought the condemned man might as well have a last cigar and a rather good brandy, even if the circumstances were a little lively.' He indicated the movement of the ship by a wave of his free hand.

'We've got company,' Sandys called through the door, before Stuart could answer.

'Any guns?' Stuart called back.

'The arms are locked in the captain's cabin,' Falcone cut in. 'Spare the crew, Thomas. They are just seamen, not soldiers . . . The ship is in your hands. Who has died up top?'

'Mario and the captain; couple of others bent a bit,' Stuart answered, taking pleasure in the flicker in Falcone's eyes when Mario's name was mentioned.

'You lot! Back down the stairs and stay there until we come down,' Sandys could be heard shouting in the background.

'You see, Thomas? This is not a warship.'

'Why the delaying tactics? What's the end game-plan, Falcone? I'm sick of playing and being played with,' Stuart finished, keeping the rifle levelled at the old man's chest.

'Thomas, Thomas. Like all men with guns, you *are* the game now. We must all play by your rules until the weapon changes hands again.' He stopped as the ship gave another mighty heave and rocked everyone standing or seated. 'Is anyone in charge up there, or are we steaming around blind?'

'We're OK. What was it you were about to say?'

'Oh nothing, Thomas. I grow weary also, but remember, weapons come in many different forms, and even if you kill me, nothing will change with *my* game, as you call it. My family is a big family; I am but its head. My successor already makes most of the day-to-day decisions, referring to me only for guidance and important strategic planning. Think of me as the chairman of the board!' he chuckled, taking a massive swig out of the brandy glass. 'It will be the managing director who hunts you down like the dog you are!'

Stuart's fingers tightened on the trigger, but he didn't pull it. 'I haven't got time for this. John! Lock this old bugger in here and make sure the outside door onto the boat deck is locked as well. Follow me down the stairs. I'll wait at the bottom.'

The stairs finished at the main deck level and Stuart didn't have to go looking for the crew, they were all gathered there waiting to see what was going to happen next.

'Who's in charge here?' he asked.

'The captain, of course,' an officer called out. 'Where is he?'

'He's dead, and anyone here can join him, now or in the future. All you have to do is disobey my instructions and, hey presto, you're an angel.'

Sandys joined Stuart and they stood together on the last step of the wide staircase. The crew looked around at each other, and then a short fat man came forward. He turned out to be Australian.

'You might as well know it. I think you're a filthy murdering bastard, but I'm chief engineer of this gin palace, and because of your handiwork I'm the senior officer on board. The chief officer is in charge of the bridge and acting captain, but I can tell you now that all we want to do is to get out of this blasted storm and see the back of you lot.'

'Good speech, Chief.' Stuart smiled. 'Get this *gin palace*, as you call it, to Las Palmas as quick as possible and in one piece, and you'll get your wish.'

'Right, you lot.' The chief turned to the rest of the crew. 'Back to your duties – you heard the man!'

'Oh, Chief,' Stuart added, as the men began to move away, 'you'd better send a couple of your people to the bridge to collect the wounded and dispose of their bodies.'

The engineer didn't answer directly, he just gave the order and then turned back to Stuart. 'Anything else? Where's the owner?'

'Locked up in his cabin, getting pissed.'

'Well, we'll all look forward to doing that when you murdering sons of bitches have departed, won't we?' the chief replied.

'Just watch the lip,' Sandys cut in.

'Oh, leave him, John. He's an Aussie – they talk to their mothers like that, down there.'

The ship corkscrewed over another swell as Stuart and Sandys turned and made their way back to the bridge, followed by the crew members detailed to recover the wounded and the bodies. When they were a few steps from the door, Sandys called out to Cappricci and Marker.

'Come on in,' Cappricci shouted back.

The chief engineer, the two crewmen and the bridge watchman busied themselves helping the wounded third officer and the sparks.

'What d'you reckon then, Chris?' Stuart asked.

'Well, we're still taking a few lumps of water, but the swell is generally reducing. The big radar is smashed, but the little one in the chart room is working OK. We should start to get the island on the forty-eight mile range very shortly. The point is, what are we going to do when we get there?'

'You been there before?' Stuart asked.

'Long time ago, but things could be a lot different by now. They should have a large-scale chart on board, though, if they carry world-wide charts.'

'Hey, Engineer!' Stuart called. 'Get that other chief up here . . . the bridge officer.'

'Ring two-one on the phone over there,' the chief engineer called back. 'I'm busy tidying up your handiwork.'

Marker picked up the phone and dialled. 'Is that the mate? Could you come to the bridge, please? Thank you.'

'Very polite,' Stuart commented, as he strained to see through the salty windows. 'How d'you see through these damned things?'

'Open the little valve above the most starboard of the windows and all the glass will be washed by freshwater sprays,' Marker answered.

Stuart obeyed and slowly the salt was washed away. He turned the water off and tried again. The grey sea was covered in long streaks of salty white spindrift trails, and the bridge windows began to salt over almost immediately. 'Jesus, who'd do this for a living?' he said, out loud to himself.

'Too rough for you?' the chief officer, known as the mate on board ships the world over, asked from the bridge door.

'Yeah, something like that. Chris?'

'Have you got a large-scale chart of Las Palmas harbour?'

'Probably. D'you want me to look?'

'Go ahead,' Marker answered.

The mate opened the top drawer of the chart table and shuffled through a canvas chart folio. 'Here it is, in the voyage folio. It's an insert on the approaches to the harbour chart. Who's keeping the watch, by the way?'

'I was,' Marker answered, 'but now that you're here, you'd better take over.'

'I think you're right,' the mate answered. 'Chief, you got things in hand up here?'

'Yeah, Charlie. The old man is in the second body bag, Mario in the first one. The third mate's lost a lot of blood and we need to land him ASAP. Sparks has just got sore balls. Get us in somewhere as quick as you can. I'll go below and see if we can get any more speed out of the old lady as the swell comes down.'

'Las Palmas?' the mate asked.

'Las Palmas,' Marker confirmed.

The mate slipped into well-practised procedures and left Stuart and his group to their own devices. Marker studied the chart that had been left on top of the chart table.

'The best place to put her alongside is on this pier here,' he said to Stuart, pointing at the long harbour wall that was a famous landmark of the port.

'We can't be on board then,' Stuart replied. 'We have to get off before. Isn't there anywhere we could put in? A bay, or something like that, that would allow us to get off by small boat?'

'Lots of bays around the island. It's take your pick.'

'Somewhere where there's a shelving beach, or even a small harbour.'

'Here, here, here, or here. Like I say, there's lots of them.'

'Where's the airport . . . here?' Stuart asked.

'Yes, but you can bet your bottom dollar that Hess will have people there, watching at the very least.'

Stuart nodded. 'Yeah, you're right, and once we get into an airport we would have to be clean – no weapons.'

'We also have no passports or money,' Marker continued.

'There will be money on board here, believe me. Passports are a problem, and we mustn't forget that on top of being involved with us, you're also wanted for a murder you didn't commit.'

'What d'you propose then?' Marker asked.

'Yeah,' Cappricci interrupted, 'what d'you plan to do when we get there?'

'We land and split up, make our own way out. It's the only thing we can do, because each of us has different problems once we get back into the real world. Every cop in the Western world has a description of Chris. Hess and his cronies are after all of us, and I believe that whatever is at risk for them, it's big enough to kill us for it. I suppose, at a pinch, John and I could find the embassy and hope that past favours will see us through. Falcone's family are going to be on my case for the rest of my life.'

'Along with a long list of others,' Sandys added.

'Yeah, but they've got tentacles everywhere. What will you do, Cap?'

'I've spent a lot of time thinking about that since we got on the ship. I know some people who can get me false papers and I can get hold of a fair amount of cash, but Falcone, as well as Hess, is going to be after me. We're all in the crapper really, aren't we.'

Stuart smiled, the tension gone from his face. 'Makes you creative, Cap. 'Well if no one else has got any bright ideas, that's it. We land and split up, somewhere not too far from the harbour and the town. You've got a few hours to get your thinking cap on. John, I think we could stick together for a while, if you want to. Any ideas?'

324

'Steal a small plane and get to the mainland. No more boats for me!'

The discussion was cut short by the mate, who called out to them from the chart room. 'We've got an island on the radar . . . forty-five miles. We could be in a bay in the south in about four hours at our current speed. Sorry, couldn't help overhearing.'

'I reckon this is the best place,' Marker said, pointing at the chart with the end of the 9 mm pistol.

'The safety's still off, Chris, if you don't mind,' Stuart said, holding out his hand.

Marker gave him the gun. 'Cristobal Bay. Very apt, isn't it?'

'I'll get the *Salamander 1* swung out when we get into shelter. I can send the crew for her after we have berthed. Somehow I think we're going to be in Las Palmas for some time,' the mate continued.

Gomez had been in Las Palmas for some time as well. The three days had seemed like three years. He had spent most of his time at San Carlos Point, scanning the horizon for the *Salamander* with a cheap pair of binoculars he'd bought in a gift shop. The last two days he'd got soaking wet, but a fire was burning in his belly and the money he was going to get for the extra killings was a comfort. When he finally saw her through the murk, he was surprised at the course she seemed to be taking. Instead of running out to the west, she was heading straight for the coast, about two and a half miles to the east of him. He jumped into the canvas-topped Jeep he had hired and pulled away, down the narrow road which ran the length of the southern coast.

As he got almost opposite the ship, he saw a signpost which pointed down an even narrower road, marked Cristobal. He turned and followed the road down. It was steep and winding. Before he got into the small hamlet, he stopped the Jeep and left it at a passing place on one of the corners. Out of the back he took the briefcase that Falcone's people had spirited into his hotel room. In it was a hybrid 9 mm sniper's pistol. It had a standard barrel which could be interchanged for a 14 inch barrel with a powerful scope attachment. A detachable butt completed the kit, providing a weapon that could be used as a pistol, or as an accurate rifle.

Keeping it in its pistol mode, he took the gun out of the case and slipped it inside his trouser belt, and taking the case with him, he made his way towards the tiny harbour.

By the time he got there, a motor launch could be clearly seen making its way ashore. Looking through the cheap binoculars, it was only when the boat was within a hundred metres of the harbour that Gomez recognised Marker in the stern.

Quickly, he mounted the longer barrel and the butt and found a vantage point on a small rise by the side of the track. The scope sucked Marker's face in to Gomez, being more powerful than the binoculars and having the best of lenses. There had to be others with him in the cabin, but his target was coming in to him like a lamb to the slaughter.

The boat pulled in alongside the small stone quay and Marker jumped out to tie it up. Another two men appeared. The tall one had an AK47 in his hand, but he left it behind as he jumped down off the boat's deck onto the quay. A last man, smaller but clearly giving orders, also jumped down, and three of them grouped with their backs to Gomez, talking amongst themselves and to Marker.

It seemed to Gomez that Marker could have brought these men ashore and could return to the ship. What happened then was anybody's guess. Nothing that had happened so far was what was supposed to have happened. He couldn't risk losing Marker again, and these other men were probably the ones Falcone wanted killed.

Taking careful aim, he lined the crosshairs up in the middle of Marker's face and pulled the trigger. At the same moment, Mark Cappricci leaned forward to shake Marker's hand in a farewell gesture, as he was about to do with the others. The bullet passed into Cappricci's back, ten inches below the nape of his neck, shattering his spine instantly. Terribly distorted, it then passed upwards and burst through the top of his forehead, spraying a cloud of death over Marker. His body jumped forward onto Marker, taking Gomez's second bullet as they fell to the ground.

The assassin looked up from the scope, just as bullets from Stuart's pistol started to kick up the soil around him. Gomez slid back down the slight rise and disappeared from view. Sandys was back into the boat in seconds to retrieve a rifle, but by the time he had aim on the hill, Gomez was well on his way back to the Jeep, out of sight. Nobody moved, they just watched and listened.

'Reckon he's gone, Trap?' Sandys shouted.

'Bring two AKs. We'd better check the hill out.'

'And the company,' Sandys added, pointing to some of the local menfolk who had left their homes to see what the noise was.

'What d'you think . . . fishermen?' Stuart asked.

'Yeah, but watch for shotguns,' Sandys replied as he dropped down next to Stuart, with the AKs.

'You sort this lot out, Chris. We're going to check the hill out,' Stuart shouted across to Marker. 'Come on, get a grip! *He's* dead, *you're* not. Keep these locals off our back. Tell them we're marines, or something . . . Just keep them away from a phone.'

Stuart and Sandys snaked their way up the hill from the small quay, leaving Marker to explain, in broken Spanish and nervous English, that they were special Nato forces hunting a terrorist group who must have seen them coming ashore. He began to ask them question about any strangers they had seen around recently. Surprisingly, quite a few of the community had seen untrustworthy characters in the area during the last few days and wanted to help. They were so sorry about the soldier who had died.

When Stuart reached the rise that Gomez had shot from, only empty shell casings were there to greet him.

'He's legged it.'

'Any sign?' Sandys asked, as he reached the rise as well.

'Couple of nine mill casings, that's all. Hang on, listen . . . *Motor!* Hit the other side of the road, quick!'

The two men took positions on either side of the track, ready to take out any approaching vehicle, but the noise got fainter not louder, as Gomez powered the Jeep up the track and onto the coast road.

'Whoever it was has gone the other way,' Sandys called, as he stood up.

'Right then, we know one of the groups after us is here, so let's collect Chris and get the hell out of here.'

Back down at the harbour, Marker had learnt that there were no telephones in the small hamlet. There were, however, three trucks.

'Total population fifteen, no phones, three trucks, only two working,' Marker said to Stuart as he arrived back on the quay.

'We'll put Cap in the launch and tell these people that we need to borrow both their trucks. Tell them we'll radio for someone to come for the body. They must stay in their houses, for safety, until our people arrive.'

Marker started to explain to the villagers, while Stuart and Sandys lifted Cappricci's body into the launch.

'Disable the radio, John. We'll take the AKs for the time being. Normally I would set fire to the boat, but this little lot will leave the don with even more problems to wriggle out of.'

'D'you think Chris will get the trucks off them?'

'He can talk the hind legs off a donkey when he has to! He's a broker, don't forget . . . That's it then.'

Sandys went first, but Stuart paused before he left the cabin and looked back at Cappricci. 'How does it go, Cap?' *It is a far far better thing that I do now* – or something like that?' He turned and followed Sandys, the famous line from *A Tale of Two Cities* drifting on the wind.

'They've gone to get the trucks,' Marker reported, as the others returned. 'Not before time, either. Look.' He pointed out to sea. The *Salamander* had turned and was making way to the west. She would be in Las Palmas harbour within the hour.

'They've got a lot of explaining to do. We've got time to disappear,' Stuart commented.

'The trucks are here,' John Sandys said, breaking their thoughts as the bow wave on the ship seemed to grow visibly.

The trucks consisted of an ancient Citroën one-ton pick-up and a Second World War vintage Mercedes ten-tonner.

'John, you drive the big one and follow Chris and me in the small one,' Stuart instructed.

Marker gave the villagers theatrical thanks as they left, reminding them to return to their houses for safety. The small pick-up may have looked as though it might fall apart at any moment, but it was fleet of foot and Marker had to slow down to let the lumbering Mercedes catch up, its ancient diesel spewing black smoke from its rotting exhaust pipe as it struggled up the steep hill. When they got to the top and joined the coast road, Stuart flagged them all to stop, and got out.

'This is it, old lad,' he said to Marker. 'You take this one, it's less conspicuous. Got any ideas?'

'No,' Marker answered. 'I'm just going to go into town and wing it. I'll tell you what – I'll meet you in Trader Vic's at the Hilton in London in three months, if we make it.'

'Why not? You take care of yourself, you old pirate, and, well, I'm sorry. Complete balls-up from start to finish!'

'I know you are . . . Three months then?'

'What date?'

'It'll be March. Make it the fifteenth. I see you on the Ides of March. Twenty-two hundred hours.'

Marker gunned the Citroën and disappeared around the next corner before Stuart had reached the Mercedes.

'Just the A team left, then,' Sandys quipped, as Stuart climbed into the cab.

'What's an Ide? He said he'd see me on the Ides of March.'

'Shakespeare,' Sandys replied. '*Julius Caesar*. They murdered Caesar on the fifteenth of March – the Ides in Latin.'

'Julius Caesar . . . *Caesar* Falcone. Cute. Let's go!'

17

Chameleons and Snakes

'Drop it?' Hess repeated. 'Just drop it? No explanation, no nothing – just drop it?'

'That's right, Carlton. Drop it,' the President repeated.

'At least tell me why. What's happened?'

There was a pause, but the phone line remained open.

'Tel Aviv.'

'The *Israelis*? What the hell do they have to do with this?'

'You asked . . . you've been told.'

The telephone went dead. Carlton Hess was absolutely furious. Never, in his whole career had he been dropped in it so deeply and so easily. The Israelis, the goddamned Israelis, he thought. They certainly had the capabilities to pull off such an operation but how did they get involved and why?

More than anything, he felt like a fool. It was as if he had only been given the most limited information right from the beginning. Had the agency been used just to protect an administration, rather than the country? It wouldn't be the first time, but what was required *now* was the protection of Admiral Carlton Hess. He wasn't going to go down for a politician, whoever he might be . . . He punched his intercom.

'Nancy?'

'Yes, Admiral?'

'Any news from Jackson on that boat?'

'He called while you were on the phone to the President.

330

Also, you have a meeting with the internal investigation group regarding Mr Cappricci and Miss Christie, at ten.'

'Get Jackson up here, now,' Hess ordered, without his usual pleasantries.

Where were they? *Who* were they? Everything seemed to be piling up at the same time. Obviously it was all connected, but those two had been with the agency for years, particularly Cap. If they'd been sleepers, it must have been something real important to somebody to press their buttons and blow their cover for ever. Everything now pointed to the Israelis, but he was lost for reasons. The Masada weapon and its accidental, momentous, seeping effect on the world could have no practical use for them. The formula for the weapon itself was not available to them, just the knowledge that it had existed and an attempt had been made to recover the evidence – a million years too late! Could it just be simple blackmail? The blackmail of a president, by another state? *This game isn't finished, Mr President, and neither is Carlton Hess . . .* There was a knock on the door.

'Come in,' he shouted. 'Oh, Jackson, it's you. Sit down, sit down. Tell me about the ship. Has she arrived at Las Palmas?'

'Well, from what we can piece together, she got there but sailed on straight past. The weather was bad, as you know, so we only picked her up again at four in the morning, our time.'

'So where is she?'

'Sailing north for Europe, it looks like. We should have a good idea what region tomorrow, when she gets off Gibraltar.'

'Yeah, a right turn, or straight on north,' Hess agreed. 'What's the weather forecast now?'

'We should have clear skies for at least forty-eight hours. It shouldn't be a problem keeping tabs on her.'

'Well, at least we still know where Stuart and his crew are. Good work, Jackson. Keep me informed of any changes in her route. I think I'll take a trip to Europe and meet the *Salamander* myself.'

'Well, I think you should be on the other side of the pond by tomorrow, to make sure you have the best chance of catching her if she turns in somewhere quickly.'

'You're right. I'll get Nancy to get me out of the States tonight. I suppose Heathrow is the best bet. It's got the best connection options and I can be anywhere in the Mediterranean within, say, six hours after I get your call. OK then, I'll let you know where I am going to be as soon as I'm booked.'

'Good luck, sir,' Jackson offered, as he left the room.

It took Nancy only a matter of ten minutes to get Hess confirmed on a United States flight to London Heathrow that evening and a room in the Ramada Hotel at the airport. It had a personal chauffeur service as well as regular buses to terminals 1, 2 and 3.

'Take it easy,' Maclazowitz scolded, as Rider slipped trying to get out of the wheelchair.

'I can make it.' Rider grimaced, pushing up onto the elbow crutches that Michelle Christie had removed from the hospital store. 'What's this guy's name again?'

'Sharon,' Michelle supplied.

'And who is he? Wasn't there a cabinet minister of that name once?'

'He's in charge of one of security departments, based here in Tel Aviv, not Jerusalem. It's just routine. He's already spoken with Chet, but your file is a little thin and he wants to know what you know about why you were in Sierra Laputu, and what might have happened to the others.'

'That's an easy one. If they're not plastered all over the newspapers by now, they've bought it.'

'Ah, gentlemen,' Yani Bar-David greeted them as he walked around the corner of the office corridor. 'There you are. Michelle, would you take them through to the briefing room, down there and to the left? It's marked – you can't miss it. I'll go and tell him that you're here.'

'Seems like a nice boy,' Rider quipped as he hobbled down the shiny corridor.

Maclazowitz just shook his head and smiled at Michelle. She returned it with instant warmth, the smile on her face sending out the signals that he wanted to receive. These few short days since they had arrived had been enough for both Michelle and Chet to know that the chemistry that bubbled into action every time they were in each other's company was made of special ingredients. Neither had said anything to the other, but the looks and the odd touches had been like white-hot steel.

'Excuse me, you two,' Rider called back over his shoulder. 'Are you coming, or are you going to stand there all day?'

'Ah, we were just watching to see how you were doing. Don't worry, you're still in catching range if you fall over,' Maclazowitz assured him.

They slowly followed Rider down the corridor and then held the briefing room door open for him to hobble through.

'You know, I think I can manage with just the one crutch. The leg's sewn up, not broken.'

'Well, you'll do what you want to do, no matter what we say,' Michelle replied. 'Come on, sit down over there. I'll organise some drinks. Hot or cold?'

'Cold for me,' Rider answered. 'I've had a raging thirst ever since I started to get about again.'

'Fine by me,' Maclazowitz confirmed.

'And I'll have a black coffee,' Sharon said from behind them. 'Welcome to Israel, Mr Rider. My name is Avraham Sharon. I run an organisation which looks after certain security aspects of the state.'

'Mossad,' Rider stated.

Sharon didn't confirm or deny it. 'I wonder, Mr Maclazowitz, Michelle, would you leave me to have a short chat with Mr Rider? I'm sure you can find something to busy yourself with for half an hour or so. I don't intend to tire him out. Don't forget the drinks, though.'

It actually took over an hour for Sharon to be sure that Rider, like Maclazowitz, didn't know the deep background to the reason for their mission.

'Well, that would appear to be that, Steve.' Sharon got up and opened the briefing room door. Maclazowitz and Michelle were talking to Yani Bar-David about the intricacies of the political situation. Sharon waved, and they came in and joined him and Rider.

333

'Well, I may have some news for you all. Information from the country in question indicates that there is a possibility that one or more of your colleagues may still be alive and may even have escaped from Sierra Laputu. I'm not going to go into details at this time. I just think that you should know.'

'If anyone got out, it has to be Stuart and Sandys. Those two have got more than nine lives,' Maclazowitz mused.

'Sandys – he's the pilot, yes?' Sharon asked, glancing for a second at Yani.

'That's right,' Rider answered. 'He's a bloody good one as well!'

'Could he pilot a hovercraft?'

'Anything!' Rider confirmed.

'Then I think that our suspicions have more credance. Time will tell. What we must do now is decide what we do with you two. Where d'you want to go? The UK? The States?'

'The UK will do fine, and the sooner the better,' Rider answered quickly. 'Don't get me wrong. I'm eternally grateful for the way you guys plucked me out of there and patched me up, but home is the best place for a sick man.'

Chet instinctively looked at Michelle.

'Take your time,' Sharon cut in, rescuing Maclazowitz from his silence. 'This is a beautiful country, with much to see. This is your first time here. Take a few days to see the sights, and then we can make whatever arrangements suit. You will need new passports as well, so leave these arrangements to us and rest. Tomorrow is Shabbat, so you can join in the holiday. Now, I have some business with Michelle and then she can take you off somewhere.'

Bar-David led the rest of them out of the room and closed the door behind him.

'You like this man Maclazowitz?' Sharon asked immediately.

'Sir, I've only known him a few days!'

'Answer the question, please.'

'Well, yes, I like him, but we haven't . . .'

'I am not interested in what you have or haven't done with him. I have something in mind for your future and a man like that could be of use to us.'

334

'You're not ordering me to have a relationship with this man, are you, sir?'

'Miriam – Michelle – if it was for the good of Israel I would have no hesitation in doing so, but I think that nature is way ahead of me.'

'Everybody seems to know my business better than I do!'

'Not everybody, Michelle – just me. Now listen to me, I'm thinking of sending you to the Far East ... Hong Kong, actually.'

'*Tripoli!*' Hess screamed down the telephone to Jackson. 'I don't fucking believe it. I just don't fucking believe it. Probably the one place in the fucking world I can't catch up with the son of a bitch.'

'We don't actually know for sure who was, or is, on board, sir.' Jackson attempted to calm the fury that was reaching out of the telephone and choking both him and Hess.

'It doesn't matter any more. We've lost him. He'll be on his way to some lair or other, to recuperate and spend my money. You put him on the wanted terrorist list and circulate it to every agency we do business with. If he does so much as show his face anywhere, I want to know.'

'But all the agencies know about Stuart. A mercenary, yes – but not a terrorist, sir,' Jackson objected.

'Perhaps you're right. Look, I'm getting the next plane home. I'll work something out on the journey. Jesus, Tripoli, I still can't believe it!'

As Hess fumed, Caesar Falcone's Lear jet was taking off from Tripoli airport. It quickly left the Libyan coast behind. Falcone ordered a large brandy and gave the cabin attendant a telephone number to call. He used a prearranged name, and the senior White House official took the call immediately.

'We heard there had been some problems?'

'Minor details,' Falcone dismissed the concern. 'Tell me, have you made the President aware of his, ah, situation?'

'Yes, he's thinking about it.'

'He can think about it as long as he likes. I have only one requirement. He must be seen to lose the next election. My

335

man is waiting in the wings. Make it happen!' With that, Falcone cut the line off.

LONDON

'Vasco,' Stuart said in a level voice which would have been recognised as a greeting only by his closest associates.

'Trap,' Marker replied, with a smile. 'Welcome back to England.'

'Ides of March!'

'Scotch?'

'Don't mind if I do.'

Marker signalled the waitress. Before she reached the table, Marker held up the Scotch and held up two fingers. She smiled and nodded.

'So, how did you get out?' Stuart asked.

'Well, I hung around the port for a couple of days. I couldn't understand it – there was nothing in the papers, or on the TV about the mess we left in San Cristobal . . . nothing.'

The young waitress delivered the drinks and smiled again.

'Cheers!' Marker raised his glass.

'Cheers.' Stuart smiled, taking a large pull at the glass. 'So what did you do?'

'Went to the American Express office, told them I had been robbed, had no passport or card, blah, blah, blah, and they sorted the whole thing out for me. After a few checks, they organised money, a passport, everything. I couldn't believe it – it was brilliant.'

'You always were a lucky bugger!'

'Not quite, Trap. It was OK at that end, but I walked straight into the arms of three plain-clothes coppers from the Yard when I got to Heathrow, and they had a couple of uniformed boys with machine pistols with them.'

'And?'

'And I spent that night at Her Majesty's pleasure, and the next one, until I could arrange a good solicitor to get me out. They were going to put me on remand, but the Swiss have to prove extradition grounds, and apparently the story I gave has attracted some witnesses to my movements and their case isn't as strong as they thought. My guy is over there now. He thinks the charges will be dropped finally, but I'll probably have to jump through a few hoops yet. What about you?'

'Nicked a plane.'

Marker's jaw dropped. 'Stole a plane?'

'Only a small one! John had us out of there in minutes, just on dusk, and we landed in Casablanca during the night. We just got out, left the engine running, and by the time the locals had sorted it out we were on our way to Rabat. We took a week to get to Algiers, as Arabs. Once there, an old friend of mine from the Legion fixed us up with French and Greek papers and we got into France through Marseilles, drove up into Switzerland, made a quick visit to old man Bonhoff at the bank, and that was that – back in control.'

'Where's John?' Marker asked.

'Canada, bush piloting, crop spraying or something like that. They're all mad those guys, so he'll fit in quite well. He speaks French, so he can get drunk in two languages over there.'

'What about the others?'

'Chet called Silas. He and Steve made it. Strange, though, he wouldn't go into details – just said he would be in touch one day.'

'So that's it, then. The rest are dead. What a waste.' He took another large pull at the drink. 'What are you going to do now? What *have* you been doing?'

'Me? Oh, I've been asking a few questions, putting a few pieces together.'

'What do you mean?' Marker asked.

'Come on, let's take a walk.'

Stuart didn't wait for an answer. He just got up and left the table. Marker struggled with his wallet and dropped a ten-pound note on the table. The waitress smiled again. There wasn't a large tip in there, at their prices, but every little helped.

At the top of the stairs, the evening breeze was chilly, but it was good weather for a walk. Their Crombie-style overcoats almost matched: two London businessmen leaving the Park

337

Lane Hilton after a meeting. Taxis were drawing up in a regular stream and the humdrum of the hotel's foyer kicked in and out of gear as customers came and went.

They walked quickly across Park Lane, narrowly avoiding the scurrying traffic and into Hyde Park at the south-east corner of the Serpentine Road. There were quite a few people about, walking dogs or making their way with purpose to some venue on the opposite side of the park.

'I've always liked London,' Stuart said. 'To visit, anyway. Don't think I could live here permanently, though, or any city really. I like the sun on my back too much. It's a fun town . . . Haven't had a lot of fun, these past years.'

Marker didn't interrupt. He just let Stuart get it out of his system. It had been Marker that Stuart had turned to after his young American wife, Kelly, had taken a bullet meant for him and died in his arms all those years ago.

'Fancy Italian?' Stuart asked, as he turned to cut south across Rotten Row, to be in hailing distance of a passing cab plying its trade around the beautiful people's area of Knightsbridge.

'You were saying?' Marker reminded him, as silence fell.

'Falcone might be mad, but he's a businessman. No, there has always been an underlying calling card somewhere in this mess. Look at old Shanks; he was whacked before we even got off the ground. Day one . . . bang! Just like that! We didn't have time to figure it out, only to throw a curved ball onto the ball park and see what fell out. Get rid of Hess's replacement sharpish and pull in John Sandys. It had to be Hess, but why? I just can't accept any explanation I can think of.'

'Perhaps there was a whole different operational deal, which you never had time to find out about because you got rid of Hartman,' Marker offered.

'Maybe. I've thought of that, but . . . Taxi!'

The conversation ended abruptly as a black taxi cab pulled up quickly and Stuart leapt into the back seat, giving an instruction that Marker didn't hear.

The taxi rolled left and right, around the tight streets of London, towards San Lorenzo's, the fashionable restaurant frequented by rock stars, television and movie stars, royalty, diplomats and just ordinary millionaires. Cars were parked all along the street as they approached, but there was a small gap opposite the restaurant's door.

'Stay in the cab,' Stuart ordered. 'I'll just check, first.'

'No chance, mate!' the cabby commented. 'I'll keep the meter running.'

'You do that.' Stuart smiled as he stepped past Marker onto the sidewalk, bounced up the steps and through the glass door.

Two couples were sitting at the few seats in the reception bar. Three men were being served by the barman. They noticed Stuart but turned away in a supercilious manner. The restaurant was on three levels. Stuart walked straight through the bar and started downstairs to the busy and noisy lower floor.

'Yes, sir,' a waiter said when he reached the bottom.

'Meeting a friend,' Stuart said.

'And the name, sir?'

'It's OK, sonny, I see him over there.'

Carlton Hess was sitting with his back to Stuart, stuffing himself with an excellent veal dish. Sitting with him was a member of the Australian Embassy staff, talking rapidly and laughing at his own humour.

Stuart walked slowly up to and past the table, turning as he came level with the loud cheerful Australian.

'Good evening, Carlton,' Stuart said quietly with a beaming smile. 'Haven't seen you for ages. When I saw you sitting here, I thought I would just pop over and give you *this!* Excuse me for interrupting,' he added to the Australian, who was just about to say it was no problem, when he watched in slow-motion horror as Stuart brought a silenced .32 pistol from his coat pocket and squeezed off five rapid rounds into an extremely startled Admiral Carlton Hess. The second round hit him squarely in the mouth, and the veal, with its rich mushroom sauce, exploded all over the wood-chip wallpaper and onto the back of a rather expensive-looking lady on the next table. Stuart pressed the magazine release, caught it and then gave the gun to the Australian.

'Hold this, would you?' he said with a winning smile, and

walked past Hess's twitching body, up the stairs and out into the street.

The majority of the customers in the restaurant hadn't the slightest notion what had happened. Many, on the adjacent tables, only looked up as the expensive-looking lady jumped up to complain about having some food spilt onto her. The reality of the situation only struck home as Stuart and Marker's taxi was turning the corner at the bottom of the road. Two customers and a waiter grabbed the gun-holding Australian.

'You'll probably get in at Pontevecchios,' the taxi driver said.

'The veal looked good,' Stuart said. Pontevecchios sounds fine.'

At the traffic lights at the junction of Queen's Gate and Old Brompton Road, Stuart suddenly shouted through to the driver.

'Turn left, please. We'll get out here.'

'We'll be there in two ticks, guv. It's only a hundred metres down the road from here.'

'It's OK, we've changed our minds. Thanks a lot.'

After Marker paid the fare, the taxi sprang off down Onslow Street and onto the Fulham Road. It was thirty minutes later before he heard about the killing on his radio. By that time Marker and Stuart were eating salt beef sandwiches in Fino's wine bar, just off Berkeley Square.

'So you reckon it was all down to Hess then?' Marker finished.

'Enough of it,' Stuart answered.

'Have you spoken to him at all?'

'Who, Hess?' Stuart asked. 'No, I haven't heard hide nor hair of him since we got out. I suppose he's sitting on his fat behind in Langley, blaming everybody else for the cock-up!'

'Maybe he got fired.'

'Maybe,' Stuart agreed, a slight smile appearing on his lips. 'Maybe he did. His boss certainly looks as if he isn't going to make it for a second term in the White House anyway.'

Marker shrugged. 'He certainly left the world a legacy, in any event.'

'Not his fault really, Chris. Just happened to be the man in

340

the chair when the scientists shouted *Eureka*! The rest was an accident of fate.'

'Must be a hell of a cross to bear, though – knowing that you had a part in causing the creation of the AIDS virus.'

'That's what presidents and prime ministers are there for, to take the wrap for what the people who actually run the country make a mess of. Come on, get another drink in and then you can give me an update on this Gomez chap. We can't have him running around the world having a potshot at you every time he feels like it, can we?'

'You're going to be pissed at this rate. Never seen you pissed before, except when, sorry!'

'Forget it. Mine's a large Scotch – and I mean a *real* dram! Three fingers in the glass it's poured in.'

The two men toured the bars and nightclubs until they closed at 3 a.m. the next morning. Marker poured Stuart into a cab and took him back to his flat in Eaton Place, threw him into the guest room, undressed untidily and collapsed into the familiar snoring sleep of the drunken male. It was 11.30 a.m. when he woke, desperate for the toilet and freezing cold. The central heating was off.

After relieving himself, he stumbled downstairs. *The Times* was on the doormat and he retrieved it on the way to the kitchen and the life-saving coffee that awaited him there.

As his body entered the room, it went into automatic. Press a button here, open a cupboard there. Within five minutes he had orange juice and coffee, and toast was only a few seconds away from burning when he picked up the paper and read the headlines.

'You bastard!' he shouted out loud, adrenaline flooding through his veins and clearing even the far reaches of his brain. 'How dare you! You rotten stinking bastard!'

Marker crushed the paper in his hand and stormed out of the kitchen and up the elegant staircase to Stuart's room.

'What the fucking hell d'you mean by this,' he shouted, as he burst through the door. 'You absolute bastard! After everything I've d—'

The room was empty. Stuart was gone.

18

Spinning Tops and Turning Wheels

Don Falcone walked along the side of the ten-acre ornamental lake, half a mile from the mansion. Summer had come late and gone early, but the crisp November sun still held warmth when there was no wind. Two bodyguards traced his steps 50 metres behind, but Falcone was so used to them that they weren't really there. He thought of his dream and the players in the game.

Today the news had been good. The President had been beaten at the polls and a young new president, with a dozen skeletons in his cupboard, had been elected. A man like this could be tricked and controlled, if the game was played well. There had never been an opportunity like this in his lifetime.

Cassa remained President in Sierra Laputu and the PRC's privatisation plans were being well laid by Falcone's advisers. Only the death of Carlton Hess had been a partial worry. He was sure that Stuart was behind it, but the reports from the so-called witnesses were so varied and unreliable that they became useless. More work had to be done there because the flow of information from Langley was severely curtailed by the loss of Cappricci and even Hess himself, although the admiral had never known it.

The lake had several seats around it, on the side next to the house. As he approached the nearest, the small figure sitting on it turned and smiled.

'Come walk with me,' Falcone said, offering his arm to her.

'Caesar! I didn't hear you. I was watching the mallard on the lake. Isn't it beautiful?'

'Almost as beautiful as the harbour when we were children in Sicily, *Nancy*. Do you remember sitting and watching the fishermen mend their nets?'

'Yes, and stealing a little wine from their bottles when they weren't looking,' she chuckled.

'What do you plan to do today, little one? Now that your job is done, you can't spend the rest of your life thinking about the past.'

Nancy sighed and rested her arm heavily on the old man. He balanced his weight with his stick and continued to walk. 'I thought I might come into town with you. Perhaps you will find time to be gracious and buy your cousin some lunch?'

'So be it! Today there will be no business. Today is a beautiful day and we will spend time together and enjoy it.'

Much later, as the black Cadillac pulled into the traffic to return to the estate, Nancy laid her head back and dozed. Falcone's eyes were partially hidden behind the dark prescription glasses, but they were open and alert.

Shortly after they pulled off the freeway, the car slowed as it came up to a small line of traffic, obeying some temporary road traffic lights that the electric company had been using up and down the road, as they laid a new cable for the estate and the surrounding properties.

The old cables had been built only for the main house and there had been trouble with the supply as long as Falcone could remember. Finally, after a little persuasion, the mayor's office had insisted that a new cable was run, big enough to carry the load for the estate and the large new houses that the don had allowed to be built, for the selected rich and worthy of the city.

'What's the problem?' Falcone asked.

'It's the electric company again,' the driver replied. 'I'll be glad when they've finished,' he continued. 'At least they've finished around the estate gates. It was a pain in the backside having to use the north gate when the main gate was blocked by that trench.'

343

Falcone didn't answer; he emulated Nancy and rested his eyes. A couple of minutes later they were on their way again and five minutes after that approaching the estate entrance.

The driver noticed an old man on an old bicycle peddling slowly towards them. It reminded him of pictures of his grandfather, just after he and his wife arrived on Ellis Island all those years ago. Dino was third-generation American and very proud of his roots. At the gates he slowed and pushed the remote control to open them. Nothing happened.

'Goddamned electric company,' he said, as he pulled up to them and got out of the car.

A split second before he reached the gates, the electric company's trench, which had been backfilled over ten days before, erupted in a massive explosion. The force of the blast lifted the rear end of the car first, igniting the petrol tank in a supplementary addition to the holocaust. Dino was blasted through the middle of the gates as they burst open. He landed unconscious on the grass by the side of the drive, some 50 metres from where the car had been, debris showering around his prone body. Bits of the Don of Dons, Caesar Falcone, and his cousin Nancy would be found around the site for many days to come.

Three hundred metres away from the explosion, Silas Urquart took the cotton wool plugs out of his ears. Along with the remote control trigger, he carefully placed them securely in his saddlebag. He then mounted the bike unsteadily and peddled slowly away from the scene. Silence came back to the countryside; and he thought that while it was a beautiful area, his home at Castle Stuart was more beautiful. Mallards spiralled above him, returning to the lake. Doesn't take long for nature to get back to normal, does it? Silas thought, as he started to get in his stride with the bike and pick up a bit of speed. The car was only a mile away; he'd be back in the hotel within the hour and home tomorrow. Nigger would be pleased to see him.

'I'm pleased to see you awake, Yank,' Michelle whispered into Chet's ear. She was naked and straddled across his body, letting her long hair brush across his forehead in an annoying, tickling motion.

'I'll let *Yank* go, but never Yankee!' the big Texan replied equally softly, spinning round and grabbing her sides at breast level, to lift her above him and then slowly lower her down onto his body. He was under the sheet, and as they kissed his erection fought to get free of the crisp linen.

'Wait a minute, for God's sake. I'm all caught up.'

'You see, Maclazowitz, even big men can be brought to their knees by clever women!' Michelle laughed, wriggling higher up on his chest and grabbing the member through the sheet, behind her.

'I'm surprised it can even rise to the occasion,' he said, joining in the laughter, 'especially after the last two days.'

Since they reached Hong Kong, they had spent all their time in the Mandarin Hotel bedroom. Sex, sleep, sex, room service, sex and sleep, in various combinations and order. She wondered when the right time would come to tell him about the job Sharon wanted them to do.

'I'm red raw,' he said, crushing her in his arms. 'Don't you ever have enough?'

'Not with you, cowboy. I've never had sex like this before . . . I never want to get up.'

'I am pretty special, I suppose,' Maclazowitz replied, in a mock serious voice.

'And what about me?' Michelle demanded, leaping up and prancing about in front of him like a siren from *The Odyssey*. 'This is some body, I tell you. Men would kill to have a woman like me spinning on their manhood for days and days.'

She pulled the sheet off and started to crawl up the bed.

'Oh no!' Chet cried in a stage whisper. 'Mercy!'

She ran her tongue along the inside of his leg and watched his penis throb as if it was about to burst the knotted veins that spiralled round it. She ran up its side and onto the tip, but she didn't take it in her mouth, preferring to rise up and lower herself slowly onto it in a swaying motion. They made love slowly this time, rolling back and forth; first her on top and then him.

There was a knock on the door. The erection disappeared as quickly as it had arrived.

Chet's instinctive warning bells were not in full working order under their current circumstances, but he lifted her off him carefully and went to the door.

'Yeah, who is it?' he called.

'Room service, sir.'

'We didn't order any,' Chet replied, looking through the peephole in the door. It was the regular waiter so he turned to Michelle and shrugged. 'Might as well see what we didn't order.'

'Champagne?' he said, surprised, as the waiter whisked past with a smirk on his face.

'Oh darling, you shouldn't have . . . not again! I'm drowning in the stuff. Oh, look there's a card and something in an envelope.'

She reached over to the table as the waiter retreated, the cover slipping from her breasts to reveal their perfect form: firm, with erect nipples that tipped ever so slightly upwards.

'What does it say?' Chet asked, as he poured the wine into chilled glasses.

She ran her hand through her hair and pushed back to lean against the bed head. 'Just listen to this: *"Love each other every day, as if it's your last. The safety deposit box key is the wedding present I hope you will need! Trap."*'